ENGLAND, ENGLAND

ENGLAND, ENGLAND

Julian Barnes

VINTAGE CANADA
A Division of Random House of Canada

Published in Canada by Vintage Canada, a division of Random House of
Canada. First published in hardcover in the United Kingdom by Jonathan
Cape, a division of Random House UK Limited, and in Canada by Random
House of Canada Limited, Toronto.

Canadian Cataloguing in Publication Data

Barnes, Julian
England, England

ISBN: 0-679-30997-7

I. Title.

PR6052.A6657E53 1999a   823'.914   C99-930223-X

Printed in the United States of America
First Canadian Edition

TO PAT

1: ENGLAND

'WHAT's your first memory?' someone would ask.
And she would reply, 'I don't remember.'

Most people assumed it was a joke, though a few suspected her of being clever. But it was what she believed.

'I know just what you mean,' sympathisers would say, preparing to explain and simplify. 'There's always a memory just behind your first memory, and you can't quite get at it.'

But no: she didn't mean that either. Your first memory wasn't something like your first bra, or your first friend, or your first kiss, or your first fuck, or your first marriage, or your first child, or the death of your first parent, or your first sudden sense of the lancing hopelessness of the human condition – it wasn't like any of that. It wasn't a solid, seizable thing, which time, in its plodding, humorous way might decorate down the years with fanciful detail – a gauzy swirl of mist, a thundercloud, a coronet – but could never expunge. A memory was by definition not a thing, it was . . . a memory. A memory now of a memory a bit earlier of a memory before that of a memory way back when. So people assertively remembered a face, a knee that bounced them, a springtime meadow; a dog, a granny, a woollen animal whose ear disintegrated after wet chewing; they remembered a pram, the view from a pram, falling out of a pram and striking their head on an upturned flower-pot which their brother had placed to climb up on and view the new arrival (though many years later they would begin to wonder if that brother had not wrenched them out of sleep and dashed their head against the flower-pot in a primal moment of sibling rage. . .). They remembered all this confidently, uncontradictably, but whether it was the report of others, a fond imagining, or the softly calculated attempt to take the listener's heart between finger and thumb and give it a tweak whose spreading bruise would last until love had struck – whatever its source and its intent, she mistrusted it. Martha Cochrane was to live a long time, and in all her years she was never to come across a first memory which was not in her opinion a lie.

So she lied too.

Her first memory, she said, was of sitting on the kitchen floor, which was covered in loosely woven raffia matting, the sort with holes in, holes she could poke a spoon into and make bigger and get smacked for – feeling safe because her mother was singing to herself in the background – she always sang old songs when she cooked, not the ones she liked listening to at other times – and even today when Martha turned on the radio and heard anything like 'You're the Top' or 'We'll All Gather at the River' or 'Night and Day' she would suddenly smell nettle soup or frying onions, wasn't that the strangest thing? – and that was another, 'Love Is the Strangest Thing', which always meant the sudden cut and seep of an orange for her – and there, spread out on the matting, was her Counties of England jigsaw puzzle, and Mummy had decided to help her by doing all the outside and the sea to begin with, which left this outline of the country in front of her, this funny-shaped piece of raffia floor, a bit like a bulgy old lady sitting on a beach with her legs stretched out – the legs being Cornwall, though of course she hadn't thought that at the time, she didn't even know the word Cornwall, or what colour the piece was, and you know what children are like with jigsaws, they just pick up any old piece and try to force it into the hole, so she probably picked up Lancashire and made it behave like Cornwall.

Yes, that was it, her first memory, her first artfully, innocently arranged lie. And there was often someone else who had had the same jigsaw as a child, and a passage of soft competitiveness would ensue, about which piece they would do first – it usually was Cornwall, but sometimes it was Hampshire, because Hampshire had the Isle of Wight attached to it and stuck out into the sea and you could match the hole easily, and after Cornwall or Hampshire it might be East Anglia, because Norfolk and Suffolk sat on top of one another like brother and sister, or clutched one another like husband and wife, lying fatly coupled, or made the two halves of a walnut. Then there was Kent pointing its finger or its nose out at the Continent in warning – careful, foreigners over there; Oxfordshire playing spoons with Buckinghamshire and squashing Berkshire flat; Nottinghamshire and Derbyshire like side-by-side carrots or pine-cones; the smooth, sea-lion curve of Cardigan. They would remember how most of the large, clear counties were round the edge, and when you'd put them in it left an awkward muddle of smaller, odd-shaped counties in the middle, and you could never remember where Staffordshire went. And then they would try to recall the colours of the pieces, which had seemed so important at the time, as important as the names, but now, so long afterwards, had Cornwall been mauve, and Yorkshire yellow, and Nottinghamshire brown, or was it Norfolk that was yellow – unless it was its sister, Suffolk? And these were the sorts of memories which, even if wrong, were less untrue.

But this, she thought, might be a true, unprocessed memory: she had progressed from the floor to the kitchen table, and her fingers were swifter with the counties now, neater and more honest – not trying to force Somerset to be Kent – and she would usually work her way round the coastline – Cornwall, Devon, Somerset, Monmouthshire, Glamorgan, Carmarthen, Pembrokeshire (because England included Wales – that was the bulgy old lady's stomach) – all the way back to Devon, and then fill in the rest, leaving the messy Midlands till last, and she would get to the end and a piece would be missing. Leicestershire, Derbyshire, Nottinghamshire, Warwickshire, Staffordshire – it was usually one of them – whereupon a sense of desolation, failure, and disappointment at the imperfection of the world would come upon her, until Daddy, who always seemed to be hanging around at this moment, would find the missing piece in the unlikeliest place. What *was* Staffordshire doing in his trouser pocket? How could it have got there? Had she seen it jump? Did she think the cat put it there? And she would smile her Nos and head-shakes at him, because Staffordshire had been found, and her jigsaw, her England, and her heart had been made whole again.

This was a true memory, but Martha was still suspicious; it was true, but it wasn't unprocessed. She knew it had happened, because it had happened several times; but in the resulting amalgamation the distinguishing marks of each separate time – which she would now have to make up, like when her father had been out in the rain and gave Staffordshire back to her damp, or when he bent the corner of Leicestershire – had been lost. Memories of childhood were the dreams that stayed with you after you woke. You dreamed all night, or for long, serious sections of the night, yet when you woke all you had was a memory of having been abandoned, or betrayed, caught in a trap, left on a frozen plain; and sometimes not even that, but a fading after-image of the emotion stirred by such events.

And there was another reason for mistrust. If a memory wasn't a thing but a memory of a memory of a memory, mirrors set in parallel, then what the brain told you now about what it claimed had happened then would be coloured by what had happened in between. It was like a country remembering its history: the past was never just the past, it was what made the present able to live with itself. The same went for individuals, though the process obviously wasn't straightforward. Did those whose lives had disappointed them remember an idyll, or something which justified their lives ending in disappointment? Did those who were content with their lives remember previous contentment, or some moment of well-arranged adversity heroically overcome? An element of propaganda, of sales and marketing, always intervened between the inner and the outer person.

A continuing self-deception as well. Because even if you

recognized all this, grasped the impurity and corruption of the memory system, you still, part of you, believed in that innocent, authentic thing – yes, thing – you called a memory. At university Martha had made friends with a Spanish girl, Cristina. The common history of their two countries, or at least the contentious part, lay centuries back; but even so, when Cristina had said, in a moment of friendly teasing, 'Francis Drake was a pirate', she had said No he wasn't, because she knew he was an English hero and a Sir and an Admiral and therefore a Gentleman. When Cristina, more seriously this time, repeated, 'He was a pirate', Martha knew that this was the comforting if necessary fiction of the defeated. Later, she looked up Drake in a British encyclopaedia, and while the word 'pirate' never appeared, the words 'privateer' and 'plunder' frequently did, and she could quite see that one person's plundering privateer might be another person's pirate, but even so Sir Francis Drake remained for her an English hero, untainted by this knowledge.

When she looked back, then, she saw lucid and significant memories which she mistrusted. What could be clearer and more remembered than that day at the Agricultural Show? A day of frivolous clouds over serious blue. Her parents took her softly by the wrists and swung her high into the sky, and the clumpy grass was a trampoline when she landed. The white marquees with striped porticos, as solidly built as vicarages. A rising hill behind, from which careless, scruffy animals looked down on their pampered, haltered cousins in the show ring below. The smell from the back entrance to the beer tent as the day's heat rose. Queuing for the portable toilets, and the smell not much different. Cardboard badges of authority dangling from buttons on shirts of Viyella check. Women grooming silky goats, men trundling proudly on veteran tractors, children in tears slipping from ponies while in the background swift figures repaired the shattered fences. St John's Ambulance men waiting for people to faint or fall over guy-ropes or have heart attacks; waiting for things to go wrong.

But nothing had gone wrong, not that day, not in her memory of that day. And she had kept the book of lists for many decades, knowing most of its strange poetry by heart. The District Agricultural and Horticultural Society's Schedule of Prizes. Just a couple of dozen pages in a red paper cover, but to her much more: a picture book, though it contained only words; an almanac; an apothecary's herbal; a magic kit; a prompt-book of memory.

Three Carrots – long
Three Carrots – short
Three Turnips – any variety
Five Potatoes – long
Five Potatoes – round
Six Broad Beans
Six Scarlet Runners
Nine Dwarf Beans
Six Eschalots, large red
Six Eschalots, small red
Six Eschalots, large white
Six Eschalots, small white
Collection of Vegetables. Six distinct kinds. Cauliflowers, if included, must be shown on stalks.
Tray of vegetables. Tray may be dressed, but only parsley may be used.
20 ears of wheat
20 ears of barley
Sward of Re-seeded pasture in Tomato Box
Sward of Permanent pasture in Tomato Box
Scheme goats must be halter led and there must be a two-yard space *maintained at all times* between them and non-scheme goats.
All goats entered shall be female.
Goats entered as Classes 164 and 165 shall have borne a kid.
A Kid is defined as birth to 12 months.
Jar of Marmalade

Jar of Soft Fruit Jam
Jar of Lemon Cheese
Jar of Fruit Jelly
Jar of Pickled Onions
Jar of Salad Cream
Friesian Cow in milk
Friesian Cow in calf
Friesian Heifer in milk
Friesian Heifer Maiden not showing more than 2 broad teeth
Attested cattle must be halter led and there must be a three-
yard space *maintained at all times* between them and non-
attested cattle.

Martha did not understand all the words, and very few of the
instructions, but there was something about the lists – their calm
organisation and their completeness – which satisfied her.

Three Dahlias, decorative, over 8" – in three vases
Three Dahlias, decorative, 6"–8" – in one vase
Four Dahlias, decorative, 3"–6" – in one vase
Five Dahlias, miniature ball
Five Dahlias, Pompom, under 2" diameter
Four Dahlias, Cactus, 4"–6" – in one vase
Three Dahlias, Cactus, 6"–8" – in one vase
Three Dahlias, Cactus, over 8" – in three vases

There was the whole world of Dahlias accounted for. None
missing.

She was swung up to the sky by her parents' safe hands. She
walked between the two of them on duckboards, under canvas,
through hot, grassy air, and she read from her booklet with a
creator's authority. She felt as if the items laid out before them
could not truly exist until she had named and categorised them.

'So what do we have here, Miss Mouse?'

'Two seven oh. Five Cooking Apples.'

'That looks about right. Five of them. Wonder what sort they are.'

Martha looked at the booklet again. 'Any variety.'

'Right-oh. Any Variety Cooking Apples – we must look out for them in the shops.' He would pretend to be serious, but her mother would laugh and fiddle with Martha's hair quite unnecessarily.

They saw sheep clamped between the legs of sweating, big-biceped men and slipped out of their woolly car-coats in a whirr of buzzing clippers; wire cages held anxious rabbits so large and laundered they did not seem real; then there was the Parade of Stock, the Mounted Fancy Dress Competition and the Terrier Racing. Inside hot marquees were lardy cakes, drop scones, eccles cakes and flapjacks; Scotch eggs halved like ammonites; parsnips and carrots a yard long, tapering to the thinness of a candlewick; slick onions with their necks bent over and tied into submission with twine; clusters of five eggs, with a sixth broken into a judging dish beside them; beetroot cut to show rings like trees.

But it was Mr A. Jones's beans that glowed in her mind – then, later, and later still – like holy relics. They gave out red cards for first prize, blue for second prize, and white for commended. All the red cards on all the beans belonged to Mr A. Jones. Nine Runner Beans Any Variety, Nine Climbing Beans Round, Nine Dwarf Beans Flat, Nine Dwarf Beans Round, Six Broad Beans White, Six Broad Beans Green. He also won Nine Pods of Peas and Three Carrots Short, but these interested her less. For Mr A. Jones also had a trick with his beans. He laid them out on pieces of black velvet.

'Looks like a jeweller's window, eh, love?' her father said. 'Pair of earrings, anyone?' He reached towards Mr A. Jones's Nine Dwarf Beans Round, her mother giggled, and Martha said, 'No,' quite loudly.

'Oh, all right then, Miss Mouse.'

He shouldn't have done that, even if he hadn't meant it. This wasn't funny. Mr A. Jones could make a bean look perfect. Its colour, its proportions, its evenness. And nine beans that much more beautiful.

At school they had chanted. They sat four abreast in their green uniforms, beans in a pod. Eight legs round, eight legs short, eight legs long, eight legs any variety.

Each day would begin with the chants of religion, falsified by Martha Cochrane. Later came the dry, hierarchical chants of mathematics, and the dense chants of poetry. Stranger and hotter than either were the chants of history. Here they were encouraged to an urgency of belief out of place at morning Assembly. The chants of religion were said in a hurrying mumble; but in history Miss Mason, hen-plump and as old as several centuries, would lead them in worship like a charismatic priestess, keeping time, guiding the gospellers.

55BC (clap clap) Roman Invasion
1066 (clap clap) Battle of Hastings
1215 (clap clap) Magna Carta
1512 (clap clap) Henry the Eighth (clap clap)
    Defender of Faith (clap clap)

She'd liked that last one: the rhyme made it easier to remember. Eighteen fifty *fower* (clap clap) Crimean *Wower* (clap clap) – they always said it like that, no matter how many times Miss Mason corrected them. And so the chant proceeded, down to

1940 (clap clap) Battle of Britain
1973 (clap clap) Treaty of Rome

Miss Mason would lead them down the ages and then return them, from Rome to Rome, back to the beginning. This was how she warmed them up and made their minds supple. Then she would tell them tales of chivalry and glory, plague and famine, tyranny and democracy; of royal glamour and the sturdy virtues of modest individualism; of Saint George, who was patron saint of England, Aragon and Portugal, as well as protector of Genoa and Venice; of Sir Francis Drake and his heroic exploits; of Boadicea and Queen Victoria; of the local squire who went to the Crusades and now lay in stone beside his wife in the village church with his feet on a dog. They listened, the more intently because if she was satisfied Miss Mason would end the class with more chanting, but different this time. There would be actions which called for dates; variations, improvisations and tricks; the words would duck and dive while they all clung to a scrap of rhythm. Elizabeth and Victoria (clap clap clap clap), and they would reply 1558 and 1837 (clap clap clap clap). Or (clap clap) Wolfe at Quebec (clap) and they would have to answer (clap clap) 1759 (clap). Or instead of cueing them in with Gunpowder Plot (clap clap), she would switch it to Guido Fawkes Caught Alive (clap clap), and they would have to find the rhyme, 1605 (clap clap). She led them in and out of two millennia, making history not a dogged progress but a series of vivid and competing moments, beans on black velvet. Much later, when everything that would happen in her life had happened, Martha Cochrane could still see a date or a name in a book and hear Miss Mason's clappy response in her head. Poor Old Nelson Not Alive, Trafalgar 1805. Edward Eight Lost the Nation, 1936 Abdication.

Jessica James, friend and Christian, sat behind her in history. Jessica James, hypocrite and betrayer, sat in front of her during Assembly. Martha was a clever girl, and therefore not a believer. In morning prayers, her eyes tight shut, she would pray differently:

Alfalfa, who farts in Devon,
Bellowed be thy name.
They wigwam come.
Thy swill be scum
In Bath, which is near the Severn.
Give us this day our sandwich spread,
And give us our bus-passes,

As we give those who bus-pass against us,
And lead us not into Penn Station,
Butter the liver and the weevil.
For thine is the wigwam, the flowers and the story,
For ever and ever ARE MEN.

She was still working on one or two lines, which needed improvement. She didn't think it was blasphemous, except perhaps for the bit about farting. Some of it she thought was rather beautiful: the bit about the wigwam and the flowers always made her think of Nine Climbing Beans Round, which God, had He existed, would presumably have approved of. But Jessica James had denounced her. No, she'd done something cleverer than that: arranged for Martha to denounce herself. One morning, at a signal from Jessica, everyone nearby had fallen silent, and Martha's solo voice could be clearly heard intently urging the significance of sandwich spread, liver and weevils, at which point she had opened her eyes to meet the swivelled shoulder, hennish bosom and Christian glare of Miss Mason, who sat with their class.

For the rest of the term she had been made to stand apart and lead the school in prayer, forced to articulate clearly and to counterfeit an ardent faith. After a while, she found she did it rather well, a born-again convict assuring the parole board that he was now washed free of his sins and would they kindly think of letting him out. The more suspicious Miss Mason became, the more it pleased Martha.

People began to take her on one side. They would ask her what she meant by being so contrary. They would tell her that there was such a thing as being too clever by half. They would advise her that cynicism, Martha, is a very lonely virtue. They would hope she was not pert. They would also hint, in less or more obvious ways, that Martha's home was not as other homes, but that trials were there to be overcome, just as character was there to be built.

She did not understand about building character. It was

surely something you had, or something that changed because of what happened to you, like her mother being brisker and more short-tempered nowadays. How could you build your own character? She looked at village walls for bewildered comparison: blocks of stone, and mortar in between, and then a line of angled flints which showed that you were grown-up, that you had built your character. It made no sense. Photographs of Martha would show her frowning at the world, pushing out a lower lip, her eyebrows clenched. Was this disapproval of what she saw, was it showing her unsatisfactory 'character' – or was it merely that her mother had been told (when she was a child) that you should always take pictures with the sun coming over your right shoulder?

In any case, building her character was not her chief priority at this time. Three days after the Agricultural Show – and this was a true, single, unprocessed memory, she was sure of that, she was almost sure of that – Martha was at the kitchen table; her mother was cooking, though not singing, she remembered – no, she knew, she had reached the age where memories harden into facts – her mother was cooking and not singing, that was a fact, Martha had finished her jigsaw, that was a fact, there was a hole the size of Nottinghamshire showing the grain of the kitchen table, that was a fact, her father was not in the background, that was a fact, her father had Nottinghamshire in his pocket, that was a fact, she looked up, that was a fact, and the tears were dripping off her mother's chin into the soup, that was a fact.

Secure within her child's logic, she knew not to believe her mother's explanations. She even felt slightly superior before such incomprehension and tears. To Martha it was perfectly simple. Daddy had gone off to find Nottinghamshire. He thought he had it in his pocket, but when he looked it wasn't there. That was why he wasn't smiling down at her and blaming the cat. He knew he couldn't disappoint her, so he'd gone off to hunt for the piece and it was just taking longer than he'd imagined. Then he'd be back and all would be well again.

Later – and later came all too soon – a terrible feeling entered her life, a feeling she did not yet have words to describe. A sudden, logical, rhyming reason (clap clap) why Daddy had gone off. *She* had lost the piece, *she* had lost Nottinghamshire, put it somewhere she couldn't remember, or perhaps left it where a thief could come and steal it, and so her father, who loved her, who said he loved her, and never wanted to see her disappointed, never wanted Miss Mouse to stick out her lip like that, had gone off to find the piece, and it would be a long, long search if books and stories were anything to go by. Her father might not come back for years, by which time he would have grown a beard, and there would be snow in it, and he would look – how did they put it? – emaciated by malnutrition. And it was all her fault, because she'd been careless or stupid, and she was the cause of her father's disappearance and her mother's misery, so she must never ever be careless or stupid again, because this was the sort of thing that happened afterwards.

In the corridor off the kitchen she had found an oak leaf. Her father was always bringing leaves in on his feet. He said it was because he was in such a hurry to get back and see Martha. Mummy used to tell him in an irritated voice to stop being so plausible, and that Martha could very well wait until he had wiped his feet. Martha herself, afraid of provoking similar disapproval, always wiped her shoes carefully, feeling rather smug as she did so. Now she held an oak leaf in her palm. Its scalloped edge made it seem like a piece of jigsaw, and for a moment her heart lifted. It was a sign, or a coincidence, or something: if she kept this leaf safe as a reminder of Daddy, then he would keep Nottinghamshire safe, and then he would come back. She didn't tell her mother, but tucked the leaf into the little red booklet from the Agricultural Show.

As for Jessica James, friend and betrayer, the chance for revenge presented itself in time, and Martha accepted it. She was not a Christian, and forgiveness was a virtue others practised. Jessica James, pig-eyed and pious, with a voice like morning service, Jessica James, whose father would never disappear, began seeing a tall, gawky boy whose red hands had the damp and flabby inarticulacy of a boned joint. Martha quickly forgot his name but always remembered the hands. Had she been older, Martha might have thought the cruellest thing to do was let Jessica James and her smirking courtier continue in knees-together smugness until the day they walked up the aisle past the Crusader with his feet on the dog and into the sunset of the rest of their lives.

But Martha was not yet so sophisticated. Instead, Kate Bellamy, friend and conspirator, let the boy know that Martha might possibly be interested in going out with him if he was thinking of trading up. Martha had already discovered that she could make almost any boy fancy her as long as she didn't fancy him. Various plans now had to be discussed. She could simply steal the boy, flaunt him for a while and humiliate Jessica James before the entire school. Or they might organize a little dumb-show: Jessica James would be taken for an innocent walk by Kate, and chance would lead her to a place where her prim little heart would be shredded by the sight of a porky hand clamped to a mild breast.

Martha, however, settled for the cruellest revenge, and the one in which she had to do the least. Kate Bellamy, innocent of voice, duplicitous of heart, convinced the boy that Martha might truly learn to love him – once she got to know him – but that since she was serious in matters of love, and all else that love meant, he would have to break irrevocably and publicly with Miss Piety before he stood a chance. After a few days' thought and lust, the boy did so, and Jessica James was duly seen in gratifying tears. More days passed, Martha appeared everywhere in laughing profile, and yet no message came. Anxiously, the boy approached her co-conspirator, who played dumb and said he must have misunderstood: Martha Cochrane go out with *him*? The very idea of it. Furious and humiliated, the boy waylaid Martha after school; she mocked his presumption in anticipating her feelings. The boy would recover; boys did.

As for Jessica James, she never identified the engineer of her misery, which pleased Martha until the day she left school.

As winters passed, it slowly became clear to Martha that neither Nottinghamshire nor her father were going to return. She still believed they might as long as her mother wept, used one of the bottles from the high shelf, hugged her too tightly and told her that all men were either wicked or weak and some of them were both. Martha cried as well on these occasions, as if their joint tears might bring her father back.

Then they moved to another village, one further from school, so that she had to take the bus. There was no high shelf for bottles; her mother stopped weeping and had her hair cut short. No doubt she was building her character. In this new house, which was smaller, there were no photographs of her father. Her mother told her less often that men were either wicked or weak. She told her instead that women had to be strong and look after themselves because nobody else could be relied upon to do it for them.

In response to this, Martha made a decision. Each morning, before leaving for school, she pulled the jigsaw box from beneath her bed, opened the lid with her eyes closed, and took out a county. She never looked in case it was one of her favourites: Somerset or Lancashire perhaps. Of course she recognized Yorkshire as the one she could hardly get her fingers round, but then she'd never had particularly strong feelings about Yorkshire. On the bus, she would reach behind her and push the county down the back of the seat. Once or twice, her fingers encountered another county clamped between the tight upholstery, one she had left there days or weeks before. There were about fifty counties to dispose of, and so it took her almost the whole term. She threw the sea and the box into the dustbin.

She did not know whether she was meant to remember or to forget the past. As this rate she would never build her character. She hoped there was nothing wrong with thinking so much about the Show; in any case, she could not stop it glowing in her mind. Their last outing as a family. Swung high to the heavens in a place where, despite the noise and the pushing, there was order, and rules, and wise judgment from men in white coats, like doctors. It seemed to her that you were often wrongly judged at school, as you were at home, but that at the Show a superior justice was available.

She did not, of course, put it like that. Her immediate apprehension, when she asked if she could go in for the Show, was that her mother might be cross, and that the Schedule of Prizes might be confiscated for having 'given her ideas'. This was another of childhood's sins which she could never quite anticipate. Are you being pert, Martha? Cynicism is a very lonely virtue, you know. And what's been giving you ideas?

But her mother just nodded and opened the booklet. The oak leaf fell out. 'What's that?' she asked.

'I'm keeping it,' replied Martha, fearing rebuke, or recognition of motive. But her mother merely tucked the leaf back into the pages, and with the new briskness she was using nowadays began to look up categories in the Children's Section.

'A Scare Crow (maximum height 12")? An article made from Salt Dough? A Greetings Card? A Knitted Hat? A Face Mask made from any material?'

'Beans,' said Martha.

'Let's see, there's Four Shortbread Biscuits, Four Butterfly Cakes, Six Marzipan Sweets, A Pasta Necklace. That sounds nice, A Pasta Necklace.'

'Beans,' repeated Martha.

'Beans?'

'Nine Climbing Beans Round.'

'I'm not sure you can go in for that. It's not in the Children's Section. Let's look at the regulations. Section A. Open to Householders and Allotment Holders within a radius of 10 miles of the Show Site. Are you a Householder, Martha?'

'What about an allotment?'

'There aren't any around here, I'm afraid. Section B. Open to All. Ah, that's just flowers. Dahlias? Marigolds?' Martha shook her head. 'Section C. Confined to gardeners residing within 3 miles of the Show Site. I don't see why we don't qualify. Are you a gardener, Martha?'

'Where do we get the seeds?'

Together they dug up a patch of ground, put in some horse manure, and built two wigwams. Then it was up to Martha. She worked out how many weeks before the Show to plant her seed, pushed in the beans, watered them, waited, weeded, watered, waited, weeded, lifted clumpy bits of soil away from where they might be coming up, saw the glistening, whippy sprouts break from the soil, encouraged the tendrils in their spiralling climb, saw the red flowers form and break, watered just as the tiny pods appeared, watered, weeded, watered, watered, and there, an exact few days before the Show, she had seventy-nine Climbing Beans Round to choose from. When she got off the bus from school she would go straight out to examine her plot. For thine is the wigwam, the flowers and the story. It didn't seem blasphemous at all.

Her mother praised Martha's cleverness and green fingers. Martha pointed out that her beans didn't look much like those of Mr A. Jones. His had been flat and smooth, and the same colour green all over, as if they'd been sprayed. Hers had regular bumps like bunions where the beans were, and speckly yellow bits on the skin here and there. Her mother said this was just the way they grew. The way they built their character.

On the Saturday of the Show they got up early and her mother helped pick the beans at the top of the wigwam. Then Martha made her selection. She had asked for black velvet but the only piece in the house was still attached to a dress, so instead there was black tissue paper which her mother ironed, though it still looked rather crumpled. She sat in the back of somebody's car, thumbs on tissue paper, watching the beans stir and roll across the plate as they went round corners.

'Not so fast,' she said sternly at one point.

Then they bumped their way over a furrowed car-park and she had to rescue her beans yet again. In the horticultural tent a man with a white coat gave her a form with just a number on it so that the judges wouldn't know who she was, and showed her to a long table where everybody else was laying out their beans as well. Ancient gardeners with jolly voices said, 'Look who's here!' even though they'd never met her, and 'Have to look to your laurels now, Jonesie!'. She couldn't help noticing that no-one else's beans looked like hers, but that must have been because they were growing different varieties. Then they all had to leave because it was time for the judging.

Mr A. Jones won. Somebody Else was second. Somebody Else was commended. 'Better luck next time!' everyone said. Enormous hands with knotted knuckles solemnly reached down to console her. 'Have to look to our laurels next year,' the old men repeated.

Later, her mother said, 'Still, they taste very nice.' Martha didn't reply. Her lower lip stuck out, wet and stubborn. 'I'll have yours, then,' said her mother, and a fork reached towards her plate. Martha was too miserable even to join in the game.

Men with cars would sometimes come for her mother. They couldn't afford a car themselves, and to see her mother taken away so quickly – a wave, a smile, a toss of the head, and then her mother turning to the driver before the car was even out of sight – to see this happen always made Martha think of her mother disappearing as well. She didn't like the men who came to call. Some tried to ingratiate themselves, patting her as if she were the cat, and others stared from a distance, thinking there's a pot of trouble. She preferred the men who saw her as a pot of trouble.

It wasn't just about being left. It was about her mother being left. She looked at these occasional men, and whether they squatted on their haunches to ask her the usual questions about homework and television, or whether, standing, they jiggled their keys and muttered, 'Let's be off,' she saw them all in the same way: as men who would hurt her mother. Perhaps not tonight, or tomorrow, but some time, without any doubt. She was skilled at developing fevers and aches and menstrual pain of a kind which demanded her mother's attendance.

'You're a proper little tyrant, you are,' her mother would say, in tones ranging from affection to exasperation.

'Nero was a tyrant,' Martha would reply.

'I'm sure even Nero let his mum go out once in a while.'

'Actually, Nero had his mum killed, Mr Henderson told us.' Now that, she knew, was being pert.

'I'm the one more likely to poison *your* food if this goes on,' said her mother.

One day they were folding sheets, air-dried from the line. Suddenly, as if to herself, but loud enough for Martha to hear, her mother said, 'This is the only thing you need two people for.'

They carried on in silence. Stretch wide (arms not long enough yet, Martha), up, grip at the top, drop the left hand, catch without looking, stretch sideways, pull, over and again and catch, then pull, pull (harder, Martha), then across to meet, up to Mummy's hands, down and pick up, one last pull, fold, hand it over and wait for the next.

The only thing you needed two people for. When they pulled, there was something which ran through the sheet which wasn't just pulling the creases out of the sheet, it was more, something between the two of them. A strange sort of pulling, too: you pulled first as if wanting to get away from the other person, but the sheet held you, and then seemed to yank you back off your heels and towards one another. Was that always there?

'Oh, I didn't mean *you*,' said her mother, and suddenly hugged Martha.

'Which one was Daddy?' asked Martha later that day.

'What do you mean, which one? Daddy was . . . Daddy.'

'I mean, was he wicked or weak. Which one?'

'Oh, I don't know . . .'

'You said they were one or the other. That's what you said. Which one was he?'

Her mother looked at her. This obstinacy was something new. 'Well, I suppose if he was one or the other, then he was weak.'

'How can you tell?'

'That he was weak?'

'No, how can you tell if they're wicked from if they're weak?'

'Martha, you're not old enough for things like that.'

'I need to know.'

'Why do you need to know?'

Martha paused. She knew what she wanted to say, but feared it. 'So that I won't make the same mistakes as you.'

She had paused because she expected her mother to cry. But that part of her mother had gone away. Instead, she gave the dry laugh she specialized in nowadays. 'What a wise child I've given birth to. Don't get old before your years, Martha.'

That was a new one. Don't be pert. What's been giving you ideas? Now it was, Don't get old before your years.

'Why won't you tell me?'

'I'll tell you all I know, Martha. But the answer is, you don't know until it's too late, if my life's anything to go by. And you won't make the same mistakes as me because everyone makes different mistakes, that's the rule.'

Martha looked at her mother carefully. 'That's not much help,' she said.

But it was in the long run. As she grew up, as her character was built, as she became headstrong rather than pert, and clever enough to know when to hide her cleverness, as she discovered friends and social life and a new kind of loneliness, as she moved from country to town and began amassing her future memories, she admitted her mother's rule: they made their mistakes, now you make your mistakes. And there was a logical consequence of this, which became part of Martha's creed: after the age of twenty-five, you were not allowed to blame anything on your parents. Of course, it didn't apply if your parents had done something terrible – had raped and murdered you and stolen all your money and sold you into prostitution – but in the average course of an average life, if you were averagely competent and averagely intelligent, and more so if you were more so, then you were not allowed to blame your parents. Of course you did, there were times when it was just too tempting. If only they'd bought me roller-skates like they promised, if only they'd let me go out with David, if only they'd been different, more loving, richer, cleverer, simpler. If only they'd been more indulgent; if only they'd been more strict. If only they'd encouraged me more; if only they'd praised me for the right things . . . None of that. Of course Martha felt it, some of the time, wanted to cuddle such resentments, but then she would stop and give herself a talking-to. You're on your own, kid. Damage is a normal part of childhood. Not allowed to blame anything on them any more. Not allowed.

But there was one thing, one tiny yet ineradicably painful thing for which she could never find the cure. She had left university and come to London. She was sitting in her office, pretending to be excited about her job; she had heart-trouble, nothing too serious, just a man, just the usual mild catastrophe; she had her period. She remembered all that. The phone went.

'Martha? It's Phil.'

'Who?' Someone over-familiar in red braces, she thought.

'Phil. Philip. Your father.' She didn't know what to say. After a while, as if her silence doubted his identity, he reconfirmed it. 'Daddy.'

He wondered if they could meet. What about lunch one day. He knew a place he thought she might like, and she suppressed the question, 'How the hell would you know?' He said there was a lot to talk about, he didn't think they should either of them get their expectations up too high. She agreed with him about that.

She asked her friends for advice. Some said: say what you feel; tell him what you think. Some said: see what he wants; why now rather than before? Some said: don't see him. Some said: tell your mother. Some said: whatever you do, don't tell your mother. Some said: make sure you get there before him. Some said: keep the bastard waiting.

It was an old-fashioned, oak-panelled restaurant, with elderly waiters who took world-weariness close to sardonic inefficiency. The weather was hot, but there was only heavy, clubman's food on the menu. He urged her to have as much as she wanted; she ordered less. He suggested a bottle of wine; she drank water. She answered him as if filling in a questionnaire: yes, no, I expect so; very much, no, no. He told her she had grown into a most attractive woman. It seemed an impertinent remark. She did not want to agree or disagree, so she said, 'Probably.'

'Didn't you recognize me?' he asked.

'No,' she replied. 'My mother burnt your photographs.' It was true; and he deserved that wince, if nothing more. She looked across the table at an elderly, red-faced man with thinning hair. She had deliberately tried not to expect anything; even so, he looked shabbier than she would have thought. She realized that all along she had been working on a false assumption. She'd been imagining for the last fifteen or more years that if you disappeared, if you abandoned a wife and child, you did so for a better life: more happiness, more sex, more money, more of whatever was missing from your previous life. Examining this man who called himself Phil, she thought he looked as if he'd had a worse life than if he'd stayed at home. But maybe she wanted to believe that.

He told her a story. She absented herself from judging its truth. He had fallen in love. It had just happened. He didn't say that to justify himself. He had thought at the time a clean break was fairer all round. Martha had a half-brother, name of Richard. He was a nice boy, though he didn't know what he wanted to do with his life. Normal enough at that age, probably. Stephanie – the name was spilt suddenly into Martha's half of the table, like a knocked-over wine glass – Steph had died three months ago. Cancer was a brute of an illness. She'd been diagnosed first five years ago, then there'd been a remission. Then it came back. It's always worse when it comes back. It just takes you.

This all seemed – what? – not untruthful, but irrelevant, not a way of filling the exact, unique, fretsaw-cut hole within her. She asked him for Nottinghamshire.

'Sorry?'

'When you went off, you had Nottinghamshire in your pocket.'

'I thought that's what you said.'

'I was doing my Counties of England jigsaw.' She felt awkward as she said it; not embarrassed, but as if she were showing too much of her heart. 'You used to take a piece and hide it, then find it in the end. You took Nottinghamshire with you when you left. Don't you remember?'

He shook his head. 'You did jigsaws? I suppose all kids love them. Richard did. For a while, anyway. He had an incredibly complicated one, I remember, all clouds or something – you never knew which way up it was until you were half finished . . .'

'You don't remember?'

He looked at her.

'You really, really don't?'

She would always blame him for that. She was over twenty-five, and she would go on getting older than twenty-five, older and older and older than twenty-five, and she would be on her own; but she would always blame him for that.

2: ENGLAND, ENGLAND

One

PITMAN HOUSE

had been true to the architectural principles
of its time. Its tone was of secular power tempered by
humanitarianism: glass and steel were softened by ash and
beech; licks of eau-de-nil and acid yellow gave hints of
controlled passion; in the vestibule a dusty-red Corb drum
subverted the dominion of hard angles. The supernal atrium
objectified the aspirations of this worldly cathedral; while
passive ventilation and energy-saving showed its commitment to
society and the environment. There was flexibility of spatial use
and candid ductwork: according to the architectural team of
Slater, Grayson & White, the building combined sophistication
of means with transparency of intent. Harmony with nature was
another key commitment: behind Pitman House was an area of
specially-created wetland. Staff on the decking (hardwood from
renewable sources) could eat their sandwiches while inspecting
the transient birdlife of the Hertfordshire borders.

The architects were accustomed to client intervention; but
even they lost a little fluency when glossing Sir Jack Pitman's
personal contribution to their design: the insertion at board-
room level of a double-cube office with moulded cornices,
shagpile carpet, coal fires, standard lamps, flock wallpaper, oil
paintings, curtained *faux* windows and bobble-nosed light
switches. As Sir Jack musingly proposed, 'Rightly though we
glory in the capabilities of the present, the cost should not, I feel,
be paid in disdain for the past.' Slater, Grayson & White had
tried to point out that building the past was, alas, nowadays

considerably more expensive than building the present or the future. Their client had deferred comment, and they were left to reflect that at least this sealed sub-baronial unit would probably be considered Sir Jack's personal folly rather than an element in their own design statement. As long as no-one congratulated them on its ironic post-post-modernism.

Between the airy, whispering space created by the architects and the snug den demanded by Sir Jack lay a small office – no more than a transitional tunnel – known as the Quote Room. Here Sir Jack liked to keep visitors waiting until summoned by his PA. Sir Jack himself had been known to linger in the tunnel for more than a few moments while making the journey from outer office to inner sanctum. It was a simple, austere, underlit space. There were no magazines, and no TV monitors dispensing promo clips about the Pitman empire. Nor were there gaudily comfortable sofas covered with the hides of rare species. Instead, there was a single high-backed Jacobethan oak settle facing a spotlit slab. The visitor was encouraged, indeed obliged, to study what was chiselled in Times roman:

JACK PITMAN

is a big man in every sense of the word.
Big in ambition, big in appetite, big in generosity.
He is a man whom it takes a leap
of the imagination fully to come to terms with.
From small beginnings, he has risen like a meteor
to great things. Entrepreneur, innovator,
ideas man, arts patron, inner-city revitaliser.
Less a captain of industry than a very admiral,
Sir Jack is a man who walks with presidents
yet is never afraid to roll up his sleeves
and get his hands dirty.
For all his fame and wealth, he is yet
intensely private, a family man at heart.
Imperious when necessary, and always forthright,
Sir Jack is not a man to be trifled with;

> he suffers neither fools nor busybodies.
> Yet his compassion runs deep.
> Still restless and ambitious,
> Sir Jack makes the head spin with his energy,
> dazzles with his larger-than-life charm.

These words, or most of them, had been written a few years previously by a *Times* profiler to whom Sir Jack had subsequently given brief employment. He had deleted references to his age, appearance and estimated wealth, had the whole thing pulled together by a rewrite man, and ordered the final text to be carved on a swathe of Cornish slate. He was content that the quote was no longer sourced: a few years ago the acknowledgment 'The Times of London' had been chiselled out and a filler rectangle of slate inserted. This made the tribute more authoritative, and more timeless, he felt.

Now he stood in the exact centre of his double-cube snuggery, beneath the Murano chandelier and equidistant from the two Bavarian hunting-lodge fireplaces. He had hung his jacket on the Brancusi in a way that – to his eye, at least – implied joshing familiarity rather than disrespect, and was displaying his roundedly rhomboid shape to his PA and his Ideas Catcher. There had been some earlier institutional name for this latter figure, but Sir Jack had replaced it with 'Ideas Catcher'. Someone had once compared him to a giant firework, throwing out ideas as a Catherine wheel throws out sparks, and it seemed only proper that those who pitched should have someone to catch. He pulled on his after-lunch cigar and snapped his MCC braces: red and yellow, ketchup and egg-yolk. He was not a member of the MCC, and his brace-maker knew better than to ask. For that matter, he had not been to Eton, served in the Guards, or been accepted by the Garrick Club; yet he owned the braces which implied as much. A rebel at heart, he liked to think. A bit of a maverick. A man who bends the knee to no-one. Yet a patriot at heart.

'What is there left for me?' he began. Paul Harrison, the

Ideas Catcher, did not immediately activate the body-mike. This had become a familiar trope in recent months. 'Most people would say that I have done everything a man is capable of in my life. Many, indeed, do. I have built businesses from the dust up. I have made money, few would deny that. Honours have come my way. I am the trusted confidant of heads of state. I have been the lover, if I may say so, of beautiful women. I am a respected but, I must emphasize, not *too* respected member of society. I have a title. My wife sits at the right hand of presidents. What is there left?'

Sir Jack exhaled, his words swirling in the cigar smoke which fogged the lower droplets of the chandelier. Those present knew the question to be strictly rhetorical. An earlier PA had naively imagined that at such moments Sir Jack might be in search of useful suggestions, or, even more naively, consolation; she had been found less demanding employment elsewhere in the group.

'What is real? This is sometimes how I put the question to myself. Are *you* real, for instance – you and you?' Sir Jack gestured with mock courtesy to the room's other occupants, but did not turn his head away from his thought. 'You are real to yourselves, of course, but that is not how these things are judged at the highest level. My answer would be No. Regrettably. And you will forgive me for my candour, but I could have you replaced with substitutes, with . . . simulacra, more quickly than I could sell my beloved Brancusi. Is money real? It is, in a sense, more real than you. Is God real? That is a question I prefer to postpone until the day I meet my Maker. Of course I have my theories, I have even, as you might say, plunged a little into futures. Let me confess – cut your throat and hope to die, as I believe the saying goes – that I sometimes imagine such a day. Let me share my suppositions with you. Picture the moment when I am invited to meet my Maker, who in His infinite wisdom has followed with interest our trivial lives in this vale of tears. What, I ask you, might He have in store for Sir Jack? If I were He – presumptuous thought I admit – I would naturally be obliged to punish Sir Jack for his many human faults and vanities. No, no!' Sir Jack held up his hands to quell the likely protests of his employees. 'And what would I – He – do? I – He – might be tempted to keep me – oh, for not too long a stretch, I trust – in a Quote Room of my own. Sir Jack's very personal limbo. Yes, I would give him – me! – the hard settle and spotlight treatment. A mighty tablet. And *no magazines*, not even the holiest!'

Sotto chuckles were appropriate, and were duly provided. Sir Jack walks with the deity, Lady Pitman dines at the right hand of God.

Sir Jack strolled heavily across to Paul's desk and leaned towards him. The Ideas Catcher knew the rules: eye contact was now required. Mostly, you preferred to pretend that working for Sir Jack required hunched shoulders, lowered lids, unbreakable concentration. Now, he panned upwards to his employer's face: the wavy, boot-black hair; the fleshy ears, the left lobe pulled long by one of Sir Jack's negotiating tics; the smooth convexity of jowl which buried the Adam's apple; the clarety complexion; the slight pock-mark where a mole had been removed; the mattressy eyebrows with their threads of grey; and there, waiting for you, timing how long it took to get your courage up, the eyes. You saw so many things in those eyes – benign contempt, cold affection, patient irritation, logical anger – though whether such complexities of emotion in fact existed was another matter. Reason told you that Sir Jack's technique of personnel-management consisted in never offering the mood or expression obvious to the occasion. But there were also times when you wondered if Sir Jack was merely standing before you holding in his face a pair of small mirrors, circles in which you read your own confusion.

When Sir Jack was satisfied – and you never quite knew what did satisfy Sir Jack – he took his bulk back to the middle of the room. Murano glass above his head, shagpile lapping his laces, he swilled another grave question around his palate.

'Is my name . . . real?' Sir Jack considered the matter, as did his two employees. Some believed that Sir Jack's name was not real in a straightforward sense, and that a few decades earlier he had deprived it of its Mitteleuropäisch tinge. Others had it on authority that, though born some way east of the Rhine, little Jacky was in fact the result of a garage liaison between the shire-bred English wife of a Hungarian glass manufacturer and a visiting chauffeur from Loughborough, and thus, despite his upbringing, original passport, and occasional fluffed vowel, his blood was one hundred percent British. Conspiracy theorists and profound cynics went further, suggesting that the fluffed vowels were themselves a device: Sir Jack Pitman was the son of a humble Mr and Mrs Pitman, long since paid off, and the tycoon had allowed the myth of continental origin slowly to surround him; though whether for reasons of personal mystique or professional advantage, they could not decide. None of these hypotheses received support on this occasion, as he supplied his own answer. 'When a man has sired nothing but daughters, his name is a mere trinket on loan from eternity.'

A cosmic shudder, which may have been digestive in origin, ran through Sir Jack Pitman. He swivelled, puffed smoke, and eased into his peroration.

'Are great ideas real? The philosophers would have us believe so. Of course, I have had great ideas in my time, but somehow – do not record this, Paul, I am not certain it is for the archive – somehow, sometimes I wonder how real they were. These may be the ramblings of a senile fool – I do not hear your cries of contradiction so I presume you agree – but perhaps there is life in the old dog yet. Perhaps what I need is one last great idea. One for the road, eh, Paul? That you may record.'

Paul tapped in, 'Perhaps what I need is one last great idea', looked at it on the screen, remembered that he was responsible for rewrites as well, that he was, as Sir Jack had once put it, 'my personal Hansard', and deleted the wimpish 'Perhaps'. In its more assertive form the statement would enter the archive, timed and dated.

Sir Jack good-humouredly lodged his cigar in the stomach-hole of a Henry Moore maquette, stretched and pirouetted lightly. 'Tell Woodie it's time,' he said to his PA, whose name he could never remember. In one sense, of course, he could: it was Susie. This was because he called all his PAs Susie. They seemed to come and go at some speed. So it was not really her name he was unsure of, but her identity. Just as he'd been saying a moment ago – to what extent was she real? Quite.

He retrieved his jacket from the Brancusi and shrugged it past his MCC braces. In the Quote Room he paused to read again the familiar citation. He knew it by heart, of course, but still liked to linger over it. Yes, one last great idea. The world had not been entirely respectful in recent years. Well then, the world needed to be astonished.

Paul initialled his memorandum and stored it. The latest Susie rang down to the chauffeur and reported on their employer's mood. Then she picked up his cigar, and returned it to Sir Jack's desk drawer.

'DREAM A LITTLE

with me, if you please.' Sir Jack raised the decanter interrogatively.

'My time, your money,' replied Jerry Batson of Cabot, Albertazzi and Batson. His manner was always agreeable and always opaque. For instance, he made no evident response, by word or gesture, to the offered drink, yet it was somehow clear that he was politely accepting an armagnac which he would then politely, agreeably and opaquely judge.

'Your *brain*, my money.' Sir Jack's correction was an amiable growl. You didn't jerk someone like Jerry Batson around, but the residual instinct to establish dominance never left Sir Jack. He did so by his heartiness, his embonpoint, his preference for staying on his feet while others sat, and his habit of automatically correcting his interlocutor's first utterance. Jerry Batson's technique was different. He was a slight figure, with greying curly hair and a soft handshake he preferred not to give. His manner of establishing, or contesting, dominance was by declining to seek it, by retreating into a little Zen moment where he was a mere pebble washed briefly in a noisy stream, by sitting there neutrally, just feeling the *feng shui* of the place.

Sir Jack dealt with the *crème de la few*, so he dealt with Jerry Batson of Cabot, Albertazzi and Batson. Most people assumed that Cabot and Albertazzi were Jerry's transatlantic and Milanese associates, and imagined they must resent the way in which the international triumvirate effectively meant nothing but Batson. Neither, in fact, resented the primacy of Jerry Batson, since neither of them – despite having offices, bank accounts and monthly salaries – in fact existed. They were early examples of Jerry's soft-handed skill with the truth. 'If you can't present yourself, how can you be expected to present a product?' he had been inclined to murmur in his earlier, candid, pre-global days. Even now, twenty or more years on, he was still inclined, in post-prandial or reminiscing mood, to accord real existence to his sleeping partners. 'Bob Cabot taught me one of the first lessons of this business . . .' he would begin. Or, 'Of course, Silvio and I never used to agree about . . .' Perhaps the reality of those monthly Channel Island transfers had invested the account-holders with lingering corporeality.

Jerry accepted the glass of armagnac and sat quietly while Sir Jack went through the swirling and snuffling, the gum-rinse and the ecstatic eyes. Jerry wore a dark suit, spotted tie and black loafers. The uniform was easily emended to murmur youth, age, fashionability or gravitas; cashmere polo-necks, Missoni socks and designer specs with plain-glass lenses all offered nuance. But with Sir Jack he displayed no professional accessories, human or mechanical. He sat there smiling a nominal subservience, almost as if waiting for his client to define the terms of employment.

Of course, the time was long past when 'clients' 'employed' Jerry Batson. A key prepositional switch had taken place a decade back, when Jerry decided that he worked with people rather than for them. Thus, at different periods (though also sometimes not) he had worked with the CBI and the TUC, with animal liberation and the fur trade, with Greenpeace and the nuclear industry, with all the main political parties and several splinter groups. At about the same time he had begun discouraging such crude labels as ad-man, lobbyist, crisis manager, image-rectifier and corporate strategist. Nowadays Jerry, mystery man and black-tied alumnus of the party pages, where they hinted that he was soon to become Sir Jerry, preferred to position himself differently. He was a consultant to the elect. Not to the elected, he liked to point out, but the elect. Hence his presence in Sir Jack's city penthouse, sipping Sir Jack's armagnac, with the whole of darkened, sparkling London behind a curtain-wall of glass against which his loafered feet gently tapped. He was here to crunch a few ideas. His very presence provoked synergy.

'You have a new account,' announced Sir Jack.

'I do?' There was the mildest, opaquest frown in the voice. 'Silvio and Bob handle all the new accounts.' Everyone knew this. He, Jerry, was above the battle. He used to think of himself as a kind of superior lawyer, one arguing his cases in the higher, wider courts of public opinion and public emotion. Lately, he had promoted himself to the judiciary. That was why talk of accounts in his presence was frankly a touch vulgar. But then you did not expect delicacy from Sir Jack. Everyone agreed that he was a little short – for whatever reason – of *finesse* and *savoir*.

'No, Jerry, my friend, this is both a new account and a very old one. All I ask, as I say, is for you to dream a little with me.'

'Will I like this dream?' Jerry affected a slight nervousness.

'Your new client is England.'

'England?'

'Just so.'

'Are you buying, Jack?'

'Let's dream that I am. In a manner of speaking.'

'You want me to dream?'

Sir Jack nodded. Jerry Batson took out a silver snuff-box,

sprang open the lid, launched the contents of a tensed thumb-hollow up each nostril, and sneezed without conviction into a paisley handkerchief. The snuff was darkened cocaine, as Sir Jack probably knew. They sat in matching Louis Farouk armchairs. London was at their feet, as if waiting to be discussed.

'Time is the problem,' Jerry began. 'In my judgment. Always has been. People just don't accept it, not even in their daily lives. "You're only as old as you feel," they say. *Correction*. You are as old, and exactly as old, as you are. True of individuals, relationships, societies, nations. Now, don't get me wrong. I'm a patriot, and I bow to none in admiration of this great country of ours, I love the place to bits. But the problem can be put in simple terms: a refusal to face the mirror. I grant you we're not unique in this respect, but among those in the family of nations who paste on the slap every morning whistling *You're only as old as you feel*, we are an egregious case.'

'Egregious?' queried Sir Jack. 'I am a patriot too, you forget.'

'So England comes to me, and what do I say to her? I say, "Listen, baby, face facts. We're in the third millennium and your tits have dropped. The solution is not a push-up bra."'

Some people thought Jerry Batson a cynic; others merely a scoundrel. But he was not a hypocrite. He considered himself a patriot; what's more, he had the memberships where Sir Jack had only the braces. Yet he did not believe in mindless ancestor-worship; for him, patriotism should be pro-active. There were still old-timers around nostalgic for the British Empire; just as there were others soiling their pants at the idea that the United Kingdom might break up. Jerry had not gone on public record – and caution might prevail until he was safely Sir Jerry – with opinions he would happily express when mixing with free-thinkers. He didn't, for instance, see anything except historical inevitability in the notion that the whole of Ireland should be governed from Dublin. If the Scots wanted to declare independence and enter Europe as a sovereign state, then Jerry – who in his time had worked with both the Scotland For Scots campaign and the Union Forever lads, and was well-placed to see all the arguments – then Jerry would not stand in their way. Ditto Wales, for that matter.

But in his view you could – and should – be able to embrace time and change and age without becoming a historical depressive. He had been known on certain occasions to compare the fair land of Britain to the noble discipline of Philosophy. When the study and elaboration of philosophy had begun, back in Greece or wherever, it had contained all sorts of skill-zones: medicine, astronomy, law, physics, aesthetics, and so on. There wasn't much the human brain churned out which wasn't part of philosophy. But gradually, down the centuries, each of these various skill-zones had spun off from the main body and set up on its own. In the same way, Jerry liked to argue – and did so now – Britain had once held dominion over great tracts of the world's surface, painted it pink from pole to pole. As time went by, these imperial possessions had spun off and set themselves up as sovereign nations. Quite right too. So where did that leave us now? With something called the United Kingdom which, to be honest and facing facts, didn't live up to its adjective. Its members were united in the way that tenants paying rent to the same landlord were united. And everyone knew that leaseholds could be turned into freeholds. But did philosophy cease to address life's central problems just because astronomy and its chums had set up house elsewhere? By no means. You could even argue that it was able to concentrate better on the vital issues. And would England ever lose her strong and unique individuality established over so many centuries if, just for the sake of argument, Wales and Scotland and Northern Ireland decided to bugger off? Not in Jerry's book.

'Tits,' said Sir Jack remindingly.

'My point. Quite. You have to face facts. This is the third millennium and your tits have dropped, baby. The days of sending a gunboat, not to mention Johnny Redcoat, are long gone. We have the finest army in the world, goes without saying, but nowadays we lease it for small wars approved by others. We are no longer mega. Why do some people find that so hard to admit? The spinning jenny is in a museum, the oil is drying up. Other people make things cheaper. Our friends in the City still coin it, and we grow our own food: we are modest capitalists with corn. Sometimes we are ahead of the game, sometimes behind. But what we *do* have, what we shall always have, is what others don't: an accumulation of time. Time. My keyword, you see.'

'I see.'

'If you're an old geezer in his rocker on the porch, you don't play basketball with the kids. Old geezers don't jump. You sit and make a virtue of what you have. And what you also do is this: you make the kids think that anyone, *anyone* can jump, but it takes a wise old buzzard to know how to sit there and rock.

'There are some people out there – classic historical depressives in my book – who think it's our job, our particular geopolitical function, to act as an emblem of decline, a moral and economic scarecrow. Like, we taught the world how to play cricket and now it's our duty, an expression of our lingering imperial guilt, to sit back and let everyone beat us at it. Balls, as it were. I want to turn around that way of thinking. I bow to no-one in my love of this country. It's a question of placing the product correctly, that's all.'

'Place it for me, Jerry.' Sir Jack's eyes were dreamy; but his voice lustful.

The consultant to the elect helped himself to another thumbful of snuff. 'You – we – England – my client – is – are – a nation of great age, great history, great accumulated wisdom. Social and cultural history – stacks of it, reams of it – eminently marketable, never more so than in the current climate. Shakespeare, Queen Victoria, Industrial Revolution, gardening, that sort of thing. If I may coin, no, copyright, a phrase, *We are already what others may hope to become.* This isn't self-pity, this is the strength of our position, our glory, our product placement. We are the new pioneers. We must sell our past to other nations as their future!'

'Uncanny,' muttered Sir Jack. 'Uncanny.'

PA-PA-PA-PA PUM PUM PUM

went Sir Jack as Woodie, cap under arm, opened the limo door, '*Pum pa-pa-pa-pa pumm pumm pumm.* Recognize it, Woodie?'

'Could it be the mighty Pastoral by any chance, sir?' The chauffeur still pretended a little uncertainty, earning his employer's nod and a further display of connoisseurship.

'Awakening of serene impressions upon arriving in the country. Some translators say "happy"; I prefer "serene". Meet me at The Dog and Badger in two hours.'

Wood drove off slowly towards the rendezvous at the other end of the valley, where he would pay the pub landlord to give his employer drinks on the house. Sir Jack straightened the tongues of his walking boots, hefted his blackthorn stave from hand to hand, then stood squeezing out a long slow fart like a radiator being bled. Satisfied, he tapped his stick against a stone wall regular as a Scrabble board, and set off through the late-autumn countryside. Sir Jack liked to speak in praise of simple pleasures – and did so annually as Honorary President of the Ramblers' Association – but he also knew that no pleasures were simple any more. The milkmaid and her swain no longer twirled the maypole while looking forward to a slice of cold mutton pie. Industrialization and the free market had long since disposed of them. Eating was not simple, and historic recreations of the milkmaid's diet involved the greatest difficulty. Drink was more complicated nowadays. Sex? Nobody except dunderheads ever thought that sex was a simple pleasure.

Exercise? Maypole-dancing had become work-out. Art? Art had become the entertainment business.

And it was all a jolly good thing too, in Sir Jack's opinion. *Pa-pa-pa-pa pum pum pum.* Where would Beethoven be if he were living today? Rich, famous, and under a good doctor, that's where. What a shambles it must have been that December night in Vienna. 1808, if memory served. Bloody hopeless patrons, under-rehearsed players, a dim and shivering audience. And which bright spark imagined it a good idea to première the Fifth *and* the mighty Pastoral on the same night? Plus the fourth concerto? *Plus* the Choral Fantasia. Four hours in an unheated hall. No wonder it was a disaster. Nowadays, with a decent agent, a diligent manager – or better still, with an enlightened patron who might dispel the need for these grubbing ten-per-centers ... A figure who would insist on adequate rehearsal time. Sir Jack felt for the mighty Ludwig, he truly did. *Pa-PA-pa-pa-pa-pum-diddy-um.*

And even a pleasure as supposedly simple as walking had its complications: logistic, legal, sartorial, philosophical. No-one just 'walked' any more, strode for striding's sake, to fill the lungs, to make the body exult. Perhaps no-one ever really had, except a few rare spirits. Just as he doubted whether in the old days anyone had ever really 'travelled'. Sir Jack had interests in many leisure organizations, and was sick to death of the self-opinionated claim that genteel 'travel' had been superseded by vulgar 'tourism'. What snobs and ignoramuses the complainers were. Did they imagine all those old-style travellers on whom they fawned were such idealists? That they hadn't 'travelled' for much the same reasons as today's 'tourists'? To get out of England, to be somewhere else, to feel the sun, to see strange sights and stranger people, to buy things, to quest for the erotic, to return home with souvenirs and memories and boasts? Exactly the same in Jack's book. All that had happened since the Grand Tour was the democratization of travel, and quite right too, as he regularly told his shareholders.

Sir Jack enjoyed marching out across land belonging to

others. He would raise his stick approvingly at the cut-out cows on the hillside, the shire horses in bell-bottoms, the rolls of hay like Shredded Wheat. But he never made the mistake of imagining that any of it was simple, or natural.

He entered a wood, nodding to a couple of young hikers coming the other way. Did he hear a snicker pass between them? Perhaps they were surprised by his tweed deerstalker, hunter's jacket, cavalry twills, gaiters, hand-crafted doe-skin boots and fell-walker's stave. All made in England, of course: Sir Jack was a patriot in his private moments too. The receding hikers were dressed in shell-suits of industrial colour, with rubber trainers below, baseball caps above and nylon day-packs behind; one wore earpieces and in all probability was not listening to the mighty Pastoral. But again, Sir Jack was not a snob. There had been a motion before the Ramblers' Association a few years ago proposing that walkers be obliged to wear colours which blended with the landscape. Sir Jack had fought that motion tooth and nail, root and branch. He had described the proposal as fantastical, élitist, unworkable and undemocratic. Besides, he was not without his interests in the leisurewear market.

The path through the wood, several generations of springy beech leaves, was quilted underfelt. Layered fungi on a rotting log made a Corbusier maquette of workers' dwellings. Genius was the ability to transform: thus the nightingale, the quail and the cuckoo became the flute, the oboe and the clarinet. And yet was not genius also the ability to see things as with the eyes of an innocent child?

He left the wood and climbed a small hill: below him, an undulating field led down past a copse to a thin river. He leaned on his stick and brooded on his meeting with Jerry Batson. Not exactly a patriot, in Jack's view. Something a bit evasive about him. Didn't meet you man to man, didn't look you in the eye, sat there in a trance like an haute-couture hippie. Still, if you crossed his palm with silver, Jerry would usually put his finger on it for you. Time. You are as old, and exactly as old, as you are. A statement so apparently obvious that it was almost mystical. So how old was Sir Jack? Older than it said on his passport, that was for sure. How much time did he have? There were moments when he felt strange misgivings. In his personal bathroom at Pitman House, athwart his porphyry toilet, a sense of frailty would sometimes come upon him. An ignoble end, to be caught with your trousers down.

No, no! This was not the way to think. Not little Jacky Pitman, not Jolly Jack, not Sir Jack, not the future Lord Pitman of wherever he chose. No, he must keep moving, he must act, he must not wait for time, he must seize time by the throat. On, on! He swiped at a thicket with his stave and disturbed a pheasant, which rose heavily into the air, its fairisle sweater aflap, whirring off like a model aeroplane with a wonky propeller.

The clean October breeze was sharpening as he followed the edge of an escarpment. A rusting wind-pump offered itself as a cheeky cockerel by Picasso. He could already see a few early lights in the distance: a village of commuters, a pub returned to authenticity by the brewers. His journey was ending too quickly. Not yet, thought Sir Jack, not yet! He felt at times such kinship with old Ludwig, and it was true that magazine profiles of Sir Jack frequently used the word genius. Not always embedded in flattering contexts, but then, as he said, there were only two kinds of journalist: those he employed, and those employed by envious rivals. And they could have chosen another word, after all. But where was his Ninth Symphony? Was this it, stirring within him at the moment? It was surely the case that if Beethoven had died after completing only eight, the world would still have recognized him as a mighty figure. But the Ninth, the Ninth!

A jay flew past, advertising the new season's car colours. A beech hedge flamed like anti-corrosion paint. If only we could dip ourselves in that . . . *Muss es sein?* Any Beethovenian – and Sir Jack counted himself among their number – knew the reply to that one. *Es muss sein.* But only after the Ninth.

He cross-fastened his hunter's collar against the rising wind, and set course for a gap in a distant hedge. A double brandy at The Dog and Badger, whose mutton-chopped host would patriotically waive the bill – 'A pleasure and an honour as always, Sir Jack' – then the limo back to London. Normally, he would fill the car with the Pastoral, but not today, perhaps. The Third? The Fifth? Dare he risk the Ninth? As he reached the hedge, a crow took silk and wing.

'OTHERS MAY LIKE

to surround themselves with yes-men,' said Sir Jack, as he interviewed Martha Cochrane for the post of Special Consultant. 'But I am known to value what I like to call no-people. The awkward squad, the nay-sayers. Isn't that so, Mark?' He beckoned to his Project Manager, a blond, puckish young man whose eyes followed his employer so quickly that at times they seemed to precede him.

'No,' said Mark.

'Ho, ho, Marco. Touché. Or, on the other hand, thank you for proving my point.' He leaned across his double-sided partners' desk, treating Martha to some benign *Führerkontakt*. Martha waited. She was expecting attempts to wrong-foot her, and Sir Jack's double-cube snuggery had already done so, with its wrenching stylistic change from the rest of Pitman House. Crossing the room, she had nearly turned an ankle in the tussocky shagpile.

'You will note, Miss Cochrane, that I emphasize the word people. I employ more women than most in my position. I am a great admirer of women. And it is my belief that women, when they are not more idealistic than men, are more cynical. So I am looking for what might be called an Appointed Cynic. Not a court jester, like young Mark here, but someone unafraid to speak their mind, unafraid to oppose me, even if they should not expect their advice and their wisdom necessarily to be heeded. The world is my oyster, but I am seeking in this instance not a pearl but that vital piece of grit. Tell me, do you agree that women are more cynical than men?'

Martha thought for a few seconds. 'Well, women have traditionally accommodated themselves to men's needs. Men's needs being, of course, double. You put us on a pedestal in order to look up our skirts. When you wanted models of purity and spiritual value, something to idealize while you were away tilling the soil or killing the enemy, we accommodated ourselves. If you now want us to be cynical and disillusioned I dare say we can accommodate ourselves to that as well. Though of course we may not mean it, any more than we meant it before. We might just be being cynical about being cynical.'

Sir Jack, who interviewed in democratic shirt-sleeves, plucked his Garrick braces in a rubbery pizzicato. 'Now that is *very* cynical.'

He looked at her application file again. Forty, divorced, no children; a degree in history, then graduate work on the legacy of the Sophists; five years in the City, two at the Department of Heritage and the Arts, eight as freelance consultant. When he switched from her file to her face, she was already eyeing him back steadily. Dark brown hair cut in a severe bob, a blue business suit, a single green stone on her left little finger. The desk kept her legs out of his view.

'I must ask you some questions, in no particular order. Let's see . . .' Her fixed attention was oddly disconcerting. 'Let's see. You are forty. Correct?'

'Thirty-nine.' She waited for his lips to part before cutting him off. 'But if I said I was thirty-nine you'd probably think I was forty-two or -three, whereas if I say I'm forty you're more likely to believe it.'

Sir Jack attempted a chortle. 'And is the rest of your application as approximate to the truth as that?'

'It's as true as you want it to be. If it suits, it's true. If not, I'll change it.'

'Why do you think this great nation of ours loves the Royal Family?'

'Gun law. If we didn't have it, you'd be asking the opposite question.'

'Your marriage ended in divorce?'

'I couldn't stand the pace of happiness.'

'We are a proud race, undefeated in war since 1066?'

'With notable victories in the American Revolutionary War and the Afghan Wars.'

'Still, we defeated Napoleon, the Kaiser, Hitler.'

'With a little help from our friends.'

'What do you think of the view from my office window?' He waved an arm. Martha's eye was guided to a pair of floor-length curtains held back by gilded rope; between them was an evidently false window on whose glass was painted a prospect of golden cornfields.

'It's pretty,' she said non-committally.

'Ha!' replied Sir Jack. He marched across to the window, seized its trompe-l'oeil handles, and, to Martha's surprise, wrenched it upwards. The cornfields disappeared to reveal the atrium of Pitman House. 'Ha!'

He sat down again, with the complacency of one who has got the upper hand. 'Would you sleep with me to get this job?'

'No, I don't think so. It would give me too much power over you.'

Sir Jack snorted. Watch your tongue, Martha said to herself. Don't start playing to the audience – Pitman is already doing that for both of you. Not much of an audience anyway: the blond court jester; a hunky 'Concept Developer'; a small, bespectacled fellow of indeterminate function crouched over a laptop; and a mute PA.

'And what do you think of my mighty Project, such as it has been outlined?'

Martha paused. 'I think it will work,' she replied, and lapsed into silence. Sir Jack, suspecting an advantage, came round from behind his desk and stood looking at Martha's profile. He tugged at his left earlobe and examined her legs. 'Why?'

As he asked the question, he wondered whether the candidate would address one of his subordinates, or even his empty chair. Or would she half-turn and squint awkwardly up at him? To Sir Jack's surprise, she did none of these. She stood up, faced him, crossed her arms easily over her chest, and said, 'Because no-one lost money encouraging others to be lazy. Or rather, no-one lost money encouraging others to spend well on being lazy.'

'Quality Leisure is full of activities.'

'Exactly.'

Sir Jack moved slightly between each of his next questions, seeking to disconcert Martha. But she remained standing, and simply turned to face him wherever he was. The rest of the interview board was ignored. At times, Sir Jack almost felt as if he were the one moving round in order to keep up with her.

'Tell me, did you have your hair cut in that way especially for this interview?'

'No, for the next one.'

'Sir Francis Drake?'

'A pirate.' (Thank you, Cristina.)

'Well, well. How about Saint George, our patron?'

'Patron saint also of Aragon and Portugal, I believe. And protector of Genoa and Venice. A five-dragon man, by the sound of it.'

'What if I suggested to you that England's function in the world was to act as an emblem of decline, a moral and economic scarecrow? For example, we taught the world the ingenious game of cricket, and now it's our job, our historical duty, an expression of our lingering imperial guilt, to sit back and let everyone else beat us at it, what would you say to that?'

'I'd say it doesn't sound much like you. Naturally I've read most of your speeches.'

Sir Jack smiled to himself, though such private gestures were always generously available for wider consumption. He had by now completed his circumambulation, and eased himself back into his presidential chair. Martha also sat down.

'And why do you want this job?'

'Because you'll pay me more than I deserve.'

Sir Jack laughed openly. 'Any further questions?' he asked his team.

'No,' said Mark pertly, but the reference back was lost on his employer.

Martha was shown out. She paused in the Quote Room and pretended to cast her eye over the spotlit slab; there might be a furtive camera to be satisfied. In fact, she was trying to think what Sir Jack's office reminded her of. Half gentleman's club, half auction house, the product of imperious but erratic taste. It felt like the lounge of some country-house hotel where you met to commit half-hearted adultery, where the edge of nervousness in everyone else's demeanour disguised your own.

Meanwhile, Sir Jack Pitman pushed back his chair, stretched noisily, and beamed at his colleagues. 'A piece of grit *and* a pearl. Gentlemen – I speak metaphorically, of course, since in my grammar the masculine always embraces the feminine – gentlemen, I think I'm in love.'

A BRIEF HISTORY OF SEXUALITY

in the case of Martha Cochrane:

1. Innocent Discovery. A pillow clamped between the thighs, mind throbbing, and the crack of light still hot beneath her bedroom door. She called it Getting a Feeling.

2. Technical Advance. The use of one finger, then two; first dry, then wetted.

3. Socialisation of the Impulse. The first boy who said he liked her. Simon. The first kiss, and wondering, where do the noses go? The first time, after a dance, against a wall, that she felt

something bodge into the curve of her hip; the fleeting idea that it might be some deformity, at any rate a reason for not seeing more of the boy. Later, seeing more of the boy: visual display, causing moderate panic. It'll never go in, she thought.

4.   Paradox of the Impulse. In the words of the old song: Never had the one that she wanted, Never wanted the one that she had. Intense and unadmitted desire for Nick Dearden, whose forearm she never even brushed. Complaisant submission to Gareth Dyce, who fucked her three times in a row on a gritty carpet, while she smiled and encouraged him, wondering if this was as good as it got and half-embarrassed by the oddness of male weight-distribution: how he could be light and floaty down there, while pressing the air out of her lungs with his heavy boniness up here. And she hadn't even liked the name Gareth when she'd spoken it before and during.

5.   The Funfair. So many rides on offer while serpentine strings of lights flashed, and swirly music blared. You flew high, you were stuck to the walls of a revolving drum, you defied gravity, you tested the possibilities and limits of the flesh. And there were prizes, or there seemed to be, even if, more often than you expected, the thrown hoop skimmed off the wooden cylinder, the gimcrack fishing rod hooked nothing, and the coconut was glued to its cup.

6.   Pursuit of the Ideal. In various beds, and sometimes by renouncing or avoiding bed. The assumption that completeness was possible, desirable, essential – and attainable only in the presence and with the assistance of Another. The hope for that Possible in: a)   Thomas, who took her to Venice where she found his eyes glowed before a Giorgione more than they did when she stood before him in her specially-bought night-blue bra and knickers while the back canal went slap-slap outside their window; b)   Matthew, who really liked to shop, who could tell what clothes would suit her when they were still on the rail, who brought his risotto to a perfect pitch of sticky dampness, but couldn't do the same for her; c)   Ted, who showed her the advantages of money and the softening

hypocrisies it encouraged, who said that he loved her and wanted to marry her and have kids with her, but never told her that between leaving her flat every morning and reaching his office he always spent an intimate hour with his psychiatrist; d) Russell, with whom she ran away light-headedly in order to fuck and love, halfway up a Welsh mountain with hand-pumped cold water and udder-warm goat's milk, who was idealistic, organized, community-minded and self-sacrificing, whom she admired to death until she began to suspect she couldn't survive without the complacency, the distraction, the laziness and corruption of modern urban living. Her experience with Russell also caused her to doubt whether love was ever attained by striving or by active decision; whether individual worthiness was relevant. Further, where was it laid down that anything beyond a sweet companionable piggishness was possible? (In books, but she didn't believe books.) A light, almost heady despair accompanied her life for several years after these realizations.

6 a) Appendix. Not to forget: several married men. It's your choice, Martha, from the following: mobile phones, carphones, answering machines; feelings uncommitted to paper, credit card slip caution; sudden sex, and the door to your flat closing too soon after sudden sex; intimate e-mail, empty Easters; the brio of light uninvolvedness, the request not to wear any scent; the joy of larceny, the lowered hopes, the uncauterisable jealousy. Also: friends you thought you could fuck. Also: fucks you thought could be friends. Also: (nearly) Jane (except for being too tired and falling asleep).

7. The Pursuit of Separateness. The necessity of dreaming. The reality of that dream. Another might be there and helping, his own contingent presence adding to a supposedly shared reality. But you detached yourself from his reality, as you did from his ego, and in that separation lay your hope. Is that what you mean, Martha, she sometimes asked herself, or are you just dressing up a decision to fuck for yourself?

7 a)   Not to forget: ten and a half months of celibacy. Better, worse, or merely different?

8.   The Current Situation. This one, for instance. A good provider, as they used to say. As he had been before. Nice whippy unproblematic cock; good torso, with rather female limpety nipples; short legs, but he wasn't standing up now. And he busied himself, how he busied himself, sure that he knew exactly what he was up to, fitting her to some eternal female template of his previous devising. As if you were a cash-point – tap in the right code and the money gushes. The sleek confidence, the smug knowledge that what had worked before would work again.

Where did such confidence come from? From not thinking too much; also, from her predecessors, who had approved his doings. And she too approved in her different way: it meant she could safely leave him busying away. And the smugness meant he wouldn't notice as she separated herself from his reality. If he noticed any absence on her part, he would cockily presume it was his doing, that he was translating her to a further plane of pleasure, to seventh, eighth, ninth heaven.

She slid a finger into her mouth, then into the top of her cunt. He paused, as if criticized, readjusted himself, growled to imply that such blatancy excited him, and resumed his busyness, his business once more. She left him below, alone down there with his fluids and hydraulics, his stop-watch timing and his victor's place on the podium. She would pretend to applaud, when the time came.

Parenthesis: (The mystery of the female orgasm, once hunted like some rare species, the narwhal or sea-unicorn. Was it out there, in the impenetrable seas, on the frozen tundra? Women hunted it, then men joined in the chase. The squabble for ownership. Men, for some peculiar reason, seemed to believe it belonged to them, and could never have been found without their help. They wanted it dragged in triumph through the streets. But they had lost it in the first place, so it was right to take it away from them now. A new mystery was necessary, a new protectionism.)

She recognized the signs. She felt the increasing tenseness of his body, heard the strangulated noises: deep ones, like faecal straining; lighter ones, like trying to free blocked ears on an aeroplane. She offered her own contribution, the dulcet protests and raucous approval of one being sweetly stabbed; and then, in the same time location but in different sectors of the universe, he came and she came.

After a while, he murmured, 'Enjoy?'

It was probably a joke, but it still made him sound like a waiter. Safe behind the ambiguity of words, she replied, 'I had a good time.'

He chuckled. 'Don't tell me, tell your friends.'

Where were the swear words when you really needed them? The trouble was, most of them referred to what she'd just done. Either that, or they weren't strong enough. She'd even heard his glib line before, somewhere along her route. Actually, she probably would: she would tell, though doubtless not in the way he imagined. A little about this night, and this partner; but more about the lilting, lifting, soaring, floating, sweet fucking power of deception.

THE FINEST TAX-DEDUCTIBLE MINDS

were brought in to address the Project's Co-ordinating Committee. The French intellectual was a slight, neat figure in an English tweed jacket half a size too big for him; with it he wore a pale blue button-down shirt of American cotton, an Italian tie of flamboyant restraint, international charcoal wool trousers, and a pair of tasselled French loafers. A round face tanned by several generations of desk lamps; rimless glasses; receding hair cut close against the skull. He carried no briefcase and hid no notes in the cupped palm. But with a few suave gestures he drew doves from his sleeve and a line of flags from his mouth. Pascal led to Saussure via Laurence Sterne; Rousseau to Baudrillard via Edgar Allan Poe, the Marquis de Sade, Jerry Lewis, Dexter Gordon, Bernard Hinault and the early work of Anne Sylvestre; Lévi-Strauss led to Lévi-Strauss.

'What is fundamental,' he announced, once the coloured scarves had floated to the ground and the doves had perched, 'what is fundamental is to understand that your great Project – and we in France are happy to salute the *grands projets* of others – is profoundly modern. We in our country have a certain idea of *le patrimoine*, and you in your country have a certain idea of *'Eritage*. We are not here talking of such concepts, that is to say we are not making direct reference, although of course in our intertextual world such reference, however ironic, is of course implicit and inevitable. I hope we all understand that there is no such thing as a reference-free zone. But that is by the by, as you say.

'No, we are talking of something profoundly modern. It is well established – and indeed it has been incontrovertibly proved by many of those I have earlier cited – that nowadays we prefer the replica to the original. We prefer the reproduction of the work of art to the work of art itself, the perfect sound and solitude of the compact disc to the symphony concert in the company of a thousand victims of throat complaints, the book on tape to the book on the lap. If you are to visit the Bayeux Tapestry in my country, you will find that in order to reach the original work of the eleventh century, you must first pass by a full-length replica produced by modern techniques; here there is a documentary exposition which situates the work of art for the visitor, the pilgrim as it were. Now, I have it on authority that the number of visitor minutes spent in front of the replica exceeds by any manner of calculation the number of visitor minutes spent in front of the original.

'When such discoveries were first made, there were certain old-fashioned people who expressed disappointment, even shame. It was like the discovery that masturbation with pornographic material is more fun than sex. *Quelle horreur!* Those Barbarians are within the gates once more, they cried, the fabric of our society is being undermined. But this is not the case. It is important to understand that in the modern world we prefer the replica to the original because it gives us the greater *frisson*. I leave that word in French because I think you understand it well that way.

'Now, the question to be asked is, why is it that we prefer the replica to the original? Why does it give us the greater *frisson*? To understand this, we must understand and confront our insecurity, our existential indecision, the profound atavistic fear we experience when we are face to face with the original. We have nowhere to hide when we are presented with an alternative reality to our own, a reality which appears more powerful and therefore threatens us. You are familiar I am sure with the work of Viollet-Le-Duc, who in the early part of the nineteenth century was charged with rescuing many of the crumbling chateaux and *forteresses* of my country. There have traditionally been two ways of looking at his work: first, that he was seeking as far as possible to save the old stones from total destruction and disappearance, that he was conserving them as best he could; second, that he was attempting something much more difficult – to recreate the edifice such as it had been when originally built – a task of the imagination which some judge successful and others the contrary. But there is a third way of approaching the matter, and it is this: Viollet-Le-Duc was seeking to *abolish the reality* of those old edifices. Faced with the *rivalization* of reality, with a reality stronger and more profound than that of his own time, he had no choice, out of existential terror and the human instinct for self-preservation, except to destroy the original!

'Permit me to cite one of my fellow-countrymen, one of those old *soixante-huitards* of the last century whose errors many of us find so instructive, so fruitful. "All that was once directly lived", he wrote, "has become mere representation." A profound truth, even if conceived in profound error. For he intended it, astonishingly, as criticism not praise. To cite him further: "Beyond a legacy of old books and old buildings, still of some significance but destined to continual reduction, there remains nothing, in culture or in nature, which has not been transformed, and polluted, according to the means and interests of modern industry."

'You see how the mind may proceed so far and then lose courage? And how we may locate that loss of courage in the movement, the degeneration, from a verb of neutral description, "transform" into one of ethical disapproval, "pollute". He understood, this old thinker, that we live in the world of the spectacle, but sentimentalism and a certain political recidivism made him fear his own vision. I would prefer to advance his thought in the following way. Once there was only the world, directly lived. Now there is the representation – let me fracture that word, the re-presentation – of the world. It is not a substitute for that plain and primitive world, but an enhancement and enrichment, an ironisation and summation of that world. This is where we live today. A monochrome world has become Technicolor, a single croaking speaker has become wraparound sound. Is this our loss? No, it is our conquest, our victory.

'In conclusion, let me state that the world of the third millennium is inevitably, is ineradicably modern, and that it is our intellectual duty to submit to that modernity, and to dismiss as sentimental and inherently fraudulent all yearnings for what is dubiously termed the "original". We must demand the replica, since the reality, the truth, the authenticity of the replica is the one we can possess, colonise, reorder, find *jouissance* in, and, finally, if and when we decide, it is the reality which, since it is our destiny, we may meet, confront and destroy.

'Gentlemen and ladies, I congratulate you, for your enterprise is profoundly modern. I wish you the courage of that modernity. Ignorant critics will no doubt assert that you are merely attempting to recreate Olde Englande, an expression whose feminine endings are of particular interest to me, but that is another matter. Indeed, if you will permit, it is a joke. I say to you, in conclusion, that your Project must be very Olde, because then it will be truly novel and it will be modern! Gentlemen and ladies, I salute you!'

A Pitco limousine took the French intellectual to central London, where he spent part of his fee on waders from Farlow, flies from House of Hardy, and aged Caerphilly from Paxton and Whitfield. Then he departed, still without notes, via Frankfurt, to his next conference.

THERE WERE MANY DIFFERENT OPINIONS

about Sir Jack Pitman, few of them compatible. Was he villain and bully, or born leader and force of nature? Inevitable and gross consequence of the free-market system, or a driven individual who nevertheless kept in touch with his essential humanity? Some ascribed to him a deep, instinctive intelligence which gave him equal feel for the tidal fluctuations of the market and the susceptibilities of those he dealt with; others found him a brute and unreflecting junction between money, ego and lack of conscience. Some had watched him put calls on hold while he proudly showed off his collection of Pratt ware; others had taken calls from him in one of his favourite negotiating positions, athwart his porphyry toilet, and heard their impertinences treated to ripostes of colonic wrath. Why such conflicting judgments? Naturally, there were divergent explanations. Some thought Sir Jack simply too big, too multi-faceted a being for lesser mortals, often of an envious aspect, to fully grasp; others suspected that a tactical withholding, which deprived the scrutineer of key or consistent evidence, lay behind his technique of dominance.

The same duality afflicted those who examined his business

dealings. Either: he was a chancer, a gambler, a financial illusionist who for that brief and necessary moment convinced you that the money was real and before your eyes; he exploited every laxness of the regulatory system; he robbed Peter to pay Paul; he was a mad dog, digging each new hole to use the soil for filling in the hole he had just left behind him; he was, in the still-echoing words of an Inspector from the Department of Trade and Industry, 'unfit to run a whelk-stall'. Or: he was a dynamic merchant venturer whose success and energy naturally incited malice and rumour among those who thought business was best transacted between small, dynastic firms playing by the venerable rules of cricket; he was an archetypal transnational entrepreneur working in the modern global market, who understandably minimized his tax liabilities – how else could you hope to remain competitive? Either: look at the way he used Sir Charles Enright to gain entrée to the City, fawned on him, flattered him, then turned round and chewed him up, dumping him from the board the moment Charles had his first heart attack. Or: Charlie was one of the old school, decent enough but frankly a bit off the pace, the firm was due for a damn good shake-up, the pension offer was more than generous, and did you know Sir Jack put Charlie's youngest through school at his own expense? Either: no-one who worked for him ever had a bad thing to say about him. Or: you have to admit Pitman's always been a master of the gagging writ and the secrecy clause.

Even something as seemingly unambiguous as the twenty-four storey, steel-and-glass, beech-and-ash, architectural fact of Pitman House yielded to variant readings. Was its location – in an enterprise zone reclaimed from green belt to the north-west of London – a canny piece of cost-cutting, or an indication that Sir Jack was bollock-scared of mixing it with the City's heavy hitters? Was the hiring of Slater, Grayson & White a mere kow-tow to architectural modishness, or a clever investment? A more basic question was: did Pitman House even belong to Jack Pitman? He may have paid for the building of it, but there were stories that the last blip of recession had caught him badly overstretched and he'd had to go cap in hand to a French bank for a sale and leaseback. But even if this were true, you could take it one of two ways: either Pitco was undercapitalized, or Sir Jack was one step ahead of the game as usual, and aware that tying up capital in the wasting asset of flagship offices was what mugs did.

Even those who loathed the owner (or lessee) of Pitman House agreed that he was good at getting things done. Or at least, good at getting others to get things done. Here he stood, beneath his chandelier, turning slightly to different members of his Co-ordinating Committee, tossing out orders. Profilers, especially those from his own newspapers, frequently mentioned how light on his feet he was for such a big man, and Sir Jack was known to profess an unfulfilled desire to learn the tango. He also, at such moments, compared himself to a gunslinger, turning to outdraw the next uppity young pup on the block. Or might he rather be a lion-tamer snapping his whip at a semi-circle of brawling cubs?

Martha, sceptically impressed, now watched him instruct his Concept Developer. 'Jeffrey, survey please. Top fifty character-istics associated with the word England among prospective purchasers of Quality Leisure. Serious targeting. I don't want to hear about kids and their favourite bands.'

'Domestic? Europe? Worldwide, Sir Jack?'

'Jeffrey, you know me. Worldwide. Top dollar. Long yen. Poll the Martians as long as they've got the price of the entrance ticket.' He waited for the appreciative laughter to subside. 'Dr Max, I want you to find out how much people know.'

He was turning again, middle finger notionally tapping holster, when Dr Max cleared his throat. The Official Historian was a recent appointment, and this was Martha's first sight of him: trim, tweedy, bow-tied and languidly pert. 'Might you be a little more spe–cific, Sir Jack?'

There was a heavy pause before Sir Jack rephrased his command. 'What they know – find it out.'

'Would that be, well, Do–mestic, Europe or Worldwide?'

'Domestic. What Domestic doesn't know the Rest of the World won't be shagged to find out.'

'If you don't mind my saying so, Sir Jack,' – though Martha could already tell from their employer's melodramatic frown that, yes, he minded very much – 'It seems rather a b–road b–rief.'

'That is why you receive a rather broad salary cheque. Jeff, hold Dr Max's hand, will you? Now, Marco, you are going to have to live up to your name.' The Project Manager knew enough to wait for Sir Jack's meaning. Sir Jack chuckled before he made the hit, 'Marco Polo.'

Again, the Project Manager, as if instructing Dr Max, replied with no more than a blue-eyed, cheeky-yet-subservient gaze. Sir Jack then moved across to what he called his Battle Table, thus announcing a new phase of the meeting. With a mere inward flex of a fleshy hand, he gathered his troops around him. Martha was closest, and he laid fingers on her shoulder.

'We are not talking theme park,' he began. 'We are not talking heritage centre. We are not talking Disneyland, World's Fair, Festival of Britain, Legoland or Parc Asterix. Colonial Williamsburg? Excuse me – a couple of old-style turkeys roosting on a picket fence while out-of-work actors serve gruel in pewter plates and let you pay by credit-card. No, gentlemen – I speak metaphorically, you understand, since in my grammar the masculine embraces the feminine, as I seem to be doing Miss Cochrane – gentlemen, we are talking quantum leap. We are not seeking twopenny tourists. It is world-boggling time. We shall offer far more than words such as Entertainment can possibly imply; even the phrase Quality Leisure, proud though I am of it, perhaps, in the long run, falls short. We are offering *the thing itself.* You are looking doubtful, Mark?'

'Only in the sense, Sir Jack, that as I understood it from our French *amigo* the other day, isn't it . . . I mean, his thing about preferring the replica to the original. Isn't that what we're up to?'

'God, Mark, there are times when you make me feel less than English, though England is the air I live and breathe.'

'You mean . . .', Mark struggled with some schoolroom memories, 'something like we can approach the real thing only by means of the replica. Sort of, Plato?' he added, for himself as much as in appeal to the others.

'Warmer, Marky-Mark, tootsies getting toastier. Can I perhaps help you the final few yards down the track? Let me try. You like the countryside, Mark?'

'Sure. Yes. I like it. I like it enough. That's to say, I like driving through it.'

'I was in the countryside quite recently. *In* the countryside, I stress that. I do not wish to pull rank, but the point of the countryside is not to *go through* it but to *be in* it. I make this point every year when I address the Ramblers' Association. Even so, Mark, when you *go through* it, presumably, in your modest, inattentive way, you like the way it looks?'

'Yes,' said the Project Manager, 'I like the way it looks.'

'And you like it, I suppose, because you think it an example of Nature?'

'You could put it that way.' Mark wouldn't have done so himself, but he knew he was now enlisted in his employer's more bullying version of the Socratic dialogue.

'And Nature made the countryside as Man made the cities?'

'More or less, yes.'

'More or less, no, Mark. I stood on a hill the other day and looked down an undulating field past a copse towards a river and as I did so a pheasant stirred beneath my feet. You, as a person *passing through*, would no doubt have assumed that Dame Nature was going about her eternal business. I knew better, Mark. The hill was an Iron Age burial mound, the undulating field a vestige of Saxon agriculture, the copse was a copse only because a thousand other trees had been cut down, the river was a canal and the pheasant had been hand-reared by a gamekeeper. We change it all, Mark, the trees, the crops, the animals. And now, follow me further. That lake you discern on the horizon is a reservoir, but when it has been established a few years, when fish swim in it and migrating birds make it a port of call, when the treeline has adjusted itself and little boats ply their picturesque way up and down it, when these things happen it becomes, triumphantly, a lake, don't you see? It becomes *the thing itself.*'

'Is that what our French *amigo* was driving at?'

'He was disappointing, I thought. I told Payroll to give him dollars instead of pounds, and cancel the cheque if he complained.'

'Pounds being the real thing, and dollars the replica, but after a while the real thing becomes the replica?'

'Very good, Mark. *Very* good. Worthy of Martha, to offer praise.' He squeezed his Special Consultant's shoulder. 'But enough of this jolly cut-and-thrust. The question we have to address is *where.*'

A map of the British Isles had been laid out on the Battle Table, and Sir Jack's Co-ordinating Committee stared at the jigsaw of counties, wondering if it were better to be completely wrong or completely right. Probably neither. Sir Jack, now perambulating behind their backs, gave them a hint.

'England, as the mighty William and many others have observed, is an island. Therefore, if we are serious, if we are seeking to offer *the thing itself,* we in turn must go in search of a precious whatsit set in a silver doodah.'

They peered at the map as if cartography was a dubious new invention. There seemed either too much choice or too little. Perhaps some daredevil conceptual leap was called for. 'You're not, by any chance, thinking ... Scotland, are you?' A heavily bronchial sigh indicated that, No, dunderhead, Sir Jack was not thinking Scotland.

'The Scillies?'

'Too far.'

'The Channel Islands?'

'Too French.'

'Lundy Island?'

'Refresh my memory.'

'Famous for its puffins.'

'Oh, fuck the puffins, for God's sake, Paul. And no boring mud-flats in the Thames estuary, either.'

What could he be thinking? Anglesey was out. The Isle of Man? Perhaps Sir Jack's idea was to construct his own purpose-built offshore island. That would not be untypical. Mind you, the thing about Sir Jack was that nothing, in a way, was untypical except what he didn't want to do.

'There,' he said, and his curled fist came down like a passport stamp. '*There*.'

'The Isle of Wight,' they answered in straggly unison.

'Ex*act*ly. Look at her, snuggling into the soft underbelly of England. The little cutie. The little beauty. Look at the shape of her. Pure diamond, that's what struck me straight away. A pure diamond. Little jewel. Little cutie.'

'What's it like, Sir Jack?' asked Mark.

'What's it like? It's perfect on the map, that's what it's like. You been there?'

'No.'

'Anyone?'

No; no; no; no and no. Sir Jack came round to the other side of the map, parked his palms on the Scottish Highlands and faced his inner circle. 'And what do you know of it?' They looked at one another. Sir Jack pressed on. 'Let me help clarify such ignorance, in that case. Name five famous historical events connected with the Isle of Wight?' Silence. 'Name one. Dr Max?' Silence. 'Not your period, no doubt, ho, ho. Good. Name five famous listed buildings on the island whose renovation might cause ructions at Heritage.' 'Osborne House,' replied Dr Max in quiz-show mode. 'Very good. Dr Max wins the hair-drier. Name another four.' Silence. 'Good. Name five famous and endangered species of plant, bird or animal whose habitat might be disturbed by our saintly bulldozers?' Silence. 'Good.'

'Cowes Regatta,' a sudden voice suggested.

'Ah, the phagocytes stir. Very good, Jeff. But not, I think, a bird, plant, listed building or historical event. Any more offers?' A longer silence. 'Good. Indeed, perfect.'

'But Sir Jack . . . isn't it, well, presumably, full of *inhabitants*?'

'No, Mark, it is not full of inhabitants. What it is full of is grateful future employees. But thank you for volunteering to put your curiosity to the test. Marco Polo as I said. On your horse. Report back in two weeks. I understand there is some famously inexpensive bed-and-breakfast accommodation on the island.'

'SO WHAT DO YOU THINK?'

asked Paul as they sat in a wine lodge half a mile from Pitman House. Martha had a tumbler of mineral water, Paul a goblet of preternaturally yellow white wine. Behind him, on the oak-veneer panelling, hung a print of two dogs behaving like humans; around them, men in dark suits yelped and barked.

What did she think? For a start, she thought it surprising that he was the one who had asked her for a drink. Martha had become skilled at anticipating moves in predominantly male offices. Moves and non-moves. The fat pads of Sir Jack's fingers had been laid meaningfully upon her at moments of professional elucidation, but the touch registered to her as command rather than lust – though lust was not ruled out. Young Mark, the Project Manager, flashed his quick blue eyes at her in a manner she recognized as largely self-referring; he would be a flirt with no follow-through. Dr Max – well, they had shared sandwiches on the deck overlooking the artificial wetland more than once, but Dr Max was delightedly and transparently interested in Dr Max, and when he wasn't Martha Cochrane doubted she would be his preferred species. She had therefore expected an approach from Jeff, hunky, solid, married Jeff, with baby-seats strapped into his Jeep; surely he would be the first with the sly, joined-up murmur of fancy-a-drink-after-work? In the zoo-cage of egos at Pitman House, she had overlooked Paul, or taken him for a patch of quiet straw which occasionally shuddered. Paul behind his laptop, the mute scribe, the Ideas Catcher, fielding Sir Jack's nickel-plated banalities and hoarding them for posterity, or at least for some future Pitman Memorial Foundation.

'What do I think?' She also thought it felt like a set-up: Paul as office-boy sounding her out for Sir Jack, or possibly someone else. 'Oh, it doesn't really matter. I'm just the Appointed Cynic. I merely react to other people's ideas. What do *you* think?'

'I'm just the Ideas Catcher. I catch ideas. I don't have any of my own.'

'I don't believe that.'

'What do you think of Sir Jack?'

'What do *you* think of Sir Jack?'

Pawn to king four, pawn to king four, black follows white until white varies. Paul's variation came as a surprise.

'I think of him as a family man.'

'Funny, I've always considered that phrase an oxymoron.'

'He's a family man at heart,' repeated Paul. 'You know, he's got an old auntie out in the sticks somewhere. Visits her as regular as clockwork.'

'Proud father, devoted husband?'

Paul looked at her as if she were perversely sustaining her professional mode outside office hours. 'Why not?'

'Why?'

'Why not?'

'Why?'

Temporary stalemate; so Martha waited. The Ideas Catcher was an inch or two shorter than her five nine, and younger by a few years; a pale, round face, earnest blue-grey eyes behind glasses which made him look neither studious nor nerdy, just a sufferer from bad vision. He wore the uniform of business a little uneasily, as if someone else had chosen it for him, and twirled his goblet on a characters-from-Dickens coaster. Peripheral awareness told her that when she looked away he focused on her intently. Was this timidity or calculation – was she perhaps meant to notice? Martha sighed to herself: nowadays even simple things were rarely simple.

In any case, she waited. Martha had learned to be good at silence. Long ago she had been taught – more by social osmosis than by anyone in particular – that it was part of a woman's function to bring men out, to put them at their ease; then they would entertain you, tell you about the world, let you know their inner thoughts, and finally marry you. By the time she had reached her thirties, Martha knew that this was seriously bad advice. In most cases it meant giving a man licence to bore you; while the idea that they would tell you their inner thoughts was naive. Many had only outer thoughts to begin with.

So instead of approving male conversation in advance, she held back, savouring the power of silence. This unnerved some men. They claimed such silence was intrinsically hostile. They told her she was passive-aggressive. They asked if she was a feminist, not a term uttered as neutral description, still less as praise. 'But I haven't said anything,' she would reply. 'No, but I can *sense* your disapproval,' said one. Another, drunk after dinner, turned to her, cigar still in his mouth, rage in the eyes, and said, 'You think there are only two kinds of men, don't you, those who've said something crappy already and those who are going to say something crappy in the future. Well, fuck *you*.'

Martha, therefore, was not going to be out-silenced by a sideways-glancing boy with a glass of yellow wine in front of him.

'My father played the oboe,' he said eventually. 'I mean, he wasn't professional, but he was good enough, played in small amateur groups. I used to get dragged round to cold churches and village halls on Sunday afternoons. Mozart's Wind Seren-ade here we go again. That sort of thing.

'Sorry, that's not really relevant. He told me a story once. About a Soviet composer, I can't remember which. It was in the war, what they called the Great Patriotic War. Against the

65

Germans. Everyone had to put their shoulder to the wheel, so the Kremlin told Soviet composers they had to write music which would inspire the people and make them throw out the aggressor. None of your art music, says the Kremlin, we need music for the people which comes from the people.

'So the top composers were all packed off to various regions and told to come back with cheerful suites of folk music. And this one was sent to the Caucasus – at least, I think it was the Caucasus, anyway it was one of those regions which Stalin had tried to wipe out a few years earlier, you know, collectivization, purges, ethnic cleansing, famine, I should have said that earlier. Anyway, he travels around looking for peasant songs, the old fiddler who plays at weddings, that sort of thing. And guess what he discovered? There wasn't any authentic folk music left! You see, Stalin had wiped out the villages, and scattered all the peasants, so he'd wiped out the music in the process.'

Paul took a sip of his wine. Was he pausing or had he stopped? This was another social skill women were meant to learn: when a man's story had come to an end. Mostly, it wasn't a problem, as the end was thumpingly obvious; or else the narrator started snorting with laughter in advance, which was always a pretty good clue. Martha had long ago decided only to laugh at things she found funny. It seemed a normal sort of rule; but some men found it rebuking.

'So he had a problem, the composer. He couldn't very well go back to Moscow and say I'm afraid the Great Leader has unfortunately by mistake wiped out all the music down there. That wouldn't have been wise. So this is what he did instead. He invented some new folk songs. Then he wrote a suite based on them and took it back to Moscow. Mission accomplished.'

Another sip, followed by a half-glance at Martha. She took it as a sign that the story was probably over. This was confirmed when he said, 'I'm a bit shy of you, I'm afraid.'

Well, that, she supposed, was better than being leaned heavily against by a red-faced, chalk-striped bruiser with suspiciously perfect teeth who said in a jolly, bantering way, 'Of course, what I *really* want to do is shag the tits off you.' Yes, it was better than that. But she had heard this one before as well. Perhaps she had passed the age when there could be new beginnings; only familiar ones.

Martha's tone was deliberately brisk. 'So what you're saying is that Sir Jack's rather like Stalin?'

Paul stared at her in bewilderment, as if she had slapped him. 'What?' Then he peered suspiciously around the wine lodge, as if for some deft KGB skulker.

'I thought that was the point of the story.'

'Christ, no, whatever gave . . .'

'I can't imagine,' said Martha, smiling.

'It just came into my head.'

'Forget it.'

'Anyway, there's no comparison . . .'

'Forget it.'

'I mean, just to take a simple point, present-day England is hardly Soviet Russia at that time . . .'

'I never said a word.'

The progressive softening of her tone encouraged him to raise his eyes, though not to meet hers. He looked past her, in little swerves and dabs, first on one side, then on the other. Slowly, as warily as a butterfly, his glance settled on her right ear. Martha was confused. She had become so used to plots and ploys, to complicit directness and confident hands, that a simple shyness pierced her.

'And what was the reaction?' she found herself asking, in almost a panic of tenderness.

'What reaction?'

'When he took his suite of peasant songs back to Moscow and had it played. I mean, that's the real point, isn't it? They'd asked him for some patriotic music to inspire the workers and such peasants as were left after all the purges and famines and whatever, so did this music, this music he'd completely invented, was it as useful and uplifting as the music he would

67

have found if there'd been any? I suppose that's the real question.'

She was over-elaborating, she knew. No, she was burbling. This wasn't how she normally talked. But she'd pulled him back from wherever he was going. He dropped his gaze from her ear and seemed to retreat behind the frames of his spectacles. He was frowning, though more at himself than at her, she felt.

'History doesn't relate,' he finally replied.

Wouf. Well done, Martha. Just got out of that alive.

History doesn't relate.

She liked the way he couldn't remember the name of the composer. And whether or not it had been the Caucasus.

DR MAX

was, of all the assembled theorists, consultants and implementers, the slowest to grasp the principles and demands of the Project. This was initially ascribed to scholarly isolationism – and yet Dr Max had been appointed precisely because he seemed not to smell of the cloister. He had always moved easily between his professorial chair and the broadcasting studios; he was adept at the posher game-shows, and first-named half a dozen TV anchors as they serenely waited for him to lay out his dapper controversialism. While appearing quite urban, he contributed the Nature Notes column to *The Times* under the well-leaked pseudonym Country Mouse. His sartorial preference was for tweed suits with a range of toning suede waistcoats, topped off by a trademark bow-tie; he was an early choice for style columns such as 'My Mufti'. However far his trouser leg rode up as he ostentatiously relaxed amid the sneaky subversions of a TV studio's furniture, bare calf was never glimpsed. He was the obvious choice.

Dr Max's first expression of tactical naivety had been to ask where the Project's library could be found. His second was to circulate offprints of his article in *Leather Trash* entitled 'Did Prince Albert Wear a Prince Albert? – A Hermeneutic Study in Penile Archaeology'. More serious was his tendency to address Sir Jack at Executive Committee with a friskiness which even an Appointed Cynic would not have risked. Then there had been his – as some felt – rather over-personalized homoerotic reading of Nelson and Hardy's kiss during the brain-storming session on Great British Heroes. Sir Jack had ringingly listed the family newspapers under his pastoral control, before inviting Dr Max to fuck off and stuff his bow-tie up his arse, advice that was not recorded in the minutes.

Jeff didn't like his new role as minder to the Official Historian, mainly because he didn't like the Official Historian. Why should Dr Max come under Concept Development, except because it amused Sir Jack? Jeff didn't think his reluctance sprang from homophobic prejudice. It was more a prejudice against dandies, egotists and gadflies, against people who looked at Jeff as if he was some great, slow, brain-damaged plodder and asked, in a manner they deemed witty, how many Concepts he'd Developed over the weekend. Jeff always answered such questions in a straightforward, literal manner, which reinforced Dr Max's assumptions. But it was either that or throttling the fellow.

'Max, if I may.' They were in the Oasis, a ferny, palmy, waterfally zone of Pitman House, which probably had some architectural theorizing behind it. No doubt he lacked a grasp of metaphor, but the sound of running water always made Jeff want to pee. Now he stood looking down at the Official Historian, at his silly little moustache, his poncey fob-chain, his wanky TV waistcoat, his smug cuffs. The Official Historian looked up at Jeff, at his bullocky shoulders, his horsily long face, his donkey hair, his glistening sheepy eyes. They had placed themselves awkwardly, as if some choreographer had told Jeff to throw his arm round Dr Max's shoulders in a spirit of camaraderie, but neither could bring himself to effect, or accept, the gesture.

'Max. Look.' Jeff had a feeling of weariness. He never knew where to start. Or rather, he found that each time he needed to start at an even more basic level of assumption than previously. 'It was bound to be a change of pace for you, coming here.'

'Oh, I wouldn't say that.' Dr Max was feeling generous. 'There are one or two of you I m–ight accept into my classes as m–ature students.'

'No, I didn't mean it that way, Max. Change of pace up, not down.'

'Ah. Yes. Boo-boo time again, I see. Instruct me then.'

The Concept Developer paused. Dr Max, as he liked to be called on television, since formality and informality were thus combined, was poised before him, ready to sparkle at a floor-manager's thumbs-up. 'Let me put it this way. You are our Official Historian. You are responsible, how can I put it, for our history. Do you follow?'

'Clear as a b–ell, so far, my dear Jeff.'

'Right. Well, the point of *our* history – and I stress the our – will be to make our guests, those buying what is for the moment referred to as Quality Leisure, *feel better.*'

'Better. Ah, the old e–thical questions, what a snake-pit they are. Better. Meaning?'

'Less ignorant.'

'Precisely. That's why I was a–ppointed, I assume.'

'Max, you missed the verb.'

'Which one?'

'Feel. We want them to *feel* less ignorant. Whether they *are* or not is quite another matter, even outside our jurisdiction.' Dr Max now had his thumbs stuck in the pockets of his taupe waistcoat, a gesture indicating to viewers humorous scepticism. Jeff would have happily hung the fellow out to dry, but he pressed on. 'The point is that most people don't want what you and your colleagues think of as history – the sort you get in books – because they don't know how to deal with it. Personally, I've every sympathy. With them, that is. I've tried to read a few history books myself, and while I may not be clever enough to enroll in your classes, it seems to me that the main problem with them is this: they all assume you've read most of the other history books already. It's a closed system. There's nowhere to start. It's like looking for the tag to unwrap a CD. You know that feeling? There's a coloured strip running all the way round, and you can see what's inside and you want to get at it, but the strip doesn't seem to start anywhere no matter how many times you run your fingernail round it?'

Dr Max had taken out a little notebook and his silver propelling pencil was poised. 'Do you mind if I a–ppropriate that? It's frightfully good. The bit about the CD wrapper, I mean.' He scribbled a note. 'Yes? So?'

'So we don't threaten people. We don't insult their ignorance. We deal in what they already understand. Perhaps we add a little more. But nothing unwelcomely major.'

'And having recently had my bow-tie relocated by our i–llustrious leader, what, might I solipsistically enquire, would be the function of that larger body, namely the Official Historian, within which the bow-tie has been instructed to reside?'

Jeff's sigh was a sound from the marshalling yard. A simpleton with fancy phrases – the worst of both worlds. 'The Historian is there to advise us on how much History people already know.'

'Right,' said Dr Max, with a professional languor.

'Oh, for Christ's sake, Max, people won't be shelling out to *learn* things. If they want that, they can go to a sodding library if they can find one open. They'll come to us to enjoy what they already know.'

'And it's my job to tell you what that is.'

'Welcome aboard, Dr Max. Welcome aboard.' Behind them an unseen windjet stirred the palm-fronds. 'And a tad more advice if I may.'

'W–illingly.' Dr Max aped the first-year student.

'Too much scent. Nothing personal, you understand. I'm thinking of the Chairman.'

71

'So glad you n–oticed. *Eau de toilette*, of course. Petersburg. Perhaps you guessed? No? I thought it somehow appropriate.'

'You mean, you're a Russian in disguise?'

'Ho ho, Jeff, I do like it when you pretend to plod. You need me to explain, evidently.' Jeff raised his eyes to the atrium of Pitman House too late; Dr Max had already done the switch from student to professor. 'The secrets of the great *p–arfumiers* were, as you may be aware, always closely guarded. Handed down from man to boy in secret ceremonies, written in code if ever trusted to paper. Then – imagine – a change of fashion, a break in the chain, a premature death, and they are gone, vanished on the air. It is the catastrophe that no-one notices. We read the past, we hear its music, we see its graphic images, yet our nostrils are never activated. Think what a point of entry it would be for one's students if one could take the cork from a flask and say, Versailles smelt like this, Vauxhall Gardens like this.

'You recall newspaper reports of the find in Grasse two years ago?' Jeff evidently did not. 'The blending-book in the blocked-up chimney? So romantic one almost didn't believe it. The constituent parts and proportions of numerous forgotten scents listed in a decipherable manner. Each identified by a Greek letter which matched an order book already in the local museum. Incontrovertibly the same hand. So this, *this*,' Dr Max cocked his neck in Jeff's direction, 'is Petersburg, last worn by some aristocrat at the court of the Tsar two centuries ago. Thrilling, yes?' Dr Max could see that Jeff was plainly unthrilled, so offered a helpful comparison. 'It's like scientists cloning animals lost to the planet for millennia.'

'Dr Max,' said Jeff, 'It makes you *smell* like a cloned animal.'

'THE CENTRAL FACTS,

Mr Polo, that is all we need. You know how sedimentary rock and flint arrowheads bore me.'

'All too well, Sir Jack.' Mark enjoyed such occasions, the display and the joust of them, the spirit of subservient dominance that was involved. No notes, no documents, just a set of curly blond facts in a curly blond head. Showing off to the others while gauging Sir Jack's shifting response. Though 'gauge' implied precision; in reality, you entered the dark tunnels of his mood like a potholer with a short-beamed torch.

'The island,' he began, 'as Sir Jack pointed out two weeks ago, is a diamond. Otherwise a lozenge. Some have compared it to a turbot. Twenty-three miles in length, thirteen across at its widest point. One hundred and fifty-five square miles. Each corner at a cardinal point of the compass, more or less. Was once joined to the mainland, back in the days of sedimentary rock and flint arrowheads. Could find out, but pre-television, anyway. Topography: mixture of rolling chalk downland of considerable beauty and bungaloid dystopia.'

'Mark, again this false distinction between Nature and Man. I have warned you. Also the long words. What was that last phrase again?'

'Bungaloid dystopia.'

'So undemocratic. So élitist. I might have to borrow it.'

Mark knew he would. It was one of Sir Jack's ways of complimenting you. And he had tartishly sought the compliment. So far, so good. He picked up his narrative. 'The place is pretty flat on the whole. Good-looking cliffs. I thought the Committee might like a souvenir.' From his pocket he took a small glass lighthouse filled with bands of differently coloured sand. 'Local speciality. From Alum Bay. Twelve or so colours. Easy to replicate, I'd say. The sand, I mean.' He placed the lighthouse on Sir Jack's desk, inviting the possibility of comment. None came.

'Otherwise, some things called chines, which are a bit like ravines where streams have cut away the chalk cliffs on their way to the sea. Much used by smugglers, *vide infra*, or rather, *audi infra*. Flora and fauna: nothing particularly rare and endangered. A detail about squirrels: they only have the red variety because it's an island and the grey buggers never managed to catch the boat. But I can't see anyone making a fuss about them. Oh yes, and *slightly* bad news, Sir Jack.' He waited for a tufty, black, grey-threaded eyebrow to lift. 'They do have puffins.'

'All together now,' cried Sir Jack merrily, '*Fuck the puffins!*'

'Right,' Mark continued. 'What else has it got? Oh yes, the filthiest cappuccino in the whole country. I found it in a small seafront café in Shanklin. Worth preserving the machine if we are planning a Museum of Torture.'

Mark paused, then felt the silence. Idiot. Done it again. He'd known it even as he'd done it. Idiot. You never followed Sir Jack's joke with one of your own. You could precede, so that he could top you, but following implied competition rather than sycophancy. When would he learn?

'What's it got we can use? A little bit of everything, I'd say, yet at the same time nothing too mega. Nothing we can't dispense with if need be. So. One castle, rather nice: ramparts, gatehouse, keep, chapel. No moat, but we could bung one in easily enough. Next, one royal palace: Osborne House, as noted by Dr Max. Italianate. Opinions differ. Two resident monarchs: Charles the first, in captivity at the said castle before his execution; Queen Victoria, in residence at the said palace, where she died. Feature possibilities in either, I'd say. One resident famous poet: Tennyson. A couple of Roman villas, famous mosaics, which seemed to me and to greater authorities crude in comparison with European equivalents. A large number of manor houses of different periods. Various parish churches; bits of wall-painting, some monumental brasses, a quantity of fine tombs. Many thatched cottages, perfect for tea-shops. Correction: most of which already *are* tea-shops, but suitable for upgrade. No modern buildings of note except Quarr Abbey, circa 1910, a masterpiece of early twentieth-century Expressionism, Belgian brick out of Gaudi, Catalonia, Cordova, Cluny, designed by a Benedictine monk, I take such opinions from Pevsner, as you know. But specialist change of user, I would recommend.

'What else? Cowes Regatta indeed, as Jeff pointed out. King Charles's bowling-green, Tennyson's tennis-court. A vineyard or two. The Needles. Various obelisks and monuments. Two large prisons, complete with prisoners. Apart from boat-building, the main industry used to be smuggling. And wrecking. Nowadays it's tourism. Not a top-dollar destination as you might have inferred. Old proverb to the effect that there were no monks, lawyers and foxes on the island. Tennyson said that the air on the Downs was worth sixpence a pint – I wish I had sixpence, or a pint, for every time I've read that. Swinburne the poet buried there. Keats visited, so did Thomas Macaulay. George Morland if you're interested. H. de Vere Stacpoole anyone? Offers on the table? *The Blue Lagoon*? No, I thought not. Novelist and resident of Bonchurch. Anyway, you'll be pleased to know that H. de Vere Stacpoole donated the village pond to Bonchurch in memory of his late wife.' Mark reported this final fact in a neutral tone, hoping to set something up for Sir Jack. He was not disappointed.

'Fill it in!' chortled Sir Jack. 'Concrete it over!'

Mark had a moment of silent satisfaction. At the same time, he felt there was something ritualistic and inauthentic about Sir Jack's cry. It was Sir Jack being 'Sir Jack'. Not, in one sense, that he wasn't always 'Sir Jack'.

'And yet, pause awhile. Who are we, I ask myself, to lightly mock a man's devotion to his wife? We live in a cynical age, and that, gentlemen, is not my trade. Tell me, Mark, did Stacpoole's wife die tragically? Shredded on a railway track? Raped and butchered by a gang of vandals perhaps?'

'I'll find out, Sir Jack.'

'It might make a feature. Good God, it might make a movie!'

'Sir Jack, I should say that some of the research material I've been working from was sourced a bit on the antique side. I haven't actually seen the pond. For all I know it might have been filled in ages ago.'

'Then, Marco, we shall dig it out again, and recreate this moving legend. Perhaps the famous red squirrels gnawed through a telegraph pole which decapitated her?' Sir Jack was Jolly Jack indeed this morning. 'Summarize, Mr Polo. Summarize your exotic travels for us.'

'Summary. I've put all the history stuff in my report. Hope it passes muster with Dr Max. But to cite a writer by the name of Vesey-Fitzgerald' (he left a micro-pause in case Sir Jack wanted to revel in the pomposity of old-style names), '"Once the Garden Isle, it is now purely a tourist resort." That of course was some time ago. And now . . .' He looked across at Sir Jack, begging the compliment. Sir Jack did not fail him.

'And now, if I might make so bold with a phrase, it is a bungaloid dystopia where you can't even get a decent cappuccino.'

'Thank you, Sir Jack.' The Project Manager gave a bow into which those present could read irony if they wished. 'In short, perfect for our purposes. A location dying for makeover and upgrade.'

'Excellent.' Sir Jack thumped his foot-bell and a barman appeared. 'Potter! H. de Vere Potter, you know that magnum of Krug I asked you to put on ice? Well, return it to the cellar. We'll have cappuccinos all round, with the finest froth your machine can deliver.'

ANOTHER DRINK, A DINNER INVITATION BASED ON OBVIOUSLY FRAUDULENT PREMISES, A FILM, ANOTHER DRINK, AND, MUCH LATER THAN WITH MOST MEN,

they were at a point of decision. Or if not that, then the point at which a decision had to be taken about whether or not a larger decision had to be taken. To her surprise, Martha felt no impatience, none of the restless, psoriatic self-consciousness of some previous visits to this location. Two nights ago, he had kissed her on the cheek, except that the part of her cheek he chose, or ended up with, had been the corner of her mouth; yet she didn't feel, as she might once have done, make up your mind, stop sitting on the fence, kiss me or don't kiss me. Instead, she just thought, that was nice, even if I did sense you almost getting on tiptoe. Well, lower heels next time.

They were on her sofa, fingers half touching, still room for escape, for sensible second thoughts. 'Look,' she said, 'I'd better make it clear. I don't get involved with men I work with, and I don't go out with younger men.'

'Not unless they're shorter than you and wear glasses,' he replied.

'Nor with men who earn less than me.'

'Unless they're shorter than you.'

'Nor with men who are shorter than me.'

'Unless they wear glasses.'

'I actually haven't got anything against glasses,' she said, but he was kissing her before she got to the end of the sentence.

In bed, when words started again, Paul found his brain a sponge for happiness, his tongue a tearaway. 'You didn't ask *me* about *my* principles,' he said.

'Which ones?'

'Oh, I have principles too. About women I work with, women who are older than me, women who earn more than I do.'

'Yes, I suppose you must.' She felt chastened, as if she had been not so much predatory as crass.

'Certainly do. I have principles in favour of all of them.'

'As long as they're not taller than you.'

'Now that I can't abide.'

'And have, oh, darkish brown hair cut rather short.'

'No, must be blonde.'

'And like sex.'

'No, I much prefer a woman who just goes through the motions.'

They were murmuring twaddle, but she felt that in any case there weren't rules about what you couldn't say. She felt he wouldn't be shocked, or jealous, he'd simply understand. What she said next wasn't meant to test him.

'Someone once had his hand where yours is.'

'Bastard,' muttered Paul. 'Well, bastard with good taste.'

'And do you know what he said?'

'Anyone with five percent of a human heart would be lost for words. They wouldn't be able to say anything.'

'Accurate flattery,' she said. 'It's amazing how good it makes you feel. Every country should have it. There'd be no more wars.'

'So what did he say?' It was almost as if his hand asked the question.

'Oh, I expected he was going to say something nice.'

'Accurate flattery.'

'Exactly. And I could almost hear him thinking. And then he said, "You must be a 34C."'

'Idiot. Moron. Anyone I know?'

She shook her head. No-one you know.

'Complete moron,' he repeated. 'You're obviously a 34B.'

She hit him with a pillow.

Later, coming out of a half-doze, he said, 'Can I ask a question?'

'All questions answered. That's a promise.' It was a promise she was also making to herself.

'Tell me about your marriage.'

'My marriage?'

'Yes, your marriage. I was there when you came for interview. I was the one you didn't notice. When you were doing your dance with Sir Jack.'

'Well, if you don't tell anyone . . .'

'Promise.'

'I always allow myself one tactical lie per interview. That was it.'

'So you don't have to get divorced before you can marry me.'

'I think there are bigger impediments than that.'

'Such as?'

'Not liking sex much.'

When he came back from peeing, she said, 'Paul, how did you know I was a 34B?'

'Just my incredible instinctive knowledge and understanding of women.'

'Go on.'

'Go on?'

'Sorry. I mean, apart from that.'

'Well, you may have noticed I was all thumbs undoing your bra. I'm afraid I couldn't help reading the label. I mean, I wasn't trying to.'

Before they went to sleep, he said, 'So, to summarize the minutes of the meeting, if I change my job and get a salary rise and falsify my birth certificate and hang on a door to make myself taller and get contact lenses, you might think of going out with me.'

'I'll consider it.'

'And in return you'll work on your impediments.'

'Which ones?'

'Oh, like being married and not liking sex.'

'Yes,' she said, and felt a sudden, unjustifiable melancholy come over her. No, a justifiable one, since it said, you don't deserve this, whatever it might be. It's just come by to mock you.

'Unless . . . I mean, I don't know, perhaps you're going out with someone.'

'Yes, I think I am,' she replied, and feeling his arm tense up, added quickly, 'now.'

The next morning, after she had woken him early so that he could cross London and arrive at Pitman House from the

normal direction and in the normal clothes, she thought: well,
yes, maybe.

THE SUBJECT
                of Dr Max's test was a 49-year-old man.
Caucasian, middle-class, of English stock though unable to trace
his ancestry beyond three generations. Mother's origin Welsh
borders, father's North Midlands. State primary education,
scholarship to public school, scholarship to university. Had
worked in liberal arts and professional media. Spoke one foreign
language. Married, no children. Considered himself cultured,
aware, intelligent, well-informed. No educational or professional connection with History, as requested.

The purpose of the interview was not explained. There was
disguising mention of market research and a prominent soft
drinks company. Dr Max's presence was not alluded to. The
questions were put by a woman researcher in neutral clothes.

The Subject was asked what happened at the Battle of
Hastings.

Subject replied: '1066.'

Question was repeated.

Subject laughed. 'Battle of Hastings. 1066.' Pause. 'King
Harold. Got an arrow in his eye.'

Subject behaved as if he had answered the question. Subject
was asked if he could identify other participants in the battle,
comment on military strategy, suggest possible causes of the
conflict or its consequences.

Subject was silent for twenty-five seconds. 'Duke – I think
Duke – William of Normandy, came over with his army, by sea
from France, though it might not have been France then, the bit
he came from, won the battle and became William the
Conqueror. Or he was William the Conqueror already and
became William the First. No, I was right before. First proper

king of England. I mean, Edward the Confessor and the king who burnt the cakes, Alfred, but they don't really count, do they? I think he was related to Harold in some way. Possibly cousins. Most of them were related at that time, weren't they? They were all sort of Normans. I mean, unless Harold was a Saxon.'

Subject was asked to reflect on the matter of whether or not he considered Harold to have been a Saxon.

Subject silent for twenty seconds. 'He might have been. I think he was. No, on second thoughts I'd bet against it. I think he was another kind of Norman. On account of being William's cousin. If he was.'

Subject was asked where exactly the battle took place.

Subject: 'Is that a trick question?'

Subject was assured there were no trick questions.

Subject: 'Hastings. Well, not in the town, I don't think. Though I suppose there wasn't much of a town then. On the beach?'

Subject was asked what happened between the Battle of Hastings and the Coronation of William the Conqueror.

Subject: 'Not sure. I imagine there was some sort of march on London, like Mussolini's March on Rome, with some skirmishes and maybe another battle, and the locals flocking to the victor's flag as they tend to on such occasions.'

Subject was asked what happened to Harold.

Subject: 'Is that a . . . no, you said there weren't any. He got an arrow in the eye.' (*Aggressively*:) 'Everyone knows that.'

Subject was asked what happened after this incident.

Subject: 'He died. Of course.' (*In a more conciliatory mood*:) 'I'm pretty sure he must have died from the arrow, but I don't know how long after receiving the wound. I shouldn't think there was much you could do in those days about an arrow in the eye. It's pretty unlucky when you think about it. I suppose the course of English history might have been different if he hadn't looked up at that moment. Like Cleopatra's nose.' Pause. 'Mind you, I don't actually know who was winning the battle at the time

Harold got the arrow in his eye, so perhaps the course of English history would have remained exactly the same.'

Subject was asked if there was anything he could add to his account.

Subject was silent for thirty seconds. 'They wore chainmail and pointy helmets with noseguards and had broadswords.' Asked which side he was referring to, Subject replied: 'Both sides. I think. Yes, because that would tie in with them all being Normans, wouldn't it? Unless Harold was a Saxon. But Harold's boys definitely weren't running about in leather jerkins or whatever. Hang on. They might have been. The poorer ones, the cannon-fodder.' (*Cautiously:*) 'Not that I'm saying they had cannon. The ones who weren't knights. I can't imagine everyone could afford chainmail.'

Subject was asked if that was all.

Subject (*excited:*): 'No! The Bayeux Tapestry, I've just remembered. That's all about the Battle of Hastings. Or part of it is. It's also got the first sighting, or the first recording, of Halley's Comet. I think. No, the first representation, that's what I mean. Is that any use?'

Subject agreed that he was now at the full limits of his knowledge.

We believe that this is a fair and accurate account of the interview, and that the Subject is representative of the target group.

Dr Max uncapped his fountain-pen and leaked his reluctant initials on to the report. There had been many others like this, and they were beginning to depress him. Most people remembered history in the same conceited yet evanescent fashion as they recalled their own childhood. It seemed to Dr Max positively unpatriotic to know so little about the origins and forging of your nation. And yet, therein lay the immediate paradox: that patriotism's most eager bedfellow was ignorance, not knowledge.

Dr Max sighed. It wasn't just professional, it was also personal. Were they pretending – had they always been pretending – those people who flocked to his lectures, called his phone-in, laughed at his jokes, bought his books? When he splashed down in their minds, was it as useless as a flamingo landing in a birdbath? Did they all know bugger all about bugger everything like this ignorant 49-year-old bugger in front of him, who considered himself cultured, aware, intelligent and well-informed?

'Bugger!' said Dr Max.

THE PRINTOUT OF JEFF'S SURVEY

was laid before Sir Jack on his Battle Table. Potential purchasers of Quality Leisure in twenty-five countries had been asked to list six characteristics, virtues or quintessences which the word England suggested to them. They were not being asked to free-associate; there was no pressure of time on the respondents, no preselected multiple choice. 'If we're giving people what they want,' Sir Jack had insisted, 'then we should at least have the humility to find out what that might be.' Citizens of the world therefore told Sir Jack in an unprejudiced way what in their view the Fifty Quintessences of Englishness were:

1. ROYAL FAMILY
2. BIG BEN/HOUSES OF PARLIAMENT
3. MANCHESTER UNITED FOOTBALL CLUB
4. CLASS SYSTEM
5. PUBS
6. A ROBIN IN THE SNOW
7. ROBIN HOOD AND HIS MERRIE MEN
8. CRICKET
9. WHITE CLIFFS OF DOVER
10. IMPERIALISM

11. UNION JACK

12. SNOBBERY

13. GOD SAVE THE KING/QUEEN

14. BBC

15. WEST END

16. TIMES NEWSPAPER

17. SHAKESPEARE

18. THATCHED COTTAGES

19. CUP OF TEA/DEVONSHIRE CREAM TEA

20. STONEHENGE

21. PHLEGM/STIFF UPPER LIP

22. SHOPPING

23. MARMALADE

24. BEEFEATERS/TOWER OF LONDON

25. LONDON TAXIS

26. BOWLER HAT

27. TV CLASSIC SERIALS

28. OXFORD/CAMBRIDGE

29. HARRODS

30. DOUBLE-DECKER BUSES/RED BUSES

31. HYPOCRISY

32. GARDENING

33. PERFIDY/UNTRUSTWORTHINESS

34. HALF-TIMBERING

35. HOMOSEXUALITY

36. ALICE IN WONDERLAND

37. WINSTON CHURCHILL

38. MARKS & SPENCER

39. BATTLE OF BRITAIN

40. FRANCIS DRAKE

41. TROOPING THE COLOUR

42. WHINGEING

43. QUEEN VICTORIA

44. BREAKFAST

45. BEER/WARM BEER

46. EMOTIONAL FRIGIDITY

Jeff watched Sir Jack's expression move between wise self-congratulation and acrid dismay as he worked through the list. Then a fleshy hand dismissed him, and Jeff knew the bitterness of the messenger.

Alone, Sir Jack considered the printout again. It frankly deteriorated towards the end. He crossed off items he judged the result of faulty polling technique and pondered the rest. Many had been correctly foreseen: there would be no shortage of shopping and thatched cottages serving Devonshire cream teas on the Island. Gardening, breakfast, taxis, double-deckers: those were all useful endorsements. A Robin in the Snow: where had that come from? All those Christmas cards, perhaps. The Magna Carta was currently being translated into decent English. *The Times* newspaper was no doubt easily acquired; Beefeaters would be fattened up, and the White Cliffs of Dover relocated without much linguistic wrenching to what had previously been Whitecliff Bay. Big Ben, the Battle of Britain, Robin Hood, Stonehenge: couldn't be simpler.

But there were problems at the top of the list. Numbers 1, 2, and 3, to be precise. Sir Jack had put out early feelers to Parliament, but his initial offer to the nation's legislators, put at a working breakfast with the Speaker of the House of Commons, had been insensitively received; the word contempt might even have been used. The football club would be easier: he'd send Mark up to Manchester with a team of top negotiators. Little blue-eyed Mark who looked like a soft touch and then flattered you into signing your life away. No doubt there would be matters of local pride, civic tradition, and so on – there always were. Sir Jack knew that in such cases it was rarely just a question of price: it was price combined with the necessary self-deception that price was finally less important than principle. What principle might apply here? Well, Mark would find one. And if they dug their little studs in, you could always buy up the club's title behind its back. Or simply copy it and tell them to fuck off.

Buck House would need a different approach: less carrot and stick, more carrot and carrot. The King and Queen had been taking a lot of flak lately from the usual mixture of cynics, malcontents and nay-sayers. Sir Jack's newspapers had been under orders to patriotically refute all such treasonable libels while reproducing them in mournfully extensive detail. Ditto that squalid business with Prince Rick. King's cousin in drug-crazed lezzie sex-romps – was that the headline? He'd fired the journalist, of course, but sadly dirt had a tendency to adhere. Carrot and carrot; they could have a whole bunch of carrots if that was what it took. He would offer them improved pay and conditions, less work and more privacy; he would contrast the carping ingratitude of their current subjects with the guaranteed adoration of their future ones; he would stress the decay of their old kingdom and the bright prospects of a precious jewel set in a silver sea, Mark II.

And how would that jewel glitter? Sir Jack prodded a forefinger down Jeff's list again, and his loyal growl intensified with each item he'd crossed off. This wasn't a poll, it was bare-faced character assassination. Who the *fuck* did they think they were, going around saying things like that about England? His England. What did *they* know? Bloody tourists, thought Sir Jack.

CAREFULLY, AWKWARDLY,
                                        Paul laid out his life before Martha. A suburban upbringing on a mock-Tudor estate: prunus and forsythia, mown grass and neighbourhood watch. Car-washing on Sunday mornings; amateur concerts in village churches. No, of course not every Sunday: that was just how it

felt. His childhood had been peaceful; or boring, if you preferred. Neighbour would report neighbour for using a sprinkler during a hosepipe ban. At one corner of the estate there was a mock-Tudor police station; in its front garden stood a mock-Tudor bird-box on a long pole.

'I wish I'd done something bad,' said Paul.

'Why?'

'Oh, so that I could confess it to you, and you would understand, or forgive, or whatever.'

'That's not necessary. Anyway, it might make me like you less.'

Paul was silent for a few moments. 'I used to wank a lot,' he said with an air of hopefulness.

'Not a crime,' said Martha. 'So did I.'

'Damn.'

He showed her photographs: Paul in nappies, in shorts, in cricket pads, in black tie, his hair gradually darkening from straw to peat, his glasses patrolling the outer parameters of fashion, his adolescent plumpness fading as the anxieties of adulthood took hold. He was the middle child of three, between a sister who mocked him and a feted younger brother. He had been good at school, and good at escaping notice. After college, he had joined Pitco as a management trainee; then steady promotion which offended nobody until one day he was in the gents and realized that the figure next to him, so broad it seemed to lever out the wings of the stand-up, was Sir Jack Pitman himself, who must have decided to forsake the splendour and privacy of his porphyry toilet for an exercise in democratic urination. Sir Jack was humming the second movement of the 'Kreutzer' Sonata, which made Paul so nervous that his pee had dried up. For some reason he never understood, he started telling Sir Jack a story about Beethoven and the village policeman. He didn't dare look at the Chairman, of course, just told the story. At the end of it, he heard Sir Jack zip himself up and wander off, whistling the third movement, the *presto*, very inaccurately, Paul couldn't help

87

noticing. The next day he'd been summoned to Sir Jack's private office, and a year later had become his Ideas Catcher. At the end of each month he would present the Chairman with his own personal Hansard. Sometimes he even managed to surprise Sir Jack with items of forgotten wisdom. The jowly nod would be primarily of self-approval, but it also served to congratulate the Catcher of the Idea for his nimbleness in recuperating the crystal aphorism before it hit the ground.

'Girls,' Martha said. She'd had enough of Sir Jack Pitman.

'Yes,' was all he replied. By which he meant: from time to time, carefully, awkwardly. But never like now.

She answered with a preliminary version of her own life. He listened tensely when she recounted her father's betrayal and the Counties of England. He relaxed with the Horticultural Show and Mr A. Jones, laughed uncertainly at the story of Jessica James, went solemn about not blaming your parents after the age of twenty-five. Then Martha told him her mother's opinion that men were either wicked or weak.

'Which am I?'

'The jury's still out.' She was teasing, but he looked downcast. 'It's all right, you're not meant to agree with your parents after the age of twenty-five either.'

Paul nodded. 'Do you think there's a connection?'

'Between what?'

'Between your father sodding off, as you put it, and you working for Sir Jack?'

'Paul, look me in the eye.' He did so, reluctantly; he had graduated beyond her ears by now, but there were times when he preferred her cheeks and her mouth. 'Our employer is not a substitute for a lost father, all right?'

'It's just that he sometimes treats you like a daughter. A rebellious one who questions him all the time.'

'That's his problem. And that's cheap psychology.'

'I didn't mean . . .'

'No . . .' But he must have meant something. Martha, having

constructed her life, having built her character, resisted contrary interpretation.

There was a silence. Eventually Paul said, 'Do you know the story of Beethoven and the village policeman?'

'You're not auditioning for a job now.' Oh, watch your tongue, Martha, it was meant to be a joke, but he's blushing. You've murdered relationships with that tongue before. She softened her voice. 'Tell me another time. I've a better idea.'

He kept his eyes away from her.

'I'll be weakly wicked and you can be wickedly weak. Or the other way round if you prefer.'

It was their fourth time in bed together. The first careful awkwardnesses were disappearing; they had stopped banging knees. But on this occasion, as she felt them about to take their separate journeys, he half-raised himself on an elbow and said quietly, 'Martha.'

She turned her head. His glasses were on the bedside table and his gaze was naked. She wondered if she was out of focus for him, and if this made it easier for him to look her in the eye.

'Martha,' he repeated. In a way, he didn't need to say anything more, but he did anyway. 'I'm still here.'

'I can see that,' she said. 'I can feel that.' She tightened herself around his cock, but knew she was being defensive, jaunty.

'Yes. But you know what I mean.'

She nodded. She'd got out of the habit of being there. She smiled at him. Maybe things could be simple again. In any case, she was grateful to him for taking the risk. She stayed with him, watching, attending, following, leading, approving. She was careful, she was honest; so was he.

And yet, it wasn't the best sex she'd ever had in her life. Still, who said there was a connection between human decency and good fucking? And who kept a league-table of lovers? Only the insecurely competitive. Most people couldn't remember the best sex of their lives. Those who did were exceptions. Like Emil. Good old Emil, a gay friend of hers. He remembered. She'd once sent him a postcard from Carcassonne. By the time she got home, his swift and exultant reply was on her mat. His letter began: 'Had the best fucky-fuck of my life in Carcassonne. Way back when. A hotel room in the old city with a balcony overlooking cooked roofs. A tremendous storm was brewing, like in an El Greco, and as the heavens went about their business, so did we, until the gap between the lightning and the thunder grew to nothing, and the storm was overhead, and all we seemed to be doing was following the guidance of the skies. Afterwards we lay on the bed listening to the storm head off towards the hills, and as we paused, we heard a cleansing rain begin to fall. Enough to make you believe in God, eh, Martha?'

Well, enough for Martha to believe that God, if He existed, didn't have any prejudice against gays. But God – and man, for that matter – had never arranged such grand counterpoint for her. The best fucky-fuck of her life? Pass. She snuffled her face into Paul's armpit. She'd settle for good.

ROAST BEEF OF OLD ENGLAND

was naturally approved on the nod by the Gastronomic Sub-Committee, as were Yorkshire pudding, Lancashire hotpot, Sussex pond pudding, Coventry godcakes, Aylesbury duckling, Brown Windsor Soup, Devonshire splits, Melton Mowbray pie, Bedfordshire clangers, Liverpool Christmas loaf, Chelsea buns, Cumberland sausages, and Kentish chicken pudding. A swift tick was given to fish and chips, bacon and eggs, mint sauce, steak and kidney pudding, ploughman's lunch, shepherd's pie, cottage pie, plum duff, custard with skin, bread and butter pudding, liver and bacon, pheasant, game chips and crown roast. Approved for their picturesque nomenclature (contents could be adjusted later if necessary) were London Particular, Queen of puddings, Poor Knights of Windsor, Hindle Wakes, stargazey pie, wow-wow sauce, maids-of-honour, muffins, collops, crumpets, fat rascals, Bosworth jumbles, moggy and parkin. The Sub-Committee banned porridge for its Scottish associations, faggots and fairy cakes in case they offended the pink dollar, spotted dick even when renamed spotted dog. Devils- and angels-on-horseback were in; toad-in-the-hole and cock-a-leekie out. Welsh rarebit, Scotch eggs and Irish stew were not even discussed.

There would be a fine range of ales from the planned micro-brewery at Ventnor; Island wines would be served by the jug, provided the Adgestone vineyards survived the final Strategic Plan. But top dollar and long yen were also to be lured by the tinkling *tastevins* of master sommeliers; oenophiles would be flattered by guided visits to cellars deep in the chalk cliffs ('once the hidey-hole for smugglers' booty, now the resting-place for classic vintages') before being suckered with a quadruple mark-up. As for after-dinner drinks: there might be a gentle recommendation of Great Aunt Maud's Original Shropshire Plum Brandy, but a range of single malts, none with aggressively Hibernian names, would also be available. Sir Jack would personally oversee the armagnac list.

'And that leaves sex,' said the Project Manager, after the patriotic menus had been approved by the Co-ordinating Committee.

'I beg your pardon, Marco.'

'Sex, Sir Jack.'

'I have always run family newspapers.'

'Family newspapers', said Martha, 'are traditionally obsessed with extramarital and transgressive relationships.'

'Which is *why* they are family newspapers,' replied her employer exasperatedly. He snapped his Garrick Club braces and sighed. 'Very well. Given the democratic rules of these meetings, proceed.'

'I assume we have to provide some kind of sex angle, don't we?' said Mark. 'People go on holiday to have sex, it's a well-known fact. Or rather, when they think about holidays, some part of their brain thinks about sex. If they're single, they hope to meet someone; if they're married, they hope to have better sex than in the domestic bed. Or even *some* sex.'

'If you say so. Oh, you young folk . . .'

'So as I see it, if your twopenny tourist is looking for threepenny sex, then those purchasing Quality Leisure will be looking for quality sex.'

'It would have a historical logic to it,' said Martha. 'The British always used to go abroad for sex. The Empire was built on the inability of the British male to find sexual satisfaction outside of marriage. Or inside it, for that matter. The West always treated the East as a brothel, upmarket or downmarket. Now the position's reversed. We're chasing Pacific Rim dollars, so we have to offer a historical *quid pro quo.*'

'And what says the Official Historian to this scandalous analysis of our nation's glorious past?' Sir Jack pointed his cigar at Dr Max.

'I'm f–amiliar with it,' he replied. 'If not always as pithily put. It can be argued.' Dr Max's languor implied that he personally could not be fished to argue the matter one way or the other.

'Ah,' his employer replied. 'It can be argued. Spoken like an historian, if I may be permitted a little *lèse-majesté*. So what is being argued is . . . what, exactly? The offering of English virgins in the marketplace, chained naked to a tumbril, sold into sexual slavery by the hour in high-price brothel hotels equipped with waterbeds, tilting mirrors and pornographic videos? I speak, you understand, figuratively as it were.'

There was an embarrassed silence which Mark moved swiftly to counter. 'I think we're getting a little off the point. I just said I wondered if there shouldn't be a sexual angle. I don't know what it might be. I'm not an ideas man, I'm just the Project Manager. I merely put to you the proposition: Quality Leisure, top dollar, long yen, market expectation, England and sex. May I offer that cocktail to the meeting?'

'Very well, Marco. Let us place that on the vibrating bed, to coin a phrase. And let us start simply. Sex and England, any takers?'

'Swiss Navy,' said Martha.

'My condolences, Miss Cochrane.' Sir Jack gave a heavy chuckle. 'Though that's not what a little birdie tells me.' He was looking blandly away by the time Martha snapped a glance at him. She didn't dare look at Paul. 'Any advance on that?'

'OK, OK.' Martha took up the challenge irritatedly. 'I'll go first. The English and sex. What comes to mind? Oscar Wilde. The Virgin Queen. Lloyd George Knew My Father. Lady Godiva.'

'One Irishman and a Welshman so far,' Dr Max observed, in a public murmur.

'Plus one virgin and a stripper,' added Mark.

'The English vice,' Martha continued, looking firmly at Dr Max. 'Sodomy or flagellation, take your pick. Child prostitution in the Victorian era. A number of multiple sex murders. Do we hear the turnstiles clicking? What about an English Casanova? Lord Byron, I suppose. A club-footed nob with a taste for incest. It's such a tricky area, isn't it? Oh, we invented the condom, if that's any help. Supposedly.'

'None of that is any help,' said Sir Jack. 'Even more obstructive than usual, which is saying something. What we are looking for, if I may make so obvious a point, is a woman who gave sex a good name, a nice girl everybody's heard of, god dammit a cutie with big knockers, figuratively as it were.' The Committee found unprecedented interest in the grain of the table, the flock of the wallpaper, the glitter of the chandelier. Sir Jack suddenly bounced his palms off his forehead. 'I have her. I have her. The very woman. Nell Gwynn. Of course. A cat may look at more than a king. Charming girl, I'm sure. Won the hearts of the nation. And a very democratic story, one for our times. Perhaps a *little* massaging, to bring her into line with third millennium family values. Then there's the orange franchise, of course. Well? Do I hear good? Do I hear more than good?'

'More than good,' said Mark.

'Good,' said Martha.

'Dubious,' said Dr Max.

'How?' asked their employer grumpily. Did he really have to shoulder all the creative burden, only to find himself carped at by a pack of nay-sayers?

'It's not really my p—eriod,' the Official Historian began, a disclaimer which rarely led to a briefer lecture, 'but as I recall, little Nell's background was not exactly riddled with family values. She referred to herself openly as a "Protestant whore" – the King being Catholic at the time, you understand. Two bastard children by him, shared the pleasures of his mattress with another favourite whose name temporarily escapes me . . .'

'You mean, three-in-a-bed stuff,' muttered Sir Jack, envisaging the headlines.

'. . . and obviously I would have to check, but her career as King's mistress did start at a relatively tender age, so we might have to factor in the child-sex angle.'

'Good,' said Martha. '*Very* good. Western paedophiles traditionally went East for their satisfaction. Now Eastern paedophiles can come West.'

'Disastrous,' said Sir Jack. 'I have always run family newspapers.'

'We could make her older,' suggested Martha brightly, 'lose the children, lose the other mistresses, and lose the social and religious background. Then she could be a nice middle-class girl who ends up marrying the King.'

'Bigamously,' annotated Dr Max.

'Things were so much simpler in my day,' sighed Sir Jack.

'DO YOU THINK

Sir Jack's on to us?' They were in bed; the lights were out; their bodies were tired, their minds still fretful with caffeine.

'No,' said Paul. 'He was just fishing.'

'It didn't feel like fishing. It felt more like . . . goosing. I told

94

you, it's always the family men who are the worst.'

'He's fond of you, can't you see?'

'He can keep his fondness for the invisible Lady Pitman. Why do you always defend him?'

'Why do you always attack him? Anyway, you provoked him.'

'I *what*? You mean, my charcoal suit with the shirt buttoned to the neck?'

'With your unpatriotic views on sex.'

'Provocative *and* unpatriotic. Better and better. It's what I'm paid for.'

'You know what I mean.'

They were on a nervous run of talk edging towards aggression. Why was it like this, Martha wondered. Why did love seem to come with a subversive edge of boredom attached, tenderness with irritation? Or was that just her? 'I only said the English weren't famous for sex, that's all. Like the Boat Race, in out, in out, in out, then everyone collapsed over their oars.'

'Thanks.'

'Didn't mean *you*.'

'No, I can recognize accurate flattery when I hear it. What everyone needs, I seem to remember. Prevents wars, we were saying.' Paul thought: what have I done wrong? Why are we here, suddenly, like this, growling at one another in the dark? A moment ago it was fine. A moment ago I liked you and loved you; now I just love you. That's frightening.

'Oh, tell me another story, Paul.' She didn't want to fight.

He didn't want to either. 'Another story.' He let a little resentment burn off in the silence. 'Well, I was going to tell you about Beethoven and the village policeman. The one I told Sir Jack.'

Martha stiffened. She liked to leave Sir Jack in the office. Paul kept bringing him home. Now he was in bed with them. Well, maybe this once.

'Right. I picture the scene. Side by side in the gents. What was he humming?'

'The Kreutzer. Second movement. *Adagio espressivo*. Not that that's directly relevant. Anyway, what happened. One morning, back whenever it was, eighteen something I suppose, the point is, he was already famous as a composer, Beethoven got up early and went for a walk. He was a bit scruffy, as you may know. He put on this ragged old coat, and he didn't have a hat, which all respectable people who weren't great composers did have, and he set out along the canal towpath near where he lived. He must have been thinking about his music, hearing it in his head, and not paying attention to anything else, because he walked and walked and all of a sudden found himself at the end of the canal, at the canal basin. He didn't know where he was, so he started looking in at people's windows. Well, this was a respectable part of Germany, or whatever it was called then, and naturally instead of asking what he wanted or offering him a cup of coffee, they called the local constable and had him arrested as a vagrant. He was surprised by this turn of events, to say the least, and protested to the policeman. He said, "But Officer, I am Beethoven." And the policeman replied, "Of course you are – why not?"'

He stopped, but Martha's instinct for the rhythms of male narration didn't fail. She waited.

'And then – that's right – and then the constable explained why he was arresting him. He said, "You're a tramp. *Beethoven doesn't look like this.*"'

Martha smiled in the dark, realized he couldn't see her, and reached an arm across to him. 'That's a good story, Paul.'

They had pulled back from wherever they were heading because they'd both wanted to. What if one of them hadn't? What if both? As she fell asleep, she wondered about two things. Why, even in bed, they still referred to Sir Jack by his title. And why Beethoven thought he was lost. All he had to do was turn round and follow the canal back to where he lived. Or was that the logic of lesser mortals?

Later that night she awoke to thoughts of sex. She listened to an echo of own voice. I'll settle for good, she had said. Settling already, Martha, isn't it a bit early for that? Oh, I don't know, after all, everyone settles. Not you, Martha, you've always lived your life not settling, that's why you're not . . . settled.

— Look, I only said that the sex was very enjoyable but it wasn't Carcassonne. Why's that keeping you awake? It's not as if it's the opposite of Carcassonne, whatever that might be. Chernobyl. Alaska. The Guildford by-pass. And anyway, relationships aren't just about sex.

— Yes they are, Martha, that's exactly what they're about, this early. It's not as if your previous relationships had their beginnings in pottery classes or bell-ringing, is it? Then it might not matter.

— Look, it's just getting going, this relationship.

— It's just getting going and instead of all that old hopefulness and lovely self-deception and . . . ambition you used to have, you're making sensible adjustments and sensible excuses.

— No I'm not.

— Yes you are. You're using words like *very enjoyable*.

— Well, maybe I'm getting middle-aged.

— You said it.

— Then I'll unsay it. Maybe I'm getting mature. And not so self-deceiving. It's different now. It feels different. I respect Paul.

— Oh dear. Doesn't it feel like settling down to hear the Lives of the Great Composers?

— No, it feels like this: no games, no deceptions, no pretence, no betrayal.

— Four negatives make a positive?

— Shut up, shut up. Yes, by the way, they might. So shut up.

— Didn't say a word, Martha. Sleep well. Just out of interest, why do you think you woke up?

A BRIEF HISTORY OF SEXUALITY

in the case of Paul Harrison would be briefer than in the case of Martha Cochrane:

— inchoate yearnings for girls in general, and since girls in general, or at least girls en masse in his particular vicinity, wore white ankle socks, green plaid skirts to mid-calf because their mothers knew they would grow into them, and white blouses with green ties, this was his initial paradigm.

— specific yearning for Kim, a friend of his sister's, who was learning the viola, who came round to the house one Sunday morning and made him realize (which he had not done on the mere evidence of his sister) that girls not dressed in school uniform could make the lips parch, the mind fog, and the underpants bulge in a way that girls at school never could. Kim, who was two years older than he was, took no notice of him, or appeared not to, which amounted to the same thing. He once said to his sister, nonchalantly, 'How's Kim?' She had looked at him carefully, then giggled almost enough to make herself throw up.

— the discovery of girls in magazines. Except that they clearly weren't girls but women. Women with large perfect breasts, medium-sized perfect breasts, and small perfect breasts. The sight of them made his brain press outwards against his skull. They were all of unimpeachable beauty, even the rough, slaggy-looking ones; perhaps especially them. And the parts which weren't their breasts, and which initially rendered him quite dumb with wonder, were also surprisingly various in layout and physiology, but never less than wholly perfect. These women seemed to him as inaccessible as goat crags to a mole. They were the deodorized, depilated aristocracy; he was a smelly, ragged peasant.

— he still loved Kim though.

— but he found that he could also love magazine women at the same time. And among them he had his favourites and his fidelities. The ones he thought would be kind and understanding, and show him how to do it; and then the others, who once he had learnt how to do it would *really* show him how to do it; and then a third category, of fauns, waifs and innocents, whom, in the fullness of time, he would show how to do it. He tore out photo-spreads of the women who pierced his heart, and kept them under his mattress. To avoid crushing them (an impracticality as well as a sacrilege) he stored them in a stiff-backed manilla envelope. After a while he had to buy another one.

— as the girls at school grew older, their skirts rose from mid-calf to knee level. He hung around in groups of boys looking at groups of girls. He didn't think he would ever, ever be able to handle being alone with a girl (who wasn't his sister). It was much easier to be alone with magazine women. They always seemed to understand him when he had sex with them. And another thing: you were meant to feel sad after sex, but he never did. Just disappointment that he had to wait a few minutes before he could crank the old system up again. He bought a third manilla envelope.

— one day in the playground Geoff Glass told him an intricate, confidential story about a travelling salesman away from home for long periods of time and what he did when he couldn't find a woman. There was this, and then there was that, and sometimes for a change, because he didn't want the landlady spying on him, he would do it in the bath. Well, you know what it looks like in the bath – whereupon Paul, not wanting the story to stop, had said 'Yes' instead of 'No', whereupon Geoff Glass started shouting to the playground, 'Harrison knows what it looks like in the bath.' He realized that sex meant pitfalls.

— he realized this further when he came home from school and discovered that his mother, in the course of spring-cleaning, had decided to turn his mattress.

— for a time he kept in cryptographic form, in the back of a maths textbook where his mother would never look, a graph of dermal eruption plotted against the sex he had with the lost magazine women. The conclusions were inconclusive, or at least not dissuasive. He found that he remembered Cheryl and Wanda and Sam and Tiffany and April and Trish and Lindie and Jilly and Billie and Kelly and Kimberley in startling detail. Sometimes he took their memories into the bath with him. In bed, he didn't have to worry about keeping the light on. He worried instead about whether he would ever meet a real woman, or girl, who would inspire in him the same ferocious carnality. He understood how men died for love.

— someone told him that if you did it left-handed, it felt like someone else doing it to you. Perhaps; except that it felt like someone else's left hand, and you wondered why they didn't use their right.

— then, quite unexpectedly, there was Christine, who didn't mind the fact that he wore glasses, and at seventeen years and one month was three months older than him, which she thought was a nice sort of difference. He agreed, as he did with everything she said. He found himself, in the parallel universe of real life, allowed to do the things he had previously dreamed of. With Christine he burst into a world of condom-unrolling and menstruation, of being allowed to put his hands anywhere (anywhere within reason, and nowhere dirty) while helping baby-sit her youngest brother; of dizzying joy and social responsibility. When she pointed at some bauble in a lighted shop window and cooed with a strange longing he found uniquely feminine, he felt like Alexander the Great.

— Christine wanted to know where they were going. He said, 'I thought the cinema.' She burst into tears. He realized that agreement and misunderstanding could easily co-exist.

— when he mentioned condoms to Lynn, she said 'I hate them', and fucked him just like that, towards the end of a party, both of them drunk. He discovered that being drunk meant he could go on a long time without coming. On a later occasion, he discovered that the correlation and the benefit did not increase exponentially. His parents considered Lynn a bad influence, which she certainly was, and why he liked her. He would do anything for her, which is why she quickly tired of him.

— after he broke up with Christine, there were semi-encounters, near-misses, yearnings which disappeared into self-contempt, liaisons he wanted to get out of before he'd got into them. Women who looked at him as if to say: you'll do for now. Others who took him firmly by the arm from the moment of the first kiss, and who made him feel, as their fingers squirmed in the crook of his arm, that he was being marched first to the altar and then to the grave. He began to look at other men with envy and incomprehension. None but the brave deserved the fair, according to some stupid old poet. Real life wasn't like that. Who got what they deserved? Shits and philanderers and horrible pushy bastards nabbed the fair while the brave were away at battle. Then the brave came home and got second pick. People like Paul had to make do with the leftovers. They were meant to come to terms with this, to settle down and breed foot-soldiers for the brave, or innocent daughters for the shits and philanderers to despoil.

— he went back to Christine for several hours, which was clearly a mistake.

— but Paul resisted his tacit destiny, both in a general sense, and in the person of Christine. He didn't believe in justice where sex and the heart were concerned: there was no system whereby your merits as a human being, companion, lover, husband or whatever could be fairly assessed. People – specifically women – gave you a quick look and passed on. You couldn't very well protest, try handing over a list of your hidden selling points. But if there was no system, that logically meant there was luck, and Paul was a tenacious believer in luck. One minute you're a mid-ranking Pitco employee, the next you're standing beside Sir Jack in the gents and he happens to be whistling the right tune.

— when he first set eyes on Martha, with her sculpted bob, blue suit, and calm yet disconcerting silences, when he found himself thinking You've a dark brown voice to match your dark brown hair and you can't possibly be forty, when he watched her turn elegantly and dance her cape in the nose of the pawing, snorting Sir Jack, he thought: she seems very nice. He realized that this was rather an inadequate response, and probably not one he should ever confide in her. Or if he did, without the following annotation: after he'd left home and gone back to buying magazines for a while, he increasingly found, as he gazed at a double-page woman laid out for him as the personification of availability, that sidling into his head would come the thought, '*She* seems very nice.' Perhaps he wasn't really cut out for magazine sex. Fuck me, the women were meant to urge, and he kept replying, 'Well, I'd really like to get to know you better first.'

— in the past he had noticed how being with a woman changed your sense of time: how lightly poised the present could be, how trudging the past, how elastic, how metamorphic the future. He knew even better how not being with a woman changed your sense of time.

— so when Martha asked him what he'd thought of her when they first met, he wanted to say: I felt you would change my sense of time irrevocably, that future and past were going to be packed into present, that a new and indivisible holy trinity of time was about to be formed, as never before in the history of the created universe. But this wasn't completely true, so instead he cited the clear feeling he had in Sir Jack's double-cube office and later as he sat across from her in the wine lodge and realized she was slightly guiding the conversation. 'I thought you were very nice,' he said, all too aware that it was not the sort of hyperbole employed by shits and philanderers and assorted horrible pushy bastards. Yet it appeared to have been the right thing to say, or to have thought, or both.

— Martha made him feel more intelligent, more grown-up, funnier. Christine had laughed abidingly at his jokes, which in the end made him suspect she had no sense of humour. Later, he knew the humiliation of the raised eyebrow and the implicit Don't try unless you know how to tell them. For a while, he gave up making jokes except under his breath. With Martha he started again, and she laughed when she found something funny, and not when she didn't. This seemed extraordinary and wonderful to Paul. Also symbolic: he had previously been living his life under his breath, not daring to voice it. Thanks to Sir Jack, he had a proper job; thanks to Martha he had a proper life, a life out loud.

— he couldn't believe how falling in love with Martha made things simpler. No, that wasn't the right word, unless 'simpler' also included the sense of richer, denser, more complicated, with focus and echo. Half his brain pulsed with gawping incredulity at his luck; the other half was filled with a sense of long-sought, flaming reality. That was the word: falling in love with Martha made things real.

Two

SIR JACK'S CHOICE OF THE ISLAND had not been a matter of cartographical serendipity. Even his whims had costing behind them. In the present instance, relevant factors had been: the size, location and accessibility of the Island, plus the extreme unlikelihood of it being spot-listed by UNESCO as a World Heritage Site. Access to labour pool, elasticity of planning regulations, malleability of locals. Sir Jack did not anticipate too much trouble getting the Wighters on board: his experience in the developing world had taught him how to exploit historical resentment, even how to engender it. He also had the Island's MP in his pocket. A series of well-publicized inward investments to the constituency, plus the signed affidavits of three London rent-boys in a solicitor's safe near Lincoln's Inn Fields, would ensure that Sir Percy Nutting QC MP would continue to show the correct enthusiasms. Carrot and stick – it always worked; while stick and carrot worked even better.

At first he had planned simply to buy the Island. Several thousand acres of farmland had been acquired from pension funds and the Church Commissioners in exchange for bonds in his new venture; the next step was to persuade Westminster to sell him sovereignty. It did not seem an improbable idea. The last bits of Empire were currently being disposed of in this – to Sir Jack – entirely rational way. Earlier colonies had departed in a flurry of sudden principle hastened by guerrilla warfare. With the final outposts, sensible economic criteria applied: Gibraltar was sold to Spain, the Falkland Islands to Argentina. Of course, this was not how the handovers were presented, by either vendor or purchaser; but Sir Jack had his sources.

These sources also reported, disappointingly, that Westminster had hardened its position on selling the Isle of Wight to a private individual. Specious objections of national integrity had been adduced. Despite pressure from Sir Jack's loyal group of backbenchers, the Government simply refused to put a price on sovereignty. Not for sale, they said. This had made Sir Jack a little huffy at first, but he soon regained his humour. There was something inherently unsatisfactory about the straight deal, after all. You wanted to buy something, the owner fixed a price, and you eventually got it for less. Where was the fun in that?

Indeed, wasn't there something old-fashioned about the whole concept of ownership, or rather its acquisition by formal contract, in which title is received in exchange for consideration given? Sir Jack preferred to rethink the whole notion. It was certainly true that ownership was irrelevant as long as you had control: and yes, for the moment he had all the land options and planning concessions he needed. He had the banks, the pension funds and the insurance companies onside; his debt-equity ratio was uncontroversial. Naturally, none of his own capital had been ventured, beyond seed-corn level; Sir Jack believed in putting other people's money where his own mouth was. And yet, beyond and beneath all this legitimate buccaneering, there lay a more primal urge, an atavistic yearning to cut through the red tape of contemporary life. It would have been unfair to call Sir Jack Pitman a barbarian, though some did; but there stirred within him a longing to revisit pre-classical, pre-bureaucratic methods of acquiring ownership. Methods such as theft, conquest and pillage, for example.

'Peasants,' said Martha Cochrane. 'You're going to need peasants.'

'Low-cost labour, we call it nowadays, Martha. Not a problem.'

'No, I mean peasants. As in straw-chewing yokels. Men in smocks, village idiots. Fellows with scythes over their shoulders winnowing chaff, if that's what you winnow. Flailing and threshing.'

'Agriculture,' replied Sir Jack, 'is certainly catered for both as Backdrop and as a secondary-visit option. You country girls will not be forgotten.' His smile mixed impatience and insincerity.

'I'm not talking about agriculture. I'm talking about *people*. We spend our time discussing product placement, Visitor profiling, showtime structures, throughput and leisure theory, but we seem to be forgetting that one of the oldest lures in this business is to advertise the people. The warm, friendly, natural people. Irish eyes are smiling, we'll keep a welcome in the hillsides and all that stuff.'

'Fine,' said Sir Jack, a little suspiciously. 'We can focus on it. A very positive suggestion. But your manner implies that you foresee a problem.'

'Two, actually. First, you don't have any raw material. That's to say, none of your low-cost labour on the Island has ever set eyes on corn except in flake form in a bowl.'

'Then they will take to flailing, or whatever you said, with the enthusiasm of a new generation making a fresh start.'

'And the traditional warm-hearted hospitality?'

'That too can be learned,' replied Sir Jack. 'And by being learned, it will be the more authentic. Or is that too cynical a notion for you, Martha?'

'I can live with it. But there's a second problem. It's really, how do we advertise the English? Come and meet representatives of a people widely perceived, even according to our own survey, as cold, snobbish, emotionally retarded and xenophobic. As well as perfidious and hypocritical, of course. I mean, I know you guys like a challenge ...'

'Good, Martha,' said Sir Jack. 'Excellent. I was for a moment afraid that you were being helpful and constructive. So, *you guys*, earn your corn, hand-winnowed or industrially-processed as it might be. Jeff?'

Martha, watching the Concept Developer pause for thought, realized that Jeff was the odd man out on the Co-ordinating

Committee. He seemed to have no private agenda; he seemed devoted to the Project; he seemed to approach problems as if they needed solutions; he also seemed to be a married man who hadn't made a pass at her. It was all very strange.

'Well,' said Jeff, 'off the top of my head I'd say the best approach is to flatter the client rather than the product. As in: sip your pint of Jolly Jack ale in the Old Bull and Bush, meet the colourful regulars, and see how that fabled English reserve just fades away. As in: they don't give their hearts easily, but once given, their friendship is good for life and will throw a girdle round the earth.'

'Bit threatening, that one, isn't it?' said Mark. 'People don't go on holiday to make friends.'

'I think you're wrong there, actually. All the surveys we've done suggest that other people, that's to say non-English people, frequently regard making friends on holiday as a bonus, dare I say it an enrichment of their lives.'

'How quaint.' Mark gave a disbelieving laugh and danced his eyes over Sir Jack's impassive bulk, looking for clues. 'Is that what they'll be coming to the Island for? All this top dollar and long yen is going to chummy up to our low-cost labour, exchange Polaroids and addresses and all that. "This is Worzel from Freshwater demonstrating the old English custom of downing a pint of Old Skullsplitter with a twiglet up each nostril . . ." No, I'm sorry, I can't handle it.' Mark offered a blurry eye to the Committee and quietly snorted to himself.

'Mark is usefully displaying those very English characteristics I was just describing,' commented Martha.

'Well, why not,' said Mark between snorts. 'After all, I *am* English.'

'To business,' said Sir Jack. 'We might or might not have a problem. Let's solve it anyway.'

They got down to work. It was mainly a question of focus and perception. They had already established that agriculture would be represented by true-life dioramas clearly visible to passing traffic, whether it be London taxi, double-decker bus or pony and trap. Shepherds lolling beneath wind-angled trees would point their crooks and whistle *falsetto* to old English sheepdogs hustling their flocks; smocked rustics with wooden pitchforks would toss hay on to stacks sculpted like topiary; gamekeeper would arrest poacher outside a Morland cottage and place him in the stocks beside the wishing-well. What they needed was merely a conceptual leap from decorative status to bonding possibilities. The lolling shepherd must later be discovered in The Old Bull and Bush, where he would gaily accompany the pipe-playing gamekeeper in a selection of authentic country airs, some collected by Cecil Sharp and Percy Grainger, others written half a century back by Donovan. The haymakers would leave off their tourney of skittles to make menu suggestions, the poacher would explain his dodges, whereupon Old Meg crouching in the inglenook would lay down her clay pipe and disburse the wisdom of the generations. It was, they decided, all about foregrounding the background. Technical stuff, really.

'On the other hand,' said Mark.

'Yes, Marco. Another unpatriotic outburst about to fall upon us?'

'No. Maybe yes. I seem to be taking over from Martha today. It's just that . . . don't you think we should be wary of the Californian Waiter Syndrome?'

'Enlighten a parochial mind,' said Sir Jack.

'The guy who instead of standing there with a notepad writing down what you want to eat and *shutting the fuck up*,' said Mark violently, 'takes the next chair to you and talks about the non-violent way they cracked the hazel nuts and wants to share with you about your allergies.'

Sir Jack affected astonishment. 'Marco, is this a common experience for you? Are you choosing the right sort of restaurant? I confess, my experience is so narrow that I have yet to meet a waiter enquiring about my allergies.'

'But you get the general point? You go into a pub for a quiet pint and find some foul-smelling old skittle-player spilling his beer over you and chatting up your wife?'

'Well, it's an authentically English experience,' Martha remarked.

Jeff coughed. 'Look, this is all quite improbable. Our hygiene requirements and sexual harassment rules preclude such a scenario. In any case, they have chosen to go to a pub, haven't they? There are many other dining options being developed. They can have anything from Country House Weekend Banquet to room service.'

'It's just . . . I'm not being snobbish,' said Mark. 'Well, maybe I am. You're asking some guy who's worked in a sock factory or something to stand around all day threshing and then go down the pub and instead of talking about sex and football with his mates as he wants to, you're going to make him work even harder at being a yokel with visitors who are, dare I whisper it, quite possibly a little more intelligent, and fragrant, than our trusty employee?'

'Then they can have dinner with Dr Johnson at the Cheshire Cheese,' said Jeff.

'No, it's not that. It's more like . . . have you ever been to a play and when it's over the actors come off the stage and walk through the audience shaking hands with you – like, hey, we were only figments of your imagination up there but now we're showing how we're flesh and blood the same as you? It just makes me uneasy.'

'That's because you're English,' said Martha. 'You think being touched is invasive.'

'No, it's about keeping reality and illusion separate.'

'That's very English too.'

'I fucking *am* English,' said Mark.

'Our visitors won't be.'

'Children,' said Sir Jack chidingly. 'Gentlemen. Lady. A modest proposal from the chair. How about an Island espresso bar, as I believe they're known, to be called The Filthy Cappuccino. Proprietor, Signor Marco?'

The obligatory communal guffaw brought the meeting to a close.

'TELL WOODIE

it's time,' said Sir Jack. He was wearing his
Académie Française braces that afternoon, which in retrospect
he judged fully appropriate: the meeting had been studded with
Pitmanesque *bons mots* and *aperçus*. The Committee had been
treated to a *tour d'horizon* of exceptional girth.

The current Susie was a new Susie, and at times he couldn't
remember why he had appointed her. The surname, of course,
and her father, and her father's money, and so on, and her
somewhat cheeky smile, and a sort of ductile sexuality he
suspected beneath those crisp outfits . . . But those were all the
usual reasons for such appointments. What you also wanted
from a Susie was a touch of subcutaneous instinct, of ESP, of *je
ne sais quoi*. Anyone would think the job consisted merely of
relaying accurate information in a polite fashion.

'Oh,' said Susie into the phone, and then, with an inappropriate smile, 'I'm afraid Woodie's had to go home, Sir Jack. I
think his back's been playing up.'

He'd correct her on another occasion about 'Woodie'. Sir
Jack called him Woodie. She should know to call him Wood.
'Get one of the others.'

A further murmuring in quite the wrong tone: that of bright
factuality rather than gross distress at her employer's inconven-
ience. 'They're all out, Sir Jack. The Outreach Conference. I
could call you a cab.'

'A cab, girl? A *cab*?' This was so wide of the mark it almost
amused Sir Jack. 'Can you imagine how the market would react
if I were photographed getting into a cab? Fifty points? *Two
hundred* points? You must be off your tiny head, woman. A *cab*!
Get me a limo, a *limousine*' – he gave it a French twirl, to show
that incredulous disapproval and humour could cohabit. 'No.'
He pondered briefly. 'No, Paul will drive me. Won't you, Paul?'

'Actually, Sir Jack,' said Paul, not looking at Martha but
thinking of the immediate area behind and above her left knee,
of the difference between finger and tongue, between silkily

112

covered flesh and pure flesh, between leg and raised leg, 'Actually, I have a date.'

'You do indeed. You have a date with me. You have a date to drive me to see my Auntie May. So get yourself a fucking cap, de-garage your fucking company Jaguar, and take me to Chorleywood.'

Paul's incipient erection scuttled back into its mousehole. He didn't dare look at Martha. He didn't care about being humiliated in front of the others – they all knew what Sir Jack could be like – but Martha . . . Martha. Three minutes later, he found himself bending to open the rear door of his own car. Sir Jack paused heavily, and waited until Paul produced an awkward salute, a stiff memory of some army film.

'So kind of you,' said the voice behind his ear as the gatekeeper raised his pole with a more practised salute. 'A few points I'm sure you won't mind my mentioning. Your car – which is *my* car, when we come down to it – looks as if it has just been driven backwards across a ploughed field after a fox. The unwashable in pursuit of the inedible, if I may turn a phrase. Always change the tie before driving me, something simpler, plain black in fact. And the order of events is as follows: remove the cap, place it under the left arm, open the car door, stand erect, salute. *Capito?*'

'Yes, sir.' Except that Paul would rather counterfeit an epileptic fit than go through this again.

'Good. And I'm sure Martha will be waiting up for you later, and will give you an even bigger kiss.' Paul's eyes went instinctively to the mirror, but Sir Jack's were there already, contemptuously triumphant. 'Keep your attention on the road, Paul, that's most unchauffeurlike behaviour. Of course I *know*. I know everything I need to know. For instance – and this may be of some comfort to you – I know that there are very few things in the world that spoil by being kept waiting. Rice, of course, and soufflées, and fine old burgundy. But women, Paul? Women? In my experience, no. In fact, I would say, without any undue indelicacy, on the contrary.'

Sir Jack chuckled like a stage lecher and unsnapped his briefcase. As they did slow spurts amid the damp blink of brake-lights, the Ideas Catcher ran through the rationalisations he knew so well. Sir Jack's ego required so much oxygen that it seemed both logical and just to him that it should be extracted from the lungs of those nearby. Sir Jack was a normally demanding employer who paid well and expected perfection: when he didn't get it, someone had to suffer. It just happened to be your turn that week, that day, that microsecond, it didn't mean anything. Conclusion: the humiliation was quite unjusti-fied, but the very injustice, the extremity of disapproval, demonstrated that Sir Jack didn't really have it in for you. Alternatively: the fact that he did have it in for you, had singled you out for this treatment, made you special, in his eyes and your own. If he didn't care he wouldn't have bothered. It was almost his way of showing affection.

Paul told himself all this as the stalled traffic began to loosen. Because otherwise he would be obliged to lightly swing the wheel, just like *that*, say, and take the Jaguar into an approaching lorry and kill them both. Except that any Pitco employee could have told him what would happen: Paul would end up as steak tartare, while Sir Jack would walk energized from the wreckage, eager to philosophize about Providence's generosity to the first TV crew on the scene.

After an hour's silent drive, during which Paul felt his sense of self dwindle, they reached a suburb of dripping beech trees where carriage-lamps illuminated burglar alarms.

'Just here. Two hours. And my drivers never drink.'

'It's raining, Sir Jack. Can't I run you to the door?'

'Umbrella. Package.'

Paul managed the awkwardness of the cap, the door and the salute, then watched Sir Jack walk off with a wrapped bottle of sherry beneath his arm. He climbed back into the car, threw his cap on to the passenger seat, and reached for the phone. I'm sorry, Martha, I'm sorry I couldn't look at you. I hope you don't hate and despise me. I love you, Martha. And you're right about Sir Jack, you always have been, it's just that I didn't like to admit it. I may say something different tomorrow but you're right today. Is everything still OK? Have I lost you? I haven't, have I?

In mid-dial, as blood and self returned, Paul stopped. Of course: his employer probably got a printout of numbers called from all company cars. It was just the sort of detail Sir Jack never overlooked. That could have been how he'd guessed about Martha. And if Paul phoned her now, Sir Jack would find out, and retain it in his elephantine, retaliative memory, waiting for some moment, some unwelcome public moment.

So, a phone box. Rare things nowadays. Paul drove the empty streets, taking turns at random. An occasional dog-walker, a respectable alcoholic limping home with supplies, no sign of a box, and then, twenty yards ahead, in a curving avenue of detached houses quarter-lit by replica Victorian gas-lamps, his headlights spotted a stripey golf umbrella. Sod it. What now: drive past, or brake suddenly? Whatever he did would be wrong, or Sir Jack would find a reason for it being wrong. As it was, he'd probably noted the car mileage before getting out and would bill Paul for excess petrol.

Driving past might seem a greater impertinence: best to stop. Paul braked as softly as possible, but the umbrella with legs did not break stride. It marched on and disappeared up a driveway. After a few minutes Paul released the handbrake and gentled the car down the avenue. Auntie May lived in a tile-hung Domestic Revival house with neat banks of shrubs and a carved wooden name-plate screwed to a fir tree. 'Ardoch', the house was called. Paul imagined a frail maiden lady with a scrap of lace at the neck offering seed cake and a glass of madeira. Then she became large, perfumed, Jewish and Viennese, spooning extra whipped cream on the Sachertorte. Then – perhaps Sir Jack's braces were a clue – an ironical, fine-boned Parisienne, the sleeve of her tweed jacket pulling elegantly up her forearm as she poured a delicate tisane through a silver spout. He might be a brute at times, but Sir Jack's piety towards his Auntie May, his unmissable monthly visits, did him credit.

Paul gazed balefully at the house and tried not to think of Martha. He wondered if 'Ardoch' was an official Pitco property. It would be just like Sir Jack to put his Auntie on the payroll, with a large house thrown in. Time passed. Rain fell. Paul looked across at his chauffeur's cap on the passenger seat. Was Sir Jack jealous of Martha? Of him and Martha? Was that it? Then he did something in a moment of unthinking rebellion. He took the recorder out of his pocket, half-pretending to himself that it was a phone on which he could call Martha, and activated Sir Jack's body-mike.

The specified range of the instrument was fifty feet, a capacity needed on days when Sir Jack liked to perambulate musingly in halls as broad as his thoughts. The front door of 'Ardoch' was thirty feet away, and doubtless walls reduced the strength of the signal. But the three words Paul had on tape, and which later that night he replayed to Martha, making them both lose interest in immediate sex, came through as clearly as if Sir Jack had been sitting at his desk.

The Jaguar was back at the original rendezvous; rain was still falling as the striped umbrella came into view. Paul's salute was impeccable. In the rear-view mirror Sir Jack's expression was one of benign repose. They reached his apartment at quarter to eleven, and Paul nodded gratefully as a hundred-euro note was stuffed with approximate fingers into his top pocket. But his gratitude was for another gift.

'T . . . N . . . P!'

whispered Paul as he came out of a brief post-coital doze. The downward pressure of Martha's laugh ejected his cock, and she rolled him aside to give her lungs room.

'He might just have been telling a story.' She was deliberately cautious.

'To his auntie? With that punchline? No, it's got to be true.'

Martha wanted it to be true; more importantly she wanted to keep Paul as he'd been when he returned three nights ago – quietly angry, quietly triumphant, ripping up a hundred-euro note. She didn't want him slipping back into respectful reasonableness, a piece of Pitco livestock with the company brand on his rump. She wanted him to lead for once.

'Look,' he said, 'the house isn't on the manifest of properties and you can be sure if she *was* his Auntie May it would be. And she'd be on the payroll. And I've told you, he never misses. First Thursday of every month. Wood's driven him there direct from Heathrow on occasion. Never takes her out, either.'

'She could be in a wheelchair or something.'

'No-one ever visits aunties, even if they're in a wheelchair, like that.'

Martha nodded agreement. 'Unless they're other kinds of auntie.'

'T ... N ... P!'

'Don't. You're killing me.' Laughing on her back felt almost unhealthy. She sat up in bed and looked down at Paul's inverted face. She took his lobe between thumb and finger. 'What do you think we should do?'

'Find out. I mean, get someone else to find out.'

'Why?'

'What do you mean, why?' Paul reacted as if his generalship were in question.

'Just that we ought to know what we're after.'

'Insurance.'

'Insurance?'

'Even Sir Jack's ardent admirers' – he looked up at Martha as if dissociating himself from them – 'would admit that his hire-and-fire policy isn't always merit-based.'

Martha nodded approval. 'Am I in focus when you haven't got your glasses on?'

'You're always in focus,' he said.

Gary Desmond was their chosen operative. Gary Desmond, until recently a key byline in Sir Jack's own newspaper chain. Gary Desmond, who had outed three cabinet ministers, one of them female; who had named the England cricket captain's love-child, lamented the coke habits of two weather-girls, and finally, after only a small amount of breaking-and-entering, brought his employer photographic evidence of Prince Rick's three-in-a-bed sessions with high-price escort girls.

Had he been over-confident, or just naive? Either way, he had assumed the wrong thing: that the moral parameters implicit in his stories, and enthusiastically endorsed by proprietor and readers, were somehow real; or if not real, at least immutable. But Gary Desmond, waiting, with a modest pun, to call the story his crowning achievement, discovered that it was possible to triumph too completely, in a way that challenged the supposed reality of his trade. There had been no doubting the general excitement when he'd revealed how a young man 'six heartbeats from the throne', funded out of public money and paid to represent the Nation on foreign trips, had languidly cavorted with Cindy and Petronella in one of the 'luxury palaces' provided by the tax-payer. But as each day's revelations had continued, prurient condemnation had somehow given way to embarrassment and then to a sort of patriotic self-reproach. At a more local level, this translated itself into Sir Jack Pitman picking at his House of Lords braces and fearing he might not get the ermine to match.

Gary Desmond's story stood up as solid as Pitman House; the pictorial evidence was unchallenged, and the girls didn't have a parking ticket between them. None the less, Gary Desmond was paid off. He was denounced in the very paper which had once published his exclusives as 'the sleaze-hound who went too far'. Reference was made – and this was quite out of order – to a research trip to the West Indies from which, strictly speaking, nothing publishable had resulted. He'd taken Caroline from Accounts and the bastards had printed a snap of her looking distinctly the worse for wear, with her bikini top at half-mast, which could only have been obtained by theft or severe bribery. All of which had rendered Gary Desmond a bit hard to employ for the foreseeable.

Martha and Paul met him in the lounge of a tourist hotel.

'The deal is this,' said Martha. 'We own the story. We decide whether it runs or not. It might be more useful not to publish. We'll pay your fee, a bonus for a good result, and a second bonus for either publication or secrecy, whichever we decide. So either way you don't lose. Deal?'

'Deal,' said the reporter. 'Except, what if the trail gets over-populated?'

'It can't unless you blow it. We know, you know, that's it. That remains it. Deal?'

'Deal,' Gary Desmond repeated.

With hindsight, he could understand how Pitman House had behaved over the Prince Rick business. There had been 'unusual pressure', he was assured, from both the Palace and the Home Office. The pay-off had been satisfactory, even fair; his pension rights were unaffected; the secrecy clause was normal in the circumstances. Gary Desmond was not without imagination; he knew these things happened. But what Gary Desmond could not forgive, and what made him shake hands on the present business, was the comment Sir Jack had made as he stepped into his limo beneath the shadow of the saluting Wood. 'I always say,' his former employer had told the waiting hack-pack, 'I always say you can never trust a man with two Christian names.' The quote made the front page of three newspapers, and it continued to rankle with Gary Desmond.

THE ISLAND BREAKFAST EXPERIENCE
began with the
search for a logo. The design section produced scores of them,

mostly unacknowledged revisions and quiet steals of familiar symbols. Lions in various numbers and various stages of rampancy; assorted crowns and coronets; castle keeps and battlements; a skewed Palace of Westminster portcullis; lighthouses, flaming torches, silhouettes of landmark buildings; profiles of Britannia, Boadicea, Victoria and Saint George; roses of every kind, single and double, tea and floribunda, briar, cabbage, dog and Christmas; oak leaves, apples and trees; cricket stumps and double-decker buses, White Cliffs, Beefeaters, red squirrels, and a robin in the snow; phoenix and falcon, swan and talbot, eagle and popinjay, hippogriff and hippocampus.

'All wrong, all wrong.' Sir Jack hefted a sheaf of recent suggestions from Battle Table to shagpile. 'It's all too *then*. Give me *now*.'

'We could just have your entwined initials.' Careful, Martha: don't confuse professional cynicism with amateurish contempt. But since discovering what she thought they had discovered, her attitude to Sir Jack had shifted; Paul's too.

'What we want,' said Sir Jack, ignoring her and banging the table in emphasis, 'is *magic*. We want *here*, we want *now*, we want the *Island*, but we also want *magic*. We want our Visitors to feel that they have passed through a mirror, that they have left their own worlds and entered a new one, different yet strangely familiar, where things are not done as in other parts of the inhabited planet, but as if in a rare dream.'

The Committee waited, expecting that Sir Jack's complicated demands were merely the preface to an applaudable answer. But the normal dramatic pause lengthened into an anxious silence.

'Sir Jack.'

'Max, my dear fellow. Not the first voice I would have expected.'

Dr Max gave an uneasy smile. He was in shades of barkbrown that day. He gave a superstitious touch to his bow-tie and joined church-steeple fingers to indicate his TV-anecdote mode. 'Some time in the early-to-mid-nineteenth century,' he began, 'a woman was walking to Ventnor market with a basket of eggs. She came from one of the villages along the coast, so she naturally took the clifftop path. It came on to rain, but she had wisely brought her umbrella. This being the early days of umbrella technology, it was a large and sturdy contraption. She had proceeded some distance nearer to Ventnor when a sharp gust of wind from the landward side caught her by surprise and blew her off the edge of the cliff. She thought she would die – at least, I assume this to have been the case on the grounds that any normal person so swept would have assumed they were going to die, and there is no indication that she was an abnormal person in this respect – but her umbrella began to act like a parachute, slowing her fall. Her clothes also billowed out in a way which decreased her velocity. We do not know exactly what she was wearing, but we might plausibly picture to ourselves a crinoline with stretched muslin or the like, so that in effect she had two parachutes, one above and one below. Though even as I speak, a doubt suggests itself: surely the crinoline was a garment of the fashionable and bourgeois classes, its encirclement all too obviously denoting the protect-edness, the *noli me tangere*, of such women. Could the egg-seller have been middle-class, I wonder? Or might the existence of a thriving fishing industry on the Island mean that whalebone, that essential stiffener of the female undergarment, was more socially pervasive than on the mainland? It is not, as you see, exactly my province, and I would need to do some research into the undergarments worn by the egg-selling classes in the probable decade during which the recorded incident took place . . .'

'Get on with the bloody story, man. Stop wittering,' shouted Sir Jack. 'You've left us hanging in mid-air.'

'Quite.' Dr Max took no more notice of Sir Jack than of a studio heckler. 'And so, you see, she drifted down, her basket of eggs over one arm, her umbrella and her crinoline further sustained by the upcurrents from offshore. One pictures her looking out to sea, murmuring a prayer to God, and watching the soft sand rising to meet her. She landed safely on the beach, and was quite unharmed, according to my source, the only damage done being that a few of the eggs in her basket were said to be cracked.'

Sir Jack's expression was of exasperated pleasure. He sucked on his cigar and the exasperation waned. 'I love it. I don't believe a word of it, but I love it. It's *here* and it's *magic* and we can make it into *now*.'

The logo was drawn and redrawn, in styles from pre-Raphaelite hyper-realism to a few expressionist wrist-flicks. Certain key elements persisted: the three echoing sweeps of umbrella, bonnet and spread skirts; the pinched waist and full breasts indicating a woman of an earlier period; and the hemispherical rustic basket whose circle was completed by the rounded pile of eggs. Outside Sir Jack's hearing the motif was referred to as Queen Victoria Showing Her Knickers; within it she was given a series of attempted names – Beth, Maud, Delilah, Faith, Florence, Madge – before they settled on Betsy. Someone remembered, or discovered, that there had once been a phrase 'Heavens to Betsy', which seemed to make her christening appropriate, even if no-one knew what the expression meant.

They had their logo, which contained both the *here* and the *magic*; it was Techno-development who supplied the *now*. Their initial, logical proposal was that Betsy's jump be replicated, when the wind was in the right quarter, by a stuntman in Victorian drag. A drop-zone west of Ventnor was earmarked; if trials were successful, the beach could be reclaimed and enlarged to provide a safe landing area; while Visitors might watch either from grandstands or from small boats anchored offshore. A series of experiments was undertaken to establish the optimum fall-height, wind-force, umbrella-spread and crinoline capacity. Twenty drops with dummy figures led to the day when Sir Jack, binoculars ironing his eyebrows, and legs spread against the gentle swell, witnessed the first live-action test.

Three-quarters of the way down, the heavily-built 'Betsy' seemed to lose crinoline-control, eggs cascaded from his basket, and he landed on the beach beside an impromptu omelette, breaking an ankle in three places.

'Dunderhead,' commented Sir Jack.

A few days later, a second jumper – the lightest stuntman they could find, in an attempt to counterfeit womanhood – kept his eggs intact but cracked his pelvis. It was concluded that Betsy's original fall must have been aided by freak weather conditions. Her feat had been either miraculous or apocryphal.

The next idea was the Heavens To Betsy Bunjee Experience, whose advantage was that it allowed Visitor participation. There followed a series of uniformly safe practice leaps from the modified clifftop by egg-bearing jumpers of both sexes and all sizes. But there was something unconvincing, and decidedly unmagical, and somehow altogether too *now* about the sight of a jumper pinging up and down in a harness before being slowly lowered to the beach.

Techno-development, after several personal interventions from Sir Jack, eventually came up with a solution. The props and jumper's harness would remain the same, but instead of a bunjee cord there would be the controlled unravelling of a camouflaged cable, while hidden windjet sources would simulate rising air-currents. The result would be guest-safe and all-weather. Marketing provided the clinching refinement: the Heavens To Betsy Bunjee Experience would become the Island Breakfast Experience. At the top of the cliff would be a free-range hen facility aswagger with plumed and coiffed birds; fresh eggs would be flown in daily; and the Visitor would descend to the beach with a clip-on Betsy Basket. Then he or she would be led by a mob-capped waitress to Betsy's All-Day Breakfast Bar, where the eggs would be taken from the Basket and fried, boiled, scrambled or poached, according to choice, before the jumper's very eyes. With the bill would come an engraved Certificate of Descent stamped with Sir Jack's signature and the date.

and cranes teetered, as the dull landscape became a pop-up book of hotels and harbours, airports and golf courses, as sweeteners were given to the inconveniently housed and smiling promises offered to grim environmentalists about the chalk downs and the red squirrels and any number of bloody butterflies, Sir Jack Pitman concentrated on the Island councillors. Westminster and Brussels could wait: first he had to get the locals on board and onside.

Mark would be in charge. If they saw Sir Jack they might come over all chippy and defensive, as if he were a corporate invader rather than a massive benefactor. Much better to leave it to the blue eyes and blond curls of Marco Polo.

'What will I need?' the Project Manager had asked at the outset.

'Native wit, a sack of carrots and a bundle of sticks,' Sir Jack had replied.

There were two sets of negotiations. The official consultative meetings between Pitco and the Island Council were held at the Guildhall in Newport. The public was admitted and all proper democratic procedures followed: which meant, as Sir Jack privately observed, that tokenism, special interests and minority groupings ran the show, the lawyers made a bundle, and you spent your time on all fours with your arsehole getting sunburnt. In parallel, however, there was a secret colloquium attended by key Island councillors and the small Pitco team led by Mark. These latter talks were by their nature exploratory and non-committal; they were also unminuted, so that imaginative ideas could if necessary be forcefully expressed, so that, as one tame councillor had been invited to put it, the dream could flow. Sir Jack's instructions to Mark were that the dream should flow like a canal, in a straight line to a named destination. When he outlined it, even Mark was taken aback.

'But how do you do it? I mean, this is the third millennium –

there's Westminster, there's Brussels, there's, I don't know, Washington, the United Nations?'

'How do you do it?' Sir Jack beamed. The banal question had been exquisitely put. 'Mark, I am going to let you into the greatest secret I know. Are you ready?' Mark didn't need to force a show of interest. Sir Jack, for his part, wanted to temporize but couldn't resist the moment. 'Many, many years ago, when I was as young as you are today, I asked the same question of a great man for whom I worked. The great man – Sir Matthew Smeaton – quite forgotten, now, alas – *sic transit* – was planning a coup of spectacular audacity. I asked him how he did it, and you know what he replied? He said, "Jacky" – I was called Jacky in those days – "Jacky, you ask of me how you do it. My answer is this: *You do it by doing it.*" I have never forgotten these words of advice. To this day they inspire me.' Sir Jack's voice had become almost hoarse with reverence. 'Now let them inspire you.'

Mark's exploratory dialogue began with an attempt to put the current Island development into an historical perspective, and to address a few preliminary questions. Not that he would have the impertinence to suggest answers. For instance, given the formidable amount of investment proposed by Pitco, the jobs already created and the jobs to come, and given the assurance of longterm prosperity, might this not be an appropriate time to reconsider the exact nature of the Island's links with the mainland? It was, surely, the case that the Island's requests for help from Westminster over the decades and centuries had always been grudgingly received, that levels of unemployment had traditionally been high. Why then should Westminster and the taxman be the beneficiaries of the present and forthcoming upturn?

Dr Max's historical evaluation – given stylistic refreshment and bullet points by Mark's department – had already been circulated. In addition, the routine searches which corporate lawyers naturally undertook during such large commercial ventures had already thrown up various documents and opinions which Mark felt it his duty to share with those present. In strictest confidence, of course. And without prejudice. But none the less he had to report that in the opinion of both contract lawyers and constitutional experts the original purchase of the Island in 1293, by Edward I from Isabella de Fortuibus, for the sum of six thousand marks, was manifestly dubious and quite possibly illegal. Six thousand marks was chickenfeed. It had clearly not been an arm's-length deal. Duress was still duress, even if it had taken place at the end of the thirteenth century.

At the next meeting, Mark suggested that since they were not bound by conventional procedure, they boldly move the agenda forward. If indeed it was the case – which no-one seemed to contradict – that the Island had been unlawfully acquired by the British Crown, what might be the consequences of this in the current situation? For there was, whether they liked it or not, a historical, constitutional and economic dilemma facing the Island Council. Were they to brush it under the carpet or seize it by the throat? If those Council members present would forgive him for letting the dream flow, Mark would like to propose that any logical, objective analysis of the present crisis might suggest a three-pronged attack which he would summarize as follows.

First, a formal challenge in the European courts to the Fortuibus contract of 1293; such challenge naturally to be funded by Pitco. Secondly, the elevation of the Island Council to the full status of a parliament, with appropriate premises, funding, salaries, expenses and powers. Thirdly, a simultaneous application for entry to the European Union as a full member nation.

Mark waited. He was particularly pleased to have introduced the idea of crisis. Of course there wasn't one, at least not for the moment. But no legislator, from tinpot Island councillor to President of the United States, could be seen denying that there was a crisis if someone said there was one. It looked like idleness or incompetence. So now, officially, on the island, there was a crisis.

'Are you seriously suggesting a breach with the Crown?' The question was a plant, of course. There would be objections from sentimentalists and conservatives; it was best at this stage for them to assume they were in the majority.

'On the contrary,' replied Mark. 'The royal link is in my view of paramount importance to the Island. Any breach the present crisis might force upon us would be with Westminster, not the Crown. If anything, we should seek to strengthen the royal link.'

'What do you mean?' asked the plant.

Mark appeared unready for this question. He seemed flustered. He looked to other members of his team, who offered no help. He mentioned, unconvincingly, the notion that the King might become Official Visitor to the Island. Then he felt compelled, given the candour and openness of the current talks, and the assurances of secrecy, to mention that the Palace was at this very moment seriously considering a relocation proposal. *No!* Why not? Nothing was set in concrete: that was the nature of History. There was a very fine royal palace on the Island currently undergoing renovation. Of course, not a word of this should be breathed to anybody. Which resulted in hot words being breathed to all the necessary people.

At the next meeting, sentimental conservatives and ungrateful churls expressed fears of intervention from the mainland. What about sanctions, blockade, even invasion? Pitco and its advisers took the view, first that such responses were unlikely, second that they would provide incomparable worldwide publicity, and third that since the Island would be following all proper legal and constitutional channels, Westminster would be far too apprehensive of European and even UN reprisals. Instead, it would probably come back to the negotiating table and ask for a decent price. Council members might like to share in another little secret: Sir Jack's opening offer, of half a billion pounds for sovereignty, had now been revised downwards to six thousand marks plus one euro. Which would leave a lot more in the kitty for upgrading Island facilities.

Why should Pitman House be any better masters than Westminster? A fair question, Mark conceded, grateful for the aggression. And yet, he smiled, also an unfair question. We are bound together by mutual self-interest in a manner which does not apply between central government and distant region. In the modern world, stability and longterm economic prosperity are provided more effectively by the transnational corporation than by the old-style nation state. You only had to look at the difference between Pitco and the mainland: which was expanding, and which contracting?

What's in it for you? Continued mutual benefit, as aforementioned. Putting our cards on the table, we shall probably request the revoking of certain minor items of antique planning legislation, most of which have their source in the contemptible Palace of Westminster. And what official or unofficial connection would you expect to have with our new Island parliament? None whatsoever. In the opinion of Pitman House, the separation of powers between economic driving-force and elected body was essential to the health of any modern democracy. Of course, you might find it appropriate to offer Sir Jack Pitman some nominal position, some paper title.

'Like President for Life?' suggested one churl.

Mark couldn't have been more amused. The coughing fit and the tears might even have been real. No, he'd only mentioned it on the spur of the moment, given the exploratory and non-committal nature of these exchanges. Rest assured, the matter hadn't been mentioned to Sir Jack, or by him. Indeed, probably the only way to get him to accept such a role would be by giving him no chance to refuse. Just make an Order in Council, or whatever you might choose to call it.

'An Order in Council making him President for Life?'

Oh dear, he did seem to have started a hare. But – purely off the top of his head – there might be some ceremonial title not inappropriate to whatever constitution they decided to frame.

What did those old counties of England have? Fellow with the sword and plumed helmet? Lord Lieutenant. No, that probably smacked too much of the mainland. Mark pretended to flick through Dr Max's historical résumé. That's right, you had captains and governors, did you not? One or the other would do, though Captain did have rather a junior flavour nowadays. And as long as everyone understood that Sir Jack's powers, however theoretically enunciated in slopey script on ivory vellum, would never actually be invoked. Of course, he would provide his own carriage. And uniform. Not that such matters had been discussed with him.

Meanwhile, the future Governor was surfing his vision. You always had to push the envelope. Play short but think long. Let lesser men dream nickel-and-dime stuff; Sir Jack dreamed top dollar. Boldness, and more boldness; the true creative mind played by a separate rule-book; success bred its own legitimacy. Pitco's transnational standing had persuaded the banks and the funds to pour in capital; but it had been a moment of inspiration – at times, how the financial imagination resembled that of the artist! – to secretly loan such monies (the word always sounded luscious to Sir Jack in its plural form) to one of his own subsidiaries in the Bahamas. Naturally, this meant that the first charge on any revenue would be Pitco's management fees back home. Sir Jack shook his head in mock sympathy. They were regrettably heavy nowadays, management fees; regrettably heavy.

Then there was the question of what should happen immediately after Independence. Suppose that the new Island Parliament – flying in the face, as it had every right to do, of Sir Jack's public counsel – decided on a policy of nationalization. Bad news indeed for the banks and stockholders: but what could they do? The Island, regrettably, would not yet be a signatory to any international agreements. And then – after letting them run with the ball for a while – Sir Jack might be obliged to exercise his emergency powers as Governor. At which point technically – legally, too – everything would then belong to him. Of course, he would promise to repay creditors. In due course. At some percentage. After a great deal of debt-restructuring. Oh, it made him feel good to contemplate it. Think how they'd be shitting themselves. The lawyers would be pigs in clover. There might be action against him in the big financial centres. Well, the Island wouldn't have signed any extradition treaties. He could tough it out and wait for a negotiated settlement. Or he could tell them to fuck off and simply hole up at Pitman House (II). After all, his Wanderlust Years were behind him.

And yet . . . was that all too complicated, too confrontational? Was he letting his combative nature get the better of his wise old head? Perhaps the nationalization idea was a mistake. The very word played badly among Premier tourists nowadays, and quite rightly. He mustn't take his eye off the ball, he must look at the big picture. What was his game-plan, his bottom line? To get the Island up and running. Quite. And if current forecasts were in the right ball-park, the Project had every chance of roaring success. By nature, Sir Jack always allowed for the possibility of having to disappoint investors. But what if his Last Great Idea really worked? What if they were able to meet interest repayments, even to offer dividends? What if – to reverse the dictum – legitimacy bred its own success? Now that really would be ironic.

'DID YOU MAKE THAT STORY UP,

Dr Max?' Martha asked. They were sharing pitta-bread sandwiches on the renewable hardwood decking above the wetlands area. Dr Max had a weekend look to him: V-neck fairisle slipover and yellow paisley bow-tie.

'Which story?'

'The one about the woman and the eggs.'

'M–ake it up? I am an historian. The Official Historian, you forget.' Dr Max sulked for a moment, but it was only a studio sulk, not a real one. He chewed his pitta pocket and gazed at the stretch of water. 'I'm rather miffed no-one asked me to source it, actually. It's thoroughly respectable, not to say parsonical.'

'I didn't mean . . . I mean the reason I thought you might have done is because it would have been so clever.'

Dr Max sulked again, as if what he'd actually done wasn't clever, or as if clever wasn't what you normally got from him, or as if . . .

'You see, I assumed you made it up because you thought a bogus Project ought to have a bogus logo.'

'M–uch too clever for me, Miss Cochrane. Of course, Kilvert didn't see the flying woman's underwear himself, he was only reporting it, but there's some chance something of the sort *happened*, to use the vernacular term.'

Martha sucked at her front teeth, where a rocket leaf had reduced itself to a strand of dental floss. 'Still – you do think the Project's bogus?'

'Bo–gus?' Dr Max came out of his sulk. Any direct question, not obviously insulting, which allowed the possibility of a long answer, put him in a good mood. 'Bo–gus? No, I wouldn't say that. I wouldn't say that at all. Vulgar, yes, certainly, in that it is based on a coarsening simplification of pretty well everything. Staggeringly commercial in a way that a poor little country mouse like myself can scarcely credit. Horrible in many of its incidental manifestations. Manipulative in its central philosophy. All these, but not, I think, bogus.

'Bo–gus implies, to my mind, an authenticity which is being betrayed. But is this, I ask myself, the case in the present instance? Is not the very notion of the authentic somehow, in its own way, bogus? I see my paradox is perhaps a touch too ripe and vivid for you, Miss Cochrane.'

She smiled at him; there was something touchingly pure about Dr Max's self-love.

'Let me e–laborate,' he continued. 'Take what we see in front of us, this little area of unexpected wetland suspiciously close to the Great Wen. Perhaps, however many centuries ago, there was such a splashdown zone for passing trade here, perhaps not. On the whole probably not. So it is invented. Does that make it bogus? Surely not. Its intention and purpose are merely being supplied by man, rather than by nature. Indeed, you might argue that such intentionality, rather than reliance on the brute hazard of nature, makes this stretch of water superior.'

Dr Max plunged two finger-forks towards waistcoat pockets which today did not exist, and his hands slid on down to his thighs. 'As it h–appens this water *is* superior, in the following respect. Ornithology being one of the many strings to my bow. What a curious phrase that is. Shouldn't it be strings to my violin or something? Anyway, this patch of wetland, I would have you know, has been laid out at a particular angle, and planted in a particular way, to encourage the presence of certain desirable species by *dis*couraging one great big bore of another species, *id est* the Canada goose. Something to do with that bank of reeds over there, without being too specific.

'So we might conclude that this is a p–ositive im–provement on the way things had been before. And – to broaden the argument – is it not the case that when we consider such lauded and indeed fetichized concepts as, oh, I throw a few out at random, Athenian democracy, Palladian architecture, desert-sect worship of the kind that still holds many in thrall, there *is* no authentic moment of beginning, of purity, however hard their devotees pretend. We may choose to freeze a moment and say that it all "began" then, but as an historian I have to tell you that such labelling is intellectually indefensible. What we are looking at is almost always a replica, if that is the locally fashionable term, of something earlier. There is no prime moment. It is like saying that on a certain day an orang-utan sprang upright, put on a celluloid dicky and announced that fish-knives were vulgar. Or,' he giggled for the two of them, 'that a gibbon suddenly wrote Gibbon. Not very likely, is it?'

'So why have I always assumed that you despise the Project?'

'Oh, Miss C–ochrane, *entre n–ous*, I do, I do. But that's merely a social and aesthetic judgment. To any creature of taste and discernment, it's a monstrosity planned and conceived, if I may so characterize our beloved Duce, by another monstrosity. But as an historian, I have to say that I barely object.'

'Despite the fact that it's all . . . constructed?'

The pseudonymous author of Nature Notes smiled benignly. 'R–eality is r–ather like a r–abbit, if you'll forgive the aphorism. The great public – our distant, happily distant paymasters – want reality to be like a pet bunny. They want it to lollop along and thump its foot picturesquely in its home-made hutch and eat lettuce out of their hand. If you gave them the real thing, something wild that bit, and, if you'll pardon me, shat, they wouldn't know what to do with it. Except strangle it and cook it.

'As for being c–onstructed . . . well, so are you, Miss Cochrane, and so am I, constructed. I, if I may say so, a little more artfully than you.'

Martha chewed her sandwich and watched an aeroplane pass slowly overhead. 'I can't help noticing that when you addressed the Committee the other day, your nervous hesitations quite disappeared.'

'A–stonishing, the e–ffects of a–drenaline.'

Martha laughed with a whole heart, and laid her hand on Dr Max's arm. He gave a slight shudder as she did so. She laughed again.

'Now, that little shudder you gave. Was that artful?'

'S–uch a c–ynic, Miss Cochrane. By the same token, I might ask if your question was artful. But as to my shudder, yes it was artful in that it was a learned and deliberate response to a particular gesture – not, you understand, that I took any offence. It is not a gesture I was making in my perambulator. I may, in some Jurassic period of my psychological development, have decided upon it, lifted it from the great mail-order catalogue of gestures. I may have got it off the peg. I may have hand-crafted it to fit. Larceny is not ruled out. Most people, in my opinion, steal much of what they are. If they didn't, what poor items they would be. You're just as constructed, in your own less ... zestful way, no disrespect intended.'

'For instance?'

'For i–nstance, that question. You don't say No you Fool or Yes you Sage, you merely say, For instance? You withhold yourself. My observation, and this is in the context, Miss Cochrane, of being fond of you, is that either you participate actively, but in a stylized way, portraying yourself as a woman without illusions, which is a way of not participating, or you are provokingly silent, encouraging others to make fools of themselves. Not that I am against fools exhibiting their foolishness. But either way, you make yourself unavailable for scrutiny and, I would guess, contact.'

'Dr Max, are you coming on to me?'

'That's ex–*actly* what I mean. Change the subject, ask a question, avoid c–ontact.'

Martha was silent. She didn't talk like this with Paul. Theirs was a normal, day-to-day intimacy. This was intimacy too, but grown-up, abstract. Did that make any sense? She tried to think of a question that wasn't a means of avoiding contact. She'd always thought asking questions *was* a form of contact. Depending on the answers, of course. Eventually, with a girlish hopefulness, she said, 'Is that a Canada goose?'

'The i–gnorance of the young, Miss Cochrane. Tut, indeed, tut. *That* is a perfectly ordinary and frankly rather scruffy mallard.'

MARTHA KNEW WHAT SHE WANTED:

truth, simplicity, love, kindness, companionship, fun and good sex was how the list might start. She also knew such list-making was daft;

normally human, but still daft. So while her heart opened, her mind had remained anxious. Paul behaved as if their relationship were already a given: its parameters decided, its purpose certain, all problems strictly for the future. She recognized this trait all too well, the blithe urgency to get on with being a couple before the constituent parts and workings of coupledom had been established. She had been here before. Part of her wished she hadn't; at times she felt burdened by her own history.

'Do you think I avoid contact?'

'What?'

'Do you think I avoid contact?'

They were on her sofa, drinks in hand. Paul was stroking the inside of Martha's forearm. At a certain point, just above the wrist, on the third or fourth pass, she would give a soft yelp of pleasure and jerk her arm away. He knew this, waited until it happened, then replied, 'Yes. QED.'

'But do you think I'm, oh, irritatingly silent or else putting on an act of some kind?'

'No.'

'Sure?'

Paul's expression was of amused complacency. 'Put it this way, I haven't noticed.'

'Well, if you haven't noticed, it might as likely be yes as no.'

'Look, I said it's no. What's the matter with you?' He saw that she was still unconvinced. 'I just think you're . . . real. And you make me feel real. Is that good enough for you?'

'I know it should be.' Then, as if changing the subject, she said, 'I was chatting to Dr Max at lunchtime.' Paul gave a grunt of indifference. 'You know that patch of wetland behind Pitman House?'

'You mean the pond?'

'It's a patch of wetland, Paul. I was talking to Dr Max about it. He's an amateur ornithologist. Did you know he was Country Mouse in *The Times* every Saturday?'

Paul smiled a sigh. 'That's probably the least interesting piece of information you've told me in all the time we've been together. Country Mouse, what a misnomer for a . . . poncey twat who talks at you as if he's still on television. I shouldn't be at all surprised if Jeff doesn't punch him one of these days. Oh, and I *really* dislike his l–ittle he–sitations when he sp–eaks.'

'He's interesting. You don't have to like someone for them to be interesting. Anyway, I *do* like him. In fact, I'm very fond of him.'

'I de–test him.'

'No you don't.'

'I do–hoo.' Paul reached again for her arm.

'No. He told me something fascinating. Apparently they designed that wetland in a particular way. It's to do with the landscaping, the planting of the reeds, the height of the banks, the direction of the water. The idea is to stop Canada geese landing on it. I suppose they're a pest, or they frighten other birds away. There was a very pretty mallard on the water at lunchtime.'

'Martha,' said Paul heavily, 'I know you're a country girl, but why are you telling me this? Is Dr Max planning a bird section for the Project? Doesn't he remember Sir Jack's instruction, Fuck the Puffins?'

'I thought you'd given up quoting Pitmanisms. I thought you'd been cured. No, it just set me thinking. I mean, do you think we're like that?'

'Us?'

'Not you and me. People generally. The whole business of who you . . . click with and who you don't. It's a mystery, finally, isn't it? Why do I find you attractive rather than someone else?'

'We've been into this. Because I'm younger, shorter, wear glasses, don't earn as much and . . .'

'Come on, Paul. I'm trying to move on. I'm not saying it's . . . silly that I'm attracted to you.'

'Thanks. What a relief. So how about coming to bed with me? Just to show you really are.'

'You see, if someone was trying to be objective about it, they might think it had something to do with my father.'

'Hang on.' Paul couldn't decide whether he was amused or irritated. 'But we've agreed I'm *younger* than you.'

'Quite. So, for instance, I don't trust older men. Something like that.'

'That, as you said to me not long ago, is fairly cheap psychology.'

'Sorry,' said Martha. 'Or you could say that you're a contrast to the men I've been out with in the past. Or you could say that there's simply no pattern to it.'

'Like we're both heterosexual and happen to work in the same office and Fate Threw Us Together?'

'Or you could say there *is* a pattern, but it's one we don't know, or can't understand. That there's something guiding us without our knowing.'

'Hang on. Hang on. Stop.' Paul got up and stood in front of her. He raised a finger so that she wouldn't say any more. 'I've got it, I've finally got it. I think it was the idea that Dr Mer–mer–mer–Max might have anything remotely relevant to say on the subject of human relationships that threw me. Now I'm there. *You*'re a patch of wetland, and you can't understand why all those nice big Canada geese aren't stopping by, and why you have to settle for a boring old mallard like me.'

'No. Not entirely. Not at all. Anyway, mallards are very nice.'

'If that's accurate flattery, I'm not sure I can handle it.'

'So what do you think?'

'I don't think, I quack.'

'No really.'

'Quack quack.'

'Paul, stop it.'

'Quack. Quack. Quack.' He saw Martha on the cusp of laughter. 'Quack.'

never came too soon. That is what his colleagues used to say of him, admiringly. He had good contacts, secured his sources, did the leg-work, triple-checked anything iffy, and only brought his story to the Editor when it was busting out of its bra. He also had the advantage, as an acquirer and purveyor of sex stories, that he didn't look like one. Most people imagined some coarse, collusive, blackmailing humanoid who leeringly licked a pencil between note-taking and had stains on his trench-coat which might have been beer but probably weren't.

Gary Desmond wore a dark suit and restrained tie, and on certain occasions a wedding ring; he was intelligent, civil, and rarely put discernible pressure on his informants. His approach was – or seemed – sympathetic yet businesslike. This story had come to the paper's attention, they had researched it thoroughly, and were intending to publish shortly; but first they wanted, out of courtesy, and indeed moral obligation, to check it with the key protagonist. There were some facts she or he might like to clarify, and obviously the newspaper would like to help in any way it could when rivals picked up the story and – let's be realistic about this – persuaded other parties to put a different slant on affairs. In short, there was a problem, and a problem that wouldn't go away, but Gary Desmond was there to help you. Instead of suggestive pencil-licking, he made slow notes with a gold-nibbed fountain-pen, the sort of semi-antique that could become a talking-point, and his manner was endlessly patient and faintly subservient, so that in the end it was usually you who first mentioned money. It just needed a mild 'I suppose my expenses will be covered?' or a more blatant 'Drink in it for me?' – and before you knew it you were at a 'secret hideaway under an assumed name', which sounded more exotic than a Home Counties conference hotel near a bypass but still ... And the tape-recorder would turn and turn – the likeable fountain-pen having long since been put away – as Gary Desmond went over and over things he already knew, or seemed to know, but just wanted to double check. By this time you had already signed the contract and seen the air-tickets. Indeed, such was your bonding with Gary – as you had slipped into calling him – that you even wondered, with a cute toss of your bleached hair, whether he couldn't come with you and share those five days in the sun waiting for it all to blow over. And sometimes he did and sometimes it was regrettably against the rules.

All this professional lulling did not prepare you for a front page which read MY DRUG-CRAZED LEZZIE ROMPS WITH PRINCE RICK. Inside, across two pages, you saw yourself, cleavage adangle, laid out in a French basque on a snooker table naughtily cupping a couple of balls in your hand. Then came the call from your parents, who'd always been so proud of you but now couldn't hold up their heads let alone walk into the pub; except it was only a call from Mum, because Dad couldn't bring himself to speak to you. And after that came follow-ups from loyal ex-boyfriends of several years ago ('Just lay in bed like a big fat poodle and let Mugsie do all the work ... Had even bought the ring when she upped and offed with a toff ... Always a bit of a goer but who'd have thought it would have led to hard drugs and three-in-bed romps ...'). It was all so unfair, and the papers were vicious, and it was only coke and most of it had been Petronella's idea anyway. So you looked to Gary Desmond for support, and yes, he was still there, if returning your calls a little more slowly than before; but no, alas, he didn't have time for a meal this week, working on a big story, out of town, maybe a drink some time, anyway, chin up, girl, in Gary's opinion you came out of it really well, full of dignity, and what did they say, always shoot the messenger, eh? It was only if you carried on whingeing that his tone would harden just a little and he would remind you that it was a tough old world out there, play with fire you should expect to get burnt, and if you wanted his advice you'd had the cheque so why didn't you trot along and spend a bit of it, there's no girl in his experience that wasn't cheered up by a new frock, sorry, love, gotta run. And you didn't have time to suggest that if he came to the shop with you he could say you still looked nice and not a disgusting slag like you'd been called only yesterday with no provocation. How many of these did the doctor say to take for not sleeping?

Gary Desmond's dark-blue van, which looked as if it dealt in superior maintenance of an unspecified kind, was parked across from Auntie May's house in Chorleywood for some time. The cab was always empty, and no passing dog-walker or neighbourhood watch snooper suspected that the air-vents were peep-holes, and that inside Gary was at work with notebook, tape-recorder and fast film. The identification of visitors to 'Ardoch' involved a small amount of sub-contracting; he bought an old chum a big drink for credit-card access; but he kept everything watertight and the name of the chief bumblebee, the big fat buzzer, was never mentioned.

Making the first contact was always the trickiest part, since Gary Desmond's ignorance was at its fullest, and there was always the chance that Fruitfly Number One would scream 'Fuck off you slimy bastard', run to the phone and warn off his Auntie May, thus putting the kibosh on the whole operation. But the shy and balding airline pilot, a divorced sadsack in his fifties, whom Gary Desmond chose to confront – in the fellow's local pub, where the likelihood of erratic behaviour was diminished – felt initially calmed both by Gary's manner and by his lies. Of course he was nothing as offensive as a journalist; his documentation showed him as a special investigator for HM Customs and Excise. It was a drugs case, worldwide, with a certain amount of murder attached, and one of the key figures was a frequent habitué of a certain address. Gary Desmond emphasized to his now anxious victim that this wasn't a police matter, it had nothing to do with the press, and they weren't at all bothered by Auntie May's establishment. As far as the Excise were concerned, law-abiding, tax-clean citizens could do in private whatever they liked, as long as minors, protected species and certain classified substances were not involved. Now could they perhaps go somewhere he was less well known and talk?

At the end of the evening Gary paid the restaurant bill and with a regretful gesture placed an envelope on the table. It wasn't his way of doing things, but his superiors insisted that those who helped the Excise had their expenses defrayed. The pilot refused. Gary quite understood, while adding that such monies were strictly non-accountable – no names, no receipts. Why did they call it 'petty' cash, he wondered; that was a misnomer if ever there was one. Consider it a rebate from the Chancellor. After a few moments the pilot took the envelope without looking inside. Gary Desmond was pretty sure they wouldn't need any more assistance, though of course they knew where to find him (and his employers) if necessary. Strictly off the record, the investigation might take another couple of months, at which point Auntie May would have one fewer client but in other respects everything would be back to normal.

The next stage was easier: the routine establishment of names, times, contacts, prices, choices, methods. Then came a final hard decision: did they need Auntie May or didn't they? If she panicked, or ran, or simply got loyal, things could be jeopardized. But if she co-operated for just a sweet hour or two's taping . . . Gary Desmond rethought his persona. Perhaps the security services this time, contact with a certain Arab dictator, remember those little children with their throats cut, heartbreaking the pictures, weren't they, just a question of taking out a single client, yes a well-known face, indeed a very well-known one, but then in some ways she must prefer anonymous faces. No question of expenses, by the way, absolutely no question of expenses. What they proposed instead, indeed insisted upon, was a large fee. A very large fee indeed. Just the three hours. Small aperture in the plasterwork necessary, but in, out, never see us again.

Gary Desmond thought it worth the risk.

'BUCK HOUSE,'

said Sir Jack. 'We're strapped without Buck House.'

The hotels had their carpeting and potted trees, the twin towers of Wembley Stadium were waiting to be topped off, a replica double-cube snuggery was being slotted into Pitman House (II), and three golf courses already embellished Tennyson Down. The shopping malls and sheepdog trials were ready to go. Hampton Court maze had been laid out, a White Horse cut in a chalky hillside, and on a west-facing clifftop topiarists had trimmed Great Scenes from English History which shone as a black frieze against the setting sun. They had a half-size Big Ben; they had Shakespeare's grave and Princess Di's; they had Robin Hood (and his Band of Merrie Men), the White Cliffs of Dover, and beetle-black taxis shuttling through the London fog to Cotswold villages full of thatched cottages serving Devonshire cream teas; they had the Battle of Britain, cricket, pub skittles, Alice in Wonderland, *The Times* newspaper, and the One Hundred and One Dalmatians. The Stacpoole Marital Memorial Pool had been excavated and planted with weeping willows. There were Beefeaters trained to serve Great English Breakfasts; Dr Johnson was choosing his lines for the Dining Experience at the Cheshire Cheese; while a thousand robins were acclimatising to perpetual snow. Manchester United would play all its home fixtures at the Island's Wembley, the matches being replayed immediately afterwards at Old Trafford by substitute teams, who would produce the same result. They had failed to get any members of Parliament; but even half-trained, a bunch of resting actors were proving indistinguishable from the real thing. The National Gallery had been hung and varnished. They had Brontë country and Jane Austen's house, primeval forest and heritage animals; they had music-hall, marmalade, clog- and Morris-dancers, the Royal Shakespeare Company, Stonehenge, stiff upper lips, bowler hats, in-house TV classic serials, half-timbering, jolly red buses, eighty brands of warm beer, Sherlock Holmes and a Nell Gwynn whose physique countered any possible whisper of paedophilia. But they did not have Buck House.

In one sense, of course, they had it. The palace-front and railings were complete; guardsmen in Lycra-lite bearskins had been trained not to bayonet cute toddlers smearing ice-cream into their toe-caps; colours – a whole rainbowful – were waiting to be trooped. All this went ahead under a deliberately leaky news blackout, which naturally led people to assume that the Royal Family had agreed to relocate. Regular denials from Buckingham Palace served only to confirm the rumour. But the fact was, they didn't have Buck House on board.

It ought to have been easy. On the mainland, the Family had been held in low repute for some time. The death of Elizabeth II and the subsequent fracture of the hereditary principle were widely seen as the end of the traditional monarchy. The process of public consultation over the succession further diluted the royal mystique. The young King and Queen had done their best, appearing on chat shows, hiring the best script-writers, and keeping their infidelities more or less private. A twenty-page photo-spread in *Terrific* magazine had produced a touching moment, when readers had learnt, from a cushion-cover personally designed by Queen Denise, her nickname for her husband: Kingy-Thingy. But in general the nation had grown querulous, either dismayed by the Family's normality, resentful of its cost, or simply tired from bestowing millennia of love.

This should have helped Sir Jack's cause, but the Palace was proving oddly stubborn. The King's advisers were skilled in temporization, and openly hinted that the Windsors' foreign bank accounts would see the Family through many more decades. At the end of the Mall a bunker mentality was developing, enlivened by occasional outbursts of what looked like satire. When the Prime Minister repeated the phrase 'bicycling monarchy' once too often, a Palace spokesman replied that while bicycles were not, and never could be, royal modes of transport, the King, acknowledging the economic circumstances and the dwindling supply of fossil fuels, was willing to convert the House of Windsor into a motorbicycling monarchy. And indeed, from time to time, a helmeted figure with the royal crest on the back of its leathers would power down the Mall, with silencer disconnected as if by prerogative; though whether this was the King, his wicked cousin Rick, a surrogate or a clown, no-one could discover.

For all the citizenry's disenchantment, the Palace, the Department of Tourism, and Sir Jack knew that the Royal Family was the country's top cash crop. Sir Jack's negotiating team strove to emphasize how a move to the Island would produce both financial advantage and quality leisure for the Family. There would be a fully modernized Buckingham Palace, plus, for retro weekends, Osborne House; there would be no criticism or interference, just organized adulation *ad libitum*; the Family would pay no taxes, and the Privy Purse would be replaced by a profit-sharing scheme; there could be no journalistic intrusion into their lives, since the Island had only a single newspaper – *The Times of London* – and its editor was a true patriot; boring duties would be kept to a minimum; foreign trips would be purely recreational, and dreary heads of state would have their visa applications refused; the Palace could have approval over all coins, medals and stamps issued on the Island, even postcards if they wished; finally, there would never, ever be a question of bicycles – indeed, the whole thinking behind the relocation was to restore the glamour and pizzazz which had been so insolently wrenched from the Royal Family in past decades. Transfer fees to make footballers swoon had been mentioned, yet still the Palace held out. It had been agreed – after a lot of flattery, most of it financial – that the King and Queen would fly down for the Opening Ceremony. But this was strictly without prejudice, as had been pointed out many times.

The Appointed Cynic tried to look on the bright side. 'Look,' she said, 'we've already got Elizabeth the First, Charles the First and Queen Victoria on the Island. Who needs a bunch of pricey no-talent scroungers?'

'We, alas, do,' replied Sir Jack.

'Well, if everyone around here – even Dr Max, to my surprise – prefers the replica to the original, get some replicas.'

'I think,' said Sir Jack, 'that if I hear that sentiment again I shall do someone an injury. *Of course* we have a back-up position. The "Royal Family" has been in training for months. They'll do it very well, they have my every confidence. But it's *just not the same.*'

'Which logically means that it could be better.'

'Alas, Martha, there are times when logic, like cynicism, can only take us so far. We are talking Quality Leisure. We are talking Top Dollar and Long Yen. We're *strapped* without Buck House, and don't they know it.'

A rare voice was now heard. 'What about inviting old George back from his monastery?'

Sir Jack did not even glance at his Ideas Catcher. The young man had become decidedly pert in recent weeks. Didn't he understand that his job was to catch Ideas and not proffer his own piddling semi-notions? Sir Jack attributed these sudden moments of assertiveness to Paul's stupendous good fortune in clambering into Martha Cochrane's bed. Had Pitco been reduced to this, a mere dating agency for employees? There would be pay-off time, in due course; but not today.

Sir Jack let the boy fry for a while in the expanding silence, then murmured to Mark, 'Now that really *would* be insane.' Mark's superior laughter brought the meeting to a close.

'A word, Paul, *if* you have time.'

Paul watched the others file out; or rather, he watched Martha's legs file out.

'Yes, she's a fine woman.' Sir Jack's tone was approving. 'I speak as a connoisseur of fine women. And a family man, of course. A fine woman. Goes like the proverbial clappers, I shouldn't wonder.'

Paul did not respond.

'I remember when I first set eyes on her. Likewise when I first set eyes on you, Paul. In less formal circumstances.'

'Yes, Sir Jack.'

'You've done well, Paul. Under my patronage. She's done well too. Under my patronage.'

Sir Jack left it at that. Come on, boy, don't disappoint me. Show me you've at least got something in your trousers.

'Are you saying', – the aggression of Paul's tone was new, the primness familiar – 'that my ... relationship with ... Miss Cochrane is unacceptable to you?'

'Why should I feel that?'

'Or that my work has suffered as a consequence?'

'Not in the least, Paul.'

'Or that her work has suffered as a consequence?'

'Not in the least.'

Sir Jack was content. He put his arm round Paul and felt a gratifying tightness in the shoulders as he led his protégé to the door. 'You're a lucky man, Paul. I envy you. Youth. The love of a good woman. Life before you.' He reached for the door-handle. 'My blessings on you. On you both.'

Paul was sure of one thing: that Sir Jack didn't mean it. But what did he mean?

ROBIN HOOD

and his Merrie Men. Riding through the Glen. Stole from the rich, gave to the poor. Robin Hood, Robin Hood. A primal myth; better still, a primal English myth. One of freedom and rebellion – justified rebellion, of course. Wise, if *ad hoc*, principles of taxation and redistribution of income. Individualism deployed to temper the excesses of the free market. The brotherhood of man. A Christian myth, too, despite certain anti-clerical features. The pastoral monastery of Sherwood Forest. The triumph of the virtuous yet seemingly outgunned over the epitomic robber baron. And on top of all this, no. 7 on Jeff's all-time list of The Fifty Quintessences of Englishness, as adjusted by Sir Jack Pitman.

The Hood Myth had been given priority rating from the start. Parkhurst Forest easily became Sherwood Forest, and the environs of the Cave had been arboreally upgraded by the repatriation of several hundred mature oaks from a Saudi prince's driveway. The rock-style facing to the Cave was being jack-hammered into aged authenticity, and the dormitory had received its second coat of primer. The gas-pipe to the whole-ox barbecue pit had been laid, and the hiring of Robin's Band of Merrie Men was down to its final audition. Martha Cochrane was scarcely being Cynical – it was more an idle mental doodle – when, at a Thursday committee, she said,

'By the way, why are the "Men" all men?'

'Is the Pope a Catholic?' replied Mark.

'Knock off the feminism, Martha,' said Jeff. 'Top dollar and long yen simply aren't interested.'

'I was just. . .'

But Dr Max pattered to her rescue, chivalric if ill-aimed. 'Of course, whether or not the Pope is or is not, was or was not, a Catholic, remains, despite its use as a seemingly conclusive item of tap-room repartee' – and here Dr Max glanced fiercely at Mark – 'a matter of serious concern to historians. On the one hand, the popular if fuzzy-minded view that whatever the Pontiff does is *ipso facto* a Catholic act, that Papality or Popiness is, by definition, Catholicity. On the other, the somewhat maturer judgment of my colleagues that one substantive problem of the Catholic Church down the centuries, what has landed it all too frequently in the ecclesiastical and historical mulligatawny, is precisely that the Popes have been insufficiently Catholic, and that if they *had* been . . .'

'Turn it off, Dr Max,' said Sir Jack, though his tone was indulgent. 'Fill us in on your thinking, Martha.'

'I'm not sure "thinking" isn't an exaggeration,' Martha began. 'But I . . .'

'Quite,' said Jeff. 'It's too late for all this knee-jerk stuff. There's only ever been minority money up that alley. Everyone *knows* about Robin Hood. You can't start *messing around* with Robin Hood. I mean . . .' He lifted his eyes in exasperation.

Martha had been unprepared for Jeff's attack. He was normally so solid and literal, waiting patiently for others to decide and then implementing their will. 'I just thought,' she said mildly, 'that part of our task, part of Project Development, was the repositioning of myths for modern times. I don't see what's different about the Hood myth. Indeed, the fact that it's number seven should make us examine it more carefully.'

'May I pick up a c–ouple of Jeff's c–omplacent, if I may say so, phrases?' Dr Max was leaning back, fingers loosely joined at the nape, elbows warding off doubters, already in full seminar mode. Martha looked across at Sir Jack, but the chair was feeling tolerant, or perhaps malicious, today. '*Everyone knows about Robin Hood* is a myopic formula which makes an historian's hackles rise. Everyone knows, alas, only what everyone knows, as my investigations on behalf of the Project have all too sadly shown. But the pearl richer than all his tribe is *You can't start messing around* with Robin Hood. What, my dear Jeff, do you think History is? Some lucid, polyocular transcript of reality? Tut, tut, *tut*. The historical record of the mid-to-late thirteenth century is no clear stream into which we might trillingly plunge. As for the myth-kitty, it remains formidably male-dominated. History, to put it bluntly, is a hunk. Rather like you, Jeff, in fact.

'Now, one's first thoughts on the m–atter. Miss Cochrane has raised, very pertinently, the question of whether and why the "Men" were all men. We know that one of them – Maid Marian – was clearly a certified woman. So a female presence is established from the start. Further, the name of the very leader, Robin, is sexually ambiguous, an ambiguity endorsed by the British pantomime tradition, where the outlaw is played by a young female person. The name "Hood", for that matter, denotes a garment which is ambisexual. So one might, if one wished to be provocative and somewhat anti-Jeffish, venture a repositioning of the Hood myth within the true corpus of female outlawry. Moll Cutpurse, Mary Read and Grace O'Malley might come to some, if not all, minds at this point.'

Sir Jack was enjoying Jeff's discomfiture. 'Well, Jeff, care to come back on that one?'

'Look, I'm just the Concept Developer. I develop concepts. If the Committee decides to turn Robin Hood and his Merrie Men into a band of . . . fairies, then just let me know. But I can tell you one thing: pink pound does not go through the same turnstile as top dollar.'

'It might enjoy the squeeze,' said Dr Max.

'Gentlemen. Enough for the moment. All thoughts to Dr Max, who will report to an emergency session of the Committee on Monday next. Oh, and Jeff, stop work on the dormitory for the moment. Just in case we need to build more little girls' rooms.'

The following Monday morning Dr Max presented his report. To Martha's eye he was as dapper and fussy as usual, but with a more determined air. She predicted to herself that his preliminary hesitations might disappear; she also wondered if Paul would notice. Dr Max cleared his throat, as if he, rather than Sir Jack, were in charge.

'In deference to our Chairman's known views on sedimentary rock and flint arrowheads,' he began, 'I shall spare you the none the less fascinating early history of the Hood legend, its Arthurian parallels, its possible source in the great Aryan sun-myth. Similarly, *Piers Plowman*, Andrew of Wyntoun, Shakespeare. Mere arrowheads. I shall equally spare you the results of my electronic canvass of Joe Public, who in the present instance I might rename Jeff Public. Yes, everyone does indeed "know about" Robin Hood, and they know just what you might expect. Diddly-squat, as the jargon has it.

'Leaving all that aside, how might the Band "play", as it were? Jeff Public would, I think, applaud the legend of the *ur*-freedom-fighter not just for his liberationist actions and redistributive economic policy, but also for his democratic choice of companions. Friar Tuck, Little John, Will Scarlet and Much the Miller's Son. What have we here? A rebel priest with an eating disorder; a person suffering from either restricted growth or gigantism, depending how ironic you judge the medieval mind to have been; a possible case of *pityriasis rosea*, although dipsomania can't be ruled out; and a flour operative whose personal identity is dependent upon his father's social position. Then we have Allan-a-dale, whose bursting heart might allegorically refer to a cardiac condition.

'In other words, a grouping of the marginalised led by an equal-opportunity employer who was, whether he knew it or not, one of the first implementers of an affirmative rights programme.' Martha was watching Dr Max in qualified disbelief. He couldn't mean all this stuff: he must be winding Jeff up. But sleek self-parody was close to Dr Max's normal mode; and her enquiring glance slid off his shiny carapace. 'Which leads us inevitably to consider the sexual orientation of the Band, and whether they might have been a homosexual community, thus further underlining and justifying their status as outlaws. See English kings, various, *passim*, but even so. We raised at our last pow-wow the sexual ambiguity of names – Robin and Marian being the prime examples – to which might be added the case of the Miller's Son, who appears textually both as Much, which might indicate a certain hefty masculinity or Jeffness, and as Midge, which is well attested as a term of affection applied to short women.

'As a general point, we should be aware that in pastoral communities where males greatly outnumber females, same-sex practices in a non-judgmental ethos are the historical norm. Such activities would involve a measure of transvestism, sometimes ritualized, sometimes, well, not. I should also wish to record – though would quite understand if the Committee declines to develop it as a concept – that pastoral communities of this make-up would certainly have indulged in bestiality. To take the present instance, deer and geese might seem the most likely subjects for fraternization; swans unlikely; boar, on balance, hardly at all.

'Now, in considering the historical evidence for same-sex orientation, the case of Maid Marian is fundamental. According to such imperfect narratives as have survived, Marian, originally Matilda Fitzwater, went through a ceremony of marriage to Hood performed by Friar Tuck – which presumably made it of dubious ecclesiastical validity. However, she declined to consummate the marriage until the ban of outlawry had been lifted from her spouse. In the meanwhile, she took the name Maid Marian, lived in chastity, assumed male attire, and hunted alongside the "Men". Any hypotheses, gentlemen, Miss Cochrane?'

But they were all too intent, both on Dr Max's narrative, or at least pictorial capacity, and on his audacity, not to say recklessness, *vis-à-vis* the owner of family newspapers. Sir Jack himself was ruminatively silent. 'Three possibilities spring to mind,' Dr Max went on smoothly, 'at least to my own imperfect cerebral instrument. First the neutral, non-interpretative possibility – though no true historian believes neutral non-interpretation to be possible – that Maid Marian was obeying the chivalric code of the times as she understood it. Second, that it was a marital ploy to avoid penetrative sex. Whether or not a vow of chastity would also relate to non-penetrative sex isn't clear from the historical record. Marian might have been trying, as it were, to have her cake and eat it. Third, that Matilda Fitzwater, while legally and baptismally female, was perhaps biologically male, and was employing a technical loophole in the law of chivalry in order to escape detection.

'You doubtless await my conclusions to all these matters with bated breath. My conclusions are these: that personally I could not give a toss; that in assembling this report I have rarely felt so insulted in my professional life; and that my resignation is in the post. Thank you, gentlemen, Miss Cochrane, Chairman.'

With that, Dr Max rose and tripped nattily from the room. Everyone waited for Sir Jack to pronounce judgment. But the

Chairman, untypically, declined to offer a lead. Eventually, Jeff said, 'Shot himself in the foot there, I'd say.'

Sir Jack shrugged and stirred. 'You'd say that, would you, Jeff?' The Concept Developer realized that his assumption had been too easy. 'I myself would say that Dr Max's contribution was most positive. Provocative, of course, and at times bordering on the offensive. But I did not get where I am by employing Yes-men, did I, Marco?'

'No.'

'Or do you mean Yes on this occasion? Whatever.'

Business continued. Sir Jack indicated the direction in which they should be going. Jeff sulked. Martha felt a pang for Dr Max. Mark, who sniffed every wind, seconded the proposal that there should be active recruitment among gays and ethnic minorities. He also agreed that further investigation was required into how conditions of outlawry might equip the differently-abled to make a fuller contribution than that permitted in today's marginalizing society. For who could have a stronger sense of smell than the visually impaired? Who could be more resolute under torture than the deaf mute?

A final suggestion was recorded in the minutes. Might there not be two separate 'Bands' in Sherwood Forest, ideologically linked yet autonomous: the traditional all-male, though minority-oriented organisation led by Robin Hood; and a separatist femme group led by Maid Marian? These matters were adjourned for further discussion.

As they were breaking up, Sir Jack crooked a finger at the Concept Developer. 'Jeff, by the way, you realize that I am making you personally responsible?'

'Thank you, Sir Jack.'

'Good.' The Chairman turned back to the latest Susie.

'Er. Excuse me, Sir Jack. What for?'

'What for what?'

'What exactly am I personally responsible for?'

'For ensuring that Dr Max's pertinent contributions to our ideas forum continue. Get after him, dunderhead.'

'VICTOR,'

said Auntie May. 'What a pleasant surprise.' She opened the front door of 'Ardoch' wider to let him pass. Some nephews wanted a maid – usually a very specific maid – to greet them. But nephew Victor liked doing things properly: this was Auntie May's house, so Auntie May answered the door.

'I've brought you a bottle of sherry,' said Sir Jack.

'Always a *most* considerate nephew.' Today she was an elegant, tweed-suited woman with a silver-blue rinse; respectable, affectionate yet firm. Tomorrow she would be a different Auntie. 'I'll open it later.' She knew the brown bag would also contain the correct number of thousand-euro notes. 'I feel so much better after your visits.' That was true. Some of the girls complained it wasn't worth the extra, and why was Victor allowed to when some of the others weren't? Well, they wouldn't have to bother much longer; and she wouldn't have to worry about finding a new Heidi every few months.

'May I go and play, Auntie?' Of all her nephews, Victor was the one who got down to business the quickest. He knew what he wanted, when and how. She'd miss that. Sometimes it took an age getting new nephews to articulate their desires. You'd try to help them along and then make the wrong guess. 'Now you've gone and spoiled it,' they'd whine.

'Go and play, Victor dear. I'll just put my legs up for a bit. It's been such a tiring day.'

Sir Jack's gait changed as he walked to the staircase. He became more bottom-heavy and soft-kneed; his feet pointed outwards. He went downstairs with a sideways, rolling motion, as if he might topple over at any moment. But he kept his balance; he was a big boy now, and big boys knew where to go. The first time Auntie May had tried accompanying him, but he'd soon put a stop to that.

The nursery was twelve metres by seven, brightly lit, with cheery posters on its yellow walls. It was dominated by two items: a wooden playpen one and a half metres high and three metres square; and a pram two and a half metres long, with thick-spoked wheels and hefty axles. The pram's hood was fringed with Union Jack bunting. Baby Victor adjusted the knee-level dimmer switches and the hiss on the gas-fire. He hung up his suit, then threw his shirt and underclothes over the rocking-horse. When he was bigger he would ride the horse, but he wasn't big enough yet.

Naked, he undid the big brass catch on the playpen and stepped inside. On a plastic tea-tray sat a wobbly green jelly, fresh out of its mould, half a metre high. Sometimes he liked to drop it down his tummy. Sometimes he liked to pick it up and throw it against the wall; then he would get told off and smacked. Today it didn't tempt him. He lay down on his front and burrowed into the plush pink rug, knees splayed like a frog. Then he half-turned and goggled up at the dresser. The vast pile of nappies, the metre-high bottle of baby oil, the matching powder can. Auntie May certainly knew how to do things. She'd taken some finding but it was worth every euro.

Just at the right moment, the nursery door opened.

'Baby! Baby Victor!'

'Goo-goo-goo-goo!'

'Baby botty. Baby botty need nappy.'

'Naaaapy,' purred Sir Jack, 'Naaaaapy.'

'*Nice* nappy,' said Lucy. She wore a freshly-pressed mid-brown nurse's uniform and her real name was Heather; unknown to Auntie May, she was preparing her doctorate in psycho-sexual studies at Reading University. But here she was called Lucy and was paid in cash. She took the giant powder can from the dresser and balanced it on the top rail of the playpen. Scented powder rained down from holes the size of teapot spouts; Victor gurgled and jiggled his pleasure. Nursie paused, then with a camel-hair mop attached to a broomstick she rubbed the powder into Baby's skin. He turned on his back, and she powdered his other side. Then she fetched a towelling nappy the size of a bath-sheet from the dresser. Sir Jack concealed the assistance he provided, and Lucy the amount of physical strength required, as she manoeuvred him around on the springy cloth. He parted and unparted his legs most authentically as she tucked the nappy round him and finished it off with a 50-centimetre brass safety-pin. Most babies went for ready-made padded plastic nappies with Velcro fasteners; and the mere sound of Velcro being pulled apart had an instant effect on some of them. But Baby Victor preferred terry-towelling and a safety-pin. Heather reflected on the infancy the two of them were replicating: had his parents been green, old-fashioned – or perhaps merely poor?

'Baby hungry?' asked Lucy. This one also liked old-fashioned baby talk. Others needed grown-up sentences, which perhaps denoted an infancy in which they had been treated as adults from the start, and thus denied the authentic nurturee's experiences they now sought; or it might indicate a desire for adult control over the fantasy; or again, an inability to regress further. 'Perhaps Baby would like to have his nappy changed now?' you said in all grammatical seriousness. But this Baby claimed complete Babying. Cloth nappies, naturalistic vocalization, and . . . all the rest, which she avoided thinking about for the moment. Instead she repeated, 'Baby hungry?'

'Titty,' he murmured. An advanced communicator for a three-month-old, it was true; but faithful inarticulacy would have made the job difficult.

She went to the door, opened it, and called 'Baby *hun*-gry' in a specified voice, cooing yet naughty. Two metres above her head, Gary Desmond gave himself a joyous thumbs-up about the sound quality. He watched the monitor as Lucy closed the door and Sir Jack got to his feet in the playpen. On awkward heels, he moved with his low-bottomed waddle to the dresser, wrenched open the bottom drawer, and pulled out a blue checked mobcap. He knotted its strings beneath his chin, then purposefully climbed the reinforced steps of the pram and swung himself aboard. The pram rocked on its springs like an ocean liner but otherwise did not move. Auntie May had made sure it was truly bolted to the floor.

Sitting up beneath the raised pram-hood with its Union Jack

bunting, Sir Jack began to mewl and show his teeth. After a while the grizzling stopped and in a near-boardroom voice he bawled, 'TITTY!'

At this signal, Heidi came tripping in. All the lactating mothers used by Auntie May were called Heidi; it was a house tradition. This one was getting near the end of her milk, or perhaps was simply getting fed up with having her breasts sucked on by middle-aged Babies; either way, she'd have to be replaced in a week or two. This was always a most difficult part of Auntie May's profession. Once, in desperation, she'd signed up a Caribbean Heidi. What a tantrum Baby Victor had thrown that day! It had been quite the wrong idea.

Victor also insisted on a proper feeding bra. Some Babies went for the topless-dancer look; but Baby Victor took being a Baby seriously. Heidi, who wore her highlighted hair in a French pleat, loosened her blouse a little from her dirndl skirt, climbed up to the pram's side, unbuttoned herself and then unsnapped her nipple cover. Sir Jack gurgled 'Titty' again, pulled his lips over his teeth to make a gummy mouth, and accepted the exposed nipple. Heidi gently squeezed her breast; Victor reached up a vole-like paw and rested it against the underwired bra; then closed his eyes in deep content. After a few eternal minutes, Heidi withdrew her nipple, allowing milk to splash on his cheeks, and gave him her other breast. She squeezed, he sucked again with his baby-mouth, and swallowed gurglingly. Heidi had more trouble reaching over to him with this breast, and concentrated hard on exact delivery. Finally, he opened his eyes from a deep drowse, and gently pushed her away. She dribbled some more milk on to him, and judged him almost ready. She knew he preferred to let Lucy wipe the milk off. Heidi snapped back her nipple-pouches, buttoned her blouse, and casually let her hand drift down the front of his bulging nappy. Yes, Baby Victor was well and ready.

She left the nursery. Sir Jack began to grizzle to himself, first quietly, then louder. Finally, he boomed out, 'NAPPY!' and Lucy, waiting behind the door with her hands in a bowl of iced water, came running.

'Nappy wet?' she asked worriedly. 'Baby's nappy wet? Let Nursie look.' She tickled Baby Victor's tummy, and slowly, carefully, teasingly undid his safety-pin. Sir Jack's erection was in full swing, and with cool hands Lucy felt all round it.

'Nappy not wet,' she said in a puzzled tone. 'Baby Victor not wet.' Sir Jack grizzled away again, prompting her to search for other causes. She wiped Heidi's milk from his ox-cheeks, then played gently with his balls. Finally, as it seemed, a thought came to her. 'Baby itchy?' she wondered aloud.

'Tchy,' Victor repeated. 'Tchy.'

Lucy fetched the double-magnum of baby oil. 'Itchy,' she said in a soothing voice. 'Poor Baby. Nursie make evvything better.' Upending the bottle, she squirted the oil on to Baby Victor's mountainous tummy, his elephantine thighs, and what they were both pretending was his little willy. Then she started to rub away Baby Victor's itches.

'Baby Victor like rubbing?' she asked.

'Uh ... uh ... uh,' murmured Sir Jack, dictating the required rhythm. From now on Lucy avoided eye-contact. She had tried being objective: she was, after all, Heather, and this was useful, well-paid field-work. But she found that, in a strange way, she could only become fully detached by increased involvement, by persuading herself that she was indeed Lucy, and this was indeed Baby Victor, nappy adrift, naked except for a blue mobcap, who lay sprawled beneath her.

'Uh ... uh,' he went as she ploshed more oil around his corona. 'Uh ... uh,' as he raised his hips to tell her to slicken up his balls some more. 'Uh ... uh,' in a quieter, growlier tone to indicate that she was doing it exactly right. Then, with a bigger, riper growl, he whispered, 'Poo.'

'Baby do poo?' she asked encouragingly, as if not entirely convinced that he was capable of the ultimate act of Babyhood. There were some Babies who wanted to be told they couldn't, and so didn't. There were others who wanted to be told they couldn't in order to seek the thrill of transgression. But Baby

Victor was a true Baby; there were no complications or ambiguity to his imperious demands. The final one, she recognized, was very close.

His hips pushed upwards, she squeezed her glistening hands in response, and Sir Jack Pitman, entrepreneur, innovator, ideas man, arts patron and inner-city revitalizer, Sir Jack Pitman, less a captain of industry than a very admiral, Sir Jack Pitman, visionary, dreamer, man of action and patriot, began a throaty crescendo which ended in a sforzando bellow of 'POOOOOOOOOOOOOO!' He let out a string of ploppy farts, came joltingly in Lucy's joined hands, and shat spectacularly in his nappy.

Some Babies like to be cleaned up, wiped, dried and powdered, which all cost a few thousand more euros, and was unpopular with the girls. But Lucy's duty was now over; Baby Victor preferred at this point to be left alone. The camera's closing sequence had him springing from the pram, and walking like an emerging adolescent towards the shower-room. Gary Desmond did not bother to document either the tempo, or the narcissism, of Sir Jack Pitman's dressing.

Auntie May saw Victor to the door, as she always did, thanking him for the sherry and expressing anticipation of next month's visit. She wondered if it would happen. She didn't like losing one of her most regular nephews. Still, if he did have something to do with that dreadful massacre . . . and Colonel Desmond's fee had been surprisingly generous . . . and they wouldn't have to keep remembering the bunting for the pram . . . and the girls never really approved of the crappers. They said that was taking Babyhood just a bit too far.

Sir Jack Pitman piaffed out of 'Ardoch' and whistled his way down to the limo. He felt rejuvenated. There was Woodie, cap under arm, holding open the door. Salt of the earth, people like Woodie. Damn fine driver; loyal too. Not like young Harrison, turning up his nose when offered the chance of driving Sir Jack. Wanting to get off home and canoodle with Miss Cochrane. She was a devious one, trying to subvert the Guardian of his

Ideas. Yet even the brief contemplation of their squalid coupling could not shift his good humour. Loyalty. Yes, he must give Woodie a generous tip when they got home. And what would it be on the way? The Seventh, perhaps? Kept you cheerful if you were that way inclined, cheered you up if you weren't. Yes, the Seventh. Damn fine chap, old Ludwig.

THE KING WAS PILOTING

the royal jet from Northolt to Ventnor. At least, he thought he was; and this was more or less the case. But since the sequence of royal incidents, an override system had been introduced. The official co-pilot – who had proved so inadequate during Prince Rick's tragic incineration of the day-care centre – was now just for window-dressing. He was strictly hands-off, there to smile and approve, someone to whom the royal pilot could feel superior. Instead, there was a tiny delay between the King's navigational demands and their endorsement by the Air Commander (Heritage) at Aldershot. Today, with clear skies and a light south-westerly breeze, the King was virtually in control. There was little for Aldershot to do; while the co-pilot could smile at the placid landscape and wait for the rendezvous west of Chichester.

Here they came, snub-nosed and clattery, two Spitfires and a Hurricane, waggling their roundelled wings, ready to escort the whisperjet to the Island's official opening. Aldershot briefly overrode the royal instruments and throttled back to match the agreed airspeed. The Spitfires took wing position, while the Hurricane fell in line astern.

The fighters' intercom system was the latest model, incorporating period static and crackle. 'Wing-Commander "Johnnie" Johnson reporting, Sir. On your starboard wing you have Squadron-Leader "Ginger" Baker, and on the port side Flight-Lieutenant "Chalky" White.'

'Welcome aboard, gentlemen,' said the King. 'Sit back and enjoy the show, eh? Roger, or what?'

'Roger, Sir.'

'Just out of interest, Wing-Commander, who was Roger?'

'Sir?'

'Worked for a firm called Wilco, I seem to remember.'

'You've lost me there, I'm afraid, Sir.'

'Just my joke, Wing-Commander. Over and out.'

The King looked across at his co-pilot and shook his head in disappointment. There'd been a script meeting at the Palace that morning, and he'd practised his lines with Denise as they were waiting to take off. She'd nearly peed herself. She was a real best mate, Denise. But what was the point in paying good money if the audience didn't get it?

They crossed the coast near Selsey and routed south-west over the English Channel. 'Precious jewel set in a silver sea, eh?' murmured the King.

'Indeed it is, Sir.' The co-pilot nodded as if His Majesty regularly turned such phrases.

The little squadron flew on across the waves. It always made the King a little melancholy to realize how quickly you reached the sea, and how small his realm was compared to that which his ancestors had once ruled. Only a few generations back and his great-however-many-times-granny had presided over a third of the globe. At the Palace, when they had judged his juvenile self-esteem a bit wonky, they used to dig out foxed atlases to show him how pink the world had once been, and how thumpingly important his lineage. Now it was mostly gone, all that justice and majesty and peace and power and being Bloody Number One, gone, all gone, thank you very much Johnnie Foreigner. Nowadays the place was so small you could hardly swing a cat; shrunk back to the size it had been when Old King Alfred burnt the cakes. He used to tell Denise that if the country didn't stir itself the two of them would be back to home baking, like in Alfie's time.

He was barely concentrating; there were long stretches when

this plane almost seemed to fly itself. Then his ears were tickled with a burst of static and crackle.

'Bandits three o'clock, Sir.'

The King looked where his co-pilot was pointing. A small plane was heading across their bows, towing a long banner. SANDY DEXTER AND THE DAILY PAPER GREET HIS MAJ, he read.

'Bloody bollocks,' muttered the King. He turned, and shouted through the open cockpit door, 'Hey, Denise, come and look at this bollocks.'

The Queen picked up her Scrabble pieces because she could never quite trust her lady-in-waiting not to cheat, and put her head into the cockpit.

'Bollocks,' said the Queen. 'Bloody bollocks.'

Neither of them had any time for Sandy Dexter. In the opinion of both King and Queen, Dexter was a slimeball and the *Daily Paper* not even fit for the outside bog. Of course they each separately read it, just to see what filth and lies their loyal subjects were being asked to swallow. That was how Queen Denise learned of her husband's regular visits to that bitch from hell who got her tits in America, Daphne Lowestoft. She'd need a lot more cosmetic improvement if she ever stepped foot in the Palace when Denise was around. The *Daily Paper* was also where the King discovered that his wife's recent and laudable interest in saving dolphins was also shared by someone in a wet-suit he could not even bear to name. Odd how wet-suits made everything stick out, like in an advertisement.

Now, as they watched, Dexter's little Apache turned and started heading back across their bows in the opposite direction. The King could imagine the creep chortling away and telling the photographer where to point the snout of his long lens. They probably had a shot of the royal cockpit already.

'Kingy-Thingy,' said the Queen. 'Do something.'

'Bloody *bollocks*,' repeated the King. 'How on earth can we get rid of this slimeball?'

'Roger, Sir.'

Wing-Commander 'Johnnie' Johnson climbed away from the royal jet and set course to intercept. He closed on the Apache with its trailing provocation. A little game of chicken, why not? Then he thought, what about giving the blighter a bit more of a scare? The wing cannon would still have a few rounds left after yesterday's Battle of Britain rehearsal. Put a squirt up his bum and make the fellow pee his pants. Bloody journalists.

The Hurricane closed further. With a cry to the intercom of 'This one's mine!' Johnson lined up the target in his gunsight, pressed the tit and felt the airframe shudder as he got off two eight-second bursts. He pulled the kite up into a sharp climb, just as the manual told him to do, and was chuckling to himself when he heard the unmistakable voice of 'Ginger' Baker break radio silence. 'Jesus *fuck*,' were his unambiguous words.

The Wing-Commander looked back. At first, all he could see was an expanding patch of fire. Slowly, it turned into a trail of vertical wreckage, strung lightly together, with the banner curling free and floating away unharmed. No parachutes emerged. Time slowed. Radio silence returned. Those aboard the royal squadron watched until the remnants of the light plane bounced briefly on the surface of the distant water and disappeared.

'Johnnie' Johnson took up his position in line astern again. The eastern cliffs of the Island came slowly into focus. Then Flight-Lieutenant 'Chalky' White gave his call sign. 'Log report, skipper,' he said. 'Looked like engine failure to me.'

'Jerry is inclined to sit on his own bomb,' added 'Ginger' Baker.

There was a long pause. Finally the King, having thought the matter over, came on the intercom. 'Congratulations, Wing-Commander. I'd say, bandits discouraged.' Queen Denise borrowed three letters from her lady-in-waiting and clattered down the word SLIMEBALL.

'Piece of cake, Sir,' replied 'Johnnie' Johnson, remembering his line from the Battle's end.

'But I'd say that, on the whole, Mum's the word,' added the King.

'Mum's the word, Sir.'

The squadron began its descent into Ventnor, and was cleared for landing. As the jet's door was opened and a brass band struck up his theme tune, the King tried to recall what exactly he'd said to make the Wingco go completely apeshit and blow Sandy Dexter into the middle of the English Channel. That was the trouble with being in the public eye: one's least words did get so frightfully misunderstood. The Wing-Commander, meanwhile, was wondering who could have replaced his blank ammunition with live.

A TROOP OF HEFTY SKYDIVERS,

crinolines spread and rubber eggs securely glued to their wicker baskets, descended from a windless sky towards the village green in front of Buckingham Palace.

'Heavens to Betsy!' roared Sir Jack from the reviewing stand.

The King, standing beside him, felt tired. It was a hot afternoon, and part of him was still feeling a touch guilty about yesterday's downing of Sandy Dexter. Denise had held herself together jolly well: she was a real best mate, Denise. Secretly, he'd been a trifle sickened at the idea of frying journalists, and he'd made enquiry of his ADC about an anonymous contribution for Dexter's widow. The ADC had consulted the press officer, who'd reported that Dexter was not known to be a man of domestic habit – indeed, quite the contrary – and this, in a way, had been a solace.

Then there had been the official welcome, and for all the novelty of the Island, being greeted by Sir Jack Pitman wasn't all that different from being greeted by a few heads of state he could mention, except that at least Pitman didn't try and kiss him on both cheeks. The helicopter tour of the Island – well, that at least had been rather a lark. A sort of fast-forward version of England: one minute it was Big Ben, the next Anne Hathaway's cottage, then the White Cliffs of Dover, Wembley Stadium, Stonehenge, one's own Palace, and Sherwood Forest. They had buzzed Robin Hood and his Band, who had responded by shooting arrows up at them.

'Rogues and rascals,' Pitman had shouted, 'can't do a thing with them.'

The King had led the laughter, and to show his famous royal nervelessness, had quipped back, 'Lucky you didn't arm them with ground-to-air missiles.'

Then there had been the endless line of handshakes, all sorts of odds and bods, Shakespeare, Francis Drake, Muffin the Mule, Chelsea Pensioners, a whole team of footballers, Dr Johnson, who seemed a pretty alarming cove, Nell Gwynn, Boadicea, and more than a hundred bloody Dalmatians. Gave a chap quite a turn to shake hands with his own great-however-many-times-granny, especially if you couldn't get a laugh out of her and she kept pretending she was the Queen Empress. He wasn't sure they should have introduced him to Oliver Cromwell, for that matter. Bad taste, really. Still, that Nell Gwynn had been a top girl, he thought, with her low-cut thingy, and, you know, oranges. But something about the way Denise had said, 'Are they real, do you think?' had made his ardour diminish. She could be a real bitch at times, Denise; a best mate, but a real bitch. If only she didn't have such an infallible eye for cosmetic adjustment – and His Majesty was old-fashioned enough to like cosmetic adjustment only if he wasn't aware that it had happened. He could just picture the scene – a little horsing around, the oranges rolling under the bed, old Kingy-Thingy claiming, what was that Froggy phrase, *droit de seigneur* – and then, just at the wrong moment, Denise's words, 'Are they real, do you think?' popping into his head. A real downer, that would be.

Lunch. There was always lunch, this time with rather too many glasses of that Adgestone wine of which the Island was in his opinion overproud. Then hours on the reviewing stand in the hot sun. He'd seen a march past of guardsmen and a parade of London taxis (which frankly was a bit too much like standing at the window of Buck House), pageants of history and floatfuls of myth. He'd seen Beefeaters and six-foot robins doing a co-ordinated dance on snow that declined to melt in the summer heat. He'd listened to brass bands, symphony orchestras, rock groups and opera stars all synthesized before him in cyberspace. Lady Godiva had come by on her horse, and just to make sure she wasn't in cyberspace he hoisted a pair of binox to his peepers. Feeling a stir to his left, he'd raised a regal palm to still his Queen. In public at least Denise knew her place, and this time there were no subversive little remarks about cellulite or tucks. She'd been quite a stunner, that Lady Godiva.

'Lucky old horse,' he'd murmured to the Pitman fellow on his right.

'Quite so, Sir. Though I must add, I'm a family man myself.' Gawd, why did *everyone* seem to have it in for him today? Like this morning, on the tour of the Island, there'd been a special diversion to overfly some sort of Memorial Pool. Just a village pond with a few ducks, and some weeping willows, but it had made his fat host go all misty-eyed and start prating on like the Archbishop of Canterbury.

Now these SAS men, or whatever they were, all dressed up in women's clothing, and carrying baskets of eggs, were parachuting down in front of his eyes to some patriotic soundtrack. He'd quite lost the plot as to who they were in the programme. One minute it was Royal Tournament stuff, the next a real dog's breakfast. For all he knew the whole of the human race, plus all the animal kingdom and a million people dressed up as plants were going to march past him one by one, and he was going to have to salute, shake hands, and hang a gong on every last blighter of them. The Adgestone swilled in his stomach, and the music blared.

But he didn't have the Windsor genes for nothing. His ancestors had passed on a few tricks of the trade. Always pee beforehand, that was rule Number One. Rule Number Two: stand on one foot more than the other, and switch feet after a while. Rule Number Three was Denise's: always admire things you wouldn't mind being given later on. And Rule Number Four was his very own: just when the whole bloody thing is getting unbearable and you're being bored witless, you turn to your host, as he now did to Pitman, and say, loud enough to be overheard by those around, 'Damn fine show.'

'Thank you, Sir.'

Compliments paid, the King lowered his voice. 'And damn fine Lady Godiva, if I may make so bold. Top girl.'

Sir Jack remained gazing down at the SAS transvestites stowing their chutes. Anyone would have thought he was commenting on them when he murmured, 'She's a great admirer of yours, Sir, if *I* may make so bold.'

Ker-pow! The old hypocrite. Still, maybe the day could be saved. Maybe Denise would have to fly back early.

'Absolutely no speeches,' Sir Jack continued, still in an undertone. Bloody bollocks! The old bugger seemed to be reading one's thoughts. 'Not unless you want to. No taxes. No tabloid press. Occasional exhibiting of the royal person, though very good replicas will shoulder most of the burden. No dreary heads of state coming to call. Unless you want them: I understand the pull of family commitment. And, of course, *strictly* no bicycles.'

The King had been warned against any direct negotiating with Pitman, who was held to be a tricky cove, so he contented himself with saying, 'There can be something jolly undignified about a bike, you know. The way one's knees stick out.'

'Double-glazing,' said Sir Jack, nodding towards Buckingham Palace. Somehow it looked better in the half-size version. 'Satellite, cable and digital TV. Freephone facilities worldwide.'

'So?' The King thought this last remark presumptuous. It was in his view all too direct a reference to the enforced installation of pay-phones at Buck House after the last censure motion in the House of Commons. Really, he'd *had* it with the heat and this pushy host and this bloody wine. 'What makes you think I give a toss about the effing phone bill?'

'I'm sure you don't, Sir, I'm sure you don't. All I was thinking is, it's not entirely handy if you have to go to the pay-phone every time you want to call up an airstrike. If you catch my drift.'

The King showed him a cool royal profile and twiddled his signet ring. *If you catch my drift.* Not much chance of missing it, was there? Like being downwind when one of Denise's mastiffs farted.

'Ah. Talk of the devil.'

The King wondered if this bugger Pitman had had some tip-off, or whether it was just luck. But here, as if on cue, came two Spitfires and a Hurricane, piloted, the public address system confirmed, by Flight-Lieutenant 'Chalky' White, Squadron-Leader 'Ginger' Baker, and Wing-Commander 'Johnnie' Johnson. They flew over low, buzzed the reviewing stand, waggled their wings, did slow rolls, looped the loop, fired blank ammo, and laid red, white and blue smoke.

'Just out of interest,' said the King, 'and without prejudice as my learned advisers are constantly putting it. Back at HQ I have a whole bloody army, navy and airforce ready to defend me if things get hot. Here you've got these three old museum pieces with peashooters attached. Not exactly going to make Johnnie Foreigner crap his pants, are they?'

Sir Jack, who was having their conversation recorded, was pleased with what could, if circumstances required, be turned into another royal gaffe. For the moment, he merely noted it, along with the King's boredom, querulousness, alcohol intake and lust. 'And equally without prejudice, Sir,' he replied, 'although I had intended to leave such discussions until my next meeting with your learned advisers, you would be surprised to learn how cheaply it is possible to acquire nuclear capability in this modern world of ours.'

Queen Denise returned to the mainland the next day to continue her charitable duties. The King cancelled a regimental luncheon after deciding that his personal presence was required as the Talks About Talks looked like developing into Talks. Lady Godiva turned out not to have cellulite, or tucks, as far as he could tell, and to be a whopping patriot.

According to *The Times of London*, now published from Ryde, four separate log reports described in matching detail the appearance, three days earlier, of an unidentified light aircraft ten miles south of Selsey Bill. All spoke of a sudden loss of control. There had been no possibility of survivors. *The Times* confirmed the loss of a widely-read tabloid journalist, also of a star photographer, albeit one known for run-ins with the glitterati. Sir Jack's office put out a statement confirming that the plane's wreckage had sunk inside the Island's territorial waters, and that the graves would be respected in perpetuity. Two days later, as the Talks ended satisfactorily, Sir Jack Pitman flew over the crash site in a Pitco helicopter. Beaming broadly, he dropped a generous wreath.

SIR JACK'S SIXTY-FIFTH BIRTHDAY

had been chosen as the appropriate date for action. In his replica double-cube snuggery at Island HQ, Sir Jack wore his Palace of Westminster braces with defiance. What did he care if he was finally rendering himself unavailable for the House of Lords? The various fools and dunderheads of various parties to whom he had made more than generous donations over the decades had missed their chance of draping him in ermine. Well, so be it. Small men always tried to drag down greater; hypocrites would have their day. Just because, a while back, some wet-eared Department of Trade and Industry inspector unversed in modern commercial practices chose to seek advancement through a piece of cheap phrase-making. To say of Sir Jack Pitman that he was as honourable as Taras Bulba was a shabby racial slur. The phrase 'unfit to run a whelk stall' particularly rankled. At the time, he'd had a hundredweight of whelks delivered to the inspector's modest Reigate residence with a full band of paparazzi in attendance to record the humiliation; but he wasn't sure the ploy hadn't been too subtle. Somehow the inspector had managed to turn things so that the whelks looked like an inducement. It had all got out of hand, and Sir Jack's pleasantry about the molluscs coming from his offshore fund had been quite misread.

Well, today was the day when those tinpot MPs, self-serving ministers, hypocrites and small men would realize exactly who they'd been dealing with. Soon, he could pin-cushion himself with medals, if he so desired, could create any number of titles for himself. What, for instance, had happened to the Fortuibus lineage? That could surely be revived. First Baron Fortuibus of Bembridge? And yet Sir Jack felt that, deep within him, there was always a fundamental simplicity, even an austerity. Of course you had to keep up appearances – what use would the Good Samaritan have been if he couldn't afford to pay the innkeeper? – but you should never lose touch with your essential humanity. No, perhaps it was better, more appropriate, for him to remain simple Sir Jack.

All company assets had been moved offshore, beyond the reach of Westminster's petulant revenge. The lease on Pitman House (I) had only a few months to run, and the freeholders were being stalled. A few goods and chattels would be transferred in due course, unless they were impounded by the British Government. Sir Jack rather hoped they would be: then he could take the hypocrites and small men to the International Court. In any case, he had been informed that it was time to update most of the equipment. Pretty much the same went for the human *matériel* too.

His more timid aides had argued for not striking in all directions at the same time. They claimed it would dilute the coverage. Sir Jack begged to disagree: this was Big Bang time; this was not just the day's lead item, but a rolling story. In any case, how did you do it? You did it by doing it. The events of that day would therefore unroll in swift succession at Reigate, Ventnor, The Hague and Brussels. Sir Jack would keep a small part of his mind, and a double spread in one of his newspapers, for Reigate. That DTI inspector, who seemed to have been doing so well lately, would be puzzled, over the breakfast table which he shared with his delightful wife, to find that his mail contained several registered envelopes bearing South American stamps and addressed in handwriting remarkably similar to his own. Only a few minutes would separate the visits to his front door of the amiable postman and the considerably more puritanical representatives of HM Customs and Excise. The latter had gratifyingly ferocious powers of entry and search, and also felt very strongly – the more so after a recent campaign in certain newspapers – about the filthy traffic in life-destroying drugs conducted by seemingly respectable front-men whose perverted greed dragged the nation's children into a spiral of hell.

At more or less the same time as a blanketed pair of dark trousers was seen leaving a mock-Tudor house in Reigate, while surprisingly well-informed paparazzi were shouting 'Over here, Mr Holdsworth,' Sir Jack was waving his Governor's tricorne from an open landau of his own providing. Employees lined the route to the new Island council buildings in Ventnor. First, Sir Jack, in hard hat and with gold-plated trowel aloft, assisted at the topping-out ceremony, and was pictured sharing the rough camaraderie of roofers and masons. Next, at ground level, Sir Jack cut a series of ribbons, declared the buildings open, and formally handed them over to the people of the Island, as represented by Council leader Harry Jeavons. The cameras then moved inside, where the Council swore itself in and immediately passed its final piece of legislation. Councillors unanimously declared that after seven centuries of subjugation, the Island was throwing off the yoke of Westminster.

Independence was hereby pronounced, the Council raised to the status of a Parliament, and Island patriots everywhere were invited to wave the Pitco-sponsored flags which had been tossed from the back of Sir Jack's motorcade.

Without moving seats, the Parliament then passed its first executive act, bestowing upon Sir Jack Pitman the title of Island Governor. His position was purely honorific, even if technically endowed with the residual authority – consigned to the finest vellum by a master calligrapher – to suspend Parliament and the constitution in case of national emergency and rule in his own person. These powers were expressed and delivered in Latin, which diminished their impact on those assenting to them. Sir Jack, speaking from a gilded throne, referred to a sacred trust, and evoked earlier governors and captains of the Island, notably Prince Henry of Battenberg, who had so proved his patriotism by a heroic death in the Ashanti war of 1896. His widow, the noble Princess Beatrice, had thereafter ruled as Governor – Sir Jack pointed out that in his grammar the masculine always embraced the feminine – until her own death nearly half a century later. Sir Jack confessed a modest ignorance of his own appointment with the Grim Reaper, but uxoriously advanced the name of Lady Pitman as a possible successor.

As the Ventnor bells rejoiced, across the Channel an Island maiden, personally chosen by Sir Jack to represent Isabella de Fortuibus, delivered to the International Court at The Hague a petition requesting annulment of the 1293 Island Purchase. Then a Boadicean chariot took her to the Deutsche Bank, where she opened an account in the name of 'The British People' and deposited the sum of six thousand marks and one euro. She was accompanied by a bodyguard of late-thirteenth-century yokels, whose presence was designed to emphasize that Edward I's so-called 'purchase' of the Island had been a fraud on simple folk to whom the treaty had never been properly explained. Among the yokels were various Pitco executives with rehearsed sound-bites on both the original land-grab and the subsequent, centuries-long cover-up.

Isabella de Fortuibus continued by chariot to the station, where a special Brussels express awaited her. On arrival, she was met by lawyers from Pitman Offshore International, who had prepared the Island's application for instant emergency membership of the European Union. This was a defining moment, the POI chief negotiator declared to the world's media, one which encapsulated the long struggle for liberation on the part of the Islanders, a struggle marked by courage and sacrifice down the centuries. Henceforth they would look towards Brussels, Strasbourg and The Hague for the safeguarding of their rights and freedoms. It was a time of great opportunity, but also of great peril: the Union would need to act firmly and decisively. It would be more than a tragedy if a former-Yugoslavia-style-situation were allowed to develop on Europe's northern doorstep.

While the London Stock Exchange endured such a Black Tuesday that dealing was suspended at lunchtime for the foreseeable future, Pitco shares soared worldwide. That evening, with Island oak logs flaming patriotically in his neo-Bavarian hearth, Sir Jack drank. He reviewed the evidence in video and anecdotal form. He chuckled at reruns of his own prerecorded bites. He kept half a dozen phone lines open as he switched from one awed listener to another. He permitted a few newspaper editors to be put through and offer their congratulations. The world's first bloodless *coup d'état* since whenever, they were calling it. Taking steps towards the New Europe. Breaking the Mould. Pitman the Peacemaker. David and Goliath were invoked by the pops. Robin Hood too. The whole dramatic day reminded a leader writer on one of Sir Jack's tonier titles of *Fidelio*: what a breaking of chains had there not been? Yes, indeed, the new Governor felt, a certain person might have approved. In homage – no, more with a sense of parity – he allowed the mighty Eroica to serenade his triumph.

The sweetness of victory was all the greater when those who acclaimed your victories did not know how great they really were. For instance, he had no intention of taking the Island into the European Union. The effects of their employment law and banking regulations, to name but two areas, would be disastrous. He just needed Europe to keep Westminster out of his face until everything had settled down. The offered repurchase of the Island for six thousand marks and a euro? Only a simpleton would believe this was anything more than two fingers up to the mainland: he'd had the account closed down before the media had boarded the train for Brussels. Likewise, he didn't think the legal challenge to the 1293 treaty had a snowball's chance in hell: imagine what a can of worms Europe would be opening up for itself if they let that through. And as for the fucking Island Parliament: the very sight of those jumped-up councillors behaving as if each of them were Garibaldi ... It was enough to make him rise from his Governor's throne and tell them, in English not Latin just so the fools and dunderheads understood, that he was planning to prorogue Parliament within a week. No, that was rather too complicated a word for them, so he'd keep it simple. There was a national emergency, one brought about by the Island Parliament's preposterous belief that it might be capable of running the place itself. He was closing it down because there was nothing for it to do. Nothing that he, Sir Jack Pitman, wanted it to do. And the jumped-up councillors could jump on the first boat to Dieppe as far as he was concerned. Unless they wanted to put their current brief work-experience to use. The Project was still auditioning for its House of Commons Experience. Front-bench jobs had been allocated, but they were looking for non-speaking backbenchers able to master some simple choreography – rising to their feet at a signal from the Speaker, waving their order papers in mock urgency, and then flopping back on the green leather benches. They would also be required to utter various non-verbal but interpretable noises – contemptuous baying, sycophantic groaning, rabid muttering and insincere laughter being the main categories. He thought they might be able to manage that.

Sir Jack drank more. He phoned more. He received more praise. At two in the morning he summoned Martha Cochrane and told her to bring her toyboy and snivelling note-taker, in case a vibrant dream welled up in him. Actually, he might have said fucking toyboy, the tongue did loosen after the best armagnac. At any rate, she didn't look pleased to be called from whatever business she was about. As for the boy Paul, he went into a profound sulk as soon as Jack made a mildly ribald remark about . . . Oh fuck them, fuck them. He didn't care what anyone got up to, but he wanted people around him who could *enjoy*. He didn't need insolent nay-sayers like these two, who sipped their armagnac with resentful tight mouths. Especially not on a day like this. Sir Jack was well into his peroration when he spontaneously decided to include them in his restructuring plans.

'The point about change is that no-one is ever prepared for it. The Palace of Westminster's just found that out, and the Island so-called Parliament will soon follow suit. If you don't keep one jump ahead then you're two paces behind. Most people have to run on the spot just to keep up with me while I sleep. You two, for example.' He paused. Yes, that got their attention. He gave them the searchlight glare. Just as he thought: the woman stared insolently back at him, the boy pretended to be looking for something down the side of his chair. 'I suppose you imagined once you boarded Sir Jack's gravy train that it was just a question of mopping your bread in his gravy until you pulled down your pension. Well, I've got a big surprise for you . . . pair of misery-guts. Now this Project is up and running I don't need a barrelful of whingers and moaners trying to drag it down. So let me have the honour to inform you that you are the first two employees I intend to fire. Have fired. Already. As of now. Consider yourself now fired. And what is more, under the employment legislation I might or might not put through my tinpot Island Parliament, or for that matter under new contracts which will be retrospectively valid, someone's working on it, you will receive no severance pay. You're fucking fired, you two, and if you can't get your things packed by the time the morning ferry leaves I'll throw all your shit in the harbour personally.'

Martha Cochrane looked briefly across at Paul, who nodded. 'Well, Sir Jack, you don't seem to give us any alternative.'

'No I fucking don't, and I'll tell you why.' He stood up to show his full rhomboid shape, took another slurp, pointed at each of them in turn and then, either as a climax or an afterthought, at himself. 'Because, to put the matter simply, because there is, I always feel, a fundamental simplicity within me, because I'm a genius. That's it.'

He was reaching towards the baroque bell-pull, ready to sluice out of his life this carping bitch and her ninnyish toyboy, when Martha Cochrane uttered the two words he least expected to hear.

'Auntie May.'

'I beg your pardon.'

'Auntie May,' she repeated. And then, looking up at his swaying shape, 'Titty. Nappy. Poo.'

Three

A TOURIST MECCA SET IN A SILVER SEA

Two years ago an enterprising leisure group launched a new venture off the south coast of England. It has swiftly become one of the most coveted destinations for upmarket vacationers. Staff writer Kathleen Su *asks whether the new Island state may prove a role model for more than just the leisure business.*

It is a classic springtime day outside Buckingham Palace. The clouds are high and fleecy, William Wordsworth's daffodils are blowin' in the wind, and guardsmen in their traditional 'busbies' (bearskin hats) are standing to attention in front of their sentry boxes. Eager crowds press their noses to the railings for a glimpse of the British Royal Family.

Promptly at 11 o'clock, the tall double windows behind the balcony open. The ever-popular King and Queen appear, waving and smiling. A ten-gun salute splits the air. The guardsmen present arms and cameras click like old-fashioned turnstiles. A quarter of an hour later, promptly at 11.15, the tall windows close again until the following day.

All, however, is not as it seems. The crowds and the cameras are for real; so are the clouds. But the guardsmen are actors, Buckingham Palace is a half-size replica, and the gun salute electronically produced. Gossip has it that the King and Queen themselves are not real, and that the contract they signed two years ago with Sir Jack Pitman's Pitco Group excuses them from this daily ritual. Insiders confirm that an opt-out clause does exist in the royal contract, but that Their Majesties appreciate the cash fee that accompanies each balcony appearance.

This is showtime, but it's also big business. Along with the first Visitors (as they call tourists hereabouts) came the World Bank and the IMF. Their approval – coupled with the enthusiastic endorsement of the Portland Third Millennium Think Tank – means that this ground-breaking enterprise is likely to be much copied in years and decades to come. Sir Jack Pitman, whose brain-child the Island was, takes a back seat nowadays, while still keeping a beady eye on things from his exalted position as Governor, a historic title going back centuries. The public face of Pitman House is currently its CEO Martha Cochrane. Ms Cochrane, a trim forty-something with an Oxbridge brain, a sharp wit, and an array of designer suits, explained to the *Wall Street Journal* how one of the traditional problem areas of tourism has always been that five-star sites are too rarely in easy reach of one another. 'Remember the frustration of hauling yourself from A to B to Z? Remember those nose-to-tail tourist buses?' Visitors from the US to Europe's prime locations will recognize the tune: poor infrastructure, inefficient tourist thruput, inconsiderate opening hours – everything the traveller doesn't need. Here even the postcards come pre-stamped.

Once upon a time this used to be the Isle of Wight, but its current inhabitants prefer a simpler and grander title: they call it The Island. Its official address since declaring independence two years ago is typical of Sir Jack Pitman's roguish, buccaneering style. He named it England, England. Cue for song.

It was also his original stroke of lateral thinking which brought together in a single hundred-and-fifty-five square mile zone everything the Visitor might want to see of what we used to think of as England. In our time-strapped age, surely it makes sense to be able to visit Stonehenge and Anne Hathaway's Cottage in the same morning, take in a 'ploughman's lunch' atop the White Cliffs of Dover, before passing a leisurely afternoon at the Harrods emporium inside the Tower of London (Beefeaters push your shopping trolley for you!). As for transport between sites: those gas-guzzling tourist buses have been replaced by the eco-friendly pony-and-cart. While if the weather turns showery, you can take a famous black London taxi or even a big red double-decker bus. Both are environmentally clean, being fuelled by solar power.

This great success story began, it's worth recalling, under a hail of criticism. There were protests at what some described as the virtually complete destruction of the Isle of Wight. This was clearly an exaggeration. Key heritage buildings have been saved, along with much of the coastline and parts of the central downland. But almost one hundred percent of the housing stock – described by Professor Ivan Fairchild of Sussex University and a leading critic of the project, as 'dinky interwar and mid-century bungalows whose lack of stand-out architectural merit was compensated for by their extraordinary authenticity and time-capsule fittings' – has been wiped out.

Except that you can still see it if you wish. In Bungalow Valley, Visitors may wander through a perfectly-recreated street of typical pre-Island housing. Here you will find front gardens where rockeries drip with aubretia and families of plaster 'gnomes' (dwarf statues) congregate. A path of 'crazy paving' (recycled concrete slabs) leads to a front door filled with crinkly glass. Ding-dong chimes echo in your ear as you pass into a living zone of garish carpeting. There are flying ducks on striped wallpaper, 'three-piece suites' (sofas with matching chairs) of austere design, and French windows giving on to a 'crazy-paving' patio. From here there are further vistas of aubretia, hanging baskets, 'gnomes' and antique satellite dishes. It's all cute enough, but you wouldn't want too much of it. Professor Fairchild claims that Bungalow Valley is not so much a recreation as a self-justifying parody; but he concedes the argument has been lost.

The second ground for complaint was that the Island targets high rollers. Even though most vacation costs are pre-paid, immigration officers examine arrivals not for passport irregularities or vaccination stamps but for credit-worthiness. Travel companies have been advised to warn vacationers that if their credit rating is not to the satisfaction of the Island authorities, they will be sent back on the first airplane. If there are no seats available on flights, those who are unwelcome are put on the next cross-channel ferry to Dieppe, France.

Such apparent élitism is defended by Martha Cochrane as merely 'good housekeeping'. She further explains: 'A vacation here may look expensive, but it's a once-in-a-lifetime experience. Besides, after you've visited us, you don't need to see Old England. And our costings show that if you attempted to cover the "originals" it would take you three or four times as long. So our premium pricing actually works out cheaper.'

There is a dismissive tone to her voice when she pronounces the word 'originals'. She is referring to the third main objection to the project, one initially much discussed but now almost forgotten. This is the belief that tourists visit premier sites in order to experience not just their antiquity but also their uniqueness. Detailed studies commissioned by Pitman House revealed that this was far from being the case. 'Towards the end of the last century,' Ms Cochrane explains, 'the famous statue of David by Michelangelo was removed from the Piazza della Signoria in Florence and replaced by a copy. This proved just as popular with visitors as the "original" had ever been. What's more, ninety-three percent of those polled expressed the view that, having seen this perfect replica, they felt no need to seek out the "original" in a museum.'

Pitman House drew two conclusions from these studies. First, that tourists had hitherto flocked to 'original' sites because they simply had no choice in the matter. In the old days, if you wanted to see Westminster Abbey, you had to go to Westminster Abbey. Second, and more laterally, that if given the option between an inconvenient 'original' or a convenient replica, a high proportion of tourists would opt for the latter. 'Besides,' adds Ms Cochrane with a wry smile, 'Don't you think it is empowering and democratic to offer people a wider choice, whether it's in breakfast food or historic sites? We're merely following the logic of the market.'

The project could not have had a more spectacular vindication. Both airports – Tennyson One and Tennyson Two – are approaching capacity. Visitor thruput has outperformed the most optimistic expectations. The Island itself is packed yet calmly efficient. There is always a friendly 'bobby' (policeman) or 'Beefeater' (Tower of London guard) from whom to ask the way; while the 'cabbies' (taxi-drivers) are all fluent in at least one of the major tourist languages. Most speak English too!

Maisie Bransford, of Franklin Tn, vacationing with her family, told the *Journal*, 'We'd heard that England was kind of dowdy and old-fashioned, and not really up with the cutting edge of the modern world. But we've been mighty surprised. It's a real home from home.' Paul Harrison, chief adviser to Martha Cochrane, and in charge of day-to-day strategy, explains that, 'There are two guiding principles here. Number one, client choice. Number two, guilt avoidance. We never try to bully people into having a good time, into thinking they're enjoying themselves when in fact they aren't. We just say, if you don't like these premier sites, we've got others.'

A good example of client choice is how you spend your money – literally. As Ms Cochrane points out, Pitman House could easily have eliminated any awareness of financial disbursement, either by all-inclusive packages, or by the instant crediting of a final account. But research indicated that the majority of vacationers enjoy the act of spending, and, just as importantly, that of being seen to spend. So, for those addicted to plastic, there is an Island Charge Card, diamond-shaped rather than oblong, which takes up the credit limit of your card back home.

But there is also, for the fiscally adventurous, the head-scratching complexity of real old English currency. What a rich and pocket-stretching array of copper and silver you will find at your command: farthings, ha'pennies, pennies, groats, tanners, shillings, florins, half-crowns, crowns, sovereigns and guineas. Of course, it is possible to play the traditional English pub game of shove-ha'penny, or shuffleboard, with a plastic counter, but how much more satisfying to feel the weight of a glinting copper coin against your thumb. Gamblers from Las Vegas to Atlantic City know the heft in the hand of the silver dollar. Here at the Island Casino you can play with a velvet purseful of Angels, each worth seven shillings and sixpence, and each impressed with the figure of Saint Michael slaying the Dragon.

And what dragons have Sir Jack Pitman and his team slain here on the Island? If we look at the place not just as a leisure business – whose success seems assured – but as the miniature state it has effectively been for the past two years, what lessons might it hold for the rest of us?

For a start, there is full employment, so there is no need for burdensome welfare programs. Radical critics still claim that this desirable end was produced by undesirable means, when Pitco shipped the old, the longterm sick and the socially dependent off to the mainland. But Islanders are not heard to complain, any more than they complain about the lack of crime, which eliminates the need for policemen, probation officers and prisons. The system of socialized medicine, once popular in Old England, has been replaced by the American model. Everyone, visitor or resident, is obliged to take out insurance; and the air-ambulance link to the Pitman wing of Dieppe hospital does the rest.

Richard Poborsky, analyst for the United Bank of Switzerland, told the *Wall Street Journal*: 'I think this development is very exciting. It's a pure market state. There's no interference from government because there *is* no government. So there's no foreign or domestic policy, only economic policy. It's a pure interface between buyers and sellers without the market being skewed by central government with its complex agendas and election promises.

'People have been trying to find new ways to live for centuries. Remember all those hippie communes? They always failed, and why? Because they failed to understand two things: human nature, and how the market works. What's happening on the Island is a recognition that man is a market-driven animal, that he swims in the market like a fish in the sea. Without making any predictions, let's just say that I think I've seen the future, and I think it works.'

But this is to look ahead. The Island Experience, as the billboards have it, is everything you imagined England to be, but more convenient, cleaner, friendlier, and more efficient. Archaeologists and historians might suspect that some of the monuments are not what traditionalists would call authentic. But as Pitman House surveys confirm, most people here are first-time visitors making a conscious market choice between Old England and England, England. Would you rather be that confused figure on a windswept sidewalk in dirty Old London Town, trying to find your way while the rest of the city bustles past ('Tower of London? Can't help you there, guv'), or someone who is treated as the center of attention? On the Island, if you want to catch a big red bus, you find that two or three come along in a jolly convoy before you can sort out the groats in your pocket and the dispatcher can raise her whistle to her lips.

Here, in place of the traditional cold-fish English welcome, you will find international-style friendliness. And what about the traditional chilly weather? That's still around. There is even a permanent winter zone, with robins hopping through the snow, and the chance to join the age-old local game of throwing snowballs at the bobby's helmet, and then running away while he slips over on the ice. You can also don a war-time gas-mask and experience the famous London 'pea-soup' fog. And if it rains, it rains. But only outdoors. Still, what would England, 'original' or otherwise, be without rain?

Despite all our demographic changes, many Americans still feel a kinship with, and curiosity about, the little land William Shakespeare called 'this precious stone set in the silver sea'. This was, after all, the country from which the *Mayflower* set sail (it's

Thursday mornings at 10.30 for 'The Setting Sail of the Mayflower'). The Island is the place to satisfy this curiosity. The present writer has visited what is increasingly referred to as 'Old England' a number of times. From now on, only those with an active love of discomfort or necrophiliac taste for the antique need venture there. The best of all that England was, and is, can be safely and conveniently experienced on this spectacular and well-equipped diamond of an Island.

Kathleen Su *travelled incognito and solely at the expense of the Wall Street Journal.*

FROM HER OFFICE

Martha could experience the whole Island. She could watch the feeding of the One Hundred and One Dalmatians, check throughput at Haworth Parsonage, eavesdrop on snug-bar camaraderie between straw-chewing yokel and Pacific Rim sophisticate. She could track the Battle of Britain, the Last Night of the Proms, The Trial of Oscar Wilde and the Execution of Charles I. On one screen King Harold would glance fatally towards the sky; on another posh ladies in Sissinghurst hats pricked out seedlings and counted the varieties of butterfly perching on the buddleia; on a third hackers were pock-marking the fairway of the Alfred, Lord Tennyson golf course. There were sights on the Island Martha knew so intimately from a hundred camera angles that she could no longer remember whether or not she had ever seen them in reality.

On some days she seemed hardly to leave her office. But then, if she chose to operate an open-door policy with employees, she had only herself to blame. Sir Jack would no doubt have instituted a Versailles system, with hopeful petitioners clustering in an ante-room while a Pitmanesque eye surveyed them through a spyhole in the tapestry. Since his ousting, Sir Jack had himself become a petitioner for attention. The cameras would sometimes catch him out in his landau, desperately waving his tricorne at puzzled Visitors. It was almost pathetic: he had dwindled into what he was supposed to be – a mere figurehead with no real power. Martha, out of a mixture of compassion and cynicism, had upped his armagnac allowance.

Her 10.15, she saw, was with Nell Gwynn. That was a name from the past. How far away those discussions during Concept Development now seemed. Dr Max had been making mischief that day, but his intervention had probably saved them trouble down the line. After several reports, Nell had finally been allowed to keep her place in English history; but her failure to make Jeff's list of Top Fifty Quintessences had legitimized down-sizing of her myth.

Nowadays, she was a nice, unambitious girl who ran a juicer stall a few hundred metres from the Palace railings. Yet her essence, like her juice, had been concentrated, and she remained a version of what she had once been, or at least what Visitors – even readers of family newspapers – expected her to have been. Raven hair, sparkling eyes, a white flounced blouse cut in a certain way, lipstick, gold jewellery and vivacity: an English Carmen. This morning, however, she sat primly before Martha, buttoned to the neck, and looking quite out of character.

'Nell 2 minding the Juicery?' asked Martha routinely.

'Nell 2's dahn wiv a bug,' replied Nell, at least retaining her learned accent. 'Connie's mindin' the shop.'

'*Connie?* Christ . . . what *do* . . .' Martha buzzed through to the executive office. 'Paul, can you sort this out? Connie Chatterley's running the Nell Juicery. Yes, don't ask, I know. Quite. Can you get a Nell 3 out of Props straight away? Don't know how long for. Thanks. Bye.'

She turned back to Nell 1. 'You *know* the rules. They're quite clear. If Nell 2 is sick you go straight to Props.'

'Sorry, Miss Cochrane, it's just, well, I've been rather under the weather lately. No, that's not right, I've been in a bit of a pickle.' Nell had stopped being Nell, and the screen in front of Martha confirmed that her original surname was double-barrelled and that she had been to finishing school in Switzerland.

Martha waited, then prompted. 'What sort of a pickle?'

'Oh, it's like telling tales. But it's got worse. I thought I could laugh it off, you know, make a joke of it, but I'm sorry . . .' She pulled herself upright and squared her shoulders. Her Nellness had now quite fallen away. 'I have to make an official complaint. Connie agrees.'

What Nell Gwynn and Connie Chatterley agreed on was that the current tenant of Nell's Juicery shouldn't have to put up with lewd behaviour and sexual harassment from anyone, not even if he was the King of England. Which in the present case he happened to be. At first he'd been nice, and asked her to call him Kingy-Thingy, not that she would. But then remarks had been passed, her engagement ring ignored, and stock interfered with in a suggestive way. Now he'd begun taunting her in front of customers, who just laughed as if it were all part of the show. It was unbearable.

Martha gave Nell the day off and requested the King's presence in her office at 3.00 that afternoon. She had checked his schedule: just a pro-am tournament on Tennyson Down in the morning, then nothing until decorating Battle of Britain heroes at 4.15. Even so, the King looked sulky when he turned up. He still hadn't got used to the idea of being summoned to Island HQ. At first he'd tried sitting on his throne and hoping that Martha would come to him. But all he got was Deputy Governor Sir Percy Nutting, QC ex-MP, who mixed historic grovelling with regretful insistence on the King's clear obligations under both contractual law and the executive authority which now ran the Island. Martha had called him in several times, and knew to expect a flushed, complaining presence.

'What have I done *now*?' he asked, pretending to be a child called up for chastisement.

'I'm afraid there's been an official complaint against you. Your Majesty.' Martha added the title not out of deference, but to remind him of kingship's obligations.

'Who from this time?'

'Nell Gwynn.'

'Nell?' said the King. 'Well, Lordy-Lordy, *aren't* we getting a little above ourselves all of a sudden?'

'So you acknowledge the validity of the complaint?'

'Miss Cochrane, if a fellow can't make a few jokes about marmalade . . .'

'It's more serious than that.'

'Oh all right, I did say . . .' The King looked across at Martha with a quarter-smile, inviting complicity. 'I did say she could juice my clementines any time she wanted.'

'And which of your scriptwriters gave you that one?'

'What a cheek, Miss Cochrane. It was all my own work.' He said it with evident pride.

'I believe you. I'm just working out if that makes it better or worse. And were the obscene gestures also spontaneous?'

'The what?' Martha's gaze was stern; in the face of it, he ducked his head down. 'Oh well, you know, just a lark. Talk about the morality police. You're as bad as Denise. There are times I wish I was back *there*. When I really *was* king.'

'It's not a question of morality,' said Martha.

'Isn't it?' Perhaps there was hope. He'd always had trouble with that word and exactly what it covered.

'No, it's purely contractual in my book. Sexual harassment is a breach of contract. So is conduct liable to bring the Island into disrepute.'

'Oh, you mean, like *normal behaviour*.'

'Your Majesty, I'm going to have to give you an executive instruction not to attempt relations with Miss Gwynn. There's something rather . . . controversial in her background.'

'Oh Gawd, don't say she's got the clap.'

'No, it's more that we don't want people looking into her history too closely. Some clients might not understand. You're to treat her as if she was, oh, fifteen.'

The King looked up belligerently. 'Fifteen? If that filly isn't way past the age of consent then I'm the Queen of Sheba.'

'Yes,' said Martha. 'From the birth certificate point of view. Let's just say that, on the Island, on the *Island*, Nell is fifteen. Just as on the Island . . . you're the King.'

'I'm the fucking King *anyway*,' he shouted. 'Anywhere, everywhere, always.'

Only as long as you behave, thought Martha. You are king by contract and by permission. If you disobey an executive order and we put you on a boat to Dieppe in the morning I doubt there will be an armed insurrection. Merely an organisational hitch. Someone, somewhere, always wanted the throne. And if the monarchy got too big for its boots, they could always draft in Oliver Cromwell for a bit. Why not, actually?

'The thing is, Miss Cochrane,' said the King whinily. 'I really like her. Nell. I can tell she's more than a juice-girl. I'm sure we'd click if she got to know me better. I could teach her to speak properly. It's just,' he looked down and twiddled his signet ring, 'it's just that one does seem to have got off on the wrong foot.'

'Your Majesty,' said Martha in a softer tone, 'there are lots of other women to "really like" out there. Of the right age.'

'Oh yes frinstance?'

'I don't know.'

'No you don't. Nobody knows how difficult it is being in my position. Everyone stares at you all the time and you aren't allowed to look back at them without being hauled in front of this . . . industrial tribunal.'

'Well, there's Connie Chatterley.'

'Connie Chatterley?' The King was incredulous. 'She *fucks oiks*.'

'Lady Godiva?'

'Been there, done that,' said the King.

'I didn't mean Godiva 1. I meant Godiva 2. Didn't I see you at the audition?'

'Godiva 2?' The King's face brightened, and Martha glimpsed the 'legendary charm' ritually invoked by *The Times of London*. 'You know, you're a real pal, Miss Cochrane. Not that Denise isn't a pal,' he added hastily. 'She's my best mate. But she isn't always very understanding, if you see what I mean. Godiva 2? Yes. I remember thinking, now she could be a top girl in Kingy-Thingy's book. Must give her a bell. Ask her out for a cappuccino. You wouldn't . . .'

'Biggin Hill,' said Martha.

'Eh?'

'Biggin Hill first. Medals on heroes.'

'Haven't they got enough medals, those heroes? You couldn't get Denise to do it today, could you?' He looked appealingly at Martha. 'No, I suppose not. It's in my contract, isn't it? Every sodding thing's in my sodding contract. Still. Godiva 2. You're a pal, Miss Cochrane.'

The King's departure was as jaunty as his arrival had been surly. Martha Cochrane flicked a monitor over to RAF Biggin Hill. All seemed normal: there were Visitors clustered before the little squadron of Hurricanes and Spitfires, others jabbing at battle simulators, or wandering through the Nissen huts at the runway's edge. Here they could watch heroes in sheepskin flying jackets warming their hands over paraffin stoves, dealing cards, and waiting for the dance-band music on the wind-up gramophone to be interrupted by the order to scramble. They could ask questions of these heroes, and receive period answers in authentically clipped tones. Piece of cake. Bad show. Jerry sat on his own bomb. Thoroughly browned off. Mum's the word. Then the heroes would go back to their cards, and as they shuffled, cut and dealt, Visitors might reflect on the wider hazard that filled the lives of such men: sometimes fate played the joker, sometimes it turned up the scowling Queen of Spades. Those medals the King was about to bestow were thoroughly deserved.

Martha buzzed through to her PA. 'Vicky, when BH calls for Godiva 2's number, it's authorized. Godiva 2, not Godiva 1. Thanks.'

Vicky. It made a change from Sir Jack's procession of Susies. Insisting on the PA's real name had been one of Martha's first steps on becoming Chief Executive Officer. She had also partitioned the double-cube snuggery into a cappuccino bar and a men's lavatory. The Governor's furnishings – or those deemed company rather than personal property – had been dispersed. There had been an argument over the Brancusi. The Palace had put in for the Bavarian fireplaces, which now served as indoor hockey goals for the sports room.

Martha had reduced the Governor's support staff, cut his transport to a single landau, and relocated him to more appropriate quarters. Paul had protested that some of her actions – like insisting that Sir Jack's new PA be male – were merely vindictive. There had been rows. Sir Jack's pouts had been Victorish, his sulks theatrical, his phone bill Wagnerian. Martha had declined to authorize it. Equally she had refused him permission to give interviews, not even to the newspapers he still owned. He was allowed his uniform, his title, and certain ritual appearances. That was enough in her view.

The wrangling over Sir Jack's rights and privileges – or sequestrations and humiliations, as he preferred – had helped obscure the fact that Martha's appointment as CEO actually changed very little. It had been a necessary act of self-defence to replace an egomaniacal autocracy with a relatively accountable oligarchy; yet the Project itself had scarcely been affected. The financial structures had been the work of an expert wearing HM Treasury braces; while any adjustments to Concept Development and Visitor Targeting were minimal. Stolid Jeff and twinkling Mark had remained in position. The main difference between the previous and current CEOs was that Sir Jack Pitman vociferously believed in his product whereas Martha Cochrane privately did not.

'Still, if a venal Pope could run the Vatican . . .' She had just said it, like that, at the end of a tiring day. Paul had looked at her with hot eyes. He disapproved of any flippancy about the Island.

'I think that's a stupid comparison. And anyway, I shouldn't think the Vatican did run better with a corrupt Pope. On the contrary.'

Martha had given an inward sigh. 'I expect you're right.' Once they had made common cause against Sir Jack, which should have cemented their partnership. It seemed to have had the opposite effect. Did Paul genuinely believe in England, England? Or was his loyalty a sign of residual guilt?

'I mean, we could call in your underemployed chum Dr Max and ask his views on whether large political and religious organisations are best run by idealists or cynics or down-to-earth practical people. I'm sure he'd have some long-winded opinions.'

'Forget it. You're right. We're not running the Catholic Church here.'

'That's perfectly evident.'

She couldn't bear his tone, which seemed pedantic and self-righteous. 'Look, Paul, this has turned into an argument already, and I don't know why. I usually don't nowadays. But if we're discussing cynicism, ask yourself how far Sir Jack would have got without a hefty streak of it.'

'That's cynical too.'

'Then I give up.'

Now, in her office, she thought: Paul's right in one sense. I regard the Island as no more than a plausible and well-planned means of making money. Yet I probably run it as well as Pitman would have done. Is this what offends Paul?

She crossed to her window and looked out at the Premier view which had once been Sir Jack's. Below her, in a cobbled street overhung by half-timbering, Visitors turned away from deferential hawkers and pedlars to watch a shepherd drive his flock to market. In the mid-distance, sun glinted on the solar panels of a double-decker bus parked by the Stacpoole Marital

Memorial Pool; on the village green behind, a cricket match was in progress, with someone running up to bowl. Above, in the only part of her view not owned by Pitco, an Islandair jet banked to give half its payload a farewell glimpse of Tennyson Down.

Martha turned away with a frown and a tightness in her jaw. Why was everything back to front? She could make the Project work, even though she didn't believe in it; then, at the end of the day, she returned home with Paul to something she believed in, or wanted and tried to believe in, yet didn't seem able to make work at all. She was there, alone, without defences, without distancing, irony, cynicism, she was there, alone, in simple contact, yearning, anxious, seeking happiness as best she could. Why did it not come?

MARTHA HAD BEEN INTENDING TO SACK

Dr Max for months. Not for any observable breach of contract: indeed, the Project Historian's punctuality and positive attitudes would have impressed any corporate assessor. Moreover, Martha was fond of him, and had long ago seen through his prickliness and irony. She thought of him now as someone afraid of simplicity, and that fear touched her.

His flouncing departure over the Hood repositioning had fortunately proved a mere huff, an act of rebellion which had, if anything, reinforced his loyalty to the Project. But that very loyalty had now become a problem. Dr Max had been engaged to help Develop the Concept; but once the Concept had been Developed and Pitman House transferred to the Island, he had simply come with it. In a shadow move, Country Mouse had transferred his column to *The Times of London* (published from Ryde). No-one seemed to notice or object; not even Jeff. So the Historian currently sat in an office two floors below Martha, with full research capacity at his buffed and occasionally lacquered fingertips. Anyone, Pitmanite or Visitor, could call his office for guidance on any historical matter. His presence and purpose were advertised in every hotel-room briefing pack. A bored client on the cheapest weekend break could confront Dr Max and argue Saxon strategy at the Battle of Hastings for as long as he liked, entirely free of charge.

The trouble was, nobody ever did. The Island had achieved its own dynamic; the interchange between Visitors and Experiences needed fine-tuning on a pragmatic rather than theoretical basis; and so the role of the Project Historian had simply become . . . historical. This, at any rate, was what Martha, as CEO, was preparing to tell Dr Max when she summoned him to her office. He entered it, as he always did, with one eye cocked for the size of the studio audience. Just Miss Cochrane? Well, then, a high-level tête-à-tête. Dr Max's demeanour was sleek and blithe; it seemed bad manners to remind him that his existence was precarious and marginal.

'Dr Max,' Martha began, 'are you happy with us?'

The Project Historian chuckled, settled himself professorially, brushed a probably non-existent crumb from a houndstooth lapel, stuck his thumbs in his thunder-grey suede waistcoat, and crossed his legs in a manner proposing a far longer occupancy of his chair than Martha had intended. Then he did what few other Pitco employees, from the briefest Backdrop yokel to Deputy Governor Sir Percy Nutting himself, would have done: he took the question at face value.

'H–appiness, Miss Cochrane, is very interesting from an h–istorical point of view. In my three decades as one of the most I dare not say pre-eminent but certainly visible sculptors and moulders of young minds, I have become familiar with a large variety of intellectual misconceptions, of brushwood which has to be burnt off before the soil of the mind can be tilled, of piffle and garbage frankly. Categories of error are as multi-hued as Joseph's coat, but the greatest and grossest of these tend to lodge under the following naïveté: that the past is really just the present in fancy dress. Strip away those bustles and crinolines, doublet and hose, those rather haute couture togas, and what do you discover? People remarkably like us, whose sweet essential hearts beat just like Mama's. Peer inside their slightly under-illuminated brains and you discover a range of half-formed notions, which, when fully formed, become the underpinnings of our proud modern democratic states. Examine their vision of the future, imagine their hopes and their fears, their little dreamings about how life will be many centuries after their deaths, and you will see a dimly perceived version of our own delightful lives. To put it crudely, they want to be us. All piffle and garbage, of course. Am I going too fast for you?'

'With you so far, Dr Max.'

'Good. Now it has been my pl–easure – if a rather brutal pl–easure at times, but let's not be over-moralistic about condemning it – to take my trusty little sickle and hack away at some of this brushwood of the developing mind. And in the pastureland of egregious error none is more tenacious, more unkillable – one thinks of ground elder, no, better, of the omnivorous kudzu vine – than the assumption that the swoony little heart which pitapats within the modern body has always been there. That sentimentally we are immutable. That courtly love was merely a crude forerunner of snogging in the bus-shelter, if that is what the young still get up to, don't ask *me*.

'Well, let us examine those M–iddle Ages which needless to say did not view themselves as m–iddle. Let us, for the sake of precision, take France between the tenth and thirteenth centuries. A fine and forgotten civilization which built the great cathedrals, established the chivalric ideals, tamed the vicious human beast for a while, produced the *chansons de geste* – not everyone's idea of a good night out but still – and, in short, laid down a faith, a political system, manners, taste. And all to what end, I ask my little dwellers in brushwood. To what end did they trade, marry, build and create? Because they wanted to be *happy*? They would have laughed at the pettiness of such ambition. They sought *salvation*, not happiness. Indeed, they would have viewed our modern idea of happiness as something approaching sin, and certainly an obstacle to salvation. Whereas . . .'

'Dr Max . . .'

'Whereas, if we were to fast-forward . . .'

'Dr Max.' Martha felt she needed a buzzer – no, a klaxon, an ambulance siren. 'Dr Max, we shall have to fast-forward completely, I'm afraid. And without wishing to sound like one of your students, I must ask you to address my question.'

Dr Max took his thumbs out of his waistcoat, brushed both lapels for phantom bacteria, and looked at Martha with that studio petulance – apparently good-humoured but implying severe *lèse-majesté* – which he had perfected in his struggle with hustling TV anchors. 'Which, if I may make so b–old, was?'

'I just wanted to know, Dr Max, if you were happy with us.'

'Precisely wh–ere I was h–eading. If circuitously, to your mind. To simplify what is an essentially complicated position, though I realize, Miss Cochrane, that you are no brushwood brain, I would answer thus. I am not "happy" in the bus-shelter-snogging sense. I am not happy as the modern world chooses to define happiness. Indeed, I would say that I *am* happy because I deride that modern conception. I am happy, to use that unavoidable term, precisely because I do not seek happiness.'

Martha was silent. How strange that she could be made to feel gravity and simplicity by such effervescence and delighted paradox. With only a touch of mockery, she asked, 'So do you seek salvation, Dr Max?'

'Good God, no. I'm *far* too much of a pagan for that, Miss Cochrane. I seek . . . pleasure. So much more reliable than happiness. So much better defined, and yet, so much more complicated. Its discontents so beautifully etched. You could call me, if you wished, a pragmatic pagan.'

'Thank you, Dr Max,' said Martha, rising. He evidently hadn't understood the meaning of her question; nevertheless, his answer had been one she unknowingly needed.

'I trust you enjoyed out little ch–at,' said Dr Max, as if he had been the host. One of his most reliable pleasures was talking about himself, and he also believed that pleasures should be shared.

Martha smiled at the closing door. She envied Dr Max his blitheness. Anyone else would have guessed why she had called him in. The Official Historian might disdain salvation in its higher sense, but he had just unwittingly obtained a lesser, temporal version of it.

'SOMETHING RATHER UNUSUAL,

I'm afraid.' Ted Wagstaff was standing in front of Martha Cochrane's desk. That morning, she was wearing an olive suit with a white collarless shirt held at the neck with a gold stud; her earrings were a museum copy of Bactrian gold, her tights from Fogal of Switzerland, her shoes from Ferragamo. All bought at the Tower of London Harrods. Ted Wagstaff was wearing a green sou'wester, oilskins, and waders with the tops rolled down: an outfit baggy enough to conceal any amount of electronic equipment. His complexion was poised between the bucolic and the alcoholic, though whether this came from the outdoor life, from self-indulgence, or from Props she was unable to tell.

Martha smiled. 'See where a good education gets you.'

'Beg pardon, Ma'am?' He looked genuinely puzzled.

'Sorry, Ted. Just dreaming.' Martha was cross with herself. Just because she remembered his CV. She should have learnt by now that if Ted Wagstaff, Deputy Head (Operations) of Security and Client Feedback Coordinator, arrived looking and speaking like a coastguard, then that was how she should address him. The professional disguise would wear off after a few minutes; she should just be patient.

This separation – or adhesion – of personality was something the Project had failed to anticipate. Most of its manifestations were harmless; indeed, could be taken to indicate gratifying corporate zeal. For instance, within a few months of Independence, certain members of Backdrop could no longer be addressed as Pitco employees, only as the characters they were paid to inhabit. Their case was initially misdiagnosed. They were thought to be showing signs of discontent, whereas the opposite was the case: they were showing signs of content. They were happy to be who they had become, and didn't want to be other.

Groups of threshers and shepherds – and even some lobstermen – became increasingly reluctant to use company accommodation. They said they preferred to sleep in their tumbledown cottages, despite the absence of modern facilities available at the converted prisons. Some were even asking to be paid in Island currency, having apparently grown attached to the heavy copper coins they played with all day. The situation was being monitored, and might throw up a longterm angle for Pitco – such as reduced housing costs; but it could develop into mere sentimental indiscipline.

Now it seemed to be spreading beyond Backdrop. Ted Wagstaff was a harmless case, 'Johnnie' Johnson and his Battle of Britain squadron more problematic. They claimed that since the Tannoy might honk at any moment and the cry of 'Scramble!' go up, it made sense for them to bunk down in Nissen huts beside the runway. Indeed, it would be cowardly and unpatriotic not to. So they would fire up their paraffin stoves, play a final hand of cards, and snuggle down in their fleecy flying jackets, even though part of them must have known Jerry couldn't possibly mount a surprise attack until Visitors had finished their Great English Breakfasts. Should Martha call an emergency executive about this? Or should they merely congratulate themselves on added authenticity?

Martha was aware that Ted was watching her patiently.

'Something unusual?'

'Yes, Ma'am.'

'Something that ... you're going to ... tell me about?'

'Yes, Ma'am.'

Another pause.

'Now, perhaps, Ted?'

The security man shook off his oilskin covering. 'Well, to put it bluntly, there seems to be a slight problem with the smugglers.'

'What's the problem?'

'They're smuggling.'

Martha suppressed, with great difficulty, the carefree, innocent, pure, true laugh that lay within her, something as incorporeal as the breeze, a freak moment of nature, a freshness long forgotten; something so untainted as to induce hysteria.

Instead, she gravely asked for details. There were three smugglers' villages on the Island, and reports had been coming in of activities at Lower Thatcham incompatible with Project principles. Visitors to Lower, Upper and Greater Thatcham were able to observe at close hand aspects of the Island's traditional trade: the false-bottomed barrels, coins sewn into garment hems, lumps of tobacco disguised as Jersey potatoes. Everything, it seemed, could be disguised as something else: liquor and baccy, silk and grain. As a demonstration of this truth, a piratical fellow would take his cutlass and ease apart the halves of a walnut shell, then draw from the smoothed interior a lady's glove of eighteenth-century design. Afterwards, at the Trading Centre, Visitors could buy just such a nut – or better still, a pair – whose contents were laser-encoded on its shell. Weeks later, and several thousand miles away, the nutcrackers would be brought out, and amid expressions of wonder the glove would fit the hand that had bought it.

Recently, it seemed, the Trading Centre at Lower Thatcham had been diversifying. The evidence had been circumstantial at first: the improbable appearance of gold jewellery on a number of the villagers (which at first aroused little suspicion as it was assumed to be inauthentic); a pornographic video left in one of the hotel machines; a quarter-full, unlabelled bottle whose contents were certainly alcoholic and probably toxic. Infiltration and surveillance had revealed the following: the clipping of Island coin and the minting of counterfeit; the secret distillation of a colourless, high-proof spirit from local apples; the pirating of Island guidebooks and forging of official Island souvenirs; the importation of pornography in various forms; and the renting-out of village girls.

Adam Smith had approved of smuggling, Martha remembered. No doubt he thought it a justifiable extension of the free market, one which merely exploited anomalous differentials of tax and duty. Perhaps he also applauded it as an example of the entrepreneurial spirit. Well, she wouldn't bother to discuss matters of principle with Ted, who stood there expecting reaction, praise, and orders, like any other employee.

'So what do you think we should do, Ted?'

'Do? *Do?* Hanging's too good for them.' Ted Wagstaff wanted the malefactors whipped, put on the next boat to Dieppe, and dropped off the stern for their eyes to be pecked out by seagulls. He also – his zeal for retribution confusing his grasp of freehold ownership – wanted the cottages of Lower Thatcham torched.

Justice on the Island was executive not juridical, which made it swifter and more flexible. Even so, it had to be the right justice. Not 'right' in the old-fashioned sense, but right for the future of the Project. Ted Wagstaff was over-enthusiastic but not a fool: there had to be an element of deterrence in whatever sentence Martha chose.

'Very well,' she said.

'So we chuck them on the first boat? We torch the village?'

'No, Ted. We give them temporary employment.'

'What? If I may make so bold, Miss Cochrane, that's pussy-footing. These are serious criminals we're dealing with.'

'Exactly. So I shall invoke clause 13b of their contracts.'

Ted continued to look as if some compassionate female compromise was being proposed. Clause 13b merely stated that in special circumstances, which circumstances to be decided by the executive officers of the Project, employees could be required to transfer to any other employment as designated by the said officers.

'You mean you're retraining them? That's not justice in my book, Miss Cochrane.'

'Well, you said they were criminals. That's what I'm going to retrain them as.'

The next day, Premier Visitors were invited, on payment of a supplement, to witness an authentic but unspecified example of Heritage Action at an undisclosed location. Despite a pre-dawn departure, tickets were swiftly subscribed. Three hundred Premiers, each holding a complimentary hot toddy, watched as Excise officers raided the village of Lower Thatcham. The scene was lit by flaming torches with rough fill-in from floodlights; period oaths were uttered; smugglers' doxies appeared at casement windows in a state of classic-serial undress. There was a smell of burning pitch and a subdued glitter of gilt Excise buttons; a vast contrabandist, cutlass aloft, ran menacingly at a group of Premiers until one of their number threw down his toddy, cast off his overcoat to reveal a comforting uniform, and downed the fellow. As dawn broke, twelve ringleaders in nightshirts and leg-irons were loaded on to a requisitioned hay-wain to genuine applause. Justice – or job retraining – would begin the next day at Carisbrooke Castle, where some would sit in the stocks and be pelted with rotten fruit, while others would tread the grain-wheel and append their signatures to the wrappers of the resulting convict loaves. Twenty-six weeks of this and they would have paid off the executive fines levied by Martha Cochrane. By the time they were transported to the Continent the new smugglers of Lower Thatcham, operating under more tightly-drafted contracts, would be thoroughly trained.

It would work. Everything on the Island worked, because complications were not allowed to arise. The structures were simple, and the underlying principle of action was that you did things by doing them. So there was no crime (apart from blips like this) and therefore no judicial system and no prisons – at least, not real ones. There was no government – only a disenfranchised Governor – and therefore no elections and no politicians. There were no lawyers except Pitco lawyers. There were no economists except Pitco economists. There was no history except Pitco history. Who could have guessed, back there in Pitman House (I), as they stared at the map laid out on the Battle Table and joked about bad cappuccino, what they would stumble into creating: a locus of uncluttered supply and demand, somewhere to gladden the heart of Adam Smith. Wealth was created in a peaceable kingdom: what more could anyone want, be they philosopher or citizen?

PERHAPS IT REALLY WAS

a peaceable kingdom, a new kind of state, a blueprint for the future. If the World Bank and the IMF thought so, why deny your own publicity? Electronic as well as retro-readers of *The Times* discovered immaculately good news about the Island, mixed news about the wider world, and unremittingly negative news about Old England. By all accounts the place had been in a state of free-fall, had become an economic and moral waste-pit. Perversely rejecting the established truths of the third millennium, its diminishing population knew only inefficiency, poverty and sin; depression and envy were apparently their primary emotions.

Whereas on the Island a bright and modern patriotism had swiftly evolved: not one based on tales of conquest and sentimental recitations, but one which, as Sir Jack might have put it, was here, was now, and was magic. Why shouldn't they be impressed by their own achievements? The rest of the world was. This repositioned patriotism engendered a proud new insularity. In the first months after Independence, when there were legal threats and murmurings about blockade, it had seemed daring for Islanders to take a surreptitious ferry to Dieppe, and for executives to dash across the Solent by Pitco helicopter. But this quickly came to seem wrong: both unpatriotic and pointless. Why become voyeurs of social strain? Why slum it where people were burdened by yesterday, and the day before, and the day before that? By history? Here, on the Island, they had learnt how to deal with history, how to sling it carelessly on your back and stride out across the downland with the breeze in your face. Travel light: it was true for nations as well as for hikers.

So Martha and Paul worked fifty feet away from one another at Pitman House (II), and spent their leisure – some of it Quality, some not – in a Pitco executive apartment with a Premier view over what maps still called the English Channel. Some thought the water needed rechristening, if not full repositioning.

'Bad week?' asked Paul. It was little more than a ritual enquiry, since he shared all her professional secrets.

'Oh, average. Pimped for the King of England. Tried to sack Dr Max and failed. Plus the smuggler business. At least we put the lid on that.'

'I'll ser–ser–sack Dr Max for you.' Paul's tone was enthusiastic.

'No, we need him.'

'We do? You said yourself no-one goes near him. No-one wants to know any of Dr Max's old history.'

'He's an innocent. I think he's probably the only innocent person on the whole Island.'

'Mar–tha. We *are* talking about the same fellow? TV person – or rather, ex-TV person – tailor's dummy, phoney voice, phoney mannerisms. He's an *inn*ocent?'

'Yes,' replied Martha stubbornly.

'OK, OK, as unofficial Ideas Catcher to Martha Cochrane, I

hereby record her opinion that Dr Max is an innocent. Dated and filed.'

Martha let a pause extend. 'Do you miss your old job?' By which she also meant: your old boss, how things were before I came along.

'Yes,' said Paul simply.

Martha waited. She waited deliberately. Nowadays she almost urged Paul to say things which then made her think less of him. Simple perversity, or a practical death-wish? Why did two years of Paul sometimes feel like twenty?

So part of her was satisfied when he went on: 'I still think Sir Jack's a great man.'

'Parricide's guilt?'

Paul's mouth tightened, he dropped his eyes from her, and his tone took on a pedant's sharpness. 'Sometimes you're just too clever for your own good, Martha. Sir Jack is a great man. From start to finish, this whole project was his idea. Who pays your salary really? You're *dressed* by him.'

Too clever for your own good. Martha was back in her childhood. Are you being pert? Don't forget that cynicism is a very lonely virtue. She looked across at Paul, remembering when she had first noticed him stir in his patch of straw. 'Well, then, maybe Dr Max isn't the only innocent on the Island.'

'Don't patronize me, Martha.'

'I'm not. It's a quality I like. There's far too little of it around.'

'You're still patronizing me.'

'And Sir Jack's still a great man.'

'Fuck you, Martha.'

'I wish someone would.'

'Well, count me out tonight, thank you very much.'

On another occasion, she might have been touched by Paul's habit of polite qualification. I hate you, if you'll pardon the expression. Burn in hell, you vile cow, excuse my French. But not tonight.

Later, in bed, as he pretended to sleep, Paul succumbed to

thoughts he couldn't refute. You made me betray Sir Jack, now you're betraying me yourself. By not loving me. Or not loving me enough. Or not liking me. You made things real. But only for a while. Now it's back to what it was like before.

Martha also pretended to sleep. She knew Paul was awake, but her body and her mind were turned away from him. She lay there thinking about her life. She did this in the normal way: roamingly, rebukingly, tenderly, revisingly. At work, faced with a problem or decision, her mind would work with clarity, logic, and, if necessary, cynicism. By nightfall, these qualities seemed to evaporate. Why could she sort out the King of England more easily than she could sort out herself?

And why was she being so hard on Paul? Was it just disappointment for herself? Nowadays his passivity just seemed to provoke her. She wanted to prod him, stir him out of it. No, out of more than 'it', out of himself – as if (against all the evidence) there was someone different lurking inside. She knew it made no sense. Try office logic, Martha. If you provoke someone passive into irritation, what do you get? A formerly passive, currently irritated, and soon-to-be passive-again person. To what end?

She also knew that it had been this very gentleness, this lack of ego – which she now rechristened passivity – which had been one of his attractions. She had thought . . . what, exactly? She thought (now) that she had thought (then) that here was someone who wouldn't seek to impose himself on her (well, true), who would let her be herself. Had she indeed thought that, or was this a later version? Either way, it was false. 'Be herself' – that's what people said, but they didn't mean it. They meant – she meant – 'become herself', whatever that was, and however that might be attained. The truth was, Martha – wasn't it? – that you were expecting Paul's mere presence to act as a growth hormone to the heart? Just sit over there on the sofa, Paul, and beam your love at me; then I'll turn into the mature, ripened person I've always wanted to be. Could you get more egotistical, and more naive? Or, for that matter, more passive? Who said human beings became ripe anyway? Maybe they just became old.

Her mind hopped, back to childhood, as it did more frequently these days. Her mother showing her how tomatoes ripened. Or rather, how you ripened tomatoes. It had been a cold, wet summer, and the fruit was still green on the stalk by the time the leaves curled like wallpaper and a frost was forecast. Her mother had separated the crop into two. One lot she left by themselves, to ripen naturally together. The others she put into a bowl with a banana. Within a few days the tomatoes in the second bowl were edible, the ones in the first still fit only for chutney. Martha had asked for an explanation. Her mother had said, 'That's what happens.'

Yes, Martha, but Paul isn't a banana and you aren't a pound of tomatoes.

Was it the Project's fault? What Dr Max called its coarsening simplifications – were they corrosive? No, blaming your job was like blaming your parents, Martha. Not allowed after the age of twenty-five.

Was it because the sex wasn't perfect? Paul was attentive; he stroked the inside of her arm (and more) until she yelped; he'd learnt the words she needed to hear in bed. But it wasn't Carcassonne, to use her private code. Still, why should that be a surprise? Carcassonne was a one-off: that was its point. You wouldn't keep going back there in the hope of finding yet another perfect mate and yet another El Greco thunderstorm. Not even old Emil did that. So maybe it wasn't sex.

You could always blame luck, Martha. You can't blame your parents, you can't blame Sir Jack and his Project, you can't blame Paul, or any of his predecessors, you can't blame English history. So what's there left to blame, Martha? Yourself and luck. Let yourself off tonight, Martha. Blame luck. It's just bad luck you weren't born a tomato. Things would have been much simpler. All you would have needed was a banana.

when westerlies raised heaving waves, when the stars were occluded and a wild rain fell, a group of boat-builders from a village near the Needles had been discovered standing at the water's edge waving lanterns at supply ships. One of the vessels had altered course, imagining that the lights of the harbour-bar were before them.

A few nights later, a transport aircraft reported that as it was making its final descent into Tennyson Two, it had spotted, half a mile to starboard, a rough trail of alternative landing lights.

Martha noted the details, approved Ted Wagstaff's investigations, and waited for him to leave. 'Yes, Ted? Something else?'

'Ma'am.'

'Security or Visitor Feedback?'

'Just a bit of VF I thought I should mention, Miss Cochrane. In case it's relevant. I mean, it's not like Queen Denise and the fitness trainer, which you said was none of my business.'

'I didn't say that, Ted. Just that it wasn't treason. Breach of contract at most.'

'Right.'

'Who is it this time?'

'It's that Dr Johnson. Fellow that dines with Visitors at the Cheshire Cheese. Big, clumsy fellow, floppy wig. Scruffy, if you ask me.'

'Yes, Ted, I know who Dr Johnson is.'

'Well, there've been complaints. From Visitors. Casual *and* official.'

'What sort of complaints?'

'They say he's depressing company. So the sun rises in the East, eh? Miserable bugger, don't know why they want to have dinner with him anyway.'

'Thank you, Ted. Leave me the file.'

She summoned Dr Johnson for three o'clock. He arrived at five, and was muttering to himself as he was shown into Martha's office. He was an awkward, muscular fellow with deeply scarred cheeks and eyes which barely seemed to focus on her. He continued muttering, sketched a few antic gestures, then without invitation threw himself down in a chair. Martha, who had helped audition him, and sat in on a Cheshire Cheese preview which had been a blast, was alarmed by the change. When they hired him, they had every reason for confidence. The actor – she could no longer remember his name – had spent a number of years touring a one-man show called 'The Sage of Middle England', and had full control of the necessary material. The Project had even consulted him when building the Cheese, and had engaged tavern companions – Boswell, Reynolds, Garrick – to relieve the one-on-one pressure that might have ensued had the Doctor been left alone with Visitors. Project Development also provided a bibliophilic stooge, ready with a deferential prompt to spark the Great Cham's wit. Thus the Dining Experience was choreographed to move between Johnsonian soliloquy, repartee among co-evals, and cross-epoch-bonding between the Good Doctor and his modern guests. There was even a scripted moment of subtle endorsement for the Island Project. Boswell would bring the conversation round to Johnson's travels, and ask, 'Is not the Giant's Causeway worth seeing?' Johnson would reply, 'Worth seeing? Yes. But not worth *going to see.*' The exchange often provoked a flattered chuckle from Visitors alert to irony.

Martha Cochrane scanned the file on screen which summarized the complaints against Johnson. That he was badly dressed and had a rank smell to him; that he ate his dinner like a wild beast, and so quickly that Visitors, feeling obliged to keep pace, gave themselves indigestion; that he was either bullyingly dominant, or else sunk in silence; that several times, in mid-sentence, he had stooped down and twitched off a woman's shoe; that he was depressing company; that he made racist remarks about many of the Visitors' countries of origin; that he was irritable when closely questioned; that however brilliant his conversation might be, clients were distracted by the asthmatic gasping that accompanied it, and the needless rolling-around in his chair.

'Dr Johnson,' Martha began. 'There have been complaints against you.' She looked up, but her employee seemed to be paying little attention. He shifted mammothly and mumbled something that sounded like a phrase from the Lord's Prayer. 'Complaints at your lack of civility towards those who share your table.'

Dr Johnson stirred himself. 'I am willing to love all mankind,' he replied, '*except an American.*'

'I think you will find that an unhelpful prejudice,' said Martha, 'Given that thirty-five percent of those who come here are American.' She waited for a reply, but Johnson had apparently mislaid his taste for argument. 'Are you unhappy about something?'

'I inherited a vile melancholy from my father,' he replied.

'After the age of twenty-five you're not allowed to blame anything on your parents,' said Martha crisply, as if this were company policy.

Johnson gave a vast heave, an asthmatic wheeze, and bellowed back at her, 'Wretched un-idea'd girl!'

'Are you unhappy about those you work with? Any tensions? How are you getting along with Boswell?'

'He fills a chair,' replied Johnson gloomily.

'Is it the food, perhaps?'

'It is as bad as bad can be,' replied the Doctor with a jowl-wobbling shake of the head. 'It is ill-fed, ill-killed, ill-kept and ill-dressed.'

Martha considered all this to be rhetorical exaggeration, if it wasn't an early strike for improved pay and conditions. 'Let's get to the point,' she said. 'I have a screenful of complaints about you. Here, for instance, is Monsieur Daniel of Paris. He says that he paid his Dining Experience supplement expecting to hear examples of high-class traditional British humour from you, but that you uttered barely a dozen words all evening, none of them worth repeating.'

Johnson wheezed and snorted, and threw himself around in his chair. 'A Frenchman must always be talking, whether he knows anything of the matter or not. An Englishman is content to say nothing, when he has nothing to say.'

'That's all very well in theory,' Martha replied, 'but it's not what we pay you for.' She scrolled on. 'And Mr Schalker of Amsterdam says that in the course of dinner on the twentieth of last month he made a number of enquiries of you, to none of which you gave any response.'

'Questioning is not the mode of conversation among gentlemen,' replied Johnson with heavy condescension.

Really, this was getting nowhere. Martha called up Dr Johnson's contract of employment. Of course: it should have been an early warning. Whatever the actor's original name, he had long ago changed it by deed-poll to Samuel Johnson. They had engaged Samuel Johnson to play Samuel Johnson. Perhaps this explained things.

All of a sudden there was a rolling and a scrabbling and a muttering and then a thump as Johnson fell to his knees, reached under the desk, and with a heavy yet bearishly precise flick, removed Martha's right shoe. Alarmed, she looked across the surface of her desk to the top of his soiled wig.

'What *do* you think you're up to?' she asked. But he took no notice. He was staring at her foot and gabbling to himself. She recognised the words. '. . . not into temptation, but deliver us from evil . . .'

'Dr Johnson, *Sir!*'

The edge to her voice brought him out of his reverie. He got off his knees and stood swaying and panting in front of her.

'Dr Johnson, you must pull yourself together.'

'Why, if I *must*, Madam, I have no choice.'

'Do you not understand what a contract is?'

'By all means, Madam,' Johnson replied, his attention suddenly focused. 'It is, firstly, an act whereby two parties are brought together; secondly, an act whereby a man and woman are betrothed to one another; and thirdly, a writing in which the terms of a bargain are included.'

Martha was taken aback. 'I'll accept that,' she said. 'Now you in turn must accept that your . . . moodiness, or melancholy, or whatever we choose to call it, is disagreeable to those you dine with.'

'Madam, you cannot have the warm sun of the West Indian climate without the thunder, the lightning, and the earthquakes.'

Really, how could she get through to the fellow? She'd heard of method acting, but this was the worst case she'd ever come across.

'When we hired Dr Johnson,' she began, and then stopped. His great bulk seemed to cast her desk into darkness. 'When we engaged you . . .' No, that wasn't right either. She was no longer a CEO, or a business woman, or even a person of her time. She was alone with another human creature. She felt a strange and simple pain. 'Dr Johnson,' she said, her voice softening without effort as she looked up his line of fat buttons, beyond his white stock, to his broad, scarred, tormented face, 'We want you to *be* "Dr Johnson", don't you understand?'

'When I survey my past life,' he replied, his eyes pointing without focus at the wall behind her, 'I discover nothing but a barren waste of time, with some disorders of body, and disturbances of the mind very close to madness, which I hope He that made me will suffer to extenuate many faults, and excuse many deficiencies.' Then, with the struggling walk of one confined to fetters, he began to leave Martha's office.

'Dr Johnson.' He stopped and turned. She stood up behind her desk, feeling lop-sided, one foot bare and one shod. She felt like a girl lonely before the world's strangeness. Dr Johnson was not just two centuries older than her, but two centuries wiser. She felt no embarrassment at asking: 'What about love, Sir?'

He frowned, and laid one arm diagonally across his heart. 'There is, indeed, nothing that so much seduces reason from vigilance, as the thought of passing life with an amiable woman; and if all would happen that a lover fancies, I know not what other terrestrial happiness would deserve pursuit.'

His eyes now seemed to have found their focus, which was

her. Martha felt herself blushing. This was absurd. She hadn't blushed for years. And yet it didn't feel absurd.

'But?'

'But love and marriage are different states. Those who are to suffer the evils together, and to suffer often for the sake of one another, soon lose that tenderness of look, and that benevolence of mind, which arose from the participation of unmingled pleasure and successive amusement.'

Martha kicked off her other shoe and looked at him from the level. 'So it's all hopeless? It never lasts?'

'A woman, we are sure, will not always be fair; we are not sure she will always be virtuous.' Martha dropped her eyes, as if her immodesty were known across the centuries. 'And man cannot retain through life that respect and assiduity by which he pleases for a day or for a month.'

With that, Dr Johnson rolled strugglingly out of the door.

Martha felt she had failed utterly: she had made little impression on him, and he had behaved as if she were less real than he was. At the same time, she felt light-headed and flirtatiously calm, as if, after long search, she had found a kindred spirit.

She sat down, worked her feet back into her shoes, and became a CEO again. Logic returned. Of course he would have to go. In some parts of the world they'd already be facing multi-million-dollar suits for sexual harassment, racial abuse, breach of contract in failing to make the client laugh, and God knew what else. Thankfully, Island law – in other words, executive decision – recognized no specific contract between Visitors and Pitco; instead, reasonable complaints were dealt with on an *ad hoc* basis, usually involving financial compensation in exchange for silence. The old Pitman House tradition of the gagging clause still applied.

Should they hire a new Johnson? Or rethink the whole Dining Experience with a different host? An evening with Oscar Wilde? Obvious dangers there. Noel Coward? Much the same problem. Bernard Shaw? Oh, the well-known nudist and vegetarian. What if he started imposing all that on the dinner table? It didn't bear thinking about. Hadn't Old England produced any wits who were . . . *sound?*

SIR JACK WAS EXCLUDED

from executive meetings, but allowed a decorative presence at monthly gatherings of the upper board. Here he wore his Governor's uniform: braided tricorne; epaulettes like gilded hairbrushes; lanyards as thick as knotted horse-tails; a washing-line of self-awarded decorations; a scrimshaw swagger-stick clamped in the armpit; and a sword which bounded from the side of his knee. For Martha the outfit claimed no echo of power, not even a whiff of junta; its comic exaggeration confirmed that the Governor nowadays accepted himself as a figure from operetta.

In the first months after Martha and Paul's coup, Sir Jack used to arrive late for these boards, his timing that of a busy man still in charge; but all he found was a meeting already in progress and a humiliatingly positioned chair. He would try to assert himself by making long speeches from a roving position, even issuing coherent instructions to specific individuals. But as he circled the table, he saw nothing but insolent napes. Where were the fearing eyes, the swivelling heads, the subservience of scratching pen and quietly clacking laptop? He still gave off ideas like a great Catherine wheel; but the sparks now fell upon stony ground. Increasingly, he kept his silence and his counsel.

As Martha took her place, she noticed an unfamiliar figure at Sir Jack's side. No, not exactly side: such was Sir Jack's size and sartorial clangour that the fellow seemed more in his shade. Well, one of the Governor's past conceits had been to compare himself to a mighty oak giving shelter to those beneath. Today he was keeping the rain off a mushroom: soft grey Italian suit, white shirt buttoned to the neck, grey hair cropped short on rounded skull. All pure mid-Nineties; even the spectacles dated from the same period. Perhaps he was one of those big investors still being kept sweet and yet to realize that his first dividend cheque was likely to be made out to his grandchildren.

'My friend Jerry Batson,' Sir Jack announced, more to Martha than anyone else. 'Apologies,' he added, shaking his head in gross confusion, '*Sir* Jerry nowadays.'

Jerry Batson. Of Cabot, Albertazzi and Batson. The mushroom acknowledged the introduction with a light smile. He seemed a scarcely detectable presence, sitting there mildly, Zenly. A pebble in an ever-flowing stream, a silenced windchime.

'I'm sorry,' said Martha. 'I'm not sure what your standing is here.'

Jerry Batson knew he wouldn't have to answer for himself. Sir Jack rose to his feet with an infuriated ding-dong of shaken medals. His appearance might be operetta, but his tone was Wagnerian, transporting some of those present back to Pitman House (I). 'Jerry's standing, Miss Cochrane, Jerry's standing, is that he thought up, helped think up, was *instrumental* in helping think up the whole damn Project. In a manner of speaking. Paul will confirm.'

Martha turned to Paul. To her surprise, he held her gaze. 'It was before your time. Sir Jerry was central to preliminary Project Development. The records concur.'

'I'm sure we're all grateful. My question remains: what is his standing here?'

Wordlessly, palms raised pacifically, Jerry Batson levitated himself without obvious muscular assistance. With the faintest nod towards Martha, he left the room.

'Discourtesy,' commented Sir Jack, 'heaped upon discourtesy.'

That evening the Governor, now in his simple undress uniform of tunic, Sam Browne belt and spats, sat opposite Sir Jerry with a cocked decanter. His free hand limply gestured at his modest sitting-room. Its five windows offered a clifftop view, but She had stolen his Bavarian fireplaces, and his Brancusi looked devilish cramped beside the cocktail cabinet. 'Like giving an admiral of the fleet a midshipman's quarters,' he complained. 'Humiliation heaped upon humiliation.'

'The armagnac's still good.'

'It's in my contract.' Sir Jack's tone was for once uncertain, poised between pride that he had forced through such a clause and sorrow that he had needed to do so. 'Everything's in a damn contract nowadays. It's the way the world's going, Jerry. The days of the old buccaneers are past, I fear. We have become dinosaurs. Do it by doing it, that was always my motto. Nowadays it's Don't do it unless you have witchdoctors and market researchers and focus groups holding your hand. Where's the dash, where's the flair, where's the good hard basic balls of it all gone? Farewell, oh ye merchant venturers – isn't that the melancholy truth?'

'So they say.' Batson had always found that neutrality brought Sir Jack more quickly to the point than active comment.

'But you see what I mean?'

'I hear where you're coming from.'

'About *her*. About . . . Madam. She's letting it slide. Taking her eye off the ball. A woman entirely lacking in vision. When she . . . when I appointed her CEO, I had hopes, I admit. Hopes that a man who is no longer as young as he was' – Sir Jack held up a hand against a protestation that was not in fact coming – 'might rest his weary bones. Take a back seat. Make way for younger blood, and all that.'

'But.'

'But. I have my sources. I hear of things taking place which a firmer hand would not countenance or sanction. I try to warn. But you saw for yourself the insolence with which I am treated at board level. There are times when I feel that my great Project is being undermined out of sheer envy and malice. And at such moments, I admit I blame myself. I humbly do.' He looked across at Batson, whose bland expression implied that he might reluctantly be willing to agree with such apportionment of blame; or, on the other hand, after further reflection, he might not. 'And the service contracts drawn up by Pitco were in certain respects ill-drafted. Not that these things are necessarily as binding as they appear.'

Jerry Batson gave a soft shudder which might have amounted to a nod. So Sir Jack's philosophy of business had developed a flaw. You did things by doing them – except when you didn't. Presumably because you couldn't. Eventually, Jerry murmured, 'It's a question of what we want to rule out and what we want to rule in. Plus the parameters.'

Sir Jack gave a mountainous sigh and gargled his armagnac. Why did he always have to do all the work with Batson? Smart enough chap, no doubt, and at his prices so he ought to be. But not one to delight in the cut-and-thrust of fine, masculine conversation. Either mute as a ginger biscuit or yakking away like a seminar. Ah well, to the point.

'Jerry, you have a new account.' He paused just long enough to wrong-foot Batson. 'I know, I know, Silvio and Bob handle all the new accounts. Which is very clever of them in view of what you would probably call their lack of existential reality. Not to mention the existential reality of their bank accounts in the Channel Islands.'

Batson's acknowledging smile turned into a soft chuckle. Perhaps the old rascal hadn't lost his touch. Had he known all along, and deliberately held back, or only found out since having more time on his hands? Not that Jerry would ask, as he doubted Sir Jack would tell him the truth.

'So,' the Governor concluded, 'that's enough footsie and foreplay. You have a client.'

'And does this client want me to dream some more?'

Sir Jack declined the cue, and the memory. 'No. This client requires action. This client has a problem, five letters, beginning with B, rhymes with itch. You are to find the solution.'

'Solutions,' repeated Jerry Batson. 'You know, I sometimes think that's what we're best at, as a nation. We English are rightly known for our pragmatism, but it's in problem-solving that we display positive genius. Tell you my favourite one. Death of Queen Anne. Seventeen whatever. Crisis of succession. No surviving children. Parliament wants – needs – another Protestant on the throne. Big problem. *Major* problem. Everyone in obvious line of succession is a Catholic, or married to a Catholic, which was equally bad karma at the time. So what does Parliament do? Passes over fifty – *more* than fifty – perfectly good royals with best, better and good claims, and picks an obscure Hanoverian, dull as ditchwater, can barely speak English, but one hundred and ten percent Prod. And *then* they sell him to the nation as our saviour from over the water. Brilliant. Pure marketing. After all this time the mind still boggles. *Yes.*'

Sir Jack cleared his throat to terminate this irrelevance. 'My own problem, I suspect, you will find very small beer in such exalted company.'

ALL MARTHA'S TRAINING

told her to treat the Johnson regression as a purely administrative matter. An employee in breach of his contract: dismissal, the first boat out, and a quick replacement from the pool of potential labour held on file. Public chastisement, as with the smugglers, was inappropriate. So just get on with it.

But her heart still resisted. The Project's rule-book was inflexible. Either you worked, or you were sick. If you were sick, you were transferred to Dieppe Hospital. Yet was he even a medical case? Or something quite different: like a historical case? She wasn't sure. And the fact that the Island was itself responsible for turning 'Dr Johnson' into Dr Johnson, for peeling off the protective quotation marks and leaving him vulnerable, was also irrelevant. The sudden truth she had felt as he leaned over her, wheezing and muttering, was that his pain was authentic. And his pain was authentic because it came from authentic contact with the world. Martha realized that this conclusion would strike some – Paul, certainly – as irrational, even lunatic; but it was what she felt. The way he had twitched off her shoe and started gabbling the Lord's Prayer as if in expiation; the way he had talked of his disorders and deficiencies, his hopes of salvation and forgiveness. By whatever means this vision had been put in front of her, she saw a creature alone with itself, wincing at naked contact with the world. When had she last seen – or felt – anything like that?

The church of St Aldwyn lay half-overgrown in one of the few parts of the Island still unclaimed by the Project. This was her third visit. She had the key; but the building, now sunk in scrubby woodland, was unlocked and always empty. It smelt of mould and rot; it wasn't a snug sanctuary, more a continuation, even a concentration of the dank chill outside. The petit-point hassocks were clammy to the touch; the foxed hymn pages reeked of second-hand bookshop; even the light which struggled through the Victorian glass seemed to get slightly wet in the process. And there she was, fish in a stone-bottomed, green-walled tank, inquisitive and bobbing.

The church didn't strike her as beautiful: it had neither proportion, lustre, nor even oddity. This was an advantage, since it left her alone with what the building stood for. Her eye skimmed, as on her previous visits, the list of rectors dating back to the thirteenth century. What was the difference between a rector and a vicar – or a curate, or a parson, for that matter? Such distinctions were lost on her, as were all the other intricacies and subtleties of faith. Her foot scuffed at the uneven floor where long ago a monumental brass had been removed, taken off for secularisation in some museum. The same list of hymn numbers looked down on her as last time, like some regularly winning line in the eternal lottery. She thought of the villagers who had come here and, for generation upon generation, had sung the same hymns, and believed the same stuff. Now the hymns and the villagers had vanished, as surely as if Stalin's men had passed this way. That composer Paul had talked about when they first met – they would have to send him down here to invent some new hymns, some authentic piety.

The living had been chased away, but not the dead: they were reliable. Anne Potter, beloved wife of Thomas Potter Efquire and mother of his five children Esther, William, Benedict, Georgiana and Simon, also interred nearby. Ensign Robert Timothy Pettigrew, died of the fever in the Bay of Bengal, 23rd February 1849, aged 17 years and 8 months. Privates James Thorogood and William Petty, of the Royal Hampshire Regiment, killed at the Battle of the Somme within two days of one another. Guilliamus Trentinus, who died in Latin of causes incomprehensible and with lamentations lengthy, 1723. Christina Margaret Benson, whose generous bounty permitted the restoration of the church in 1875 by Hubert Doggett, and who is commemorated in a small apsidal window featuring her initials intertwined with acanthus leaves.

Martha did not know why she had brought flowers this time. She could have guessed there would be no vase to put them in, nor water to fill it. She laid them on the altar, turned, and perched herself awkwardly in the front pew.

For thine is the wigwam, the flowers and the story . . .

She ran through her childhood text again, long forgotten, until revived by a mutter from Dr Johnson. It didn't seem blasphemous any more, just a parallel version, an alternative poetry. An airy, transportable wigwam made as much sense as a damp stone church fixed in a solid place. The flowers were a natural human offering, symbol of our own transience – and hers a quicker symbol given the lack of vase and water. And the story: an acceptable variant, even an improvement on the original. The glory *is* the story. Well, it would be, if only it were true.

If only it were true. At school her fretful scorn and clever blasphemies had come from precisely this fact, this conclusion:

that it was not true, that it was a great lie perpetrated by humanity against itself. *Thy swill be scum ...* What brief thought she had given to religion in adult years had always followed the same sleek loop: it isn't true, they made it up to make us feel better about death, they founded a system, then used the system as a means of social control, no doubt they believed it themselves, but they imposed faith as something irrebuttable, a primal social truth, like patriotism, hereditary power, and the necessary superiority of the white male.

Was that the end of the argument, or was she just a wretched unidea'd girl? If the system collapsed, if the Archbishop of Canterbury could become less known and less credible than, say, Dr Max, could belief float free? And if it did, would that make it any the truer, yes or no? What brought her here? She knew the negative answers: disappointment, age, a discontent with the thinness of life, or at least life as she had known it, or chosen it. There was something else as well, though: a quiet curiosity bordering on envy. What did they know, these future companions of hers, Anne Potter, Timothy Pettigrew, James Thorogood and William Petty, Guilliamus Trentinus and Christina Margaret Benson? More than she knew, or less? Nothing? Something? Everything?

When she got home, Paul's manner was affectedly casual. As they ate and drank, she felt him getting tenser and more self-righteous. Well, she was good at waiting. She watched him swerve away from whatever he wanted to say on three occasions. Finally, as he laid a cup of coffee in front of her, he said quietly, 'By the way, are you having an affair?'

'No.' Martha laughed with relief, which irritated him into pedantry. 'Well, are you perhaps in love with someone else and contemplating an affair?' No, not that either. She'd been in a disused church. No, that's where she'd been before, on other occasions of suspicious absence. No, she didn't meet anyone there. No, she wasn't getting religion. No, she went there to be alone.

He seemed almost disappointed. It might have been easier,

and more tactful, to say, Yes, I am seeing someone else. That would justify the dullness and the distance that had grown between them. Dr Johnson had put it better, of course: they had lost that tenderness of look, and that benevolence of mind. Yes, she could have said, blame me. Other women used this subterfuge; other men too. 'I'm falling in love with someone else' was always easier on the vanity than 'I'm falling out of love with you.'

Later, in the dark, eyes closed, she looked up at fat buttons, a white stock, and a broad, tormented face. It's true, Paul, she could have said, it's true there's someone I'm drawn to. An older man at long last. Someone I can imagine falling in love with. I won't tell you his name, you'd laugh. It's ridiculous in a way, but no more ridiculous than some of the men I've tried to love. The problem is, you see, that he doesn't exist. Or he did, but he died a couple of centuries ago.

Would that have made it any easier for Paul?

TED WAGSTAFF

stood in front of Martha's desk like a weather forecaster preparing to spoil a public holiday.

'Something unusual?' she prompted.

'Afraid so, Miss Cochrane.'

'But something you're going to tell me about. Now, preferably.'

'It's Mr Hood and his Band, I'm afraid.'

'Oh no.'

The Band ... Those other incidents could be dismissed as hiccups: pampered employees getting uppity, the criminal gene quietly reasserting itself, unforeseen personality slippage. Little more than what the King would resentfully term a bit of fun. Easily quenched by executive justice. But the Band was central to the Project, as Visitor Feedback confirmed. It was a primal myth, repositioned after considerable debate. Band personnel had been realigned with great sensitivity; offensive elements in the scenario – old-fashioned attitudes to wildlife, over-consumption of red meat – had been expunged or attenuated. All through the year Promotions had given the Band top headlining. If they had been no. 7 on Jeff's list of Quintessences, they were no. 3 in Visitor Appeal, and pre-booked solid for the next six months.

Only a couple of days ago Martha had checked the Cave onscreen, and everything was seeming honest. The ovoid rock-finished tumulus looked properly medieval; the repatriated Saudi oaks were flourishing; the man in the bear-suit entirely plausible. On either side of the Cave there were peaceful queues for the viewing windows. Through them Visitors could scrutinize the Band's domestic lifestyle: Much the Miller's Son baking ten-grain bread; Will Scarlet rubbing camomile lotion into his enflamed skin; Little John and others of his size making merrie in their miniaturized quarters. The tour continued with archery practice (participation encouraged) and a visit to the Barbecue Pit, where Friar Tuck would be found basting his 'Ox' (moulded vegetable matter oozing with cranberry juice, if anyone asked). Finally, Visitors were led to the grandstands, where an English Fool in cap and bells would warm them up with some cross-epoch satire before the climactic event: the battle – or rather, moral pageant – between the libertarian, free-market Hoodites and the wicked Sheriff of Nottingham backed by his corrupt bureaucrats and hi-tech army.

The Band was not just central to the Island's self-presentation; it was paid top whack. Recruiters had trawled high up in the theatrical profession; several Band members had negotiated a percentage on the merchandising. They had luxury apartments and a fan-club with branches from Stockholm to Seoul. What could they possibly have to complain about?

'Tell.'

'Started about a month ago. Just a little curl of the pig's tail, we thought. Nothing a good thrashing couldn't sort out.'

Was she becoming more impatient, or was Ted Wagstaff's personality slippage getting worse?

'The point, Ted.'

'Sorry, Miss Cochrane. The Band said they didn't like the ox. They said it tasted filthy. We said we'd see what we could do. We tasted it ourselves. Not great, but not too bad. We said, look, the scene where you carve chunks off it and smack your lips in appreciation isn't that long, couldn't you just pretend, either that or keep it in your mouths and spit it out later? We said we'd work on the problem. We *were* working on it, Miss Cochrane. We had a two-pronged attack. Number One, fly in a top French chef from Rouen to see if he could make it taste a bit more like meat. Number Two, fall-back position, rewrite the scenario so that the Friar Tuck is a lousy cook and so it's OK for the Band to spit it out.'

He looked at Martha, as if expecting applause for enterprise. Martha wanted to get to the point. 'But?'

'But the next thing we know, the smell from the Pit is quite different, the Band is stuffing its faces and not spitting anything out, and Dingle the Woolly Steer is missing from the Animal Heritage Park.'

'But that's on the other side of the Island.'

'I know.'

'Aren't all those animals electronically tagged?'

'We found the tag, and the ear, in Dingle's pen.'

'So they got their ox. What else?'

'They took a Devon Longwool, a couple of Gloucester Old Spots and three swans. Then last week they cleared all the ducks off the Stacpoole Memorial Pool. The fact is, they've started putting our deliveries straight in the dustbins. They're hunting their own food.'

'In our heritage parks.'

'And in our old-English farmyards. And in our woods and forests. The bastards seem to be killing anything they can hit with those arrows. Not to mention snitching vegetables from the back gardens of Bungalow Valley.'

'Are we just talking diet?'

'No way, Miss Cochrane. That Robin's got a list of complaints as long as your arm. He says that having certain members of the differently-abled in his Band slows up both their hunting and their fighting capacities. He wants them replaced with what he calls hundred-percent warriors. He says the Band insist on more privacy and are going to curtain off the viewing windows to stop everybody looking in. Yes, I know what you're going to say. He also claims that having homosexuals in the Band is detrimental to good military discipline. He says the staged fights are hopeless and wouldn't it be more realistic if the Sheriff's men were given an extra financial inducement to capture the Band, and if they, the Band, were allowed to ambush the Sheriff's men anywhere. And his final complaint, well, you'll have to pardon my language, Miss Cochrane.'

'It's pardoned, Ted.'

'Well, he said his todger was dropping off for lack of use, and what the eff did you think you were doing fixing him up with a dyke?'

Martha stared disbelievingly at Ted. She wasn't sure she could get her head round this one. 'But . . . Ted . . . I mean, for a start, Maid Marian, what's her name, Vanessa, just to be basic about it all, she's only *playing* a dyke, as Robin puts it.'

'That's as far as our information goes. I suppose she could be getting inside the skin of her role. More likely she's just using it as an excuse. To ward off his advances, as it were.'

'But . . . I mean, apart from anything else, from what I remember of Dr Max's historical report, Maid Marian wasn't sleeping with Robin anyway.'

'Well, that's as it may be, Miss Cochrane. The present state of play is that Robin's complaining that it's unfair and unjust and a crime against his manhood that he hasn't, if you'll pardon my language but it's his, he hasn't had a shag in months.'

Martha briefly wanted to call Dr Max and tell him about the behaviour of pastoral communities in the modern world. Instead, she addressed the problem. 'Right. He's contractually in breach by a long way. They all are. But that's not really the main point. He's in rebellion isn't he? Against the Project, against our repositioning of the myth, against every single Visitor who comes to see him. He's . . . he's . . .'

'A bloody outlaw, Miss?'

Martha smiled. 'Thank you, Ted.'

The Band in revolt? It was unthinkable. It was central. It played in so many other directions. What if they all took it into their heads to behave like that? What if the King decided he really wanted to reign; or, for that matter, if Queen Boadicea decided he was an upstart from some johnny-come-lately continental dynasty? What if the Germans decided they should have won the Battle of Britain? The consequences were unimaginable. What if robins decided they didn't like the snow?

'WE'VE GOT THINGS TO DISCUSS,'

said Martha, and saw Paul's cheeks tighten. The resentful face of a man called upon to discuss a relationship. Martha wanted to reassure him. It's all right, we're through with that now, the talking and the not talking. There are various things I'm unable to say, and since in any case you don't want to hear them, we can just let it go.

'It's the Band.'

She saw Paul's mood ease. It lifted even more as they discussed executive action, Visitor confidence and fast-track retraining. They agreed about the fundamental threat to the Project. They agreed it wasn't a job for Customs and Excise. It was Paul who suggested the SAS, Paul who advised a forty-eight-hour deadline, Paul who offered to liaise with the Band as technical coordinator, Paul who would see her later, perhaps a lot later, and who left in a state of relieved excitement.

They could manage this harmonious shorthand at work; at home they subsisted on a grunted routine full of polite suppressions. Once he had said that she made him feel real. Did she weep now for past flattery, or for past truth?

These were some of the things she was unable to say:

— that none of it was his fault;

— that despite Dr Max's historical scepticism, she believed in happiness;

— that when she said she 'believed in' it, she meant that she thought such a state existed and was worth trying to attain;

— that seekers after happiness tended to divide into two groups, those who sought it by fulfilling criteria laid down by others, and those who sought it by fulfilling their own criteria;

— that neither means of search was morally superior to the other;

— but that for her happiness depended on being true to yourself;

— true to your nature;

— that is, true to your heart;

— but the main problem, life's central predicament, was, how did you know your own heart?;

— and the surrounding problem was, how did you know what your nature was?;

— that most people located their nature in childhood: so their entranced self-reminiscences, the photographs they displayed of themselves when young, were ways of defining that nature;

— here was a photo of herself when young, frowning against the sun and sticking out her lower lip: was this her nature or only her mother's poor photography?;

— but what if this nature was no more natural than the nature Sir Jack had satirically delineated after a walk in the country?;

— because if you were unable to locate your nature, your chance of happiness was surely diminished;

— or what if locating your nature was like locating a patch of wetland, whose layout remained mysterious, and whose workings indecipherable?;

— that despite favourable conditions, and lack of encumbrances, and despite the fact that she thought she might love Paul, she had not felt happy;

— that at first she thought this might be because he bored her;

— or his love bored her;

— or even that her love bored her;

— but she wasn't sure (and not knowing her nature, how could she be?) that this was the case;

— so perhaps it was that love was not the answer for her;

— which was, after all, not an entirely eccentric position, as Dr Max would have reassured her;

— or perhaps it was the case that love had come too late for her, too late to make her lose her solitude (if that was how you tested love), too late to make her happy;

— that when Dr Max explained that in medieval times people had sought salvation rather than love, the two concepts weren't necessarily in opposition;

— it was just that later centuries had lower ambitions;

— and when we seek happiness, perhaps we are pursuing some lower form of salvation, though we don't dare call it by such a name;

— that perhaps her own life had been what Dr Johnson had called his, a barren waste of time;

— that she had made so little progress towards even the lowest form of salvation;

— that none of it was his fault.

THE RAID ON ROBIN'S CAVE

was quietly listed as a one-off cross-epoch extravaganza, limited to Premier Visitors on payment of a double supplement. By six o'clock the U-shaped grandstand was full and the setting sun made a natural floodlight on the Cave's mouth.

Martha and the executive board sat high up at the back of the stand. This was a major crisis, and a challenge to the very philosophy of the Project; yet at the same time, if things went pleasingly, it might throw up some useful Development ideas. Leisure Theory never stood still. She and Paul had already theorized about interfacing other non-synchronous episodes of the nation's history. Where was he, incidentally? No doubt still backstage, refining the Band's choreography.

Martha was irritated to discover Sir Jack sitting next to her. This wasn't a ceremonial event; far from it. Whose arm had he twisted to get Dr Max's seat? And was that another row of medals he'd awarded himself on his Governor's tunic? As he turned to her with his Jolly Jack grin and a waggish shake of the head, she noticed that the grey strands in his eyebrows had finally turned black. 'Wouldn't miss the fun for anything,' he said. 'Not that I'd like to be in your shoes.'

She ignored him. Once she might have bridled; now it didn't matter. Executive control was what counted. And if he wanted to play games . . . Well, she could halve the horse-power of his landau, rescind the armagnac clause in his contract, or tag him like Dingle the Woolly Steer. Sir Jack was an anachronism. Martha leaned forward to watch the action.

Colonel Michael 'Mad Mike' Michaelson had been a private fitness trainer with stuntman experience before being recruited to lead the Island SAS. The rest of his unit included gymnasts, security guards, bouncers, athletes and ballet dancers. Their shared lack of military experience was no hindrance in their bi-weekly restaging of the Iranian Embassy Siege of 1980, which demanded agility, eye and rope technique, plus a capacity to emote roughly as the stun grenades went off. But this was a new test, and as Mad Mike briefed his men in a hastily-bulldozed piece of dead ground just in front of row AA, he had authentic professional anxieties. Not about the outcome: the Merrie Men would cooperate just as the occupants of the Iranian Embassy regularly did. What worried him was that without rehearsals, the show might not have a true enough look to it.

Even he knew that in military terms a daylight assault on the mouth of a cave was absurd. The best way to take out Hood and the Band – that is, if they were really giving aggravation – would be to go in through the service entrance at dead of night with ramrods and searchlights. But provided everyone played along, he thought he could make it all quite pretty.

As at the Siege, an induction loop allowed the audience to eavesdrop by headset. Mad Mike explained his plan, backing his words with expansive gestures. The two combat groups, in full blackface, listened histrionically while continuing their preparations: one sharpening a large Bowie knife, another easing the pin on a stun-grenade, two more checking the resilience of nylon cable. The Colonel finished his briefing with terse exhortations to discipline and control, from which all military expletives had been deleted; then with an outflung arm and a cry of 'Go, go, GO!' despatched the sextet known as A-Group.

The grandstand watched contentedly and with a sense of familiarity bordering on actual knowledge as A-Group split into two, disappeared into the woods, then swung down on an instantly plausible pulley system from treetops to the roof of the Cave. Listening devices were attached to the rock surface, a microphone lowered into the Cave's mouth, and two SAS men began abseiling down each side of the Hood condo.

A-Group had just confirmed its position when a chuckle spread across the bleachers. Friar Tuck had emerged from the Cave carrying a pair of long-handled pruning shears. After much gagging, he snipped through the dangling cord, picked it up and tossed it towards the spectators. Ignoring this gross and unscripted piece of scene-stealing, Mad Mike led members of B-Group in an elbows-and-knees monkey-crawl across the open ground. In the best traditions of military thespianry, they wore leafy branches attached to their woollen balaclavas.

'Till Burnham Wood shall come to Dunsinane,' Sir Jack

announced for the benefit of the dozen rows in front of him. 'As the mighty William observed.'

B-Group were twenty yards from the Cave mouth when three arrows whizzed over them and pierced the ground a few feet in front of row AA. Huge applause acknowledged that such precise realism was what a double supplement was all about. Mad Mike looked across at his fellow gymnasts and security men, then back at the grandstand, half expecting a signal, or supplementary instructions from Paul over his headset. When none came, he murmured into his microphone, 'Red red robin. Time to go bobbing. Forty seconds, chaps.' He gave an invented gesture to A-Group on top of the Cave. Four of its six members were now poised on straining ropes above the windows, each gauging the depth and distance of his gymnastic arc. Looking down, they were surprised by what looked like the greasy sheen of real glass. At the Embassy the windows were made of low-impact, high-shatter crackle-glaze. Well, presumably Techno-Development had come up with something even more authentic.

Mad Mike and his Number Two now rose to their knees and each threw a stun-grenade into the Cave. The special thirty-second fuses were designed to stretch dramatic tension; the explosions would be the signal for A-Group to go through the windows. B-Group were still face-down in the dirt, pretending to cover their ears, when they heard another double-supplement chuckle from behind. The two grenades, now down to their final seconds of fuse, were coming back in their direction, followed by three arrows, which landed unnecessarily close. The grenades exploded thunderously among B-Group, who were relieved they were not the real thing. 'All fart and no fire,' Mad Mike commented to himself, forgetting his words were going straight into the headsets of each high roller in the grandstand.

To cover his confusion, he rose to his feet shouting 'Go, go GO!', and led the charge over the remaining twenty yards or so of ground. Simultaneously, the four roped SAS men launched themselves out from the rock's side, aiming their cleated boots at the picture windows.

Later, it was hard to decide who had screamed first: the members of A-Group who between them sustained two broken ankles and eight severely jolted knees on the Cave's reinforced double-glazing; or the members of B-Group when they saw half a dozen arrows coming in their direction. One struck Mad Mike in the shoulder; another took his Number Two through the thigh.

'Go, go GO!' shouted the recumbent Colonel as his team of athletes and actors gave most realistic flight in the opposite direction.

'Fuck, fuck FUCK!' growled Sir Jack.

'Ambulance,' said Martha Cochrane to Ted Wagstaff as unseen hands flipped the Cave windows and yanked the dangling SAS men inside.

Maid Marian's dyke bodyguard ran from the Cave and dragged Mad Mike away. 'Go, go GO!' he shouted, valiant to the end.

'Fuck, fuck, FUCK!' echoed Sir Jack. He turned to Martha Cochrane and said, 'Even you must admit you've made a complete and utter balls of this.'

Martha didn't reply at first. She'd trusted Paul to do a better job. Or maybe the choreography had been agreed and then Hood had double-crossed him. The assault had been an amateurish disaster. And yet . . . and yet . . . She turned back to the Governor: 'Listen to the applause.' Indeed. The whistling and clapping was now modulating into a rhythmical stamping which threatened the bleachers. They'd loved it, that was clear. The special effects had been terrific; Mad Mike, in his wounded heroism, was utterly convincing; any mishaps merely confirmed the action's authenticity. And after all, Martha suddenly realized, most Visitors would have wanted the Merrie Men to triumph. The SAS might be Free World heroes down at the Iranian Embassy, but here they were a snatch squad ordered in by the wicked Sheriff of Nottingham.

Robin's Band, like reluctant actors, were pulled from the Cave to take numerous bows. A helicopter ambulance dodged in to transport the Colonel's Number Two straight to Dieppe Hospital. Meanwhile, Mad Mike himself, bound with thick rope, was displayed as a hostage.

The applause continued. It had definite possibilities, Martha thought. She and Paul would have to talk it through with Jeff. The Concept needed further Development, of course, and it was a pity about the Band's over-enthusiasm; but cross-epoch conflict clearly had strong Visitor Resonance.

Sir Jack cleared his throat and turned to Martha. Ceremoniously, he placed his tricorne on his head. 'I shall expect your resignation in the morning.'

Had he lost all touch with reality?

THE NEXT MORNING,

when Martha opened her office door, Sir Jack Pitman was sitting behind her desk, thumb casually hooked through gilded lanyard. He was on the telephone; or at least, he was speaking into the telephone. Behind him stood Paul. Sir Jack pointed to a low chair drawn up on the other side of the desk. As at her first interview, Martha declined to follow instruction.

After a minute or so, having issued orders to someone who might or might not have been at the other end of the telephone, Sir Jack touched a button and said, 'Hold my calls.' Then he looked up at Martha. 'Surprised?'

Martha did not reply.

'Well, not unsurprised, then.' He chuckled, as at some obscure reference.

Martha was almost there when Sir Jack rose heavily and said, 'But my dear Paul, I forget. This is *your* chair now. My congratulations.' Aping some court chamberlain or parliamentary usher, he stiffly held the chair for Paul, then pushed it in under his thighs. Paul, Martha noted, at least had the shame to look embarrassed.

'You see, Miss Cochrane, you never learned the simple lesson. You remind me of the hunter who went after the grizzly bear. You know the story?' He did not wait for Martha to respond. 'It bears retelling, anyway. *Bears*, that's rich, excuse my unintended jocundity. It must be a product of my mood. So: a hunter heard that there was a bear on an island off the coast of Alaska. He hired a helicopter to take him over the water. After a search he found the bear, a great, big, wise old bear. He lined him up in his sights, got off a quick shot – *peeeeeooooow* – and made the terrible, the unforgivable mistake of merely wounding the animal. The bear ran off into the woods, with the hunter in pursuit. He circled the island, he criss-crossed it, he sought bear tracks up hill and down dale. Perhaps Bruin had crawled off into some cave and breathed his furry last. At any event, no bear. The day was beginning to draw in, so the hunter decided that enough was enough, and made his weary way back to where the helicopter was waiting. He got to within a hundred yards or so of it and noticed the pilot waving to him in a rather excited fashion. He stopped, put down his gun to wave back, and *that* was the moment when the bear, with a single swipe of its extraordinary paw' – Sir Jack sketched the gesture in case Martha could not imagine it – 'took off the hunter's head.'

'And the bear lived happily ever after?' Martha was unable to resist the jibe.

'Well, I'll tell you this, the hunter fucking didn't, Miss Cochrane, the hunter fucking didn't.' Sir Jack, rearing up before her, seemed more ursine by the moment, rocking and bellowing. Paul chuckled like a reinstated sycophant.

Ignoring Sir Jack, she said to the newly appointed Chief Executive Officer, 'I give you six months at the most.'

'Is that accurate flattery?' he replied coldly.

'I thought . . .' Oh, forget it, Martha. You thought you'd assessed the situation. Various situations. You hadn't. That's all.

'Pardon me for intruding upon a moment of private grief.' Sir Jack's sarcasm was lascivious. 'But there are a few contractual points to make clear. Your pension rights are revoked as per contract due to your gross misconduct over the incident at the Hood Cave. You have twelve hours to clear your desk and your quarters. Your leaving present is an economy-class one-way ferry ticket to Dieppe. Your career is at an end. But just in case you are inclined to disagree, the fraud and embezzlement charges we have prepared will lie on the record for future activation if necessary.'

'Auntie May,' said Martha.

'My mother had only brothers,' replied Sir Jack smugly.

She looked at Paul. He wouldn't accept her eye. 'There's no evidence,' he said. 'Not any more. It must have disappeared. Been burnt or something.'

'Or eaten by a bear.'

'Very good, Miss Cochrane. I'm glad to see you retain your sense of humour despite everything. Of course I have to warn you that were you to make any allegations, public or private, which I might deem harmful to the interests of my beloved Project, then I should not hesitate to use all the powers at my considerable command to discourage you. And knowing me as you do, you will be aware that I would not content myself with merely defending my interests. I would be *very* pro-active. I'm sure you understand.'

'Gary Desmond,' said Martha.

'Miss Cochrane, you *are* off the pace. Early retirement was clearly beckoning anyway. Tell her the news, Paul.'

'Gary Desmond has been appointed editor-in-chief of *The Times*.'

'At a generous salary.'

'Correct, Miss Cochrane. Cynics say that everyone has their price. I am less cynical than some I could mention. I think everyone has a proper sense of the level at which they would

234

like to be remunerated. Is that not a more honourable way of looking at things? You yourself, I seem to remember, demanded certain salary conditions when you first came to work for me. You wanted the job, but you named your price. So any criticism of the estimable Mr Desmond, whose journalistic record is second to none, would be pure hypocrisy.'

'About which you . . .' Oh, forget it, Martha. Let it go.

'You seem to be leaving a lot of sentences unfinished this morning, Miss Cochrane. Stress, I expect. A long sea voyage is the traditional remedy. Alas, we can only offer a short Channel crossing.' He pulled an envelope from his pocket and tossed it in front of her. 'And now,' he said, placing his tricorne on his head and drawing himself up less like a rearing grizzly than a ship's captain pronouncing sentence on a mutineer, 'I hereby declare you *persona non grata* on the Island. In perpetuity.'

Responses came to Martha's mind, but not her lips. She gave Paul a neutral glance, ignored the envelope, and left her office for the final time.

SHE SAID GOODBYE

to Dr Max, to Country Mouse, to the Pragmatic Pagan. Dr Max, who sought neither happiness nor salvation. Did he seek love? She presumed not, but they hadn't exactly discussed it. He claimed he wanted only pleasure, with its beautifully etched discontents. They kissed cheeks, and she got a whiff of cloned *eau de toilette*. As she turned to go, Martha suddenly felt responsible. Dr Max might have constructed his own shiny carapace, but she saw him at that moment as something vulnerable, innocent, decorticated. Who would protect him now that she was gone?

'Dr Max.'

'Miss Cochrane?' He stood before her, thumbs in the pockets

of his eucalyptus waistcoat, as if expecting another student question he could biff around.

'Look, you remember when I called you in a couple of months ago?'

'When you were planning to sack me?'

'Dr *Max*!'

'Well, you were, weren't you? An h–istorian acquires a certain nose for the mechanisms of power in the course of his studies.'

'Will you be all right, Dr Max?'

'I imagine so. The Pitman papers will take a lot of sorting. And then of course there's the biography.'

Martha smiled at him, and shook her head rebukingly. The rebuke was self-directed: Dr Max needed neither her advice nor her protection.

In the church of St Aldwyn she gazed at the lottery-line numbers. No jackpot this week, yet again, Martha. She sat on a dank, initialled petit-point hassock and seemed almost to sniff the wet light. Why was she drawn here? She didn't come to pray. There was no neat spirit of repentance. The sceptic come to heel, the blasphemer whose cataracts dissolve: her case did not replicate the old clergy-pleasing story. Yet was there a parallel? Dr Max did not believe in salvation, but perhaps she did, and felt she might find it among the remnants of a greater, discarded system of salvation.

— So, Martha, what are you after? You can tell me.

— What am I after? I don't know. Perhaps a recognition that life, despite everything, has a capacity for seriousness. Which has eluded me. As it eludes most people, probably. But still.

— Go on.

— Well, I suppose life must be more serious if it has a structure, if there's something larger out there than yourself.

— Nice and diplomatic, Martha. Banal, too. Triumphantly meaningless. Try again.

— All right. If life is a triviality, then despair is the only option.

— Better, Martha. Much better. Unless what you're meaning is that you've decided to seek God as a way of avoiding anti-depressants.

— No, not that. You misunderstand. I'm not in a church because of God. One of the problems is that the words, the serious words, have been used up over the centuries by people like those rectors and vicars listed on the wall. The words don't seem to fit the thoughts nowadays. But I think there was something enviable about that otherwise unenviable world. Life is more serious, and therefore better, and therefore bearable, if there is some larger context.

— Oh come on, Martha, you're boring me. You may not be religious, but you're certainly pious. I liked you more the way you used to be. Brittle cynicism is a truer response to the modern world than this . . . sentimental yearning.

— No, it's not sentimental. On the contrary. I'm saying life is more serious, and better, and bearable, even if its context is arbitrary and cruel, even if its laws are false and unjust.

— Now this *is* the luxury of hindsight. Tell that to the victims of religious persecution down the centuries. Would you prefer to be broken on the wheel or have a nice little bungalow on the Isle of Wight? I think I can guess the answer.

— And another thing . . .

— But you didn't answer my last point.

— Well, you might be wrong. And another thing. An individual's loss of faith and a nation's loss of faith, aren't they much the same? Look what happened to England. Old England. It stopped believing in things. Oh, it still muddled along. It did OK. But it lost seriousness.

— Oh, so now it's a nation's loss of faith, is it? This is pretty ironic stuff coming from you, Martha. You think the nation does better if it has some serious beliefs, even if they're arbitrary and cruel? Bring back the Inquisition, wheel on the Great Dictators, Martha Cochrane proudly presents . . .

— Stop. I can't explain without mocking myself. The words

just follow their own logic. How do you cut the knot? Perhaps by forgetting words. Let the words run out, Martha . . .

Into her mind came an image, one shared by earlier occupants of these pews. Not Guilliamus Trentinus, of course, or Anne Potter, but perhaps known to Ensign Robert Timothy Pettigrew, and Christina Margaret Benson, and James Thorogood and William Petty. A woman swept and hanging, a woman half out of this world, terrified and awestruck, yet in the end safely delivered. A sense of falling, falling, falling, which we have every day of our lives, and then an awareness that the fall was being made gentler, was being arrested, by an unseen current whose existence no-one suspected. A short, eternal moment that was absurd, improbable, unbelievable, true. Eggs cracked from the slight concussion of landing, but nothing more. The richness of all subsequent life after that moment.

Later the moment had been appropriated, reinvented, copied, coarsened; she herself had helped. But such coarsening always happened. The seriousness lay in celebrating the original image: getting back there, seeing it, feeling it. This was where she parted company from Dr Max. Part of you might suspect that the magical event had never occurred, or at least not as it was now supposed to have done. But you must also celebrate the image and the moment even if it had never happened. That was where the little seriousness of life lay.

She placed new flowers on the altar and took away last week's, which were crusted and fragile. She pulled the heavy door awkwardly shut, but did not lock it in case there were others. For thine is the wigwam, the flowers and the story.

238

3: ANGLIA

WITH A SERIES of wristy, metallic swipes Jez Harris sharpened his scythe. The vicar owned an ancient, petrol-driven Atco, but Jez preferred to do things properly; besides, the slewed headstones were planted in a deliberate clutter, as if to defy any mechanical mower. From across the churchyard, Martha watched Harris bend down and tighten his leather knee-straps. Then he spat on his palms, uttered a few invented oaths, and began to attack the couch-grass and rosebay willow-herb, the cornflowers and the straggling vetch. Until the weeds grew back again, Martha would be able to read the incised names of her future companions.

It was early June, a week before the Fête, and the weather was giving a false impression of summer. The wind had dropped, and slow bumblebees nosed through the scent of baked grass. A silver-washed fritillary exchanged carefree flight-paths with a meadow brown. Only a hyperactive chiff-chaff, scavenging for insects, displayed an intrusive work-ethic. The woodland birds were bolder than they had been in her childhood. The other day Martha had seen a hawfinch crack a cherry-stone right at her feet.

The churchyard was a place of informality and collapse, of time's softer damage. A cloudburst of old-man's-beard concealed the perilous lean of a flinty wall. There was a copper beech, two of whose tiring branches were propped with wooden crutches, and a lych-gate whose circumflex roof leaked. The licheny slats of the bench on which Martha sat complained even at her cautiously applied weight.

'The chiff-chaff is a restless bird, which does not form in flocks.' Where had that come from? It had just entered her head. No, that was wrong: it had always been in her head, and had taken this opportunity to flit across her mind. The operation of memory was becoming more random; she had noticed that. Her mind still worked with clarity, she thought, but in its resting moments all sorts of litter from the past blew about. Years ago, in middle age, or maturity, or whatever you called it, her memory had been practical, justificatory. For instance, childhood was remembered in a succession of incidents which explained why you were the person you had turned out to be. Nowadays there was more slippage – a bicycle chain jumping a cog – and less consequence. Or perhaps this was your brain hinting at what you didn't want to know: that you had become the person you were not by explicable cause-and-effect, by acts of will imposed on circumstance, but by mere vagary. You beat your wings all your life, but it was the wind that decided where you went.

'Mr Harris?'

'You can call me Jez, Missie Cochrane, like others do.' The farrier was a burly fellow whose knees cracked as he straightened himself. He wore a countryman's outfit of his own devising, all pockets and straps and sudden tucks, which had hints of both Morris dancer and bondage devotee.

'I think there's a redstart still sitting,' said Martha. 'Just behind that old-man's-beard. Mind you don't disturb her.'

'Will do, Miss Cochrane.' Jez Harris yanked at a loose strand of hair over his forehead, with possible satiric intent. 'They say redstarts bring luck to them as don't disturb their nests.'

'Do they, Mr Harris?' Martha's expression was disbelieving.

'They do in this village, Miss Cochrane,' replied Harris firmly, as if her comparatively recent arrival gave her no right to question history.

He moved off to hack at a patch of cow parsley. Martha smiled to herself. Funny how she couldn't bring herself to call him Jez. Yet Harris was no more authentic. Jez Harris, formerly

Jack Oshinsky, junior legal expert with an American electronics firm obliged to leave the country during the emergency. He'd preferred to stay, and backdate both his name and his technology: nowadays he shoed horses, made barrel hoops, sharpened knives and sickles, cut keys, tended the verges, and brewed a noxious form of scrumpy into which he would plunge a red-hot poker just before serving. Marriage to Wendy Temple had softened and localized his Milwaukee accent; and his inextinguishable pleasure was to play the yokel whenever some anthropologist, travel writer or linguistic theoretician would turn up inadequately disguised as a tourist.

'Tell me,' the earnest hiker with the give-away new boots might begin, 'does that clump of trees over there have a special name?'

'Name?' Harris would shout back from his forge, wrinkling his brow and banging a vermilion horseshoe like a manic xylophonist. 'Name?' he would repeat, glaring at the investigator through matted hair. 'That be Halley's copse, half-drowned dog know that.' He would toss the shoe contemptuously into a pail of water, the fizzle and fume dramatizing his rebuke.

'Halley's copse ... You mean ... like Halley's comet?' Already the disguised sipper and browser of retarded humanity would be regretting that he couldn't take out notebook or recorder.

'Comet? What comet's that? No comet's round here betimes. Ain't never heard of Edna Halley then? No, reckon it's not what folk hereabouts like to tell of. Rum business, if you ask me, rum business.'

Whereupon, with studied reluctance, and after making signs of hunger, Harris the farrier né Oshinsky the legal draughtsman would allow himself to be treated to a steak-and-kidney pudding at the Rising Sun, and with a pint of mild-and-bitter at his elbow would hint, without ever quite confirming, at tales of witchcraft and superstition, of sexual rites beneath a glowing moon and the tranced slaughter of livestock, all not so very long in the past. Other drinkers in the snug would hear phrases expire as Harris caught himself and melodramatically lowered his voice. 'Of course, the vicar has always denied ...' they would be offered, or 'Them's you meet all claim they never knew old Edna, but she'd wash 'em at birth and wash 'em after death, and in between ...'

From time to time Mr Mullin the schoolmaster would chide Jez Harris, suggesting that folklore, and especially invented folklore, should not be the subject of monetary exchange or barter. The schoolmaster was tactful and shy, so kept to generality and principle. Others in the village put things more plainly: for them, Harris's fabulation and cupidity were proof of the farrier's unAnglian origins.

But in any case Harris would decline the reprimand, and with various winks and scalp-scratchings draw Mr Mullin into his own narrative. 'Now, don't you be a-scared, Mr Mullin, Sir. Never breathed a word about you and Edna; not a word, I'd draw this very scythe across my giblets if ever my gullet started bleating about that business ...'

'Oh, come off it, Jez,' the schoolmaster would protest, though his use of the Christian name was a virtual admission of defeat. 'I just mean don't get carried away with all the guff you give them. If you want some local legends I've got lots of books I can lend you. Folk collections, that sort of thing.' Mr Mullin had been an antiquarian dealer in his previous life.

'Old Mother Fairweather and all that, you mean? Fact is, Mr Mullin, Sir,' – and here Harris gave a look of modest smugness – 'I've tried 'em on that stuff and it don't go down so well. They prefer Jez's stories, that's the truth. You and Miss Cochrane can read your books by candlelight together ...'

'Oh, for God's sake, Jez.'

'Must have been a comely one in her time, that Miss Cochrane, don't you think? They do say someone stole one of her petticoats off the line last Monday sevennight when old Brock the badger were playing by the light of the moon on Gibbet Hill ...'

Not long after this encounter Mr Mullin, earnest and

embarrassed, all pink face and leather elbow patches, knocked at Martha Cochrane's back door and declared his ignorance in the matter of the stolen underclothes, about whose loss he had been truly unaware until, until . . .

'Jez Harris?' asked Martha with a smile.

'You don't mean . . .?'

'I think I'm probably a little old for anyone to be interested in my washing.'

'Oh, the . . . the *rogue*.'

Mr Mullin was a timid, fussy man whose pupils called him Chiff-Chaff. He accepted a cup of peppermint tea and, not for the first time, allowed his complaints against the blacksmith to take slightly higher ground. 'The thing is, Miss Cochrane, in one way I can't help being on his side, telling whoppers to all those snoopers and nosey-parkers who won't even let on what they're up to. Let the deceiver be himself deceived – I'm sure that's the tag, even if I can't quite put my finger on it for certain at the moment. Could it be Martial . . .?'

'But on the other hand . . .'

'Yes, thank you, but on the other hand, I wish he wouldn't *invent* these things. I've got books of myths and legends he's welcome to. There's all sorts of tales to choose from. He could lead a little tour if he wished. Take them up to Gibbet Hill and talk about the Hooded Hangman. Or there's Old Mother Fairweather and her Luminous Geese.'

'They wouldn't be *his* stories, would they?'

'No, they'd be *our* stories. They'd be . . . *true*.' He sounded unconvinced himself. 'Well, maybe not true, but at least recorded.' Martha merely looked at him. 'Anyway, you see my point.'

'I see your point.'

'But I feel you're on his side, Miss Cochrane. You are, aren't you?'

'Mr Mullin,' said Martha, sipping her peppermint tea, 'when you get to my age you often find that you aren't on anyone's side, not particularly. Or on everyone's side. Whichever you prefer, really.'

'Oh dear,' said Mr Mullin. 'You see, I thought you were one of us.'

'Perhaps I've known too many us-es in my lifetime.'

The schoolmaster looked at her as if she were somehow disloyal, quite possibly unpatriotic. In the schoolroom he was keen to ground his pupils. He taught them local geology, popular ballads, the origin of place-names, the migratory patterns of birds, and the Kingdoms of the Heptarchy (so much easier, thought Martha, than the Counties of England). He would take them to the northern edge of the Kimmeridgean formation, and demonstrate old-fashioned wrestling holds illustrated in encyclopaedias.

It had been Mr Mullin's idea to revive – or perhaps, since records were inexact, to institute – the village Fête. One afternoon an official delegation of schoolmaster and vicar had called on Martha Cochrane. It was known that she, unlike most of the village's current occupants, had actually grown up in the countryside. Over mugs of chicory and shortbread biscuits they petitioned her for memories.

'Three carrots long,' she had answered. 'Three carrots short. Three carrots any variety.'

'Yes?'

'Tray of vegetables. Tray may be dressed, but only parsley may be used. Cauliflowers, if included, must be on stalks.'

'Yes?'

'Six broad beans. Six scarlet runners. Nine dwarf beans.'

'Yes?'

'Jar of marmalade. All goats entered shall be female. Jar of lemon cheese. Friesian Heifer Maiden not showing more than two broad teeth.'

She fetched a booklet with a faded red cover. Her visitors looked through it. 'Three Dahlias, Cactus, 6"–8" – in one vase,' they read. Then: 'Five Dahlias, Pompom, under 2" diameter.' Then: 'Five Dahlias, miniature ball.' Then: 'Three Dahlias, decorative, over 8" – in three vases.' The frail book of lists seemed like a potsherd from an immensely complicated and self-evidently decadent civilization.

'Mounted Fancy Dress Competition?' the Reverend Coleman mused. 'Two covered coat hangers? An article made from Salt Dough? Best Child Handler under 15 years of age? Dog the Judge would like to take home?'

Despite his respect for book-learning, the schoolmaster was unconvinced. 'Perhaps on the whole we'd better start from scratch.' The vicar nodded agreement. They left behind the District Agricultural and Horticultural Society's Schedule of Rules.

Later, Martha had flicked through it, remembering yet again the smell of a beer-tent, sheep being sheared, and her parents swinging her up up into the sky. Then there was Mr A. Jones and the way his beans had gleamed on black velvet. A lifetime on, she wondered if Mr A. Jones had ever cheated to arrive at such perfection. No means of knowing: he had become manure himself by now.

Pages fell from the booklet's rusted staples; then a dried leaf. She laid it, stiff and grey, against her palm; only its scalloped edge told her it was from an oak. She must have picked it up, all those years ago, and kept it for a specific purpose: to remind herself, on just such a day as this, of just such a day as that. Except, what was the day? The prompt did not work: no memory of joy, success or simple contentment returned, no flash of sunlight through trees, no house-martin flicking under eaves, no smell of lilac. She had failed her younger self by losing the priorities of youth. Unless it was that her younger self had failed by not predicting the priorities of age.

Jez Harris crept past the cascade of old-man's-beard, leaving the redstart undisturbed, and bringing himself luck, according to his own new lore. His scything and lopping left the churchyard looking attended to, rather than actually neat; birds and butterflies continued their lives. Martha's eye, and then her mind, followed a skimming brimstone southwards, across downland, over water, and past chalky cliffs to another burial ground, a place of bright drystone walls and laundered turf. There wildlife would be discouraged; if it were possible, earthworms would be banned, and so would time itself. Nothing must be allowed to disturb the resting-place of the first Baron Pitman of Fortuibus.

Even Martha did not begrudge Sir Jack his grand isolation. The Island had been his idea and his success. The Peasants' Revolt of Paul and Martha had proved a forgettable interlude, long written out of history. Sir Jack had also dealt swiftly with the subversive tendency of certain employees to over-identify with the characters they were engaged to represent. The new Robin Hood and his new Merrie Men had brought respectability back to outlawry. The King had been given a firm reminder about family values. Dr Johnson had been transferred to Dieppe Hospital, where both therapy and advanced psychotropic drugs had failed to alleviate his personality disorder. Deep sedation was prescribed to control his self-mutilating tendencies.

Paul had lasted a couple of years as CEO, which was longer than Martha had predicted; then, with professions of reluctance and great age, Sir Jack had taken up the reins once more. Shortly after this, a special vote by both Houses of Parliament created him first Baron Pitman of Fortuibus. The motion had been passed *nem con*, and Sir Jack conceded that it would have taken an arrogant man to refuse the honour. Dr Max elaborated a plausible family tree for the new baron, whose mansion began to rival Buckingham Palace in both splendour and Visitor throughput. Sir Jack would gaze down the Mall from the opposite end, reflecting that his last great idea, his Ninth Symphony, had brought him merited wealth, world fame, market applause, and a fiefdom. Truly was he acclaimed as both innovator and ideas man.

Yet even in death he had remained rivalrous. The idea of sharing common ground with lesser players seemed a little unworthy when the Island's founder came to designate his final resting-place. St Mildred's, Whippingham, the estate church for

Osborne House, was taken down and reassembled high on Tennyson Down, whose popular expanses might in future years perhaps be renamed, though of course only in response to a firm expression of Island will. The two acres of churchyard were enclosed by a drystone wall set with marble tablets bearing some of Sir Jack's more eternal *dicta*. In the centre, on a slight rise, was the Pitman mausoleum, necessarily ornate yet essentially simple. Great men should be modest in death. All the same, it would be negligent to ignore Visitor requirements at a future hotspot of England, England.

Sir Jack had divided his last months between architects' drawings and the weather forecast. Increasingly he believed in signs and portents. The mighty William had somewhere remarked that noisy laments from the sky frequently betokened the passing of great men. Beethoven himself had died while a thunderstorm crashed overhead. The last words he spoke had been in praise of the English. 'God bless them,' he had said. Would it be vain – or might it not be truly humble? – to say the same when the heavens protested at his own going hence? The first Baron Pitman was still ruminating his farewell epigram when he died, gazing complacently out at a blue and settled sky.

The funeral was an affair of orotundity and black-plumed horses; some of the grief was real. But Time, or, more exactly, the dynamics of Sir Jack's own Project, had their revenge. In the first months, Premier Visitors came to pay their homage at the mausoleum, to read Sir Jack's wall-wisdom, and depart thoughtfully. Yet they also continued to tour the Pitman mansion at the end of the Mall, if anything in larger numbers. Such loyal enthusiasm pointed up the emptiness and melancholy of the building after its proprietor's death, and it seemed to both Jeff and Mark that there was a difference between making your Visitors reflective and making them depressed. Then the logic of marketing flamed like a message on Belshazzar's wall: Sir Jack must live again.

The auditions had their disconcerting moments, but they found a Pitman who, with a little coaching and research, was as good as new. Sir Jack – the old one – would have approved the fact that his successor had played many leading Shakespearean roles. The replacement Sir Jack swiftly became a popular figure: descending from his landau to plunge into the crowds, lecturing on the history of the Island, and showing key leisure-industry executives round his mansion. The Pitman Dining Experience at the Cheshire Cheese proved a jolly Visitor option. The only marketing downside to all this was that throughput at the mausoleum dropped as fast as Betsy's egg-basket – on certain days Visitors were outnumbered by gardeners. It seemed to most people in dubious taste to smile at a man in the morning and attend his grave in the afternoon.

The Island had been on its third Sir Jack by the time Martha returned to Anglia after her decades of wandering. She stood on the foredeck of the quarterly Le Havre ferry, hooting its uncertain way into Poole harbour; as a fine spray refreshed her face, she wondered what sort of a berth she herself would find. Ropes were thrown and tightened; a gangway was hauled into place; upturned faces looked for people other than her. Martha was the last to disembark. She was wearing her oldest clothes; but even so, the mutton-chopped customs officer saluted her as she stood before his polished oak bag-table. She had retained her Old English passport, and also secretly paid taxes. These two precautions put her in the rare category of Permitted Immigrant. The customs officer, his thick blue serge suit disappearing into stout Wellington boots, pulled out the gold half-hunter strung across his belly, and timed her repatriation in a sheepskin ledger. He was certainly younger than Martha, but looked at her as if she were a long-lost daughter. 'Better one that hath strayed, if I might make so bold, Ma'am.' Then he handed back her passport, saluted again, and whistled up an urchin to carry her bags to the horse-taxi.

What had surprised her, watching from afar, was how quickly the whole thing had unravelled. No, that was unfair, that was how *The Times of London* – still published from Ryde – would have put it. The official Island line, loyally purveyed by Gary

Desmond and his successors, was gloatingly simple. Old England had progressively shed power, territory, wealth, influence and population. Old England was to be compared disadvantageously to some backward province of Portugal or Turkey. Old England had cut its own throat and was lying in the gutter beneath a spectral gas-light, its only function as a dissuasive example to others. From Dowager to Down-and-Out, as a *Times* headline had sneeringly put it. Old England had lost its history, and therefore – since memory is identity – had lost all sense of itself.

But there was another way of looking at things, and future historians, whatever their prejudice, would no doubt agree on identifying two distinct periods. The first began with the establishment of the Island Project, and had lasted for as long as Old England – to adopt the term for convenience – had attempted to compete with England, England. This was a time of vertiginous decline for the mainland. The tourist-based economy collapsed; speculators destroyed the currency; the departure of the Royal Family made expatriation fashionable among the gentry; while the country's best housing stock was bought as second homes by continental Europeans. A resurgent Scotland purchased large tracts of land down to the old northern industrial cities; even Wales paid to expand into Shropshire and Herefordshire.

After various attempts at rescue, Europe declined to throw good money after bad. There were some who saw a conspiracy in Europe's attitude to a nation which had once contested the primacy of the continent; there was talk of historical revenge. It was rumoured that during a secret dinner at the Elysée the presidents of France, Germany and Italy had raised their glasses to the words, 'It is not only necessary to succeed, it is necessary that others fail.' And if this were not true, there were enough documents leaking from Brussels and Strasbourg to confirm that many high officials regarded Old England less as a suitable case for emergency funding than as an economic and moral lesson: it should be portrayed as a wastrel nation and allowed to continue in free-fall as a disciplinary example to the overgreedy within other countries. Symbolic punishments were also introduced: the Greenwich Meridian was replaced by Paris Mean Time; on maps the English Channel became the French Sleeve.

Mass depopulation now took place. Those of Caribbean and Subcontinental origin began returning to the more prosperous lands from which their great-great-grandparents had once arrived. Others looked to the United States, Canada, Australia and continental Europe; but the Old English were low on the list of desirable immigrants, being thought to bring with them the taint of failure. Europe, in a sub-clause to the Treaty of Verona, withdrew from the Old English the right to free movement within the Union. Greek destroyers patrolled the Sleeve to intercept boat people. After this, depopulation slowed.

The natural political response to this crisis was the election of a Government of Renewal, which pledged itself to economic recovery, parliamentary sovereignty and territorial reacquisition. Its first step was to reintroduce the old pound as the central unit of currency, which few disputed as the English euro had ceased to be transferrable. Its second step was to send the army north to reconquer territories officially designated as occupied but which in truth had been sold. The *blitzkrieg* liberated much of West Yorkshire, to the general dismay of its inhabitants; but after the US backed the European decision to upgrade the Scottish Army's weaponry and offer unlimited credits, the Battle of Rombalds Moor led to the humiliating Treaty of Weeton. While attention was diverted, the French Foreign Legion invaded the Channel Islands, and the Quai d'Orsay's resuscitated claim was upheld by the International Court at The Hague.

After the Treaty of Weeton a destabilized country burdened with reparations discarded the politics of Renewal – or at least, what had traditionally been understood as Renewal. This marked the start of the second period, over which future historians would long disagree. Some asserted that at this point the country simply gave up; others that it found new strength in adversity. What remained incontestable was that the long-agreed goals of the nation – economic growth, political influence, military capacity and moral superiority – were now abandoned. New political leaders proclaimed a new self-sufficiency. They extracted the country from the European Union – negotiating with such obstinate irrationality that they were eventually paid to depart – declared a trade barrier against the rest of the world, forbade foreign ownership of either land or chattels within the territory, and disbanded the military. Emigration was permitted; immigration only in rare circumstances. Diehard jingoists claimed that these measures were designed to reduce a great trading nation to nut-eating isolationism; but modernising patriots felt that it was the last realistic option for a nation fatigued by its own history. Old England banned all tourism except for groups numbering two or less, and introduced a Byzantine visa system. The old administrative division into counties was terminated, and new provinces were created, based upon the kingdoms of the Anglo-Saxon heptarchy. Finally, the country declared its separateness from the rest of the globe and from the Third Millennium by changing its name to Anglia.

The world began to forget that 'England' had ever meant anything except England, England, a false memory which the Island worked to reinforce; while those who remained in Anglia began to forget about the world beyond. Poverty ensued, of course; though the word meant less in the absence of comparisons. If poverty did not entail malnutrition or ill health, then it was not so much poverty as voluntary austerity. Those in search of traditional vanities were still free to emigrate. Anglians also discarded much of the communications technology that had once seemed indispensable. A new chic applied to fountain-pens and letter-writing, to family evenings round the wireless and dialling 'O' for Operator; then such fashionable habits acquired authentic strength. Cities dwindled; mass transit systems were abandoned, though a few steam trains still ran; horses bossed the streets. Coal was dug again, and the kingdoms asserted their differences; new dialects emerged, based on the new separations.

Martha had not known what to expect when the cream-and-plum single-decker bus deposited her in the mid-Wessex village which had accepted her as a resident. The world's media had always followed *The Times of London*'s lead in depicting Anglia as a place of yokeldom and willed antiquarianism. Grindingly satirical cartoons showed bumpkins being hosed down at the hand-pump after over-dosing on scrumpy. Crime was said to flourish despite the best efforts of the bicycling policeman; even the reintroduction of the stocks had not deterred malefactors. Meanwhile, inbreeding was supposed to have produced a new and incomparably brain-free species of village idiot.

Of course, no-one from the Island had visited the mainland for years; though it had been a fashion for the Battle of Britain squadron to fly mock reconnaissance missions over Wessex. Through perspex goggles, and with period static in their ears, 'Johnnie' Johnson and his sheepskin-jacketed heroes would peer down in astonishment at what wasn't there: road traffic and power-lines, street-lights and billboards, the vital ductwork of a nation. They saw dead, bulldozed suburbs, and four-lane highways petering out into woodland, with a gypsy caravan titupping over the lurched, volcanic tarmac. Here and there were patches of bright reforestation, some with nature's original straggliness, others with the sharp lines of human intention. Life below seemed slow and small. Comfortably large fields had been redivided into narrow strips; wind-pumps turned industri-ously; a reclaimed canal offered up a reflection of painted traffic and straining barge-horses. Occasionally, away on the horizon, lingered the terrestrial vapour trail of a steam locomotive. The squadron liked to fly low and buzz a sudden village: scared faces turning up their inkwell mouths, a stallion shying on a toll-bridge, its rider waving a hopeless fist at the sky. Then, with superior chuckles, the heroes would give a Victory roll, tap the fuel gauge with a fraying gauntlet, and set fresh course for base.

The pilots had seen what they wanted to see: quaintness,

diminution, failure. Quieter changes evaded them. Over the years the seasons had returned to Anglia, and become pristine. Crops were once again the product of local land, not of air-freight: spring's first potatoes were exotic, autumn's quince and mulberry decadent. Ripeness was acknowledged to be a hazardous matter, and cold summers meant much green tomato chutney. The progress of winter was calibrated by the decay of racked apples and the increasing audacity of predators. The seasons, being untrustworthy, were more respected, and their beginnings marked by pious ceremonies. Weather, long since diminished to a mere determinant of personal mood, became central again: something external, operating its system of rewards and punishments, mainly the latter. It had no rivalry or interference from industrial weather, and was self-indulgent in its dominance: secretive, immanent, capricious, ever threatening the miraculous. Fogs had character and motion, thunder regained its divinity. Rivers flooded, sea-walls burst, and sheep were found in treetops when the waters subsided.

Chemicals drained from the land, the colours grew gentler, and the light untainted; the moon, with less competition, now rose more dominantly. In the enlarged countryside, wildlife bred freely. Hares multiplied; deer and boar were released into the woods from game farms; the urban fox returned to a healthier diet of bloodied, pulsing flesh. Common land was re-established; fields and farms grew smaller; hedgerows were replanted. Butterflies again justified the thickness of old butterfly books; migratory birds which for generations had passed swiftly over the toxic isle now stayed longer, and some decided to settle. Domestic animals grew smaller and nimbler. Meat-eating became popular again, as did poaching. Children were sent mushrooming in the woods, and the bolder fell stupefied from a tentative nibble; others dug esoteric roots, or smoked dried-fern roll-ups and pretended to hallucinate.

The village where Martha had lived for five years was a small agglomeration where the road forked towards Salisbury. For decades, lorries had stirred the cottages' shingly foundations and fumes darkened their rendering; every window was double-glazed and only the young or the drunk crossed the road unnecessarily. Now the split village had recovered its wholeness. Hens and geese wandered proprietorially across cracked tarmac on to which children had chalked skipping games; ducks colonized the triangular village green and defended its small pond. Washing, hung on rope lines by wooden pegs, flapped dry in the clean wind. As roof-tiles became unavailable, each cottage returned to reed or thatch. Without traffic, the village felt safer and closer; without television, the villagers talked more, even if there seemed less to talk about than before. Nobody's business went unobserved; pedlars were greeted warily; children were sent to bed with tales of highwaymen and gypsies rustling their imaginations, though few of their parents had seen a gypsy, and none a highwayman.

The village was neither idyllic nor dystopic. There were no outstanding idiots, despite the best mimicry of Jez Harris. If there was stupidity, as *The Times of London* insisted, then it was of the old kind, based on ignorance, rather than the new, based on knowledge. The Reverend Coleman was a well-intentioned bore whose clerical status had arrived by post, Mr Mullin the schoolmaster a half-respected authority. The shop opened at irregular intervals designed to fox even the most loyal customer; the pub was tied to a Salisbury brewery and the publican's wife unfit to make a sandwich. Opposite the house of Fred Temple, saddler, cobbler and barber, there was a pound for stray animals. Twice weekly a throbbing bus took villagers to the market town, passing the cottage hospital and the mid-Wessex lunatic asylum; the driver was invariably addressed as George, and was happy to do errands for stay-at-homes. There was crime, but in a culture of voluntary austerity it did not rise to much above theft of the occasional pullet. Villagers learned to leave their cottages unlocked.

At first Martha had been sentimental, until Ray Stout the publican – formerly a motorway toll-collector – leaned across the bar of the snug with her gin-and-tonic and the words, 'I suppose you find our little community *rather amusing?*' Later she was depressed by the incuriosity and low horizons, until Ray Stout challenged her with 'Missing the bright lights by now, I dare say?' Finally, she became accustomed to the quiet and necessary repetitiveness, the caution, the incessant espionage, the helpfulness, the mental incest, the long evenings. She made friends with a pair of cheese-makers, former commodity traders; she sat on the parish council and never failed the church flower roster. She walked the hills; she borrowed books from the mobile library which parked on the green every other Tuesday. In her garden she grew Snowball turnips and Red Drumhead cabbage, Bath cos, St George cauliflower and Rousham Park Hero onions. In memory of Mr A. Jones, she grew more beans than she needed: Caseknife and Painted Lady, Golden Butter and Scarlet Emperor. None of them, to her eye, looked worthy of laying on black velvet.

She was bored, of course; but then, she had returned to Anglia as a migrant bird rather than a zealot. She fucked no-one; she grew older; she knew the contours of her solitude. She was not sure if she had done right, if Anglia had done right, if a nation could reverse its course and its habits. Was it mere willed antiquarianism, as *The Times* alleged – or had that trait been part of its nature, its history, anyway? Was it a brave new venture, one of spiritual renewal and moral self-sufficiency, as political leaders maintained? Or was it simply inevitable, a forced response to economic collapse, depopulation and European revenge? These questions were not debated in the village: a sign perhaps that the country's fretful, psoriatic self-consciousness had finally come to an end.

And eventually she herself fitted into the village, because she herself no longer itched with her own private questions. She no longer debated whether or not life was a triviality, and what the consequences might be if it were. Nor did she know whether the stillness she had attained was proof of maturity or weariness. Nowadays she went to church as a villager, alongside other villagers who stooked their umbrellas in the leaky porch and sat through inoffensive sermons with stomachs calling out for the joint of lamb they had given the baker to roast in his oven. For thine is the wigwam, the flowers and the story: just another pretty verse.

Most afternoons Martha would unlatch the back door, stir the ducks to fussy flapping as she crossed the green, and take the bridle path to Gibbet Hill. Hikers – or at least, real ones – were rare nowadays, and the sunken track was overgrown again each springtime. She wore an ancient pair of jodhpurs against the briars, and kept a hand half-raised to repel the flailing hawthorn hedge. Here and there a stream trickled into the path, making the flints shine indigo beneath her feet. She climbed with a patience discovered late in life, and emerged on to a stretch of common pasture surrounding the stand of elms on Gibbet Hill.

She sat on the bench, her windcheater snagging a dulled metal plaque to a long-dead farmer, and looked down over the fields he must once have ploughed. Was it the case that colours dimmed as the eye grew elderly? Or was it rather that in youth your excitement about the world transferred itself on to everything you saw and made it brighter? The landscape she surveyed was buff and bistre, ash and nettle, dun and roan, slate and bottle. Against this backdrop moved a few fawn sheep. The little evidence of human presence also accorded to the natural laws of discretion, neutrality and fade: farmer Bayliss's purple barn, once the subject of aesthetic debate among the parish council's planning committee, was now easing to a gentle bruise.

Martha recognized that she was fading too. It had come as a shock one afternoon when she gave little Billy Temple a good telling-off for decapitating one of the vicar's hollyhocks with his willow switch, and the boy – hot-eyed, defiant, socks rolled down – stood his ground for a moment and then, as he turned to run, shouted, 'My Dad says you're an old maid.' She went home and looked at herself in the mirror: hair blown loose from her clips, plaid shirt beneath a grey windcheater, complexion whose ruddiness had finally asserted itself against decades of skin-care, and what seemed to her – though who was she to tell? – a mildness, almost a milkiness to her eyes. Well then, old maid, if that's what they saw.

Yet it was a strange trajectory for a life: that she, so knowing a child, so disenchanted an adult, should be transformed into an old maid. Hardly one of the traditional kind, who acquired the status by lifelong virginity, the dutiful care of ageing parents, and a tutting moral aloofness. She remembered when there had been a fashion among Christians, often quite young ones, to declare themselves – on what possible authority? – born again. Perhaps she could be a born-again old maid. And perhaps it was also the case that, for all a lifetime's internal struggling, you were finally no more than what others saw you as. That was your nature, whether you liked it or not.

What did old maids do? They were solitary, yet took part in village affairs; they had good manners, and appeared unaware of the entire history of sexuality; they had, sometimes, their own story, their own lived life, whose disappointments they were reluctant to divulge; they went for healthy walks in all weathers, knew about mustard baths, and brought nettle soup to invalids; they kept small souvenirs whose poignancy evaded the comprehension of outsiders; they read the newspaper.

So Martha seemed to be obliging others as well as pleasing herself when, each Friday, she boiled some milk for her morning chicory and settled down to the *Mid-Wessex Gazette*. She looked forward to its concentrated parochiality. It was better to commune with the reality you knew; duller, perhaps, but also more fitting. For many years mid-Wessex had been free of aircrashes and political coups, massacres, drug hauls, African famines and Hollywood divorces; so such matters were not reported. Nor would she read anything about the Isle of Wight, as it was still referred to on the mainland. Some years previously Anglia had renounced all territorial claim to Baron Pitman's fiefdom. It had been a necessary casting-off, even if few had been impressed. *The Times of London* had mockingly commented that this was the action of a bankrupt parent exasperatedly declaring that it would no longer underwrite the bills of its millionaire child.

There were still magazines where you could read of grosser excitements beyond the coastline; but not in the *Mid-Wessex Gazette*, or any of its stablemates. It was truly called a gazette, since it was not a paper containing novelties; rather, it was a listing of what had been agreed, and what had finished happening. The price of livestock and feed; the market rates for vegetables and fruit; proceedings from assize courts and small-claims tribunals; details of chattels sold by auction; golden, silver, and merely hopeful weddings; fêtes, festivals, and the opening of gardens to the public; sports results from school, parish, district and mid-kingdom; births; funerals. Martha read every page, even – especially – those in which she had no obvious interest. She avidly scanned lists of items sold by the hundredweight, stone and pound for amounts expressed in pounds, shillings and pence. This was hardly nostalgia, since most of these measures had been abolished before she was sentient. Or perhaps it was, and nostalgia of a truer kind: not for what you knew, or thought you had known, as a child, but for what you could never have known. So, with an attention which was artificial without being specious, Martha noted that beetroot were holding steady at thirteen and sixpence the hundredweight, while burdock had dropped a shilling in the week. She was not surprised: what on earth made people think burdock was worth eating? In her opinion, most of these retro-veg were consumed not for reasons of nutrition, or even necessity, but out of fashionable affectation. Simplicity had become confused with self-mortification.

The *Gazette* reported the outside world in only a contingent fashion: as a source of weather, as the destination of migratory birds currently quitting mid-Wessex. There was also a weekly chart of the night sky. Martha examined this as closely as she did the market prices. Where Sirius might be glimpsed, what dull red planet blinked near the eastern horizon, how to recognize Orion's Belt. This, she thought, was how the human spirit should divide itself, between the entirely local and the nearly eternal. How much of her life had been spent with all the stuff in the middle: career, money, sex, heart-trouble, appearance, anxiety, fear, yearning. People might say it was easier for her to renounce all this having once tasted it; that now she was an old woman, or maid, and that if she were obliged to lift fields of beetroot rather than idly monitor its price she might have more regrets over what she had renounced. Well, that too was probably the case. But everyone must die, however much they distracted themselves with the stuff in the middle. And how she readied herself for an eventual place in the newly-scythed churchyard was her business.

The village Fête took place on one of those gusty Anglian days in early June, when a fine spray of rain constantly threatens, and urgent clouds are late for their appointment in the next kingdom of the heptarchy. Martha looked out of her kitchen window at the sloping triangular green where a stained marquee was chivvying its guy-ropes. Harris the farrier was checking their tension and banging in tent-pegs more deeply with a wooden mallet. He did this in a showy, proprietorial manner, as if generations back his family had been granted letters patent to perform this valiant ritual. Martha was still bemused by Jez: on the one hand his inventions seemed so obviously fraudulent; on the other, this city-bred American with a joke accent made one of the most convincing and devoted villagers.

The marquee was secure; and here, riding towards it, wind in her hair, was Jez's blonde niece Jacky Thornhill. Jacky was to be Queen of the May, though as someone pointed out it was now early June, which as someone else pointed out was irrelevant because May was the tree not the month, or at least they thought so, which sent them to consult Mr Mullin the schoolmaster who said he'd look it up, and when he had he reported back that it referred to the may blossom which the Queen traditionally wore in her hair, though this must come to the same thing because presumably the may tree blossomed in

May, but in any case Jacky's Mum had made her a coronet out of gold-painted cardboard, and that was what she wore, and there the story ended.

It was the vicar's right and duty to open the Fête. The Reverend Coleman lived in the Old Rectory, next to the church. Previous vicars had lived on a plaster-board estate which had long since been bulldozed. The Old Rectory had fallen vacant when its last lay owner, a French businessman, had returned to his own country during the emergency measures. It seemed natural to villagers that the vicar should live in the rectory, just as a pullet should live in a henhouse; but the vicar was not allowed to get above himself any more than a hen should presume to be a turkey. The Reverend Coleman was not to conclude, just because he was back where his predecessors had lived for centuries, that God was back in his church or that Christian morality was the law of the village. In fact, most parishioners did live according to an attenuated Christian code. But when they came to church on Sunday it was more from a need for regular society and a taste for tuneful hymns than in order to receive spiritual advice and the promise of eternal life from the pulpit. The vicar knew better than to use his position to propose any coercive theological system; while he had soon learnt that moralising sermons were paid for on the silver plate with a trouser button and a valueless euro.

So the Reverend Coleman did not even allow himself a ritual remark about the Good Lord making the sun to shine upon the village for this special day. Ecumenically, he even made a point of shaking hands with Fred Temple, who had come dressed as a scarlet devil. When the *Gazette* photographer made them pose together, he slyly stamped on Fred's articulated tail, while ostentatiously – even paganly – crossing his fingers. Then he made a short speech mentioning almost everyone in the village by name, declared the Fête open, and made a snappy, take-it-away gesture to the four-piece band parked next to the scrumpy tent.

The band – tuba, trumpet, squeezebox and fiddle – began

with 'Land of Hope and Glory', which some villagers thought a hymn in deference to the vicar, and others an old Beatles song from the last century. An impromptu procession then toured the green at unsynchronized speeds: Jacky the May Queen, awkwardly athwart a shampooed shire horse, its mane and anklets feathering more spectacularly in the breeze than Jacky's home-permed ringlets; Fred Temple, scarlet tail wrapped round his neck, at the controls of a farting traction engine, all belts and clatter; Phil Henderson, chicken farmer, mechanical genius and suitor of blonde Jacky, at the wheel of his open-top Mini-Cooper, which he had found abandoned in a barn and converted to run off bottled domestic gas; and finally, after some satirical urging, PC Brown on his bicycle, drawn truncheon aloft, left thumb on tinkly bell, cycle clips at the ankles, false moustache on the lip. This unequal quartet lapped the green half-a-dozen times, until even close family saw no more point in cheering.

There were lemonade and ginger-beer stalls; skittles, bowling-for-a-pig and guess-the-weight-of-the-goose; a coconut shy at which, in deference to long tradition, half the coconuts were glued to the cups and sent the wooden balls ricocheting back at the thrower; a bran-tub, and ducking for apples. Rickety trestle-tables were stacked with seed cake and preserves: jams, jellies, pickles and chutneys. Ray Stout the publican, cheeks rouged and turban awry, revealing his widow's peak, crouched in a crepuscular booth offering fortunes from lime tea-leaves. Children could play pin-the-tail-on-the-donkey and have their faces bearded with burnt cork; then for a halfpenny they could enter a tent containing three antique distorting mirrors which rendered small preeners helpless with disbelief.

Later, as the afternoon drew on, there was a three-legged race, won by Jacky Thornhill and Phil Henderson, whose deftness at this disharmonious event prompted wiseacres to observe that they were well fitted for marriage. Two embarrassed youths in stout, loosely-cut linen jackets gave a demonstration of Cornish wrestling; as one prepared to try a flying mare he kept half an eye on Coach Mullin, who refereed with an open encyclopaedia in hand. For the dressing-up competition Ray Stout, retaining his crimson slap but reorganizing his turban, came as Queen Victoria; also present were Lord Nelson, Snow White, Robin Hood, Boadicea and Edna Halley. Martha Cochrane, for what it mattered, had decided to give her vote to Jez Harris's Edna Halley, despite her eerie kinship with Ray Stout's Queen Victoria. But Mr Mullin sought the farrier's disqualification on the grounds that contestants had been required to dress as real people; so an *ad hoc* meeting of the parish council was called to discuss the question of whether or not Edna Halley was a real person. Jez Harris counterclaimed by challenging the real existence of Snow White and Robin Hood. Some said you were only real if someone had seen you; some that you were only real if you were in a book; some that you were real if enough people believed in you. Opinions were offered at length, fuelled by scrumpy and ignorant certainty.

Martha was losing interest. What held her attention now were the children's faces, which expressed such willing yet complex trust in reality. As she saw it, they had not yet reached the age of incredulity, only of wonder; so that even when they disbelieved, they also believed. The tubby, peering dwarf in the distorting mirror was them and wasn't them: both were true. They saw all too easily that Queen Victoria was no more than Ray Stout with a red face and a scarf round his head, yet they believed in both Queen Victoria and Ray Stout at the same time. It was like that old puzzle from psychological tests: is this a goblet or a pair of profiles facing one another? Children could switch from one to the other, or see both at the same time, without any trouble. She, Martha, could no longer do that. All she could see was Ray Stout making a happy fool of himself.

Could you reinvent innocence? Or was it always constructed, grafted on to the old disbelief? Were the children's faces proof of this renewable innocence – or was that just sentimentality? PC Brown, drunk on scrumpy, was circling the village green again, thumb tinkling his bell, saluting all he passed with his truncheon. PC Brown, whose two months' training had been done long ago with a private security firm, who was attached to no police station, and hadn't caught a single criminal since his arrival in the village; but he had the uniform, the bicycle, the truncheon and the now-loosening moustache. This seemed to be enough.

Martha Cochrane left the Fête as the air was becoming thicker and the dancing more rough-and-ready. She took the bridle path to Gibbet Hill and sat on the bench looking down at the village. Had there really been a gibbet up here? Had corpses swung while rooks pecked out their eyeballs? Or was that in turn the fanciful, touristy notion of some Gothic vicar a couple of centuries back? Briefly, she imagined Gibbet Hill as an Island feature. Clockwork rooks? A bunjee jump from the gallows to know what it felt like, followed by a drink with the Hooded Hangman? Something like that.

Below her, a bonfire had been lit, and a conga line was circling, led by Phil Henderson. He was waving a plastic flag bearing the cross of St George. Patron saint of England, Aragon and Portugal, she remembered; also protector of Genoa and Venice. The conga, national dance of Cuba and Anglia. The band, fortified with more scrumpy, had begun to slew through its programme yet again, like a looped tape. 'The British Grenadiers' had given way to 'I'm Forever Blowing Bubbles'; next, Martha knew without thinking, would come 'Penny Lane' followed by 'Land of Hope and Glory'. The conga line, a panto caterpillar, adjusted its swaying stride to each change of tune. Jez Harris began to set off jumping jacks, which chased the children into shrieks and laughter. A slow cloud teasingly released a gibbous moon. There was a rustle at her feet. No, not a badger, despite the farrier's decorative claims; just a rabbit.

The moon went in again; the air grew cold. The band played 'Land of Hope and Glory' for the last time, then fell silent. All she could hear now was the occasional bird-impersonation of PC Brown's bell. A rocket staggered diagonally into the sky. The conga line, reduced to three, circled the weakening fire. It had been a day to remember. The Fête was established; already it seemed to have its history. Twelve months from now a new May Queen would be proclaimed and new fortunes read from tea-leaves. There was another rustle nearby. Again, not a badger but a rabbit, fearless and quietly confident of its territory. Martha Cochrane watched it for a few seconds, then got to her feet, and began to descend the hill.